Class of '78

Karen Harmon

Class of '78

Tellwell Talent
www.tellwell.ca

ISBN
978-0-2288-9572-5 (Paperback)

Table of Contents

To Joseph
Thankyou so
much for supporting
my writing
Karen

Chapter One

Class of '78

> *"The moment when everyone is laughing and you're wondering—are they laughing at me?"*
>
> —Nelson Farnsworth

Before the festivities, Kent planned with Johnny to get something a little stronger than weed for the dance. He knew all eyes would be on him, so he wanted to be in top form. As he put his flask of Southern Comfort in the pocket of his leather jacket, he winked at himself in the hallway mirror before he left for the ceremony.

The effects of the cocaine went straight to Kent's head. The wires in his brain were ignited, and his eyes lit up, as if a spotlight had been turned on, and the world before him became crystal clear. He wanted the feeling to last forever! His confidence soared, and he felt genuinely happy. But then his burst of energy became pointy and jagged as if his hair were standing on end and the roots were poking into his brain.

Instantly Kent needed to dance and move his body, or he knew he would self-combust. The melody of Earth, Wind & Fire pulsated across the gymnasium floor. Their new album *The Eternal Dance* had just come out, and the hit song "Got to Get You into My Life" was playing just when Kent spotted Tracy.

He caught himself singing along about taking a ride and suddenly seeing the woman he wanted to be with every single day for the rest of his life. Kent stopped mid-verse to laugh loudly at the vision of Tracy clad in a full-length crinkly pink dress. He wondered why it looked so stiff and shiny. Grinning, he whispered under his breath, "What the hell are you wearing, Trace?"

Unlike any other time, Kent's laugh was not a cruel cackle but a genuine heart-bursting sound with which he was unfamiliar. He instinctively knew that the laughter was not him, but a symptom of drug-induced euphoria.

At that moment as he stood still, Kent realized he had been in love with Tracy since she corrected his spelling paper with a red Crayola crayon back in fourth grade. But as he sized up the situation, taking in all her frantic, busybody tendencies, Kent knew they were an unlikely pair.

He confidently strode over to her, knowing she would turn down his request to be his dance partner. So, in his standard "old Kent" way, he decided not to ask for her hand but to forcibly grab it, figuring once he started twirling her around to the electrifying disco music, she would not pull back or refuse. He reasoned, *Who could resist someone as charming and sexy as me?*

Kent approached where she stood by the ridiculous balloon display, admiring Tracy's furrowed brow and small, delicate fingers as she expertly untangled a messy web of ribbons and string. Then he stopped suddenly when he spotted Tracy's mother, Mrs. Hansworth. His brain was buzzing, remembering how Eunice Hansworth—tall, svelte, and intense—had made a play for him two years prior when he was only in Grade 10. At the time, as self-assured as he was, he could not turn down her advances. Kent smirked at the memory and thought, *What red-blooded teenage boy would*?

Now two years later, on the verge of manhood, Kent was four inches taller, much wiser, and not about to get mixed up with a forty-year-old man-eater. So, rather than interacting with the predator mother and her cute and indisputably naive daughter, Kent walked right past the two as they fumbled with the photo opportunity archway.

He spotted Susan ahead and sized up her cheerleader phoniness, snorting and shaking his head at how she was dressed. Definitely not his type. Her short red dress, plunging neckline, red stiletto heels and fishnet stockings repulsed him. Her big hair and caked-on makeup appeared clown-like to him, which only made him laugh and shake his head.

Throughout high school, Kent had avoided Susan at all costs. He thought of her massive ponytail and cheerleader pom-poms as props to get attention, just like a proud peacock showing off its feathers, wanting everyone to see how great it was. Then the vision of her pom-poms made Kent chuckle again because he wasn't thinking about the large tufts of shredded plastic a girl shakes on the basketball court. When he approached Susan, he said loudly, "Nice poms-poms!" while jeering at her exposed cleavage.

The distraction, and getting away from Tracy, was all it took for Kent to return to his old arrogant self.

Circling around Susan, he quickly passed the balloon monstrosity and headed straight for the punch bowl. After making sure that no one was looking, he took the flask out of his pocket and poured the contents into the sickly-sweet orange beverage. He stirred the mixture with his finger, then licked it to gauge the taste. "Don't mind if I do," he drawled, filling a paper cup and downing the entire cup's worth in one gulp.

In true-blue Kent fashion, he found a cafeteria tray, filled some Dixie cups, and distributed the alcohol-laced drink to Patty and her nerdy friends. They delightedly accepted with giggles, as he knew they would.

Kent looked at the weirdos and flakes, the crappy decorations and the teenagers who would undoubtedly amount to nothing, then turned his back on the whole lot of them and walked out the big gym doors to the parking lot. Sliding into his red convertible, Kent revved the engine and made a point not to look back, yelling out of the open top, "See you on the flip side, suckers!"

The sound of Kent's car engine could be heard in the distance, growing fainter with each passing mile. The next sound was five teenage girls throwing up in the long grass lining the country road ditch. Their retching was magnified in the silence of the dry, June night air. They were no longer giggling.

***

Kent Gordon had been voted *"most likely to succeed at becoming a powerful corrupt politician while alienating everyone in the process."*

He had been the least-liked student in the whole school, although no one ever told him so to his face, as most were intimidated by him. He held the title of Preppy Rich Snob and was known for his sarcasm and meanness. His entire family was filthy rich, and he considered their wealth one of his most attractive assets. Aside from being loaded, Kent was handsome, fit, and highly intelligent.

His magnetic blue eyes were his secret weapon for getting what he wanted, and his black hair was kept short and neat, never with a hair out of place, even when driving his red TR-6 convertible sports car. Kent consistently looked like he was going to a business meeting, dressed in the latest Calvin Klein jeans, striped dress shirts and black oxford shoes. His whole outfit was tied together with socks that peeked out between his pant cuff and shoe, with a dollar sign pattern on them. As a child he idolized Reggie Mantle from the *Archie* comic book series; the only thing missing was his Veronica Lodge.

Kent had looked and acted the same way since he first entered Grade 1 and made a name for himself with his trademark cocky grin and snide comments. Unbeknownst to him, these characteristics were what everyone hated most about him.

He did well on the debate team because he was notably loud and intimidating. Even though he was feared, many secretly admired his confident, take-charge persona and hoped he would pay them just an ounce of attention.

Tracy knew nothing of Kent's secret crush on her because he annoyed her greatly. She could often be heard saying, "Argh! Kent, you have no idea!" Or most commonly, "Kent! Stop bugging me and leave me alone!"

Then, on the most monumental night of all of their lives, Kent left without saying goodbye and vowed to never look back. He would carry with him one regret—that he did not divulge his true feelings to Tracy Hansworth in all of their thirteen years at school together. Driving off into the velvet night sky on the desolate country road, he was filled with ambivalent regret and uncertain hopefulness.

***

From Kindergarten to Grade 12, everyone took Tracy's meddling with a grain of salt. They knew she meant well and could not help being in other people's business. Tracy was the go-to person for what to get someone for a birthday present or Secret Santa. If anyone was home from school sick, in the hospital, lost their dog, or their parents were getting divorced, Tracy was there with a card and a homemade container of freezer jam.

Tracy Hansworth was voted *"most likely to marry a mechanic like her dad, have five kids and be a stay-at-home mom."* The running joke was that she would probably end up managing the local flea market at the corn maze every Saturday—weather permitting.

Tracy was well known as the local MeadowBrook High busybody. She was considered average-looking with straight brown shoulder-length hair and severely cut bangs, not beautiful by Hollywood standards, but still cute, like a puppy. She had a petite frame and a big personality.

Tracy's go-to outfit was high-waisted jeans with various homemade macrame belts and hand-knitted sweaters in different shades of brown. Her favourite was a crocheted vest made of squares that she stitched together with light pink yarn, with a seashell clasp at the top. Tracy liked to use gems, embroidered patches, and shells in her handiwork and clothing whenever she could.

Tracy went to church but also read Astrid Ann's horoscope predictions in the *Gazette* newspaper every week. She always put a penny in her penny loafers because her grandma said it was good luck. She refused to walk under ladders and avoided black cats at all costs.

She promoted her hand-crafted jewellery and could often be seen in the cafeteria during lunch hour, set up to sell her wares. All proceeds were donated to an orphanage in Kenya. Unfortunately, rarely did anyone except the home economics teacher purchase any of her crafts. Tracy was also on the debate team and insisted they all wear matching berets. She reasoned that it would give them a competitive edge, and since she knitted them in the school colours, it only made sense.

Much of her time was spent in the sewing room when she was not selling her jewellery. As the Capable Craft Club creator, she had written a thirty-page handbook with rules and regulations that everyone had to adhere to, or else they would be immediately kicked out.

Some said Tracy was a gossip girl and knew everyone's business. She habitually countered that by saying, "I just like to be informed," even though her nosiness got her into trouble sometimes.

Tracy's dad was the favoured town mechanic and owned Al's Automotive and Repair Shop, with the slogan *"If it's broke, we'll fix it; if it ain't, we won't."* Tracy's mom was a homemaker and was there when needed. As a devoted parent, she was president of the PTA but still found time to help Tracy with her many crafts, school assignments, and meddling in other people's business. Many people thought Mrs. Hansworth dressed too provocatively for a mother and wondered why she spent more time chatting with teenage boys than anyone else.

On the night of graduation, Eunice Hansworth was at the dance for her daughter but continuously had her eye on everyone else.

As president of the grad committee, Tracy arrived at the gym early to oversee the decorating and set up the record player. She chose the first song of the night to be "We've Only Just Begun" by Karen Carpenter. After she put the needle down on the record, boos and hisses erupted from her fellow grads. A few hollered, "Ew, this is a wedding song!" Others chanted, "We want the Rolling Stones!" Some of the girls called out, "Hey Tracy, got any disco?" and a group of stoners situated by the back doors yelled in unison, "What about Pink Floyd?"

During the music fiasco, Tracy looked up and was horrified at the state of the balloon archway. She frantically flagged down her mother for reinforcement to address the issue.

Meanwhile, after the official presentation of diplomas, the graduating class of 1978 was loosening up and ready to party. Many separated and moved to the banquet tables without saying goodbye to their alphabetized counterparts. There was a brief hush, a silent interlude with reflections on personal accomplishments, while minds buzzed, thinking about what the future would bring. Some anticipated a future they had been planning for years, while others were at a loss. Everyone wondered what was in store for them. Many sat motionless as if waiting for the impact of a car crash. Others were hopeful that life was just about to begin, and their lottery ticket had been chosen. And then some had no thoughts on their future whatsoever and just wanted to party.

***

As the gymnasium lights dimmed, Darcie worked herself into a state of panic. She felt like a character out of an episode of *Three's Company* and wondered how Jack Tripper would have handled her debacle of wanting to spend time with two very different, but equally good-looking boys who were complete opposites. She remembered episodes of hysterical mayhem when the goofy main character had been on a date with two different women simultaneously.

Earlier, Darcie thought of being a no-show at the ceremony and dance but ultimately did not want to disappoint anyone, so she climbed into her Volkswagen Beetle, popped in an eight-track tape and listened to her favourite band on her way to the ceremony. Johnny had recently given her Fleetwood Mac's new album *Rumours*, so she sang along to "Secondhand News" and thought of Dakota.

Humming along to her favourite band, Darcie paused when Lindsey Buckingham sang *"I know I got nothing on you"* and realized that as much as she adored Dakota, she did not know how he felt about her, and there was nothing she could do about it. It wasn't like they had made a commitment for the rest of their lives and yet she longed to be alone with him in the tall grass, as the song suggested.

Darcie Richmond had been voted "*most likely to move to New York and become Andy Warhol's next protégé.*" She was considered the high-school party girl but did not think of herself that way, as she rarely drank and only pretended to inhale the skunky weed that burned her throat like a flaming torch. The part everyone got right was her artistic talent and free-spirited persona.

She was well known for her mane of thick black feathered hair, long flowing clothes, and black and silver jewelry. Extra-large hoop earrings and many silver chains graced her neck. Darcie's idol was singer and songwriter Stevie Nicks from the group Fleetwood Mac and her style reflected that. Her outfit for grad was eclectic and pure Darcie. While other girls wore white lace or pastel pink, Darcie had on a long, black, sheer skirt over a ballerina-type Lycra bodysuit. She had always been petite and willowy thin and was known for carrying around a bag of salt-and-vinegar potato chips wherever she went. Other girls were jealous that Darcie could stay thin yet eat like a truck driver.

On the night of grad, Darcie took extra time and care to blow-dry her hair, following with her ritual of turning her head upside down and dousing her tousled mane in Final Net hair spray. Then, with a few shakes, she would fling her hair back up to get the perfect look she was going for.

She tried to keep a low profile but always stood out anyway. Most of the girls admired her, the boys were intimidated by her, and the teachers did not trust her. Part of the reason for her adverse reputation was that she hung out in the halls with Johnny Fasp, the school pothead. They were often spotted leaning up against the radiators by the back entrance to the school.

Darcie and Johnny had been best friends for as long as she could remember. However, they were not a couple, even though rumours suggested otherwise.

She was unique and marched to the beat of her own drum. Her black Volkswagen bug, with yellow happy face stickers on the back window and a bumper sticker that read "Power to the People" only proved she was different from the many teenagers who followed the trends and dressed the same.

Darcie skipped out a lot and loathed P.E. She always had a note to sit on the bleachers for an ailment no one had heard of. She was a gifted artist and played the guitar. Everyone counted on Darcie to make posters that promoted the weekend parties at the local pond, which was more like a small lake near Johnny's parents' farm. The drawings included sunsets and sunrises with the instructions "Be there or be square!" written in big loopy letters.

Her single mom, Nancy, added to her mystique, as she worked at Barney's department store selling handbags, the stiff leather ones she would never dream of purchasing. Instead, Nancy preferred crocheted purses with fringes. And just like her daughter, she did not look or dress like the other moms or anyone else. Nancy was bohemian and nonconformist, and could often be spotted on Main Street picking up garbage, talking to strangers, or pulling weeds around the lamp posts. She preferred colourful floral peasant blouses and tight bell-bottom jeans.

Darcie never knew her father, and she and her mother did not talk about him. She had no siblings and was the only student living in an apartment in the centre of town.

Meanwhile, on the night of graduation, Darcie had a plan. She hoped Dakota would be there, a boy she had been in love with since Grade 9. They would drive out to the back country roads and maybe go all the way this time. But, of course, she would never tell Johnny or anyone else of her mystery boy. They never hung out at school together, but if they passed in the halls he would wink and she would bow her head and smile. Sometimes Dakota would hang out while Darcie worked at the A&W. And with her mother's approval he would also stop over late at night and the two would listen to records in Darcie's bedroom, on her mattress that was missing a box spring.

At the same time, Darcie was conflicted, because she had also promised her best friend Johnny that she would leave the grad dance early with him. They had plans to walk to the swimming hole, get high and let off fireworks. There were no fish in the pond, otherwise, Darcie would never have allowed this because she was a vegetarian and an animal activist.

***

Dakota Hillsman lived on the reservation and did not appear in the yearbook; therefore, no *"most likely to"* title or slogan was given to him. He was the Class of '78's only teenager of First Nations descent and he lived a few miles out of town on the appointed Indigenous land, even though in reality, the whole town belonged to his people.

Dakota had striking good looks. His black hair was long and straight, always clean and shiny, with a cigarette behind one ear. He maintained his cool factor in faded blue jeans, a white T-shirt, worn cowboy boots, and an oversized faded jean jacket.

He missed a lot of school days but still did well academically. Very few people spoke to him, and he, in turn, spoke to very few. Even so, he was well-liked and placed on a bit of a pedestal by students and teachers alike. Most girls had a secret crush on Dakota in a taboo kind of way. But he only had feelings for Darcie Richmond, which she reciprocated.

His home life seemed atypical. Everything about his First Nations background was unknown to the other students. They never asked, and Dakota never shared, yet he walked the halls with assurance and self-confidence.

Although he was on the honours roll, he never planned on attending the graduation. Instead, he elected to stay home. Dakota celebrated making it through an institution he wholly disagreed with by making popcorn and colouring with his little sisters and smaller cousins. He was happy doing this and would not have changed a thing.

However, he knew Darcie would be at the ceremony waiting for him. He assumed they would meet up the next day at their secret meeting place. There, Dakota would explain his absence and hoped she would not be angry. He did not know that Darcie had also promised her best friend Johnny that she would leave the grad dance early with him.

***

Johnny was the token pothead and was seemingly, permanently stoned. However, he was good-looking in a relaxed, hippie sort of way. He was known for his long blond shag-style hair, beautiful straight white teeth, and kind endearing smile. He wore his signature orange-and-pink crocheted poncho, worn leather sandals, and faded baggy blue jeans all year round. Johnny was frequently seen with his acoustic guitar slung over one shoulder for emotional support.

Johnny Fasp was undoubtedly well known and was voted *"most likely to team up with singer-songwriter Neil Young and make beautiful music together while being stoned."* He secretly supplied some of the students and even some of the teachers with marijuana.

Regardless of Johnny's extracurricular activities, he was well-liked by all as a friendly, mild-mannered soul. He was an enigma and didn't have a single enemy in the small rural town.

Johnny's friends and classmates marveled at how he got away with rarely going to class and never got in trouble or expelled for missing. Instead, he could often be spotted sitting on the grassy slope outside the school, watching the cars go by while effortlessly strumming his guitar. Sometimes girls sat near him and pleaded with him to sing "Like a Hurricane" by Neil Young, first released on his *American Stars in Bars* album. Johnny always obliged but made a point of playing the acoustic version.

Johnny's family were successful chicken farmers, and he was the middle child of seven boys. The farm was on the east side of town, next to the highway and across from the railroad tracks and local swimming hole. Even though he lived two miles from town, he never dreamed of taking the school bus. Instead, Johnny drove a blue GMC 1960s pickup truck to school, often arriving late and leaving early.

He was not keen to attend the graduation ceremony, but he had a few orders to fill from students and teachers, so he casually circulated the room and passed out the little baggies he'd carefully put together earlier that afternoon. Each pot-smoking client handed him their payment in a simulated handshake.

While scanning the room for Darcie, Johnny high-fived a few friends and smiled broadly at a few girls until he spotted her. Everyone except Darcie was happily going about signing yearbooks, hugging each other, and reminiscing about old science experiments and math tests.

Instead, Darcie stood off to the side, feeling melancholy about everything—the father she never knew, a mother she felt terrible for, and the last thirteen years that seemed like a waste of time. Disappointment took hold and settled in that Dakota was a no-show. He had said he "might be there." For a fleeting moment, she was concerned about his welfare and wrapped her black cape a little tighter around her slim shoulders. Her worried brow slackened when she spotted Johnny making his way around the tackily decorated gymnasium. Eyeing up her best friend, Darcie admired Johnny's ease in manoeuvring around teenagers she never took the time to know. She wondered what would become of their lifelong friendship now that school was ending.

As soon as their eyes met, they glanced toward the gym exit, reading each other's minds that it was time to go. Darcie and Johnny often shared the same thought at precisely the same moment, and they knew it was because of their deep-rooted closeness. Weeks before the ceremony, they had made plans to leave the dance together and walk the two miles to the pond when Johnny finished his deliveries.

Darcie's mother often warned her, "If you see a 1953 Pontiac Parisienne, run in the other direction. Always keep our door locked, and never buzz anyone into the apartment, even if you think you know them." Her advice was ominous and foreboding, and Darcie knew why. Nancy had been a little girl when the town's founder had gone missing. It had been reported that a Pontiac Parisienne was seen near the founder's home, and then the next day, he was gone. Darcie's mother grew up with pervasive rumours and hearsay that there was still a murderer hiding out somewhere in MeadowBrook.

Due to her mother's fear, Darcie never walked the back country roads alone, and she always felt safe with Johnny.

***

Just as Darcie floated past and out the door, Nelson looked up, away from his circle of goobers and other nerds like himself that he called friends—the people who "got him," his high school companions with comparable academic minds. Catching a glimpse of the only girl he had ever loved as she left the dance, Nelson slumped back in his chair, deflated.

"NUTS!" he yelled out, wondering if he would ever get a chance with Darcie Richmond again.

Nelson Farnsworth had always been on the outskirts of all school events, and truthfully, he never wanted to be involved anyway. Voted "*most likely to invent the latest, greatest pimple cream and become a millionaire,*" Nelson was aware of the murmurs and taunts behind his back.

The fact remained that he was MeadowBrook's symbolic brainiac. Many labelled him as a nerd and some called him the school geek. On the other hand, he was known more for his missing and possibly murdered grandfather than for his calculating mind. Nevertheless, he ignored the rumours that the disappearance of the town's founder, William Farnsworth, was an inside job and the cause for Nelson's strangeness.

Nelson was teased mercilessly for his thick, black-rimmed glasses, acne, and perpetually greasy hair. As a result, he was referred to as an odd duck by the teachers and a nerd by his classmates. He often retaliated and yelled at his tormentors, "I would rather be odd and a genius, than boring and dumb as a fence post!"

Without fail, Nelson wore the same short-sleeved checkered shirt, brown corduroy pants, and old tattered running shoes every day. His clothing was somewhat of a uniform. To complete his wardrobe, Nelson carried a stack of books under one arm. This aspect of his attire was more like a security blanket than a fashion accessory.

Nelson was on the chess team and could be found in the science lab, playing chess during lunch hour. He was a straight-A student in all subjects except P.E., art, and drama. He could not throw or catch a ball and often commented he could not draw a straight line. On skit day, he hid in the back of the science lab.

Nelson's father Marvin Farnsworth, son of the founder of MeadowBrook, owned and managed the local grocery store, the Red & White Frugal Grocer, which offered reasonably priced quality food, especially on outdated meat and dairy products. Marvin liked to take a black Jiffy marker and change the expiry dates. He could often be heard telling his employees and shoppers, "Those dates are just a suggestion and do not mean the food will spoil, so go ahead, shop away!" Nelson's adoring mother operated as the only florist in town and had won many awards at the country fair for her arrangements. He was an only child and liked it that way.

Part of Nelson's insecurity was due to his grandfather's disappearance back in 1953. His grandmother was the leading suspect, and many people still thought she was responsible. In addition to self-esteem issues, he was highly aware that his grandmother could possibly be a cold-blooded killer. And because she lived with Nelson and his mom and dad, he never trusted her chocolate chip cookies and poured the glass of milk she gave him down the drain when she wasn't looking.

Getting ready for graduation, Nelson took extra care to brush his teeth. He liked to meticulously clean in and around his braces to ensure there were no visible food bits.

He finished the routine by carefully applying Clearasil to his pimples, red blotchy spots, and blackheads.

Regardless of Nelson's struggles, he had looked forward to the grad ceremony all year, as he expected to win all the academic awards. More importantly, he planned to ask Darcie, the most beautiful and mysterious girl in high school, to dance. He had secretly loved her since first grade but never dared to speak to her.

When Darcie left without a word, Nelson murmured under his breath, "I could just kill that Johnny!"

***

Tim and Amanda were the school jocks; he was the captain of the boys' basketball team and she was the captain of the girls' volleyball team. The only thing they had in common was their athletics. They were not friends but recognized each other for having skill and talent.

Tim Barnes had been voted "*most likely to marry his high-school sweetheart and attend university on a basketball scholarship.*" He was the stereotypical school jock, with high expectations from his classmates and family to go into law and become a partner in his father's law firm.

As MeadowBrook High's star basketball player, Tim was also a perfect example of what a jock was—good-looking, tall, and enthusiastic. Tim only dated the cheerleaders but vehemently avoided Susan, their fearless leader.

Tim mostly wore his red-and-white gym strip in the halls but would change into the required game-day attire—black dress pants, white collared shirt, and red tie (the school colours)—when he had to. He loved to party and held the nickname "Ten Shots Tim," which stood for shot glasses, not shots on the basketball court.

Even though Tim was destined for big things, he was an average student who thought himself far more astute than his grades indicated. Secretly, Tim preferred sewing and drama class to sports. He was greatly annoyed with all the cheerleaders throwing themselves at him, but he admired their team spirit, spunk, and fun-loving cheers. Sometimes he thought being on the sidelines performing cheers and high kicks would be more fun than his role of dribbling, blocking, and shooting the ball.

Tim's father, Chuck Barnes, was a hard-nosed divorce lawyer and his mother was a homemaker who spent much of her time playing bridge and planning the family's next vacation. Tim's little sister was ten years younger and a total embarrassment to him. He often wondered what his parents were thinking when they decided to have her, and Tim avoided her at all costs. Marnie, nicknamed "Mar-Mar," wore outdated horn-rimmed glasses, was predestined for braces, and cried a lot for no apparent reason.

Tim and his family lived on a hill overlooking the vast wheat fields on the west side of town. Their home had six bedrooms, a swimming pool and a basketball court. People made a point to drive from town and neighbouring communities to view the elaborate yearly Christmas displays at the Barnes home. His mother and sister took pride in a compilation of decorations—Baby Jesus in a manger, the Grinch Who Stole Christmas, Frosty the Snowman, Charlie Brown, and Scrooge holding a lantern over his head. Tim was mortified at the tacky display and ever-increasing commercialized exhibit that he once loved as a child. Strict orders from his father on how to decorate and hours spent on a ladder had dimmed Tim's enthusiasm for a time of year lacking any reason for the season.

As he got ready for his Grade 12 high school graduation, he was not looking forward to the dance afterward, because Tim suspected that he and his girlfriend Jenny would be voted prom king and queen. He wished he could skip everything and stay home with a vegetarian pizza and an old Betty Davis movie on the TV.

Just before the buffet and dance, Tim and Jenny found a seat. He looked at his watch, tapped his foot and wished the night was ending instead of just beginning. He wanted a drink, and not the orange Fanta and pineapple juice concoction the punch bowl provided.

While they waited for their table to be called to the buffet, Jenny leaned in for a kiss, kicked Tim under the table and whined, "Hello, is anybody home?" as she knocked on his forehead. Tim's whole body tensed from the sudden pain in his shin and Jenny's annoying tap on his head. He dutifully snapped back to the presence of his date and put his alcohol craving on hold to nuzzle with Jenny. Her hair spray–starched locks scratched his cheek, and he reluctantly accepted his plight of being attached to a girl he was not interested in.

***

Amanda Marsthrop, Tim's athletic counterpart, was voted "*most likely to become a P.E. teacher, get married to another P.E. teacher, and have five athletic kids, all while saving the environment.*"

As captain of the girls' volleyball team and an award-winning all-around athlete, Amanda was fit, popular, and nice to everyone. All the teachers in the school adored her and she was lovingly nicknamed "Teacher's Pet."

She was also a natural beauty and had never worn makeup in her life. Her blond hairstyle was practical and cute, with bobby pins holding back her bangs. Two years earlier, Amanda had been the talk of the town when she cut her hair into a Dorothy Hamill short bob. She had freckles on the bridge of her nose, inspiring an additional nickname, "Spot." Amanda dressed fashionably but wasn't one to draw attention to herself. Her customary attire included blazers, wide-leg dress pants, plain button-up blouses tucked in, and brown leather clogs with a thin, matching brown leather belt.

She had an obsession with owls and started the Save the Owl Club at the high school. Amanda was often gifted owl-themed presents to add to her growing collection of earrings, figurines, posters and stuffed animals. Tracy once gave her a macrame wall hanging shaped like an owl that she spent a whole semester crocheting.

Amanda started a campaign for the entire school to use less paper and wanted all the teachers to use both sides of the foolscap. A consistent B+ student, she loved every aspect of going to school, from sports, and academics, to art, drama music, and social events.

Sometimes she would stay after school to clean the gym equipment or help out in the office to sort papers or staple report cards together. She was Principal Marple's favourite student, and he even created a marionette puppet after her. The likeness was remarkable, right down to her freckles and short blonde hair. He called the puppet "The Environmentalist." His puppeteering shows were intended to teach children about bullying, humanitarian issues and the environment.

Amanda's parents were middle class, involved in the community, and valued family togetherness. Her dad was a pharmacist and her mother worked at the local library. She had an older sister and a younger sister. All three siblings seemingly got along well and were often seen shopping around town, going to the movie theatre, and volunteering at the seniors' home. All these great attributes caused her family to be known as the *Leave it to Beaver* family, and all the Marsthrops were proud of this title. They regularly watched reruns of the show as a family on Saturday nights.

The girls' volleyball team got ready for grad at Amanda's house, and instead of wearing grad dresses, everyone thought it would be cute if they wore their volleyball uniforms, adding frills, lace, and bows to dress them up. They deservingly won the 1978 girls' volleyball championships and since they would never wear the uniforms again, they all thought, *Why not, for old times' sake?*

To add to the festivity, Amanda and the girls rented a stretch limousine (the only one in town) from the funeral hall. Her father bought them each an apple cider with six percent alcohol to drink in the limo on the way to the grad ceremony and dance. After the ceremonies,

Amanda found her girl squad, and they sat down at a long, white-clothed table. They laughed at the little egg basket centrepieces, rolled their eyes, and collectively said, "Only in MeadowBrook!"

***

Even though the teenagers tried, many could not break free from their stereotypes and the skeletons in their closets. However, two students who were seemingly oblivious to their labels were Nelson, and Patty Krakatoya. Neither was offended by their label, yet neither could rise above it. Even though Nelson retaliated periodically, most assumed he did not mind.

Patty Krakatoya was voted "*most likely to become an orthodontist*" because she had been wearing braces since Grade 6.

Most teachers at the school called Patty a wallflower, which she took as a compliment because when broken down, the word only meant she was a flower that stood by the wall. Sometimes, though, she felt more like a weed, with a wall crashing down on her head. When Patty thought about the category she had been placed in by her teachers and her peers, she felt akin to her long-standing crush, Nelson, and often wondered if she was the female version of him. She shared her observation with no one. Especially not him.

Patty was insecure about her weight and did not think she looked like the other girls her age. She spent much of her time reflecting on her classmates and perceived the entire teenage population of girls to be thinner, prettier, and more intelligent than she was. However, Patty wanted to be comfortable and did not like tight jeans, so she wore stretch pants with matching polyester blouses. Out of habit, she could always be spotted in clean white Keds running shoes. Patty had been known to buy out the whole supply of her size at Barney's department tore.

Another aspect of Patty's signature look was her prominent, thick-framed glasses that magnified her big brown eyes. Her curly dark hair framed her pretty face. For some reason, the braces on her teeth would not accomplish the desired outcome the orthodontist was going for, so even though she was old enough to graduate, her mouth was still filled with hardware.

The teasing followed Patty throughout elementary school and into high school. It started with the tuna fish sandwiches and orange soda pop in her lunches. She had taken the same lunch to school since sixth grade and could often be heard defending herself by stating, "For your information, the mushy tuna is palatable and does not hurt my teeth, because I have a hard time chewing."

As an academically average student, year after year, her report card consistently stated that she would do much better if she would only apply herself more. Patty preferred animals to people and books to social events, which was why she volunteered in the school library after school and worked on weekends cleaning up at the local vet, located in the hospital's new wing.

Her dad was a garbage man, more professionally known as a sanitation engineer. Patty's mom often said in a derogatory tone, "Garbagemen pick up other people's trash. It has nothing to do with sanitation or engineering!"

Mrs. Krakatoya, or Maybelle to her family, was a former beauty contest winner destined for pageant success. However, as a preteen, she had started finishing her parents' half-empty beer bottles after their weekend parties. It had become a family joke and was thought to be adorable until it became no longer fun and entertaining, but embarrassing and problematic.

Maybelle had entered contests most of her childhood and teenage years. The first contest she ever won was the Little Miss Peach Pit competition. Later, she became The Fasp Farms Egg Girl, Tractors and Tiaras Teen of the Year, and Barney's Department Store Representative. However, her greatest notoriety came when she was crowned the Tiger Lily Princess. Her prizes were a new car and a year's supply of tiger lilies delivered weekly to her doorstep. Tiger lilies grew wild in MeadowBrook, and so did Maybelle.

The final straw was Maybelle's last competition, MeadowBrook's Miss May Day, when her drinking had escalated and she became inebriated even before walking down the runway in a bright yellow one-piece bathing suit. She momentarily went off her rocker when she shimmied right in front of the judges and began stripping. As she was escorted off the stage, she sang her own rendition of "Happy Birthday," as Marilyn Monroe once did to the president of the United States. As they dragged her off stage, Maybelle kicked and screamed in a slurred voice, "Leave me alone, you hayseed hillbillies!"

Eventually, she crashed her prize Mustang convertible and was disqualified from ever competing again. The entire town was appalled, and the gossip mill was so intense that Maybelle became a recluse and a topic of conversation for years to follow. She stopped taking care of her appearance and eventually settled on marriage, having one child she named Patricia. Maybelle then became addicted to soap operas in addition to alcohol and was labelled the town drunk.

On the day before the graduation ceremony, Patty's mom suggested she get a perm at Helga's Hair Salon. She raved to her daughter that permanents were the trend and a simple procedure where the hairdresser wraps the hair in rods before putting perm lotion on to set the curl. Unfortunately, because Patty's hair was already naturally curly, the neutralizer designed to halt the perming process was ineffective, and Patty's hair turned into a tight frizzy mess.

Helga apologized and offered to send Patty to Barney's Barbershop to have her head shaved at no extra cost. Patty refused, left the salon and cried all the way home. Her mother was no comfort and suggested Patty have a beer and forget the whole debacle, which in turn caused Patty to weep even louder.

On the night of their graduation, Patty got ready at her friend Jan's house because her mother was soused. Jan promised to straighten Patty's hair with an iron and towel while Patty lay on the floor in her bedroom. They had both decided to wear cream-coloured matching evening gowns with different coloured sashes. Both were purchased at Barney's department store.

Patty's father drove the girls to the graduation ceremony in his garbage truck, and neither friend minded. On the contrary, Patty adored her father and shared almost everything with him, including her lifelong dream of one day becoming famous and marrying Nelson Farnsworth.

Patty and Jan sat together while the disco ball glittered and shimmered off the basketball hoops. They longed to be asked to dance. Patty stared at Nelson and whispered a silent prayer, *"Please God, let Nelson notice me."*

***

Everyone in school knew Susan Jillian. She was hard to miss from being a fixture on the sidelines as head cheerleader for the basketball team. Susan had a girl squad of friends that she paid little attention to and she worked weekends at Barney's in the lingerie department.

In keeping with her stereotypical popular girl status, Susan was more interested in the latest fashion trends and the boys on the basketball team, than getting good grades and being kind. But what took precedence over everything else was that Susan had one thing on her mind, something she had obsessed over since tenth grade and was determined to make happen on the night of graduation.

Susan Jillian's yearbook prediction stated she would "*most likely marry a wealthy and prosperous businessman, live in a mansion, and have two kids.*'" Nicknamed Suzy-Q, she was elusive and traditionally attractive. Magazine pretty, with her blond hair neatly tied up in a ponytail, Susan was well known for her thick layers of CoverGirl mascara and Bonne Bell cherry-flavoured lip gloss. Susan always smelled like Avon's *Sweet Honesty* perfume, and yet the rumours indicated she was anything but sweet and honest.

Susan wore her cheerleading uniform on game days and only dated jocks from the basketball team. She dressed in the latest trend of high-waisted wide-leg jeans, wedge platform shoes, fitted turtlenecks, and a thin gold necklace with a heart pendant nestled at her throat. Susan proudly draped her current boyfriend's letterman jacket over everything. Some called her a floozy and most assumed she slept around.

Susan's mother was a nurse in the geriatric ward of the local hospital, and her dad was an accountant. She had three younger sisters who were triplets—a phenomenon in the small town. Their names were Sylvia, Sara, and Sasha. Much attention went to them, and their family was referred to as the Four S's. As in "Here come the Four S's. I would sure hate to be their parents." Comments such as these were followed with a laugh and a slap on the back.

The entire family were avid churchgoers, and Susan's father demanded scripture readings before school and in the evening at bedtime. Susan dutifully obliged but secretly thought herself to be independent, and therefore did whatever she wanted. If she was ever not allowed to do something, she did it anyway. She got so used to sneaking out of her house that she rarely entered or left by the front door. Susan was desperate to escape from her parents' judgment, reign, and never-ending rules.

In preparation for the graduation ceremony, Susan had travelled to the town of Hillsprings by bus and bought a dress from the Suzy Creamcheese store in the Hillsprings Mall. She had decided to wear a long coat over her sequined red grad dress to hide the plunging neckline and micro-mini length, so her family was none the wiser. Susan knew they would never approve of her risqué outfit, especially her grandmother, who was already referring to her as a harlot and a Jezebel.

She was anxious and excited for the grad ceremony, but more so about what was to come afterward. Susan had planned for the outcome all year.

Lover's Lane was only known by the teenagers and was situated on a bluff overlooking the whole town. On star-studded nights it was breathtaking, and in the winter it was a cozy place to go to snuggle and steam up the windows. Susan suspected one of the boys from the basketball team would take her to Lovers' Lane after the festivities. Even though she frequented the spot regularly, she had never gone all the way with a boy before, so she had decided months earlier that she would finally give in to a teenage boy's pleading advances on grad night. Because of the suspected murder back in 1953, Susan was forbidden to be out past 9:00 p.m., especially without a chaperone. But a notorious murderer on the loose would not be a deterrent to Susan's initiation to womanhood and a ticket out of the home that was stifling her.

***

Once outside in the warm night air, Johnny and Darcie said nothing to each other as they walked side by side under the moonlit sky, occasionally bumping up against each other like they had done many times before.

The night had turned balmy and the heat complimented their sense of security as they meandered toward the pond, the old swimming hole where they grew up having family picnics as children, adventures exploring the shoreline as young teens, and drunken nights around campfires throughout high school. Both friends knew they were on the verge of an unspoken and unknown future.

In his slow, methodical way of speaking, Johnny said, "What now, Darce?"

She liked it when he called her that. She responded as non-committally as she could, "I don't know J. I'd like to leave, but I got my mom, you know. It breaks my heart when I think of her alone in this shit hole town."

They sat for a while, taking in the moment. Each silently questioned how many times they had walked the same road and how many times they had wondered about the other.

Darcie knew Johnny would date her in a second. But she had always thought of him more like a brother. The brother she never had. And he knew it, so he was not about to make a move at this stage in the game. With a rush of heat to his face, he remembered trying to kiss her back in Grade 9 and how she'd pushed him off with a gentle laugh and a friendly shove. And that was that, never again.

Besides, another boy had captured her heart years earlier. Only Johnny did not know it yet, even though he suspected there might be someone else.

As the moon slipped behind a cloud, the eeriness reminded Darcie of how safe she felt with her secret boyfriend Dakota and how Johnny could never take his place. Sitting side by side on the rickety old dock, both alone in their thought bubbles, Johnny reflected on his love for Darcie while she pondered her love for another.

Darcie remembered when she first met Dakota in Grade 1, innocently holding hands while lined up for gym class. People thought they looked like twins. Both had shaggy dark hair, big brown eyes and darker complexions—hers from swimming all summer at the pond in the glaring sunshine and his from his heritage. It wasn't until years later, at fourteen, that they shared their first intimate embrace.

When Johnny pulled out his rolling papers, Darcie glanced at him briefly and then-ignored him, closed her eyes, and allowed the flashbacks to continue.

It was in the school library back when they were in ninth grade when Darcie and Dakota felt the first sparks. She recalled his bowed head and how he peeked up at her through the hair that covered his eyes. She gave him one of her radiant smiles, a facial expression she rarely shared, not even with Johnny. Dakota smiled back just as enthusiastically.

Instinctively, they knew it was the start of something electric, even though they were so young.

The sound of gentle water ripples on the shoreline took Darcie out of the past and back to the warmth of Johnny's body next to her, which brought a flood of annoyance, and she wished Dakota was the boy sitting beside her instead of Johnny.

Darcie then wondered where Dakota was at that very moment. Her disappointment made her heart flip over and back again, aching in the process. She placed her hand on her chest, fearing her angst would leap out through her breastbone and land in the water beneath her and Johnny's feet.

Instead, Darcie said nothing and sat quietly next to Johnny, continuing to think of Dakota. The two guys were completely different in every way, from their looks to their social standing and views of the world. She knew Johnny loved her and hoped that Dakota did, too—a thought that warmed her and simultaneously frightened her.

Darcie could never see the guys being friends, even though as fellow students under the same roof, they had been cordial to one another. Their mutual connection with her was the only thing they had in common; the girl who had captured their attention and consequently their hearts from as far back as both boys could remember.

And then like cloud coverage on the star-studded prairie night, feelings of anger began to creep into Darcie's mind, eventually becoming unbearable. As sobs constricted her throat, she felt the beginning stages of tiny tears in her heart. In the calmness of the water's edge, she could almost hear them, the shredding and ripping of her love for a boy who obviously did not feel the same about her as she did about him. Sitting beside her best friend Johnny, Darcie had become hugely disheartened and greatly disappointed that Dakota had been a no-show for what might be their last night together.

***

Amanda and her gal pal volleyball crew left the dance collectively while keeping to the pact they made earlier that day. Their plan was to go home early enough to get a sober good night's sleep, as first thing the following day they would be piling into Amanda's parents' minivan to make the three-hour drive to tour their future school. With summer now before them, it was time to buckle down and make some money before starting university in September. The whole team had enrolled in the PDP Program, also known as the Teacher Education Professional Development Program. To Amanda, her teaching certificate was the only thing of importance. That, and fleeing the confines of MeadowBrook.

***

As the evening came to a close, some late-night stragglers were picked up by parents, while others headed over to the pond to pull an all-nighter and watch the sun come up.

Tracy enlisted the grad committee to help clean up, while Principle Marples oversaw the dismantling, sweeping up, and sponging down of spilled drinks and ground-up cheezies on the gym floor. When he locked up the heavy steel gymnasium doors, the principal took one last look around and whispered to himself, "Goodnight

MeadowBrook High, and good luck, grads, you're going to need it." Rolling his eyes and grimacing, Mr. Marples headed home alone to his nightcap of straight-up Scotch and a room full of puppets.

Manfred Marples had started teaching at MeadowBrook Elementary School in 1951, fresh out of university. He had been a popular puppeteer back in his college days and had introduced his decorative wood and straw marionettes shortly before the disappearance of William Farnsworth. By 1953 he had already performed in front of dozens of audiences, so it only made sense to combine his social justice hobby with his career as an educator.

Over the years, his marionette collection increased. His puppet shows addressed the dangers of smoking and drinking, and grieving the loss of a parent to death or divorce. His William Farnsworth marionette educated schoolchildren on the issues around fear and stranger danger. Especially since so many people had been traumatized, he felt it was the least he could do, considering the circumstances.

By the 1960s, Manfred Marples had been promoted to vice principal of the new high school, and in the early 1970s, he became the well-loved principal. Manfred had never dated and remained a bachelor, with all the students becoming his children.

Looking back, the 1970s brought a fashion revolution. Polyester, platform shoes, bell bottoms, leisure suits, and cowl neck sweaters were all the rage among the students and staff at MeadowBrook High. Some students drove Corvettes while others drove Chevy Chevettes. Yet, many took the school bus, hitched a ride or walked the long country roads in the small farming community known for its farm-fresh egg production. They watched *All in the Family*, *Sanford and Son,* and *Maude*. They listened to funk, soul, R&B, pop, hard rock, soft rock, and disco. Everyone had a record player at home and an eight-track tape deck in their car and were now switching to cassette tapes because they were the upcoming trend.

Be that as it may, family and social life had drastically changed for teenagers in the '70s. Gone was the innocence of rocking around the clock in penny loafers, poodle skirts and argyle sweaters. Instead, the new fad was about sex, drugs, and rock and roll. Flamboyancy, popular cliques, and showing off dominated the party scene. Teens were speaking up, and it seemed like everyone was fighting for something—women's rights, equal rights, gay rights, pollution, and the energy crisis.

Earlier in the '70s, an article in the *MeadowBrook Gazette* came out titled, "Kids Today Are Bad News." The reporter stated, "The youth today are selfish, spoiled, lazy and irresponsible. Most of them skip school and rebel in any way possible."

The local scuttlebutt had spearheaded the newspaper story about the teenagers who loitered about the small town, hung out at the local diner, walked up and down Main Street, and held weekend parties at the once family-oriented place known as the Fasp Family Pond. After the story ran, the tone and facial expressions of the townspeople changed. Many of them showed disdain and made judgmental comments about the town's young people that were very subjective in their nature.

In retaliation, a rally was held to renounce the labelling, and many teens spoke up and said the stereotypes were unfair and untrue. They worried that the undeserved titles and negative perceptions would follow them for the rest of their lives. Despite the inevitable moments of indiscretion that are common in the teen years, they were good kids overall.

The MeadowBrook class of 1978 was on their way, unabashed in its anticipation of the future. Each student had hopes and dreams. Some would have a lucky break, others would have misfortune and struggles. It was heads or tails, or a wheel of fortune because that's the way the cookie crumbles.

And yet the question remained for all of them, "Are we our stereotypes, or did our stereotypes make us?"

Tim Barnes - Jock
Nelson Farnsworth - Nerd
Johnny Fasp - Pothead
Kent Gordon - Preppie
Dakota Hillsman – Stud
Susan Jillian - Floozy
Tracy Hansworth - Busybody
Patty Krakatoya - Wallflower
Amanda Marsthrop – Teacher's Pet
Darcie Richmond - Party Girl

Chapter Two

Finding Themselves

"Once I was brave enough to leave home, then, and only then, could I ever think about returning."

—Darcie Richmond

After graduation, Tim was all set to attend law school. He had been accepted but knew his father must have pulled some strings because his grades determined he was nowhere near bright enough. Nevertheless, he went. His parents couldn't have been more happy or more proud. His father, especially.

The following year turned into a blur of failed exams and drunken stupors. Eventually, Tim left—quit law school before he was kicked out, and packed up to move to Los Angeles, California. He planned to enroll in acting school and audition for television shows and movies.

After he made the decision to leave, Tim got busy planning his escape. First, he found the *LA Times* in a newspaper box and located an apartment. Next, he wired the damage deposit and the first month's rent sight unseen. He had been saving his monthly allowance for quite some time, in addition to years of Christmas money from relatives.

In the middle of the night, he loaded up his black 1978 Toyota Celica and drove home from university, away from the worst year of his life. The car was a graduation present from his parents. Tim parked a block away from the home he grew up in, scribbled a brief note, and tried to walk urgently, but his legs felt heavy as if he were moving through quicksand. Once he found himself in front of the open front gate and perfectly manicured lawn, Tim was suddenly filled with dread and couldn't bring himself to knock. Instead, he thumb-tacked a short message to his parent's front door. All it said was, *"Your dream, not mine. Sayonara!"*

Afterward, Tim wanted to laugh. He felt an immense burden leave his shoulders and was immediately stoked and excited for his future. He ran back down the driveway and down the street to his waiting vehicle, transformed and light as a fairy. He climbed into his car and revved the engine. Near the outskirts of town, he yelled at the top of his lungs as he drove past the giant, familiar, stupid egg statue, "Just watch me now, MeadowBrook!"

Driving across the country was a time to reflect, regroup, and refocus. Tim was healing from a past he had perpetually lived for someone else, and a future he was finally making his own.

He had often heard that people reinvented themselves when they moved to California. There seemed to be something transformative about the road west, the cities on the hills and the valleys surrounded by the sea. In a magazine article, he read, *"Once people enter the golden state, they are not the same anymore."*

However, Tim wondered if he ever really knew who he was in the first place, and if that was true, how would he ever change from someone he didn't know?

He found his quaint furnished bachelor pad on Ventura Boulevard, got the key from the super and let himself in. It had seen better days and needed a few coats of paint. The whole setup reminded Tim of something straight out of an old 1950s *Dick Tracy* show. Outside the motel-like setting were faded beach umbrellas and chipped metal chairs surrounding a kidney-shaped swimming pool. Despite the age of the structure, he liked the pink doors of the apartments and how they overlooked the parking lot and pool below. Tim thought his new digs charming, and the best part was that his new home was a fresh start.

The suite came sparsely furnished, but Tim managed to spruce it up. He bleached the floors, walls, and cupboards, and bought new bedding and fabric to make curtains and pillow covers for the hard lumpy couch. Tim had no idea he had such a flair for design, so he decided to paint the whole interior in bright, bold colours as soon as he got a job.

He enrolled in acting, singing, and dance classes and signed on with a talent agent. Lastly, he found a bartending job near his new pad, at a popular discotheque.

Never had Tim done something HE wanted to do.

He knew it would take time to get discovered, so he settled into a hectic routine and was content when he landed dozens of movie extra gigs. He became the guy in the background holding a newspaper, a man sitting with a woman in a coffee shop, a young adult playing basketball behind the leading actors at Venice Beach, a police officer clad in uniform in the distance, and so on…

There was always a sea of other hopeful actors trying out just like himself. Young people from far and wide sat alongside Tim in rundown waiting rooms, anticipating their big chance at stardom.

Tim went with his coworkers—and sometimes with women he served in the club—to see stand-up comedians, poets, and bands perform. After years of listening to George Carlin's record albums in the confines of his bedroom, Tim was awestruck watching him perform live, standing in front of a dark, smoke-filled room. "California: bordering always on the Pacific and sometimes on the ridiculous. So, why do I live here? Because the sun goes down a block from my house," Carlin professed with his dry, perfect timing. As the room erupted in laughter Tim knew he was where he needed to be.

He felt as bright as the sun on the California coast.

But as time passed, a subtle familiar loneliness crept in. The Hollywood nights were losing their allure, and even though Tim found some comfort in dating a few women, none of them felt right. So, after three failed relationships, he settled on one-night stands, flings that gradually made him feel worse about himself. In the early '80s, AIDS was the number one deadly transmittable disease, and even though Tim used protection, he was terrified. Unfortunately, he could not get off the vicious cycle of sleeping around.

The terror of his sexual encounters had become addictive. Consequently, before long, Tim became mentally, physically, and emotionally exhausted. With no significant acting parts coming his way, his disappointment was mounting.

The days turned into weeks, and the weeks turned into months. Before long, the years added up, and Tim never went back to MeadowBrook. Instead, he called home occasionally and once, early on, his parents and little sister came out to visit him. They stayed at a Motel 7 near Disneyland.

Tim lied and sold the idea he was doing well, had a girlfriend, and would be getting his big break soon. His family went home, reluctantly happy for him, but there was distrust and disbelief in his mother's and father's eyes.

Eight years after leaving law school, Tim still had nothing to show for himself. He sank deeper and deeper into his anguish and despair. The auditions had become few and far between, while the booze-invested nights increased. In the spring of 1988, almost ten years after leaving MeadowBrook, Tim awoke to the sound of his clock radio blaring out the traffic report. He was instantly bombarded with an adrenaline rush of nameless panic.

He rolled over and covered his head with his bedspread that smelled like Oscar de la Renta perfume. The bile rose in his throat as he remembered the night before, causing him to feel immense remorse and humiliation. Visions of the smoke-filled discotheque, crammed with drunken partygoers clamouring to the bar, were a blur. Tim had never felt more alone as he concocted weak drinks and poured flat beer to ungrateful drunks, disco divas, pimps, and hookers. Every bartending shift blended into the next, and every woman he slept with looked and smelled the same. If hopelessness had a scent, it would have the essence of sexual activity without emotional commitment or future involvement, combined with varying body types and different shades and lengths of hair.

As desolation gripped him, Tim padded into the kitchen to make coffee, get the newspaper, and open his mail from the day before. His morning routine consisted of freshly brewed coffee with heavy cream and three teaspoons of sugar, accompanied by three aspirin for his dry, parched mouth. After the rim of his cup touched his lips, he sipped the morning delicacy and absorbed the pills as if they were his lifeline. Tim anxiously waited for his mind to clear. The combination of caffeine and pain relief decreased the risk of another ruined day due to a habitual hangover. But only momentarily, as the fogginess from drinking too much and blacking out always returned, briefly gone but never forgotten.

The day was like any other until the red flashing light on his answering machine beckoned for his attention. After having put it off for over a week, with guilt and trepidation, he pressed play.

First up was the pleading tone of his mother's voice, "Hey Timmy, I sure wish you would pick up. I am just wondering how you are doing. Miss you, please call me back as soon as possible. We're all worried about you."

He waited for the next message to be from his little sister and he was ready to delete it at the onset. Tim cringed, recalling the previous messages Marnie had sent him over the years. She always whined into the phone, with each word being held longer than the one before it for effect, "*Dummyyyy*, I've been trying to reach you about my geometry test! School is *waaaay* harder than you said! AND when you left you PROMISED you would help *meeee*!" Just before hanging up, the kid sister he never had the time of day for would blow a raspberry onto her hand and then slam down the receiver as only a spoiled brat would do.

Thinking about Marnie reminded Tim how much younger she was than him, and he speculated she would never grow up. When the next message wasn't from Marnie, Tim realized it had been years since she had called…or since he had chosen to ignore her. He felt a check in his spirit and briefly wondered how she was doing.

He let out a heavy sigh and listened to his father's message.

"I'm sick of this shit, Tim! You said you were trading in university for acting school. My ass! We haven't heard from you in months! Just pick up the damn phone, you idiot! We are all waiting to see you on the big screen, or have you messed that up too? At least a stupid toothpaste commercial for all the money that went into your braces, which reminds me, you owe me big-time, fella!"

The answering machine cut him off before Tim's dad could finish or say goodbye. In the quiet of his small 1950s-style kitchen, the long beep of Tim deleting all the nagging recordings was all that was heard, the tone flatlining as if someone's heart had stopped beating.

Tim decided he would not be returning any of their messages. *They can all go to hell*, he thought to himself. Taking a big swig of the cold coffee, Tim let the bittersweetness slide down his throat as he turned to a stack of mail. He chose not to open the electricity bill, phone bill, and long overdue cable bill. For a fleeting moment, he thought of the irony and whispered to himself, *Even if I did land a television commercial, I would not be able to watch it because my Cablevision has been cut off for months.*

At the bottom of the stack of mail was a light pink envelope peeking out from under the pile. Tim blankly stared at the corner and noticed a name on the return address. His breath caught. He squinted his eyes and pulled the envelope out, staring at it more. In the top left-hand corner, in perfect, eloquent handwriting, he read *"Tracy Hansworth, 8672 Cherrywood Drive, MeadowBrook, Canada."*

Immediately, Tim perked up with curiosity and wondered why Tracy Hansworth, the high-school busybody, was writing him a letter. He ripped open the envelope and instantly noticed it wasn't a letter at all, but an invitation.

MeadowBrook High School Ten-Year Reunion

Saturday, June 13th, Formal Dance 7
p.m. to midnight, school gym
Sunday, June 14th, Farewell Brunch 11:00
a.m. to 3:00 p.m., picnic at the pond

Cost $25.00
RSVP ASAP
Tracy Hansworth
8722 Cherry Wood Drive
MeadowBrook
Canada

After scanning the invite, Tim said to himself out loud, "No friggin' way! How could I possibly attend in the state I am in, and why would I even want to? I have nothing to say to those people." His mind raced with all the woulda, coulda, shoulda's.

Tim stared blankly at the invitation and was jolted out of his perturbed state by the sound of his pager going off. He took it everywhere, and at that moment, it vibrated in the pocket of his maroon floral bathrobe. Without urgency, he pulled it out and saw a message from his agent (the only person who ever paged him). Tim blinked in disbelief and had to read it twice.

Hey buddy, looks like you got it! You better pack up, as rehearsals start in two weeks! Call me!

Tim had been part of an auditioning process for the Broadway musical *Fame*, the stage musical that had been adapted from the 1980 film. Having seen the film a dozen times, Tim was a big fan of the story about an exceptionally talented group of students at an arts high school who shared their ambition, challenges, successes, and failures. He was inspired by their journey to become stars and found every second of the movie to be relatable.

When he got to the open casting call, he had auditioned with extremely high hopes, but weeks had passed, so he figured he hadn't been noticed, just like all the other times he had been passed up for someone taller, someone shorter, someone more handsome or less attractive.

Upon calling his agent, he was told that the casting director was impressed with his dancing skill and singing ability. In addition, he had said, "There is something about Tim Barnes that is perfect for the production. This young man definitely has the "it" factor!"

The live stage production of *Fame* was set to open in Miami, Florida, the summer of 1988.

Tim's heart rate went from zero to one hundred in the blink of his bloodshot eyes. His adrenaline rush cancelled out his hangover, leaving his mind buzzing, and he thought long and hard about travelling back to MeadowBrook for the reunion because now he would have something to show off about. *Screw them all!* he thought and then laughed out loud.

Tim promptly made a list:

- quit my job
- stop drinking
- get healthy
- no more one-night stands
- RSVP Tracy ASAP

With an immediate attitude adjustment, Tim felt like he was finally coming out on the other end of his lifelong disappointment.

Feeling so much better, Tim took his burst of energy and made it worthwhile. First, he did the dishes and then laid out his clothes for that day—a light yellow paisley shirt, white rolled-up jeans, and a pair of white thong sandals. Next, he jumped in the shower, lathered up his head with Herbal Essences shampoo, and scoured his body with an apricot body scrub. Tim stayed in the shower a little longer than usual to give the hair conditioner time to penetrate each hair shaft and to savour thoughts of his new, bright future while the hot water revived him.

Before jaywalking across the street to hand in his resignation at the club, Tim looked around at the once-fresh environment, the land of milk and honey. He remembered how no two sunsets were ever the same. He had forgotten how the tall, skinny palm trees that lined the streets and the poppies growing wild everywhere used to excite him. At that moment, Tim took note of the warm morning breeze that smelled of sand and salt water, and then tried to think back to the first day his rose-coloured glasses had lost their tint and his positive attitude had grown dark.

While taking in his surroundings just outside the disco he had worked at for almost ten years, Tim could not remember when he had lost hope and when the once blue skyline and soft white sand had turned dirty and grey. In that split second, Tim blamed his past struggles on his incessant need for fame and fortune, which had transformed into unrealistic hopes and unattainable dreams.

Finally, he would have something to show for himself.

Before entering the bar, Tim exhaled profoundly, smiled broadly, and cranked open the tinted double glass doors, entering the drinking establishment just before the 11:00 a.m. rush. Once inside, Tim was startled by how the bright lights highlighted the stained carpet, sticky tables, and dirty walls. The once glamorous discotheque now appeared like a dingy container for lost souls and dashed dreams.

He made his way to the back office and found his boss, Misty. Tim smiled to himself at her made-up name. He always wondered if her real name was Mildred, or maybe Helga.

In a tone that was lighter than usual, Tim said, "Hey, how's it going?"

Misty jumped at Tim's voice and noticed his unusually clean-shaven, fresh appearance. Before answering, she briefly thought of their relationship. She had been immediately smitten with his country-boy charm and they had dated for a while back in the early '80s—how vivacious they both had been! She had always admired Tim's neat, clean apartment and impeccable fashion sense. And then, after bearing witness to his gradual downfall, she'd dumped him like a hot potato.

Looking at him now, Misty instantly noticed how Tim's charisma and appeal had returned. The dark circles under his eyes were gone, along with the whiskered, blotchy, and bloated face.

Hanging on to her warm feelings about her long-ago boyfriend, Misty smiled and said, "It's going okay…you know the biz!" Then, letting out a sarcastic chortle, she delved into her usual complaints, "Just like any other ordinary day—the books don't add up, Shasta called in sick again, and the rum, gin, bourbon, and vodka need to be watered down again." Then in a happier mood, she said, "How's it going with you?"

Tim had at one time thought they were the perfect couple, until they became bored and grew disenchanted with each other. She had complained about his lack of affection, and he inwardly felt no love toward her, yet he could never understand why. She was a sought-after, intelligent and beautiful woman who could have any guy in any room at any time.

Misty had long, curly auburn hair, noticeably high cheekbones, full lips and thick eyelashes that were permanently plastered with layers of black mascara. She stood as tall as he did, and he admired how she could wear three-inch stiletto heels for ten hours a day and never complain about the onset of bunions.

Tim quickly bypassed his feelings of nostalgia, as old sentiments were not important and past memories did not matter anymore. Without going down the rabbit hole of love lost, Tim boldly stated, "I'm quitting, Misty. I'm handing in my two-week's notice today. Right now, in fact."

At first, Misty looked disappointed, and without even asking why he was quitting, she said, "I'm genuinely happy for you, Tim. I wish you all the best. Now, can you please call Shasta and beg her to come in? She always listens to you!"

As Tim picked up the telephone to call his coworker—another woman he had dated a few years back—he could not contain his excitement. He yelled to Misty, "I got a part in the hit Broadway musical *Fame*! Rehearsals start in a few weeks in Miami!"

Misty wanted to be happy for Tim, so she pretended she was. In reality, she was instantly jealous and felt deflated, as she had also tried to make it as an actor. Nevertheless, she mustered up as much enthusiasm as possible when she said, "Congratulations! That's so radical, Tim! You've worked so hard and look, now it's happening!" Then in a pleading tone, she added, "Now PLEASE phone that stupid waitress!"

As Tim was dialing the phone, Misty said with a smile, "Oh, and by the way, if any parts come up for an aging nightclub singer, give me a call, will ya?"

Tim grinned and said, "You better believe I will!!"

As he packed up and prepared for rehearsals, Tim whispered the chorus from the hit theme song "Fame" by Irene Cara. Tim consciously freed himself of all heaviness and wholeheartedly embraced the words about living forever and learning to fly high. Finally he was getting the chance to light up the sky, and soon everyone would be chanting his name and remembering it.

***

Johnny slept in most days. Even though the Fasp farm had an abundance of chores that started before dawn and carried on through the day past dusk, he rarely pitched in, and his brothers always picked up the slack. It was apparent and accepted that Johnny was the favourite of the seven boys. It was a given that Johnny was excused from early morning wake-up calls, roosters crowing, hens laying, and tractors revving.

However, the morning after graduation, Johnny woke up earlier than usual to the smell of bacon frying and strong coffee brewing. He'd had a fitful sleep, even though it was early morning when he finally got home from the pond with Darcie. He was unsettled, and his gut told him something was up with his lifelong friend and confidante, but he couldn't put his finger on it.

After the grad ceremony, Darcie had seemed more subdued than usual and refused his offer to smoke a joint as they'd laid down on the dock toe to toe, gazing up into the cloudless starry night—a ritual they had been doing since they first started high school.

Darcie's refusal to smoke his homegrown bud made Johnny reconsider partaking in his recreational drug of choice. He was often heard saying, "Weed is my go-to form of daily AND nightly recreation, kind of like a vitamin pill!" This statement was always accompanied by a charming smile, a wink, and an outward laugh. But he didn't smoke last night, and after Johnny had walked Darcie home and picked up his truck at the school, it was past 4 a.m. He chuckled to himself that maybe he was going through withdrawal, as a few tokes usually sent him into a peaceful La-La Land–induced sleep.

When Johnny glanced at the clock radio on his bedside table, the red digital display indicated the time was 8:07 a.m. He turned the music on and recognized one of Darcie's most loved songs, "Stairway to Heaven." The familiar opening riff and slow crooning of Led Zeppelin always reminded Johnny of her.

But this time he felt haunted by the lyrics and listened more intently, wondering if the metaphoric "sign on the wall" was Darcie's reluctance to smoke a joint with him last night. He worried that Darcie was no longer his songbird and that she was keeping something from him. He hoped his thoughts were not true.

Johnny had a sense of foreboding as he lingered in bed. He wondered why his heart was always sad about something that happened yesterday, and his head was always worried about something that might happen tomorrow.

His grandmother had always referred to him as a dreamer. To prove his point, only to himself, he thought of Darcie again, and how their usual goodnight hug felt like a split-second carved in eternal time, so prominently different from all the other *just friends* embraces in the past.

Johnny shook his head to free himself from the melancholy creeping in, and then he leapt out of bed and looked around his sparsely decorated bedroom, a room he shared with no one. This often embarrassed him, as his brothers all shared bedrooms with bunk beds, bookcases, and matching quilts their mother, grandmother, aunties and, more recently, sisters-in-law had made. He then wondered why everyone treated him just a little bit differently, even though he liked it.

Shifting gears, Johnny thought of his mother, sisters-in-law, grandmother and aunties with their laughter and hushed tones drifting up the wooden staircase or out onto the wrap-around porch. Their quilting bees filled Johnny with a serene peacefulness and profound love toward his large and growing family.

He laughed in spite of himself when the Special-K cereal commercial came on the radio, encouraging Johnny's mood to change to optimism. He decided the morning after high-school graduation was going to be "the first day of the rest of his life," just as the ad suggested.

With that, he bounded out of his bedroom and clamoured down the stairs into the kitchen, where he unexpectedly twirled his mother around and high-fived three of his brothers. As he popped some crunchy bacon into his mouth, the country-style kitchen erupted into laughter and merriment.

His usually reserved mother said, "My word, aren't you a sight for sore eyes!" His older brothers began their usual wrestling routine with their endeared middle brother, and Grandma clucked at them to settle down. Johnny professed to their kind, jovial faces, "You are now looking at a certified high-school graduate, thank you very much!" His oldest brother quickly chimed in with a mischievous tone, "Certifiable, you mean!"

Everyone was still laughing as John Fasp entered the kitchen after doing the morning chores. He tousled Johnny's hair, and with a grin, said, "What did I miss?"

John Fasp Sr. reminded Johnny of the television character John Walton, from the hit show *The Waltons*. Or perhaps it was the actor that reminded Johnny of his dad. The handsome, down-to-earth TV dad coincidently looked like Johnny's father but appeared to have fewer deep, brooding thoughts.

John Fasp, after whom Johnny was fondly named, stood six feet tall and was the family's rock. Older than most of his friends' parents in 1978, he was sixty-three. With thick silver hair and chiselled features, his weathered complexion and strong, fit body that he got from being outdoors and working the farm, revealed that his life had not been easy.

John Senior liked his coffee strong and his whiskey stronger. A man of few words, but a face that spoke of wisdom and mystique, there had always been something perplexing to Johnny about his dad, something rather abstruse and mystifying. He wondered if his brothers felt it, too. If he thought too long and hard about the man revered by his large family, Johnny became filled with an icy, cryptic rush he could not understand or begin to explain. So, he kept those thoughts fleeting and pushed them down whenever they crept up.

"No Rest for the Wicked" was a sign the family lovingly and jokingly gave their dad one Christmas many years earlier. The Fasp family, for generations, had been known for their attention to detail, immaculate upkeep of their farm, and hard work ethic. Hence the plaque was displayed over the door in the main barn. The sign was meant to be a playful reminder of their dad's insistence on never resting until the job was done. Instead, unbeknownst to the rest of the family, the sign mocked John Sr. every time he passed underneath it. Therefore, he deliberately did not look at it. The word *wicked* dismally reminded John of regrets, mistakes, and secrets—classified information, undisclosed and accountable to no one except the dark corners of his mind.

John Fasp often thought of another place and time and a woman who would eternally hold his heart. Someone other than his wife. In such a way, the endless guilt would eat away at his thoughts and remind him of the wounded heart of another and what was left of his fragmented soul.

Over that morning's breakfast of hotcakes, bacon, and maple syrup, Johnny speculated that most of his family members knew about his business venture, but they turned a blind eye. He had been discreet about his grow-op, always made good grades, and as his grandmother often said, “Our Johnny is the salt of the earth and would never hurt a flea.”

Ironically, it was Grandma Fasp who first got Johnny interested in the calming effects of marijuana. She had read a *Time* magazine article about how cannabis had been scientifically proven to relieve pain in lab rats and human guinea pigs. In addition, the news piece reported how people used it for pleasure. By the early ’70s, some doctors had even started prescribing it for specific medical conditions and symptoms.

Johnny’s grandmother struggled with severe arthritis in her joints and muscle pain in her lower back. On that account, Johnny had read the magazine article at his grandmother’s suggestion and decided to help her. He called it a win-win situation, as he was not only helping his grandmother, but he was also making some money at the same time.

Consequently, Johnny felt closer to his grandma than his mother, Rebecca Fasp. He often surmised his mother had enough on her plate with six other sons and two daughters-in-law who vied for her attention. She was the family’s matriarch and managed the books, cooked, cleaned, sewed, and worked alongside her husband, who was the love of her life and always came first.

So, grandmother and grandson took on the secret project together. They cleared and tilled a small patch of land, planted the seeds and voilà! Grandma's pain became manageable. Eventually, they built a greenhouse, because unfortunately, the cold winter months in MeadowBrook made year-round growing difficult. The warmth created inside by converting light energy into heat helped the "tomato" plants thrive in the grow-op.

Grandma Fasp became Johnny's number one customer and sales representative. She promoted their product to the entire seniors' community of MeadowBrook for their aches, pains, and insomnia.

Before Saturday night bingo in the church basement, she'd pack her purse full of necessities: a troll good luck charm, a rabbit's foot, bingo dabbers, peppermints, and her favourite grandson's homegrown bud. As a result, she became known as the "Granny with the Whammy" and Johnny's leading retail outlet.

In the parking lot before bridge tournaments and cribbage games, Grandma Fasp sold their product out of the trunk of her 1969 Skylark, like a gypsy of old selling her wares.

Johnny became untouchable by law enforcement because of his father's notoriety. In fact, the entire Fasp family was well known in the community for offering jobs, creating or supporting charity events, and donating big bucks to the police force, fire department, and political campaigns. Therefore, Johnny received somewhat of a free ride when it came to the authorities turning a blind eye.

In the midst of all these activities, Johnny and his elderly grandma never spoke about the illegal aspect of what they were doing. He developed a supply and demand system with teenagers seeking their daily high, and he often wondered if his grandmother chose to look the other way on purpose or if she was proud of his business venture, and therefore thought it okay for underage young people to be partaking.

Each of the seven Fasp sons was handed down a substantial parcel of land. Their father's one thousand acres were intended to stay in the family, and even though John Fasp Sr. was a man of few words, he could often be heard saying, "Why wait for death to take me before dividing up and passing on my land? The land is for the living, and I want to see my offspring enjoy it."

Therefore, each son received their property the day they turned thirteen, like a rite of passage. Along with the distribution were a few stipulations written into the land title agreement—they must never sell their plot, and it had to stay in the family.

Not far from the main house, Johnny's one hundred acres was situated near a cluster of alder trees and rose bushes. The trees were native to the land, but the rose bushes were planted by his grandma and himself. It was a project they worked on every day after school for an entire planting season. "Trees and sweet-smelling flowers are pretty to look at and great for camouflaging purposes," Grandma Fasp said, with a wink and a grin.

A meandering brook snaked its way throughout the community of MeadowBrook, giving the town its name. Because the brook ran through their property, Fasp Farms benefited greatly. It became a routine for Johnny and his grandmother to walk his land arm in arm, stopping every now and then at different points along the brook. At those times, Johnny divulged his hopes, dreams, and plans for the future. Grandma Fasp was there for him, listening and taking in his every word. She encouraged him to travel, see the world, and live life to the fullest, to not fall under the pressures of his family, or worse, become complacent.

In the years that followed graduation, Johnny dated a few local girls and became quite well off financially. Nevertheless, he seemingly kept his nose clean and tried to be an upstanding citizen, aside from continuing to sell weed for medicinal purposes.

Eventually, he designed a house and built it with his dad and brothers. They worked well together, like a finely oiled machine. Each family member had a role and took direction from their father, the patriarch.

Johnny still thought of his best friend Darcie and kept tabs on her through Nancy, who visited the farm once in a while. When told of Darcie's artistic successes, he was genuinely happy for her but felt wounded at her lack of communication with him, missing the bond they once shared. Johnny never took it upon himself to reach out to Darcie, yet he felt a huge loss, like a gaping hole where she used to be.

From the outside looking in, Johnny was a "go with the flow" guy. His life appeared relatively uneventful. He was a mainstay in the community, liked by just about everyone. But at the age of twenty-seven, something happened that would leave him forever changed.

In the early spring of 1988, Grandmother Fasp became ill and passed away quite suddenly.

She always had a bedroom in the main house, just off the kitchen, because at one time it had been her home. After her husband died, her eldest son John married his high school sweetheart and took over the whole farm and egg production. In the beginning, Grandma Fasp got along with John's wife Rebecca, who had once been loving and kind. However, over the years Rebecca had become bitter and standoffish toward her.

Regardless, Grandma Fasp took a back seat to the woman who married her son and chose to be especially close to Johnny for reasons unknown to everyone else. Only Rebecca and John knew why and nothing was ever spoken about it. It was the Fasp family way. They were all tight-lipped, and secrets abounded. That is, until Grandma Fasp made a deathbed confession. Her dying proclamation sent the whole family into a tailspin.

When she first became sick, only a few weeks before she passed, Johnny dropped everything to tend to her. And then, moments before the woman who raised him took her last breath, she became coherent and clear. Johnny was sitting beside her late one afternoon when suddenly Grandma Fasp sat up in bed and pulled Johnny in close by reaching up and grabbing his shirt collar. "Please listen up!" she pleaded with him.

She then spoke to Johnny plainly as if she were well. At that instant, Grandma Fasp divulged a massive family secret, a blemish on the Fasp name and a scar that would affect the entire family for the rest of their lives. Her words were direct and filled with compassion.

"My dearest grandson, I am so sorry for the sins of your father, for my son has committed a terrible act of abandonment and unfaithfulness." Then in a steady tone, she said, "I have kept your mother's and father's secret far too long. I have always felt it a disservice to you to do so. But, here on my bed in our family home that my husband's father built, I must tell you something before I leave this world. Although my confession is factual and God's honest truth, it will hurt you, my beloved grandson."

Pausing, she asked for some water, took a sip and cleared her throat. Squeezing Johnny's hand, she went on to say, "Your best friend Darcie is your twin sister, so obviously her mother Nancy is your biological mother, too."

Disbelief, shock, and stabbing pain shot directly from Johnny's brain to his heart. First, he was confused and then instantly heartbroken. At a loss for words, he said nothing, but his ordinarily calm demeanour turned rigid and sharp.

His grandmother said, "Please take this information and use it wisely."

At that point, everything became apparent—his bond with Darcie and the many visits mother and daughter made to the farm over the years. It had been under his nose the whole time, and soon it would all be out in the open.

Johnny kissed his grandmother's forehead, got up from her bedside and went outside, walking the short distance to his house. As he stepped over his mail on the front porch, he smiled briefly at the thought of his young nephew's mail delivery routine. Then Johnny saw it, a foreign-looking pink envelope. Picking up the pile, he went inside, rolled a joint, and opened a bottle of whiskey.

Johnny drank until the bottle was empty and smoked until his lungs burned. In his stupor, he reflected on his grandmother's words and shuddered at his father's act of betrayal. Far too painful to consider, Johnny pushed down everything and tried to forget the sister he thought was just a friend.

Finally, he passed out until the rooster crowed and a stream of bright light slipped through a gap in the curtains his grandmother had lovingly made many years before.

Groggy and instantly irritable, he remembered the night before and felt his stomach turn and convulse, urging him to throw up. Johnny looked around the dimly lit room, spotting the unusual pastel envelope and without getting up, he reached for it and tore it open.

MeadowBrook High School Ten-Year Reunion

Saturday, June 13th, Formal Dance 7
p.m. to midnight, school gym
Sunday, June 14th, Farewell Brunch 11:00
a.m. to 3:00 p.m. picnic at the pond

Cost: $25.00

RSVP ASAP
Tracy Hansworth
8722 Cherry Wood Drive
MeadowBrook
Canada

Immediately, Darcie came to his mind, and Johnny started to cry. First, he wept for the girl he once thought he could marry. Then the old thoughts embarrassed him. Shame took siege over his entire being, and his rounded shoulders shook with sorrow for a mother he never knew. Of necessity, Johnny curled up in the fetal position and moaned. He found comfort in rocking back and forth as he tried to visualize a childhood of happy memories. Unlike his new truth, his entire life suddenly felt like a lie.

Johnny's body eventually slackened as exhaustion took hold. Lying on his couch in the living room, he had a new perception of his mother; not his real mother, but the stern, serious woman who had raised him. The parental figure who showed little affection toward him. Her coldness suddenly made sense.

Johnny was beyond recall of love toward his father. Instead, a slow-boiling rage grew within him, unlike any emotion he had ever felt in his twenty-seven years on the planet.

At a loss for what to do next, he lit up a joint and grabbed a cold frosty beer from the refrigerator. The crisp hoppy beverage momentarily refreshed him, until he let the familiar numbness overtake him.

Johnny decided he had felt enough for one day. He fell asleep in the same blue jeans he had worn for the last two days. As he drifted in and out of oblivion, Johnny welcomed the stupor that inebriation brought.

He shrugged with disdain and thought about his name, wondering if it was Nancy or the Fasps who had given it to him. In spite of himself, he grabbed a bottle of Johnny Walker, cracked the seal and chugged the golden bitter liquid. Looking at the name on the bottle, he laughed at the label and scoffed at the irony.

Eventually, as the bright afternoon sun beckoned, Johnny methodically made his way outside to sit on the expansive wrap-around porch. He teetered before he sat down, and let out a moan of anguish. Taking in a deep breath as if it would change things, Johnny stared out at the vast wheat fields, his brothers' adjacent properties, and then back toward the main house. All he heard was dead silence. And then he said under his breath, "Your silence will not protect you anymore."

Pulling the tab on an ice-cold Pepsi, he took in the sight of his grandmother's roses and thought that the once sweet smell had now turned putrid to his senses. Instead of delicate blossoms, all he saw were prickly invasive thorns.

Johnny had never felt so alone and so full of hate.

While he was mourning his new-found truth, Johnny's grandmother silently and painlessly passed away. Unfortunately, Johnny was not at her bedside, and he would forever regret it. In place of mourning, he would seethe and plot his revenge.

***

When Kent peeled out of the MeadowBrook High School parking lot after the grad ceremony, he felt elated to be leaving the town of dweebs and hillbillies. But of course, it could have been the drugs and booze that laid claim to his upbeat mood. Then out of nowhere, in what seemed like a split second, Kent lost control of his car.

Drunk and taking a corner too fast, he ended up in old farmer Dawson's cornfield, situated on the outskirts of town. Shaken but quickly coming to his senses, Kent pried open his car door and crawled out into fresh fertilizer.

Unscathed, he immediately thought of Tracy and then of her father, who owned Al's Automotive and Repair Shop, knowing that in no uncertain terms did he want to wait around to get towed. He could not fathom showing up at Tracy's dad's auto repair shop and being the laughingstock of the community, so he decided to split.

Leaving everything behind and not saying goodbye, Kent hitch-hiked to the next town, giving him time to sober up and plot the next stage of his life. Once there, he climbed aboard a Greyhound bus headed for New York City with only the shirt on his back, as the old saying goes. In Kent's case, he wore a black tuxedo and purple cummerbund, with a matching purple bowtie.

Kent had always known he was exceptionally handsome and that an abundance of money was available to him in a trust fund, which was rightfully his. In fact, as a graduation present, his father had handed him an envelope stuffed with paperwork and said, "Congratulations, son. Invest in your future, follow your instincts and don't screw up." Slipping the envelope into his suit jacket, Kent had gone to the graduation ceremony and temporarily forgot the fortune bequeathed to him.

Arriving in New York with almost twenty-four hours of no sleep, he got a hotel, and, first thing Monday morning, went to a bank.

Kent spent the first two weeks of his new life spending money from his trust fund. He splurged on an upscale, swanky apartment overlooking Central Park, a new wardrobe, and an excessively exaggerated resume.

Every day he stood outside the World Trade Centre in the financial district. And every day, he followed people inside. When he spotted men and women wearing the most expensive clothes, he noted where they were going and trailed after them in the elevator. Kent then made the decision to apply at the most elaborately decorated offices with the best-looking employees.

His first task was charming the receptionist with his tried-and-true secret weapons: his steel-blue eyes, fit physique, and confident personality. His second task was presenting his fabricated resume while wearing his $1,000 Armani business suit. And finally, his third task was securing a position.

How could anyone refuse to hire me? he thought, then grinned as he shook hands with the lead partner of Stern, Noble & Feinstein, one of the biggest brokerage firms in the city.

Kent's mentality had always been to work hard, make money, have fun, and never take no for an answer. So, naturally, it took him no time to get hired at a prestigious brokerage firm. A month after hightailing it out of the town he professed he would never miss, he pressed the button for the eighty-eighth floor of the World Trade Centre on his first day of work.

Everything felt easy in 1978, and Kent was on the fast track to succeed in business and making it to the top.

Even though he was born with a silver spoon in his mouth, his grandfather had ignited Kent's lust for money with the stories he told. Grandpa Pete worked in the mailroom at 1882 Broad Street, the New York Stock Exchange building. He started work at fifteen years old, during the mining boom of 1905.

Much later in the 1960s, tucking Kent into bed at night, his grandpa told him detailed memories of how Broad Street back in his day was unlike any other. He painted colourful pictures of a roaring, chaotic time, sometimes glamorous and other times dismal. He was trading gold one minute and auctioning off dogs to the highest bidder the next. Taxi cabs, dance hall girls, and money brokers—he spun elaborate tales of how he painstakingly made it to the top and abruptly lost everything after the major stock market crash that precipitated the Great Depression of the 1930s. Then, in an effort to restore investor confidence, Kent's grandfather had been part of unveiling a fifteen-point program aimed at upgrading protection for the investing public.

As a six-year-old, Kent could read and write and went to bed every night with the newspaper section containing all the New York Stock Exchange stats. He studied, memorized and kept track of what was trading at what price. His grandfather was proud, and yet his parents hardly noticed him.

In Kent's mind, his grandfather was his hero and possibly the best teacher he ever had, if not the only one who truly believed in him.

Kent reasoned that he may have grown up in a farming community famous for its egg production, but he would not be another run-of-the-mill Jack and the Beanstalk. Instead, Kent knew he was destined to be the goose that laid the golden egg, no matter how hard he had to kick, scratch, and peck his way to the top, which turned out to be a seemingly easy feat.

There had never been a doubt in Kent's mind that after he settled and got on the right path, he would quickly rise up the corporate ladder. His motto was: *Be kind to everyone, unless they get in the way. Don't let anyone drag you down or be an obstacle to your success.* But then—unlike his grandfather—he also believed that corruption was not always bad, and sometimes necessary to get what you want. He often caught himself whispering, "Sorry, Pops" as he signed another deal with an intoxicated client while he wined and dined them, or lied to secure a deal. Every woman he dated became a trinket on his arm, and every one-night stand became another notch in his belt buckle.

Kent was loud and direct and his voice could be heard above and beyond anyone else's. He often joked, "I am not interrupting—I'm just collaboratively overlapping!" He would then chuckle at his own hilarity.

Over the years, Kent had kept in touch with just two people from his past. One was his kid sister, as she needed a place to crash while she attended modelling school; and the other was Johnny Fasp. Because he needed a trustworthy drug supplier.

Kent would fly Johnny out to replenish his habit. In turn, he would ply Johnny with plenty of booze, fillet mignon and lobster, and then send him back to the cornfields and henhouses. He never asked Johnny about Tracy Hansworth, even though she was never far from Kent's mind, an aspect of his past that unnerved him if he thought about it. Johnny despised the city, but he would admit to anyone who listened that Kent was a wealthy high-roller and knew how to treat people well. Provided there was a return. Kent referred to their partnership as a win-win unless they began to lose-lose. Notably in it for himself, Kent made it clear to Johnny that he would give him the heave-ho so quickly his head would spin if any of their illegal behaviour came down the pike and was revealed.

Kent told Johnny that nothing would get in the way or interfere with his career. In turn, Johnny remained the ostensibly calm, wanna-be hippie he had always been, and had no qualms with being discreet.

Miami Vice was Kent's favourite television show, and he fashioned his wardrobe after the personality of James "Sonny" Crockett, played by Hollywood actor Don Johnson. He mirrored the character's clothing of a white linen suit, pastel T-shirt, loafers without socks and a perpetual suntan from weekly tanning salon visits.

Kent was witty, charming, and narcissistic. At his office, he was considered a ladies' man, or quite a catch, as the gossip around the water cooler indicated. However, it was well known that even though Kent dated, he was not looking for a wife, soul mate, or significant other.

He only went out with secretaries from his firm or women he picked up at the discotheque, but not the flashy ones. Kent was not the type of narcissist who flocked with his own kind. He had a regular booth at Studio 54, drank excessively, partied hard, and eventually, days turned into nights, and nights turned into days. The juggling act of success and partying turned into competing requirements for Kent's greed. His primary purpose was short-term fun and long-term financial gain, and as many materialistic objects as he could obtain.

And then, one morning, everything changed.

Five years into his career, Kent woke up one day to ice on the sidewalk and ice in his breakfast vodka. All at once, he realized he perpetually felt like crap and was starting to slip financially. Subsequently, Kent's hunger for money would work in his favour to make the changes that would save his life and make him a better person. So, on that cold winter morning, Kent dumped his drink down the kitchen sink and quit cold turkey.

His revelation took him out of the disco and into the gym. After a season of abstaining from drugs and alcohol, Kent sought a therapist. In the following two years, Kent realized his old persona, lack of morals, and unethical behaviour were not his fault. Nevertheless, he delved into his patterns, past hurts, and childhood, becoming aware that his father's corruption was his biggest influence.

The unraveling of his lineage took a very patient counsellor and many hours of expensive psychoanalysis to accomplish. Kent shared with his therapist about his father's insidious behaviour and far-fetched stories of scams, personal gain, and bad influence during Kent's formative years.

Kent's most vivid and hard-hitting memory was of sitting at the dinner table one night when his dad bragged to the whole family about robbing and vandalizing the town when he was in college. It was during the funeral of the founder of the city, William Farnsworth.

Mr. Gordon had stated in his familiar, sing-song manner, "Boys will be boys, and back in my day, all the shops closed when the entire community attended the memorial service of the admirable William Farnsworth. Wouldn't you know it, the idiot shopkeepers left their cash registers full of money, and with no burglar alarms in place, my buddies and I had a heyday. Did we ever make a killing that day!" He then emitted a loud cackle, as he mocked the mom-and-pop stores and businesses of his youth.

Kent's dad became famous as a lawyer for getting guilty clients off on charges and convictions. Drunk drivers, wife beaters, and thieves hired him, the most sleazy lawyer in town, who had a record of never losing a case. Later on, when he was voted in as mayor, Kent knew that his dad's money, shady deals, and empty promises got him elected.

Even though his grandfather's teaching and mentoring stood out as being wholesome and above-board, Kent's father coloured the lens and fogged his perception of what was morally and ethically correct. Kent's memories of his grandfather's squeaky-clean image and his father's unscrupulous behaviour contradicted each other. The good tried to outweigh the bad and yet repeatedly failed.

Consequently, during Kent's therapy sessions, he unravelled his past, ripped off the Band-Aid, and gouged at the layers of hurt, deceit, and betrayal, leaving his childhood wounds open to be cleaned and stitched back up again.

At one point, he thought he might be falling in love with his psychologist, but then she explained that it was a common occurrence. Not that she thought highly of herself, but she told Kent the experience was called transference. It was when you redirected your feelings or thoughts from one individual onto another. She described how Kent had been sharing his most intimate feelings with her. She, in turn, offered unconditional attention in a safe environment and he didn't feel judged or ridiculed, but instead, comforted, leading him to believe he loved her. It turned out to be a profound way for Kent to understand more about himself. The more he reflected, the more he could remember.

When Kent was five years old, he had a soda-pop stand on the corner outside his home. He sold bottles of pop from his parents' refrigerator with a one hundred per cent markup. In elementary school, Kent organized card games at recess and won other kids' lunch money, and by the time he was in high school, he had created Ponzi schemes that never paid out. Even Principal Marples had invested in one of Kent's pyramid schemes and was too embarrassed to ask for his money back or blow the whistle on the disliked but untouchable high school student.

When Kent left at the end of Grade 12, he had no true friends because he had ripped off almost everyone in MeadowBrook.

All things considered, Kent's childhood was a mixture of bad judgment and a boy who took advantage of others for his own gain. All of his relationships were affected by these learned patterns and past hurts.

Like taking a cold shower and stepping outside naked, Kent was awakened.

What he once thought amusing and clever now disconcerted him. When Kent recalled all the people he'd scammed, he felt like a cruel shyster. He was remorseful when thinking back to the night of graduation, the smashed-up sports car, and fleeing the scene to seek wealth and personal gain at all costs. Kent wondered how he could have been so callous as to not say goodbye. Especially to Tracy.

Thoughts of Tracy had become more persistent and invaded most of his counselling sessions. It was like Tracy

Hansworth had her fingers in his brain. Or maybe it was his heart. The rude awakening shifted Kent's priorities and became the catalyst for him to make an about-face. He determined that a healthy lifestyle would spill over into his career more effectively than an unhealthy one.

Needless to say, Kent made a complete turnaround with his eating, drinking, and social habits. He started to attend morning yoga classes and evening meditation. He completely stopped dating and became celibate. And then, one afternoon, something happened that added harmony to his entire existence, which made Kent's path of self-discovery come full circle and eventually make sense.

It was early March 1988 when Tracy's invitation came directly to Kent's desk via the office mailroom.

He was alerted to how out of place the light pink envelope appeared placed next to the latest copy of *Time* magazine, *Newsweek*, and a few corporate letters. Kent quickly assumed it was from one of the stenographers he breezed past routinely on the way to and from his office every day.

Kent picked up the envelope, smelled it, turned it over in his hands, and before it registered where it was from, he went over the long list of the women he had slept with over the years and wondered if it was from one of them. He cringed and remembered a specific aroma, a whiff of bloodthirsty greed that often smelled of Ralph Lauren.

He laughed at his attention to detail, shook his head, raised his eyebrows and smirked despite himself.

When he saw the return address, he caught his breath and momentarily forgot to swallow, which sent him into a coughing fit. He leapt up and closed the door to his corner office suite, dropping down onto his overpriced Gucci couch. "Well, I'll be damned. Tracy Hansworth, what the hell?" he whispered to himself and the windows that looked out onto the massive city he now called home.

Even though Kent had quit drinking, he had the urge to pour himself a straight-up Scotch, no rocks, no soda. He suddenly craved the burn to his throat and the water it brought to his eyes.

Instead, he took a deep breath, poured a glass of Evian and opened the envelope with an ivory-handled letter opener. First, he noted how the envelope was the same pink colour as Tracy's grad dress, and then he remembered it had always been her favourite colour. Amused, he looked down at the pink tie that, ironically, he had chosen to wear that day. As he opened the envelope, Kent recognized it was not a letter or a card, but an invitation.

"Well, I guess I'm going back to Petticoat Junction to meet up with the Beverly Hillbillies again! Home sweet home!" he declared loudly. Then he hollered out to his secretary, "Hold all my calls...I have some gifts to buy!

And please clear my schedule for the entire month of June! Thanks, sweetheart!"

MeadowBrook High School Ten-Year Reunion

Saturday, June 13th, Formal Dance 7
p.m. to midnight, school gym
Sunday, June 14th, Farewell Brunch 11:00
a.m. to 3:00 p.m., picnic at the pond

Cost: $25.00

RSVP ASAP
Tracy Hansworth
8722 Cherry Wood Drive
MeadowBrook
Canada

***

The day after graduation, Darcie left MeadowBrook. Johnny would be devastated, Dakota heartbroken, but her mother was thrilled that she was getting out of the one-horse town. It had always been Nancy's plan for her one and only daughter to graduate and move on to bigger and better things. She anticipated a bright future awaited Darcie.

After the grad ceremony, Darcie got home from the pond well past 3:00 in the morning. Her mother Nancy was waiting, hands folded and not clenched. She trusted Darcie and admired who she was becoming—artistic, musical, and independent. A free spirit.

However, there was always an imminent fear in Nancy that everything could go terribly wrong at any moment. Her mother had died when she was a child and her father had worked for the Farnsworth family when Mr. William Farnsworth, the founder of the town, had gone missing back in 1953. And then, seven years later, she'd become an unwed mother with Darcie at the age of eighteen.

As far back as Nancy could remember, MeadowBrook had felt creepy. Like it had been cursed and there was evil lurking behind every weeping willow and bend in the fast-flowing brook.

She often fretted when her daughter, who seemed to have no fear, spent hours with Dakota roaming the back roads and fields. She imagined every worst-case scenario she could think of, and only relaxed when she heard the familiar hum of the elevator followed by Darcie's key in the door. On the other hand, the night after graduation was different. Nancy had a gift for her, Darcie, who had become more of a friend to her than a daughter. So as soon as she heard the lock turning, she stood up and moved toward the door to their two-bedroom apartment.

"Hey Mom," Darcie said in mid-yawn as she entered the apartment. "What are you still doing up?"

Breathlessly, Nancy exclaimed, "I couldn't go to sleep, because I have a present for you that can't wait a moment longer."

She sat down and patted the sofa cushion next to her, signaling for Darcie to sit. Nancy looked into her daughter's beautiful brown eyes, and gently reached to lift Darcie's bangs off her forehead, as she had done many times in the past.

Before she said anything, Nancy smiled and sighed. In her small gesture of touching Darcie's hair, she was reminded of all the moments she had placed a cold compress on her forehead and sat at the side of her bed nursing colds, fevers, the remark from a bully or an overly strict teacher. She adored comforting her little girl. However, thoughts of stroking little Darcie's back as sobs erupted from her chest never ceased to fill Nancy's heart with regret. She had so wanted to give Darcie everything she deserved, and carried around tremendous remorse over not being able to give her daughter a father figure, a home of their own, or an abundance of toys, trendy clothing, and vacations.

Nancy always concluded that at least they had the Fasps, who often included them in their large family and gave mother and daughter a sense of belonging. Nonetheless, deep down inside, Nancy knew they would always be outsiders.

At first, Nancy was reluctant to be invited into their tight-knit clan, but then over time, she felt they owed her. Everything about her relationship with the Fasps had a surreptitious element because she had been threatened many times to keep their little secret buried and continue with the charade *or else.*

Or else what? Nancy often pondered but never asked for clarification out of fear. The whole town was afraid of the powerful and revered Fasp family.

Nancy would never describe herself as a victim, but many people referred to her as gullible and too trusting. Meanwhile, she kept a running list of all the people who had wronged her. Nancy could remember every whisper behind her back, and the charitable handouts that made others feel better. She had gotten used to how married women grabbed their husband's hands when she strolled past, as if she was a sex fiend on the prowl to steal away good men and bring them back to her love den. It sickened Nancy and often hurt her when she was a waitress at Robinson's Diner, and certain women refused to sit at her tables, and the men who thought she was easy, would freely pat her bottom, or worse, slip her their phone numbers, sure she would call them.

Nancy knew she was the complete antithesis of what most people thought of her.

All the while, everyone in town went to the same church. But never once did Nancy refer to any of these people as hypocrites. Or repeat the same offensive, judgmental behaviour that was directed at her.

On the contrary, when Darcie was a baby, Nancy felt peace and tranquility at church. Even though she was aware of the other congregants' perceptions of her, they didn't outwardly inquire about her situation. When her name came up in their prayer circles and telephone prayer chains, she knew it was for the greater good. Even though she had no idea what they were saying about her, she hoped it was just between them and God. Because in Matthew 18:20, Nancy read that there doesn't need to be a big crowd for God to listen because Jesus promises "Where two or more are gathered in My name, I am there." This always sounded comforting to Nancy, but when she analyzed the verse it made her wonder, *What if there is only one person praying in isolation, does that mean Jesus is not there?*

Over time, Sunday school picnics and invitations to dinner parties became a part of the young mother and daughter's repertoire. Nancy looked up to the congregation and hoped to one day be like the happy-on-the-outside families that dressed up, held hands, read their Bibles, and sang in harmony from the pews.

Early on when Darcie was just a newborn, and the family-oriented church-going Fasp family stepped up to help, Nancy couldn't refuse their offer. Especially when she could see how Darcie came to depend on their visits to the farm. Nancy's heart swelled watching her daughter chase after chickens, feed the ducks, and go for bareback pony rides. Mother and daughter both enjoyed dinners, barbecues, and swims at the pond.

To the entire town of MeadowBrook, the Fasps were unequivocally a family that practiced philanthropy, and at the same time, they were down-to-earth farm folk who worked hard tending to the animals, collecting eggs, ploughing the fields, and tilling the garden. To those on the outside, the Fasps were straight out of a Norman Rockwell painting.

Deep down, Nancy knew otherwise, but she had been sworn to secrecy and was not about to blow the whistle on the people who had saved her. Even after eighteen years.

Bringing her attention back to Darcie sitting next to her on the couch, without saying any words, she handed an envelope to her daughter, with tears in her eyes and a grateful heart. Looking over at her mother's face, Darcie contemplated how their eighteen-year age gap had seemed to all but disappear, and they were closer than ever. As her mother once said, two peas in a pod, a team of two, and yoked by the heart.

She remembered dancing with her mother as a little girl to the song "Rhiannon" by Fleetwood Mac. The mournful raspy voice of Stevie Nicks made everything seem mystical. Then, floating like an angel to "Stairway to Heaven" by Led Zeppelin, and never wanting the melody and haunting, hopeful lyrics to end. Darcie's mother had explained the message behind the lyrics as one of solidarity, brother and sisterhood, and equality. Together, we can change the world around us. To be a rock, and not to roll.

She loved her mother's teachings and poetic ways.

But Darcie heard something different in the song. It filled her with wanderlust and inspired in her a desire to head west, a feeling in her spirit that wanted more.

Darcie was never annoyed or embarrassed when sometimes strangers took her and her mom for sisters. Instead, everything became a learning experience for Darcie. When older men hit on her mom or made lewd comments, Nancy responded with enough charm, wit, and appropriate rudeness that any predator would back off.

Darcie wanted to be like her mom and Stevie Nicks rolled into one human being.

Even though they had little, Darcie never felt poor or lacking. She knew they lived paycheque to paycheque but always felt rich with love and attention. Darcie knew that one day she would take care of her mother, just as her mother had always taken care of her. Which made seeing the contents of the envelope even more shocking. Darcie gasped and covered her mouth, staring bewildered at a cheque for $20,000 signed by her mother.

Alerted to her daughter's disorientation, Nancy blurted out an explanation she had been practicing for years. She spoke rapidly, "Sweetheart, all those years of me working overtime and you helping and making us both dinner, I saved almost every penny. All the field trips and movies that you missed, all the birthdays where all you got was homemade gifts… it all led to this. All the extra money I had went into a separate bank account I called 'Darcie's Freedom to Live Fund.'"

All Darcie could think to say was, "Thank you, Mom. I had no idea." Followed by, "But are you sure?"

Nancy said, "Yes, my darling. My happiness comes from giving and not from getting."

After they hugged and quietly cried together, they snuggled up on the couch and fell asleep, a mother and daughter with a bond they assumed would never be broken, and a love that would last their lifetimes.

In the morning, Darcie packed up. She had only one suitcase and a duffel bag to sling over her shoulder. She took all her worldly possessions, which were few, and some treasured items—a few meaningful record albums, her guitar, and two framed photographs. One of her and Johnny laughing as kids feeding chickens, and the other, a polaroid of Dakota taken when he wasn't looking, a side profile of him smiling while gently offering grain to one of the wild horses while on one of their outback adventures.

Before getting in her car, she gave her mother a long heartfelt hug, as she knew she was leaving for both of them. And then Darcie thought about Johnny and Dakota and realized she was leaving without saying goodbye. She already had foreboding regrets.

Darcie waved goodbye to her mother out the window of her black Beetle, drove to the bank and handed over the cheque to the teller. She already had $3,730.00 saved from working weekends at the A&W throughout high school. Darcie asked to see the bank manager about getting her money transferred to a bank in Vancouver, minus five hundred dollars cash for her journey.

Darcie was filled with melancholy as she drove out of the city limits, past the A&W, past the Fasp farm, and toward the north, where Dakota might be pointlessly waiting for her. She scarcely noticed the cracked and faded egg monument as she pressed heavily on the gas pedal, picking up speed.

The rolling hills and windswept plains reminded her of the endless love she felt for Dakota, and soundless tears streamed from her heavily made-up eyes, causing her black mascara to run. Darcie wanted to cry out loud, but the sobs stuck in her throat as though she was unwilling to release the heaviness from her heart

"I hope you can forgive me Dakota," she murmured. "Please know that I will love you forever. And please, God, keep us all safe…especially my mother."

Reluctantly driving on, she hoped that neither of the two boys in her life would see her leave.

As the open road beckoned and Darcie gathered miles, her melancholy eventually lifted. Every exit on the highway was an on-ramp to somewhere else. Within an hour of her drive, Darcie's mind was whirring with unbridled enthusiasm and excitement about what lay ahead.

Finally, she made it to Vancouver, on the west coast of Canada. With the ocean and mountains within view, it was a big city, but not too big—just the right size to lose who she was and find who she wanted to be.

The next few years were a whirlwind. Darcie dug in and spent half the money her mother gave her on music lessons, dance classes, and a down payment for a bright and sunny garden apartment near the beach. She planted a small garden to remind her of Johnny and the farm, and meditated every night under the stars to bring her closer to Dakota. She did yoga on the beach in the mornings and wrote poetry by candlelight in the evenings.

Darcie sent her mother plane tickets to visit her regularly. They ate sushi and Indian food and hung out at the Naan vegetarian restaurant. They walked on the many beaches and went to plays, concerts, and the theatre.

It filled Darcie's heart to see her mother's wonderment and joy. She loved giving back to the woman who single-handedly raised her. Their conversations were deep and meaningful, and they talked about politics, feminism, music, and current events. Mother and daughter bonded, created memories, and cherished their time together until their next visit.

However, Nancy refused her daughter's plea for her to move to the coast. It was a shot in the dark for Darcie to even bring it up because she knew her mom had strong ties to the small farming community she'd lived in all her life. She couldn't help but wonder if her mom was wasting precious time on hopes and dreams that would never come to fruition.

Darcie became a certified interpretive dance instructor and learned to play classical guitar like a pro, sometimes getting small gigs playing in pubs and a few bars throughout the Lower Mainland. However, she never gave up her Stevie Nicks obsession, and she never went back to MeadowBrook.

She tried dating occasionally but didn't have the patience. The men she met always wanted to take her to clubs, and Darcie loathed disco music. Some suggested hikes in the North Shore mountains or booze cruises in the harbour. She went occasionally and always regretted it. Once Darcie dated someone she thought might be the one, a man to fall in love with. He was a drummer in a small garage band. They went on a few walks around the seawall at Stanley Park, complete with picnics and deep discussions about what each thought the afterlife might entail.

She abruptly broke up with him after watching him play one night in a sold-out smoke-filled Gastown bar. What derailed their relationship was the feeling of having to vie for her drummer's attention alongside twenty other young women wanting the same thing. His adoration for the groupies fawning all over him embarrassed Darcie and made her remember how humble and self-sacrificing Dakota had been.

In the course of time, Darcie gave up on dating entirely and focused on her art, dance, and music—and her mother's next visit. Deep down, she knew no one could hold a candle to the two men she left back in MeadowBrook, who were both never far from her thoughts—but it was Dakota who held her heart.

Instead of dating, she had become a loner, and filled her downtime volunteering at a women's shelter and teaching dance classes to children. She grew herbs, read a lot and created beautiful art. She mostly painted water colour scenes in pastel blues and greens, depicting a rain-drenched city or foggy mountain range, and sent them home with her mother.

Darcie had a few friends, but she kept them on the periphery because she felt that no one "got her." Regardless, she was still friendly and kind, while trying not to get too close to anyone. In the true sense of the meaning, Darcie had become an introvert.

When her mother visited, she rarely asked about Dakota and Johnny, even though she always wanted to. Sometimes Nancy offered vague stories about Johnny and how he was stuck in the vicious cycle of being a pot supplier and also addicted to the drug. She mentioned that the Fasps still invited her over for Thanksgiving and a few weddings here and there. Subsequently, Nancy chose not to share how none of them ever asked about Darcie. Even though Johnny occasionally inquired, she felt wrong telling her daughter that too.

Nancy gave Darcie less information about Dakota because she had less news to report. However, she heard rumours that he had gone to university, and she saw him once at the Red & White Frugal Grocer. Nancy told Darcie he was still shy but as handsome as ever and kind to her. She was reluctant to mention that she was pretty sure he was also still single.

For the sake of her daughter's feelings, Nancy felt the need to exaggerate and told Darcie little white lies—that everyone missed her—and then truthfully said, "Darcie, as much fun as I have on my visits, I worry I made a mistake in sending you away as I did. I fear you're not completely happy in Vancouver."

In her heart, Darcie knew that her mother was probably right, but instead, she responded with conviction, "Mother, I am happy enough. Besides, I write better poetry and songs if I am a little bit lonely. True artists are like that."

Both women would smile at each other in agreement and neither noticed the faraway look in the other's eyes.

As time passed, Nancy wondered if she would ever have grandchildren or if Darcie would ever come home. In the 1980s, the small town of MeadowBrook was booming. By 1985, a new mall had been built, complete with a food court, shoe store, and separate shops selling men's, women's, and children's fashions. No longer was Barney's the only place in town to purchase items. A golf course, hotel, community centre, and two new gas stations went up seemingly overnight.

There were weddings and funerals, babies born and a brand-new community of young families. The hospital, elementary school, and high school had all been renovated and expanded.

Meanwhile, without telling her mother, Darcie had become anxious and disheartened with the big city. She could not pinpoint what was missing from her life, and she was tired of trying to figure it out. Sometimes she could feel herself slipping. Darcie wondered if she was spending too much time alone.

On Nancy's next visit to Vancouver just after Christmas in the early spring of 1988, she brought the invitation from Tracy for the ten-year grad reunion. It had been mailed to her apartment, with the expectation that she would pass it on to Darcie.

When the plane landed, the weather was dreary and overcast, comparable to Nancy's heavy heart. Shortly after arriving at Darcie's apartment, Nancy gave her twenty-eight-year-old daughter the pink envelope, and then she asked for a cup of tea and if they could sit outside in the once lush, blooming garden. Darcie took note of Nancy's demeanour and warily said, "Yes, of course, I'll grab some blankets and put the kettle on, but can you tell me what's wrong, Mom?"

It was February 14th, Valentine's Day, a commercialized time of love and roses, chocolates for sweethearts, and poetic cards with sentimental inscriptions. Soon it would be spring, and Darcie's gardenias and rose bushes would be coming to life, a vision that brought tears to Nancy's eyes.

The mother side of Nancy looked deeply into her daughter's caring, receptive eyes. Placing her hand on the side of Darcie's face, she quietly whispered, "Well, sweetheart, I haven't been feeling very good for the last few months, and I haven't wanted to worry you, but my recent prognosis is not good…" Nancy's voice trailed off, and right then and there, Darcie decided it was time to go home.

MeadowBrook High School Ten-Year Reunion

Saturday, June 13th, Formal Dance 7
p.m. to midnight, school gym
Sunday, June 14th, Farewell Brunch 11:00
a.m. to 3:00 p.m. picnic at the pond

Cost: $25.00

RSVP ASAP
Tracy Hansworth
8722 Cherry Wood Drive
MeadowBrook
Canada

Chapter Three

A Higher Education

"If you hear a voice inside you say, 'Don't do it,' then that's exactly why you should."

—Patty Krakatoya

Nelson Farnsworth spent the first two years after graduation in his parents' basement in a state of lethargy. He spent his time brooding and tuning in daily to the Phil Donahue talk show, watching cartoons and feverishly reading every comic book he could get his hands on. Without a purpose, Nelson sat in isolation and stewed, unaware of the local goings-on and the whereabouts of many of his former classmates.

He pondered not having friends because his fellow chess players and brainiacs had left for university, where they enrolled in various sciences, or were working toward business degrees. Most significantly, Nelson surmised he would never get a chance with Darcie Richmond again. High school was over, and everyone had moved on.

Nelson longed for his secret crush and could still visualize her floating through the halls of MeadowBrook High School. He obsessed about his missed opportunity to connect with Darcie at the grad ceremony. Finally, his mother and father could not stand it any longer. After much deliberation between them, they brought Nelson upstairs from the dark basement, sat him down at the kitchen table, where over a meal of chicken stew (Nelson's favourite), they gave him an ultimatum. As far as they were concerned, he had three choices: go to university; work at his father's store, the Red & White Frugal Grocer; or work at his mother's flower shop, Daisies by Diane.

They gave him a week to decide. Nelson thoughtfully considered each option. The flower shop was off the table immediately because he found the smell of flowers nauseating and they made him sneeze.

The closest university was a three-hour drive away, and without a car or a driver's license, his parents would insist that he get a place on campus. Which meant he wouldn't have a chance of running into Darcie, the only girl he had ever loved.

Alternatively, working at the grocer, stocking shelves, and collecting shopping carts, might allow him to bump into Darcie. Maybe she would need help carrying groceries to her car, he thought, and then he remembered her black Volkswagen bug and smiled to himself. He envisioned Darcie putting groceries on the conveyor belt and him touching a juicy red apple that she would later sink her teeth into. Then, maybe while packing her groceries, their hands would lightly graze, and she would notice him.

When the week was up, he sat down with his parents for another meal of chicken stew and dumplings, and without any trepidation, Nelson boldly stated that he wanted to work for his father at the grocery. Nelson's father Marvin had never been more proud. He leapt up off the kitchen chair so quickly it tipped over. Nelson's mother Diane clapped her hands enthusiastically. Each one privately thought it was about time.

Marvin had tried to be closer to his son than his father had been with him, but he did not know how. Sometimes he wished his dad was still around, even though they had never gotten along. Marvin had many regrets about his dad since the day he supposedly disappeared back in 1953. Comparing himself to his son, Marvin Farnsworth thought his own childhood to be extraordinary, whereas his son's life appeared boring and mundane, and the town now was nothing like it used to be.

He remembered MeadowBrook as being peaceful and serene, especially at night, when the only sound heard was the murmur of a neighbour's television, the hum of the streetlamps, or the song of a night bird. On the other side of the coin, MeadowBrook was so peaceful that even the slightest disturbance could be very alarming.

So, when an outbreak of disorder encapsulated the small town, the breach of public peace was monumental, and Marvin's life turned on its axis.

Marvin had grown up with a wonderful, charismatic mother and a father who put everyone else before his family. He used to refer to his father as "My dad, William Farnsworth, the phony-baloney founder of what could be a perfect little town, if not for corruption and greed."

Needless to say, Marvin felt justified in doing everything the opposite of the old geezer he was supposed to call Dad, the man he hated with a passion. The day he went missing was the best day of Marvin's life. As time went on and his father didn't return, Marvin unequivocally concluded that he didn't miss him one bit. Now he had the opportunity to invest in his own son's future, despite his own father's lack of efforts.

Nelson started his new job the following Monday. Day after day, he unpacked boxes, priced items, and meticulously placed products on the shelves, the whole time keeping one eye on the electronic door that whooshed every time it opened and whomped as it closed behind each shopper. With no sign of Darcie.

However, Nelson never gave up hope. By mid-1980 he was a full-time employee at his father's grocery store, and he knew the place like the back of his hand. If he played his cards right, one day it would all belong to him, and so would Darcie. He visualized taking on his father's role with Darcie as his wife. Before any of that could occur, however, Nelson needed to court the woman of his dreams.

He obsessively rehearsed what he'd say to her every morning in front of the bathroom mirror while brushing his teeth. He questioned if he should sound friendly and enthusiastic, or calm and kind. "Why, hello Darcie, how are you? Fancy meeting you here. A lovely day out today. So what have you been up to since grad? Are you still friends with Johnny? By the way, how is he? Any chance you would consider going out with me?"

Butterflies rose in his stomach and fluttered to his brain, causing him to feel dizzy and blush three shades of red. He was repulsed with himself, wishing he could be cool like Johnny, athletic like Tim, confident like Kent, or handsome and elusive like Dakota.

As the weeks turned into months, Nelson became more insecure and even more preoccupied with Darcie. With every flip of the calendar and every tick of his Timex wristwatch, he realized time was not on his side. Since he had hibernated for two years and worked for two years, it soon became 1982, and then '83...with no sign of Darcie.

His parents undoubtedly worried about Nelson, but they assured him he was okay, just different. He was a good son, always respectful, and helped around the house. He was a devoted employee who rarely spoke to anyone and always walked with his head down.

Nelson was promoted from box boy to inventory keeper, parking lot attendant to cashier. However, by Christmas of 1983, his father was secretly growing very concerned about his son's friendless existence and introverted behaviour.

Both of his parents tried unsuccessfully to get Nelson involved in community events. They suggested he work at the Frugal Grocer hotdog stand at the county fair, become a member of the UFO Science Club at the library, and even asked him if he wanted to go on a vacation. Nelson was not interested and begged them to let him be.

Darcie's mother came into the store periodically, but not once did Nelson have the courage to utter a word to her. Each attempt was a failure. Soon it was commonplace for Nelson to flee into the backroom at the very sight of her.

After four years of being known as "The Frugal Weirdo," Nelson started to wonder why his life was going nowhere, and then he began to think he might just die of a broken heart.

All at once, Nelson was thrown a curve ball that caused his world to drastically change. On February 10, 1984, Nelson's mother asked him if he could help at the florist shop in preparation for Valentine's Day. She was swamped and needed help with her flower deliveries. Not only that, but she had expanded and now carried houseplants in addition to flower arrangements and her acclaimed artistic bouquets. She pleaded with Nelson to ask his father for the day off at the grocery store so he could give her a hand. Initially, Nelson was indifferent to his mother's request. He had a routine, and even though it had become dismal and dull, he liked knowing exactly what he had to do and when. Besides, he worried that Darcie might come into the grocer on the exact day he wasn't there. Therefore, he was reluctant.

Then, like being hit with a ton of bricks to his noggin, Nelson had an epiphany.

Perchance the stars had aligned, or maybe he was too stupid to think of it sooner, but Nelson realized that making flower deliveries for his mother could finally be his big chance to connect with Darcie. He knew precisely where she lived, and he could imagine ringing her apartment buzzer and stating in a deep voice, "I have a special delivery for Darcie Richmond from Daisies and Plants by Diane."

Nelson took his reasoning further. If he chose to work at the florist full-time, he could spend his paycheques purchasing beautiful floral arrangements to send anonymously to Darcie. Perhaps a rose on her car windshield occasionally, or she might even enter the shop to place an order, he presumed. Nelson was amazed that, with all the pondering he did, he hadn't thought of the idea sooner!

The next day he handed in his resignation to his father. Marvin was disappointed but was sensible and figured Nelson might do better in a different environment. He had been acutely aware that his once brilliant son was not using his brain like he once had. He had gone from being on the honour roll, winning academic awards and playing intricate chess games, to obsessively turning canned corn labels to all face the same direction.

The decision was made. Nelson would change careers entirely, quit the Frugal Grocer, and become his mother's right-hand man.

It had been an exceptionally mild winter, which meant an early spring, so the roads were clear and in perfect condition to make deliveries. The night before his first shift at the flower shop, Nelson's father refurbished his son's bicycle. First, he added a large basket on the front and one on the back, using some orange crates from the store. Next, he fashioned a clipboard on the front handlebars and attached a Jiffy marker with a string for keeping track of the flower and plant orders.

Awake before his alarm, Nelson showered and put on clean clothes. His first day of work was naturally Valentine's Day, the most romantic and busy day of the year for florists, card shops, chocolatiers, lovers, and sweethearts.

Nelson carefully followed his mother's instructions. He loaded his bicycle with colourful arrangements of roses, lilies, carnations, and a few potted plants. Then, without his mother noticing, Nelson threw in an extra bouquet of tiger lilies intended for Darcie.

Shortly after the day began, while pedaling down Main Street, Nelson felt short of breath. He was not a fit person, but his breathing had never been laboured before. When he glanced down at his hands on the handlebars, they looked puffy and were unbearably itchy. Suddenly Nelson passed out and crashed his bike, deliveries and all, into a parked vehicle.

With the town as small as it was, it did not take long for a passerby to discover him. Ironically, he had smashed into Johnny's GMC pickup. Being first on the scene, Johnny ran toward Nelson, immediately checking his pulse. Thankfully he had one, but he was wheezing, and his breathing appeared laboured. Johnny picked Nelson up and hoisted him into the cab of his truck, sped the short distance toward the hospital, and once there, carried Nelson inside.

Due to Johnny's reputation, the emergency staff assumed Nelson was stoned or strung out on something. After Johnny explained the accident, it was quickly suspected that Nelson must have had an allergic reaction to one or more of the flowers he was transporting. What made matters worse was that he was terribly scraped and scratched up and bleeding profusely from his nose and a gash on his forehead.

After calling Nelson's mom, Johnny left him at the hospital in good hands, and being the nice guy he was, took it upon himself to finish the deliveries. The bike hadn't been damaged, so the job was easy. Afterward, Johnny returned the bicycle to Diane's Daisies and Plants. She tried to pay him, but he out and out refused and went on his way to make a few of his own deliveries.

It turned out that Nelson required stitches. He was a mess, with a two-inch gash on his forehead and a broken nose mixed in with many old acne scars. Additionally, he needed monitoring for signs of a concussion.

Nelson's already small ego was damaged even further, and he felt the onset of depression sinking in. Negative thoughts filled his brain and pervaded his internal monologue. "I am such a loser! Everyone is right…I am a weirdo, good-for-nothing dweeb!" He thought his self-deprecating voice was only in his head when in reality, he was yelling at the top of his lungs for all to hear. Many hospital employees and bystanders looked at him unfavourably, and then quickly looked the other way, knowing full well that Nelson had always lacked skill and dexterity, and that was probably why he was banged up and bandaged, let alone causing a ruckus.

Due to his embarrassment over the accident, Nelson refused to return to work. The days turned into weeks and weeks into months. Nelson became a gloomy hermit in his parents' basement. Again. Then one afternoon during *Phil Donahue*, Nelson was inspired by one of the guests. The show was trying something new, and they had a panel of hard-nosed punks on the program. The theme was, "What do these kids want, and aren't they all just a bunch of bums and spoiled teenagers?"

Nelson was fascinated by such a chaotic display of bad behaviour. The last words from one of the more philosophical punks resonated so much that Nelson took note. The guy said, "None of us were born this way. Society made us this way by telling us we were nothing but scum!"

Before Nelson knew what hit him, he no longer wanted to be in his parents' basement. He instantly felt like a product of his society, and he was sick of being a stereotype and deadbeat cliché.

Nelson remembered something his Grade 12 English teacher said, a quote from Robert Frost, *"The best way out is always through."* He was done with skirting the issue and camouflaging his insecurities with regret.

Nelson got up, turned off the television, and changed out of his threadbare and infantile Star Wars pyjamas. Pulling on freshly laundered corduroys and a button-up plaid shirt, he made his way up the same basement stairs he had climbed since childhood. Standing in the bright yellow kitchen, he surveyed the paisley linoleum and vinyl-covered kitchen chairs, aware of the ticking clock on the wall and the transistor radio on the countertop blaring out the farm report.

When his mother looked up from the newspaper spread out before her, she smiled pleasantly and before she could utter "Good morning," Nelson chimed in with a cheerful voice instead of his usual monotone delivery, "I'm going out, Mom, and I'm not sure when I'll be home."

With a look of surprise, Diane jumped up from the table and spilled her coffee all over the crossword puzzle section of the newspaper. Before she wiped up the brown, milky mess, she hesitantly said, “Okay, dear,” and then held her mouth open a little longer than necessary as if about to say something else. But Nelson had his sneakers on and with a determined stride, he left the house, the creaky hinge of the screen door slamming behind him. Diane just stood staring in disbelief and felt the stirrings of hope.

Nelson walked purposefully straight over to Darcie’s apartment and rang the buzzer. After a minute or two, a female voice came on the intercom and said, “Yes, who is it?”

Nelson blurted out in his loudest, clearest voice, “This is Nelson Farnsworth. I am here to see Darcie Richmond, please!”

The response he got affected Nelson like the sound of nails on a blackboard. He wanted to cover his ears and beg for it to stop. Nelson dropped to his knees beneath the intercom after Darcie’s mother simply said, “I am so sorry, Nelson, but Darcie moved away the day after graduation. Do you have a message for her that I could relay?”

His voice came out as a whisper, and all he could manage was, “No, ma’am.” Rising weakly to his feet, Nelson braced himself against the aging red bricks of the building, and then ambled home, feeling hopeless, disappointed, and deflated. So much time had gone by, wasted on unrealistic fantasies about Darcie.

Shocking his parents over dinner that night, Nelson stated that he needed to enroll in a university that instant. He decided to go into the sciences and become a great inventor. He never forgot the prediction in his high school yearbook, *"voted most likely to invent the latest, greatest pimple cream and become a millionaire."*

Nelson speculated that if he were to become rich and famous, wherever in the world Darcie was, she would surely notice him and come running back to MeadowBrook and into his arms forever.

***

At the end of the summer of 1984, Nelson left for college. He was enrolled in business, mechanical engineering, drafting and design. It was a huge workload, but Nelson was determined and ready to study hard. He settled in, joined the chess club, made a few friends, and studied. Nelson got straight A's and focused on his end goal.

Four years later, in the early spring of 1988, a pink envelope came in the mail addressed to Nelson. Since he was away at university, one Saturday morning his mother drove three hours to hand-deliver it. She filled up a thermos with Nelson's favourite chicken stew and hopped in the car to surprise her son.

It was a lovely spring day, and since Diane wasn't going to work that day and Marvin was working at the Frugal Grocer, she enjoyed having something to do. With the windows down, Diane could smell the thawing fields and see the start of the growing season. Insects were coming alive, rabbits had appeared, and the warmer weather made everything feel fresh and new. Her thoughts were light and optimistic, especially since Nelson was finally doing something substantial and on the verge of graduating. Diane was filled with tranquility, yet strangely bubbling over with joy at the prospect of soon seeing Nelson.

Pulling up to the campus, Diane steered her car toward the student residence building. After parking, she momentarily panicked, and for some unknown reason, she had a slight tinge of apprehension. She had never surprised her son before or done anything off the cuff, for that matter.

Diane got out of the car, followed a path to the front steps of Nelson's dorm, and found the main door wide open. She absent-mindedly thought of the spring weather and that perhaps the custodian was airing out the hallways.

Making her way to the third floor and down to the end of the hall, she heard loud music coming from

Nelson's room. Diane's heart rate sped up. The thumping beat of her pulse seemed to match the excruciating volume of the music. She covered her ears and considered turning back and running out to her car.

Instead, Diane timidly knocked on the door and wondered if anyone could hear her, but she kept at it anyway, waiting, but no one came. So, she pounded the door harder with her closed fist and just when she was about to give up, Nelson appeared.

Diane froze. Standing in the doorway, she recognized the song, "You Make Loving Fun," by Fleetwood Mac, blaring from the record player.

She slowly handed Nelson the thermos and pink envelope without saying anything. Nelson received them with a smile and said almost manically, "Thanks, Mom. It's cool to see you, and to what do I owe this honour?"

Diane did not answer because her words had abandoned her. She was baffled by a son she did not recognize. Looking past Nelson, she saw that his dorm room was wallpapered in photocopied images of a girl she knew from Nelson's graduating class. It appeared to be a headshot from the high school yearbook, photocopied hundreds if not thousands of times over, covering every inch of his dorm room walls—and the ceiling, too. Mother and son did not speak as Nelson turned the pink envelope over in his hands and enthusiastically opened it.

After he read it, Nelson uncharacteristically proceeded to jump up and down and hug his mother.

MeadowBrook High School Ten-Year Reunion

Saturday, June 13th, Formal Dance 7
p.m. to midnight, school gym
Sunday, June 14th, Farewell Brunch 11:00
a.m. to 3:00 p.m. picnic at the pond

Cost: $25.00

RSVP ASAP
Tracy Hansworth
8722 Cherry Wood Drive
MeadowBrook
Canada

***

Patty perpetually felt invisible. But not on the night of graduation—she felt like a princess getting ready for the King's Ball, and she visualized kissing a toad and him turning into her prince. The toad's name was Nelson Farnsworth.

However, the day after graduation, Patty was greatly deflated because the toad apparently didn't know she existed, and the fairy godmother was obviously helping out a more deserving girl. The pumpkin carriage never arrived, and when it was time to go home, Patty found herself throwing up in a ditch.

When she climbed out of bed the following day, Patty knew her mother would still be sleeping—sleeping it off was a more appropriate statement. Her father would have left hours ago on his garbage route, and she would be alone, aside from her cat and best friend, Ruskin.

Getting up at her usual time, Patty ate breakfast, spent twenty minutes brushing her teeth and picking Captain Crunch cereal out of her braces with a toothpick. With no plans for the future, and it being summer holidays, Patty was thrown off balance at what to do next. So, she turned on the television to the early morning news. Patty settled on the couch, paying little attention to the news anchor's monologue and instead, pondered the last twelve years of her life. Ruskin meowed in annoyance at his owner's preoccupation, but quickly curled up next to her, purring to his heart's content.

As Patty stroked her beloved pet and faithful confidant, she blocked out the local broadcast and instead whispered to Ruskin her disappointment in last night's event. "Oh, Ruskin, you have no idea how hard it is being me. I would trade places with you any day. To be a cat would be so much better than being human! The grad ceremony sucked. You are so lucky that you get to eat and lounge around all day, and you don't have to deal with Nelson Farnsworth!"

She then spent the next twenty minutes reliving and condensing her past and trying to make sense of Kindergarten to Grade 12, mostly in regard to Nelson. Patty recalled every trick in the book she had tried to be Nelson's friend, from offering him part of her tuna fish sandwich to letting him outscore her on exams. She'd complimented his new glasses and old, worn sweaters. She'd even tried joining his chess club, but with the no-girls-allowed policy strictly enforced, she was ousted before she could utter "checkmate."

Patty also reflected on her non-relationship with her mother, who chose to drink herself into a stupor over having a relationship with her. Patty could never understand why anyone would allow that brain-altering, body-numbing serum to enter their body in the first place, resulting in them neglecting their family in the process.

Patty's state of melancholy turned to a heavy heart when she thought about her mother's title—Mrs. Krakatoya, the MeadowBrook town drunk—and remembered how mortified she'd been when the youth pastor suggested she start attending Alateen meetings.

It happened shortly after Patty had turned sixteen, following a botched sweet sixteen birthday party when her mother forgot to plan one. She remembered being downtrodden and disappointed, which must have shown because Pastor Herman had pulled her aside at youth group while other kids were getting picked up. Patty was dutifully cleaning up Styrofoam cups and empty potato chip bags when the youth pastor said in a compassionate tone, "How are you, Patty?" Before she could respond, almost as if he knew she wouldn't, he said, "I have a wonderful idea. Taking into consideration your home life, I think you should try going to an Alateen meeting." He explained that Alateen was a worldwide fellowship founded in 1951 that offered a peer support program for teenagers who struggled with a loved one's alcohol addiction.

Patty nodded and, with her head bowed, said she would go.

But if she were honest, she didn't want to attend. When she arrived at her first Alateen meeting alone, the room fell silent, and then as if a weight had lifted off everyone else's shoulders, the small group erupted into welcoming greetings, speaking in unison.

"Wow, it's great to see you! Welcome! Come sit here!"

They all appeared overjoyed to see her. In Patty's mind, their kindness validated and magnified the fact that her family was a mess. Their acknowledgment confirmed what Patty already knew. Like a flashing neon sign, it said, "Hey, look at me! I'm an unlovable underdog, and I need all the help I can get!"

Alateen disagreed with Patty, much like the raw purple onions that gave her heartburn. But, as it turned out, the professedly intimate support group that stressed anonymity sprouted wings, and the news of Patty's attendance became known to all the town. It was no longer a secret or taboo topic that her mother was a hopeless drunk.

So that was that after her first and last Alateen meeting, the cat was let out of the bag and roamed the streets freely. Behind her back and in front of her face every time Patty was out in the community, at the Frugal Grocer or sitting by herself in the library, she overheard people say under their breath, "Poor Patty," or "That Krakatoya girl sure has it rough," and more than once, "Having a drunk for a mother is probably why that girl is such an outcast."

Meanwhile, Patty had only gone to the Alateen meetings to impress and appease Youth Pastor Herman, and she quit before she could memorize the mission statement. The worst part of the whole ordeal came the week following her awkward experience. The next Sunday at church, Youth Pastor Herman stood up in front of the whole congregation and announced his engagement to Betty Torgerson.

At the start of the service, Pastor Herman said, "Good morning. Before we commit this service to the Lord, could Betty Torgerson please come forward?" As Betty proceeded to the podium, the congregation waited eagerly, some expectantly and others, such as Patty, entirely out of the loop. Pastor Herman leaned into the microphone, and in his strong baritone voice, he said, "I would like to introduce to you my fiancée and soon-to-be bride. I proposed to Betty last night under a beautiful MeadowBrook moon, and we have already set the date for a winter wedding on December 15th. You are all invited!" The parishioners stood to applaud, and joy was felt all around. All except for Patty. Pastor Herman followed up by saying, "Please join us after the service for a celebratory lunch."

Betty was a few years older than Patty. However, to her, she was just as plain, forlorn and a little on the heavy side as Patty herself. Consequently, Patty assumed they were both in the running to become Mrs. Herman and had no idea that Pastor Herman and Betty had already been dating. Even though Nelson was Patty's first choice for a husband, her vivid imagination conjured up being a pastor's wife just as easily as being married to a scientist.

Sadly, Betty had won, and Patty had lost.

On the day after graduation, Patty pinpointed Nelson's disregard, the disastrous Alateen meeting, and the newly engaged pastor as the catalysts that were pushing her toward thoughts of leaving town.

After Patty brought her attention back to the television, she started to pay closer attention and noticed how the local news was predictable, as it rarely changed—birth announcements, the winner of the pie-eating contest, and the 4-H club member whose chicken had laid the most enormous egg. Patty ascertained how small-town news stories gave off a sense of community and filled an hour of airtime that might be of comfort to the viewer… "Youth Pastor Herman was promoted to Senior Pastor…The mayor's birthday celebration is coming; get your tickets at the courthouse…The price of chicken feed is rising… The broken sidewalk outside the bank is getting fixed; therefore, the traffic on Main Street will be affected, so please drive cautiously."

Patty preferred global news. She was fascinated with the world's current events, as the top stories were history-making. After she changed the channel, Patty's living room came alive with reports that altered people's perspectives, opened their minds, and gave them an educated view of the world.

From the world news, Patty learned about the eradication of smallpox, the first in-vitro fertilization, and the first test-tube baby. When the sports highlights came on, she was pulled into a brief moment of admiration for the incredible athletic prowess displayed by the Argentinian soccer team. The players erupted in jubilation as the ball hit the back of the net, sealing Argentina's victory in the 1978 World Cup. With elation and sheer disbelief, they embraced each other. Patty could not imagine the level of celebration and accomplishment they were feeling in that moment, expressing to her cat, "I think I will never possess such grace and agility and camaraderie with a team as I have just witnessed!"

Throughout this process while Patty watched the morning news, it became clear to her that she wanted to become a TV anchorwoman. The light bulb came on, just like in the cartoon funny papers, and Patty knew she had come up with the perfect career.

Patty had always been interested in the news and investigative programs. Her go-to TV show was *Sixty Minutes*, and her guilty pleasures were *Columbo, Kojak,* and *The Streets of San Francisco.* She subscribed to *Time* magazine, *News Week,* and *True Detective Magazine.* She figured her need to get out of town and her interest in world news were excellent qualifications for broadcasting school, and thus, her decision was made. Patty had followed the William Farnsworth murder case for most of her life and had even done a school report on his disappearance, complete with timelines and family history. She often wondered if her crush on Nelson Farnsworth had increased her interest in the notorious cold case, or vice versa.

Patty knew she was an unlikely candidate for a news reporter, but her new-found vision allowed her to see past the insecure teenage girl with an alcoholic mother and garbage truck–driving father.

That night, after a day of scheming and dreaming, Patty told her father her idea. Three weeks after high school, Patty was enrolled at the University of Southern California in their four-year Broadcasting Program.

The summer of '78 went by quickly. Patty worked at the vet, ignored her mother, and daydreamed about her upcoming education and eventual career. She was excited for the first time since Nelson borrowed an eraser in Grade 6.

On August 13, 1978, the day she left, Patty gave her father a warm and appreciative hug goodbye, followed by a weak and dutiful hug to her mother.

With one suitcase and Ruskin in an animal carrier beside her, invisible Patty Krakatoya left the confines of the hick town made famous for its eggs. She chose not to look out the window after climbing aboard the Greyhound bus, for she had seen the rolling hills and dusty fields of gold one too many times before. The further the bus motored from her past, the closer the blueprint for Patty's future came into focus.

Her father rented her a small, sparsely furnished, walk-up apartment near the university and gave her a monthly allowance. Patty arrived late at night, took a taxi to her new apartment, and immediately settled in. She and Ruskin adapted to their new surroundings quickly.

At the beginning of September, Patty began her courses: Broadcast News Writing, Television Production, Reporting and News Writing, Radio Production, and Communication Theory.

Life became one big, new, exciting educational adventure. Every weekend Patty went to Manhattan Beach, as it was the classic destination for most students at So-Cal.

Over the next four years, her braces were removed, her short curly perm grew out, her hair lightened naturally in the California sun, she became radiantly suntanned, and she lost weight. As much as Patty despised exercise, she got pulled into a beach volleyball game by accident one Saturday afternoon and surprisingly did exceptionally well. Who knew she had an athletic flair?

She started dating a fellow student in the news broadcasting program, made friends, and became well-liked. She was perhaps not the most popular person, but her tuna fish lunches and mother's reputation were gone like a disappearing act; gone without a trace, just like William Farnsworth back in 1953. When the university student body asked everyone to participate in a before and after photoshoot, Patty said she had no photos of her childhood, as they had been burned up in a fire—the one and only bald-faced lie Patty had ever told.

Even though the old Patty was gone, she was not completely forgotten, until one night in a back alley when she incinerated all her stretch polyester pants in a dumpster because the new slender and confident Patty favoured blue jeans and halter tops. However, she kept the pristine white Keds sneakers and wore them proudly. In fact, she started a fashion trend when some of the other young women and fellow students purchased white Keds running shoes too.

Aside from her new lease on life, Patty still followed the cold case. She often daydreamed about being the news reporter who solved it. Patty could visualize all the townspeople and fellow high school students who had stereotyped her, suddenly praising and admiring her on that day.

She went home occasionally for Christmas and reading breaks, and much to her relief, not one single person recognized her. She freely tootled around town like a stranger. No more name-calling, ridicule, and whispers. Patty no longer felt invisible. Instead, she was a welcomed newcomer to the farming community of her youth. People were kind and cordial, and she reciprocated. The friendly town of MeadowBrook smiled, waved, nodded and greeted Patty warmly. She relished her new persona.

On one of her visits home, Patty deliberately went into the Frugal Grocer, as she got wind from her father that Nelson worked there. She spotted him stacking boxes of canned Campbell's mushroom and tomato soup. He briefly looked up, saw her and blushed, returning to work with a furrowed brow. There was no sign of recognition on his face.

Patty's heart thumped until her ears pulsed, as her high-school crush still surprisingly affected her that way. Even though she had changed immeasurably, it was obvious Nelson had not. He appeared more insecure than Patty had remembered, with curved shoulders and a downcast gaze. Patty did not speak to Nelson, pitying him for his highly visible inferiority complex, and the extreme acne that covered his face and neck.

By 1985 Patty had graduated from broadcasting school and got a job in the mailroom of a well-known TV station in Los Angeles. She knew she had to start at the bottom and hoped to make it up the corporate ladder, if she were ever allowed to climb it.

Over the next three years, Patty became thinner, fitter, and even more confident. She loved her job, her boyfriend Albert, her cat Ruskin, and her active, health-conscious and liberal California lifestyle.

A week before the grad reunion invitation arrived in Patty's mail slot, Ruskin died. He simply fell asleep and never woke up. Albert helped her grieve, and they had Ruskin cremated. Her precious cat and lifelong confidant, reduced to ashes, now dwelt in a small urn on her fireplace mantel next to a framed photo of her broadcasting degree and a beach volleyball championship trophy.

The day before the invitation arrived, Patty was promoted to weather girl at the news station. Albert bought champagne and chocolate-dipped strawberries and they celebrated the milestone together.

The very day the invitation arrived, Patty also got a phone call from her father with remarkable news that supposedly trumped Patty's work advancement and downplayed Ruskin's demise. To Patty, it was an upsetting announcement and an oxymoron, to say the least. After picking up the receiver, Mr. Krakatoya's excited tone initially startled her when he said, "Patty dear, I have wonderful news! Your mother is no longer an alcoholic! She has been cured. Pastor Herman and I persuaded her to attend a prayer and healing circle, and like a miracle, she no longer craves alcohol! In fact, she has not had a drink in over two weeks. It's a miracle, I tell ya!"

Patty was taken aback to hear Pastor Herman's name, and instead of being jubilant about her mother's Holy Spirit encounter, Patty felt wholly irritated and was flooded with memories of her drunk mom.

Nonetheless, she adored her father, who had been her entire world during adolescence, especially throughout her years of feeling like an outcast. While listening to her father talk, Patty recalled the endless hours of being alone while her mother was out drinking and her father was at work. Her only companion had been Ruskin, and she warmly recalled her precious cat's attention after school and her father's caring conversations at the end of the day. Ultimately, her affectionate pet and faithful dad helped her survive the misery she withstood from her mother's conduct.

On the other end of the phone, Patty's father rattled on, while on her end, she silently cried.

She did not want to let on that she was anything but thrilled, so Patty responded accordingly, even though to herself her voice sounded flat and lacked emotion. "Wow, that's great news, Dad. I am happy for you…and Mom too, of course."

Before Patty could tell her dad about the death of Ruskin, her work promotion, and the upcoming high school reunion, he finished the call by saying hurriedly, "Okay, well, I gotta go! There's a huge church meeting tonight to celebrate all those who were healed at last Sunday's service. I just thought you should know. Okay, well, bye-bye, sweetheart, love you!"

Patty held the receiver to her ear long after her father hung up, listening to the sound of dead air.

MeadowBrook High School Ten-Year Reunion

Saturday, June 13th, Formal Dance 7
p.m. to midnight, school gym
Sunday, June 14th, Farewell Brunch 11:00
a.m. to 3:00 p.m. picnic at the pond

Cost: $25.00

RSVP ASAP
Tracy Hansworth
8722 Cherry Wood Drive
MeadowBrook
Canada

Looking at the invitation, Patty knew without a doubt she would attend, and then she wondered if she should bring her boyfriend Albert. Unsure of the ten-year reunion protocol, she had three months to think about it.

Patty had become a California cliché, and at the prospect of showing off her new persona to the MeadowBrook class of '78 and her one and only true love Nelson, her spirits lifted—and then dismally crashed because she knew she would have to ask for time off, take an airplane, and stay with her parents.

Unfortunately, Patty's old feelings and insecurities were fed by her dad's endorsement of a new and improved mother, which caused Patty to somehow feel sick to her stomach and wracked with anxiety.

***

Amanda knew the high school yearbook prediction stating she was most likely to become a P.E. teacher and marry another P.E. teacher was not far-fetched at all. The forecast was her plan, and her plan was the forecast.

In fact, before the publication of the 1978 MeadowBrook High School yearbook, Amanda had tipped off the grad committee and asked them to create the yearbook prediction with a few minor tweaks. As she was the well-loved student known as "Spot," the committee agreed to Amanda's request.

Amanda Marsthrop—*voted most likely to become a P.E. teacher, get married to another P.E. teacher and have five athletic kids*—eventually came to fruition. As soon as the summer of '78 was over, Amanda's parents and two sisters drove her to university in the town of Hillsprings, three hours away. Her mother set up her room, her dad hung pictures, and both sisters cried for fear of missing their beloved middle sister. Amanda reassured everyone she would be home for Thanksgiving and every other major holiday, provided they didn't interfere with her volunteer work at the homeless shelter and sorority club commitments.

She quickly settled into being a busy first-year student. Her weeks consisted of school, sorority activities, university events, sports, and charity drives. Amanda made many new friends who were called sisters and had a steady boyfriend who eventually became her fiancé.

Brad was the perfect gentleman. He had his head on straight and followed a path set out before him since he was a little boy. Both his parents had been teachers and he had been a straight-A student who excelled in academics and sports. They met in the first month of school at a sorority/fraternity party. It was a themed costume gala. Amanda was dressed as Joan of Arc, and Brad made the perfect Napoleon Bonaparte. Fortunately, he was just a little taller than his character. Brad and Amanda met by bumping into each other on the dance floor while they partook in the disco dance called *The Bump*.

After locking eyes on the dance floor, they became inseparable and saw each other every day from that night forward, adoringly nicknamed by their peers "Sandy and Danny," from the movie *Grease*. What they had in common was their abstinence from alcohol, sex, and junk food. Both were in the Save the Whales Club and the PDP teaching program.

The years that followed were filled with study dates, fondue parties, sporting events, and fundraisers for an orphanage in Guatemala. They volunteered at a soup kitchen for the homeless and took on a mentor role with some foreign exchange students.

During Christmas vacation, two years into their courtship, Brad proposed to Amanda in front of both families on a trip to Disneyland. In the lineup for the Matterhorn ride, Brad bent down on one knee, took Amanda's hand and said, "Amanda, you are the woman of my dreams and the best friend a guy could ever have. Will you marry me?" Both families cheered, jumped up and down, and squealed with delight. Amanda cried and said yes. The Disneyland staff took their photos and gave each of them complimentary Mickey and Minnie Mouse ears.

The couple continued dating as an engaged couple. In their free time, they jogged together, watched old movies, swam, rode bicycles, and roller skated. It was a campus joke that Amanda and Brad discarded their old personas portrayed by Olivia Newton-John and John Travolta, for those of Carol and Mike Brady from *The Brady Bunch*.

At the end of their five years at the university, they graduated with flying colours, and both became certified physical education teachers. One month after graduation, they got married in MeadowBrook. The whole event was put together by Tracy Hansworth and her company, Events by Tracy.

On their honeymoon to Niagara Falls, cuddling in their honeymoon suite, Brad said, "This is so nice. Did I ever tell you my lifelong dream has always been to travel? You know what we should do? Let's take a year off before settling down, and travel. We could go to Japan and teach English. Whaddya think?"

Amanda was taken aback and became silent. Tears welled in her eyes, sobs heaved from her chest, and with tightly folded arms, she said, "Are you kidding me? My parents are building us a house, and MY dream is for us both to work at my old high school, so you can just forget that idea of yours, Bradley! And furthermore, I am greatly disappointed that you didn't share this information with me sooner, like when we were dating, perhaps? If you had, it would have been a deal breaker!"

Amanda's tone and extreme reaction shocked even herself.

Since meeting, dating, and doing everything together, Brad had never seen this side of her before. It was then Brad realized he had always let Amanda steer the conversation and make most of the decisions. It had just felt comfortable to do so. She was smart and articulate, and he admired how well thought out her ideas and plans were.

He didn't like this new side of his brand-new bride. Instead of saying something comforting to quell Amanda's heavy sobs and voluminous tears, Brad threw up his arms, stomped out of their overly decorated honeymoon suite, and went for a walk.

Left alone, Amanda sat on the white lacy bedspread and thought of all the things Brad could or should have said. Such as, "I can see this is really hard for you; I'm listening" or "I'm here for you." She buried her face in the white satin pillowcase and screamed until her throat ached.

As Brad walked around the gardens surrounding the hotel, regret consumed him. He wondered if he had made a mistake getting married and if he even liked Amanda. It felt as if their entire union was beyond his control. Shuddering, Brad decided that Amanda's verbal slap in the face could only be soothed by one thing. Walking past the hotel lounge, Brad turned back and went in, sat down at the bar and ordered a drink. "Can you make it a double please?"

Amanda gave her new husband of three days the cold shoulder for the rest of their honeymoon. Neither spoke to the other. However, they kept up the facade of a happily married couple in their yellow rain jackets and gumboots, with a Kodak Instamatic camera, while they finished their honeymoon at Niagara Falls.

Once home, they swept their fight and Brad's seemingly lifelong dream under the rust-coloured shag carpet in Amanda's parents' basement. Within three months they moved into a brand new three-bedroom bungalow in a new MeadowBrook subdivision, complete with a fenced backyard, window boxes, and a sliding glass door to a deck off the kitchen.

According to Amanda's plan, they were both hired on at MeadowBrook High School. She became the girls' P.E. teacher and Brad the boys' P.E. teacher. She reconnected with Dakota Hillsman, and the three became the most well-liked teachers at school. They represented the faculty at all the MeadowBrook yearly community events and were given their own hot air balloon at the mayor's birthday party. Amanda often recalled this memorable experience as the most romantic time of her life—a time of reflection, a brief moment suspended high above the patchwork quilt of wheat fields and meandering brooks.

She used the experience to her advantage when things got tough in her marriage. Amanda would reminisce about the day she felt closest to Brad. This helped her to see past the minor annoyances that being married could often bring.

The hot air balloon day had started like any other. It was a Saturday, and there were always chores to do, but Amanda was able to put her list of household duties aside. Instead, that morning she slipped out to Barney's and purchased a yellow sundress and white sandals. She even splurged on a floppy sun hat and brand-new pair of sunglasses. At the last minute before getting to the register, she grabbed Brad a new pair of denim shorts and a yellow polo shirt to match her dress.

They drove to the field in silence, their minds on the upcoming event. Amanda thought they looked like the happiest, most attractive couple in all of MeadowBrook. Brad, on the other hand, felt ridiculous in a bright yellow shirt and wished he was at home in his rugby pants, watching a baseball game on television.

As the balloon lifted off in readiness for flight, Amanda was content in the wicker cockpit. She found significant meaning in being motionless, suspended in time with the man she loved. Drifting under the influence of the wind, she relaxed in the confined space, as her body sank into Brad's comfortable and familiar side.

Amanda held her husband's hand, shivered, and then placed her other hand on her expectant belly. Looking up at Brad's perfect jawline, she softened and thought maybe one day they *could* travel and see the world together. She cherished the sensation she felt at that precise moment, and would later describe the whole experience as feeling like a cloud in a paper bag, captivating and ethereal.

Amanda let her mind wander and remembered fundraising back in university, going door to door, and how Brad had made her laugh when he pretended to trip over a front lawn sprinkler; the late-night study dates; eating tofu hotdogs and drinking fruit smoothies when they both really wanted pepperoni pizza and thick chocolate milkshakes; the hours they spent while dating, talking, and planning their future; coming up with their not-yet-conceived children's names and talking about their hopes for teaching jobs and a dream home in MeadowBrook.

Suddenly it was over. The hot air balloons drifted down to land and the mayor's birthday celebration ended, along with Amanda's warm fuzzy thoughts and memories of why she fell in love with Brad in the first place. Once on the ground, everything about her current life seemed just like the deflated and empty hot air balloon.

Afterward, her world took on a hectic turn. Overnight, Amanda was inundated with untamed emotions and unruly thoughts, as if her dream of a lifelong loving relationship was never meant to be.

Baby number one was born shortly after a year of marriage, a son they named Bram, and then baby number two eighteen months later, a beautiful baby girl they named Branda. Both names were a combination of their own, creatively and romantically concocted years prior.

However, it was during this time of morning sickness, a long arduous delivery, dirty diapers, and sleepless nights that Brad and Amanda's marriage became even more strained. She came to the conclusion that Brad was not who he had portrayed himself to be. He had disguised the fact that he was a ruthless liar, with an outward show of innocence. Amanda speculated that he had been playing a role contrary to his real persona. This had caused her to become exceedingly disenchanted with him.

Amanda made continuous mental notes of her husband's irritating behaviours. Brad had a nasty habit of leaving used dental floss all over the house. Slimy pieces of string, with food particles attached, were left on the kitchen counter, living room coffee table, and dashboard of their Jeep Cherokee. Amanda was baffled by his pile of dirty clothes on the floor next to the laundry hamper, as if he thought each item would magically shimmy up into the basket from where it was discarded.

She was confused and hurt by Brad's recent obsession with peanut butter sandwiches, especially since she was allergic to peanuts. She wondered why he had abstained from PB & J on toast for their entire courtship and then decided he just had to have it.

What really tipped the scales and made Amanda furious was that even though they worked the same hours at school, Brad rarely did anything around the house. He had an argumentative tone whenever she asked for help, and his voice could reportedly be heard by the neighbours, hollering Amanda's name, demanding she bring him a beer, the newspaper, or clean socks, not to mention his favourite question—"AMANDA, where the hell is the *TV Guide*?"

Her adult home life was not the *Leave It to Beaver* childhood she had been accustomed to growing up.

On the other hand, Brad was regularly disappointed that his effervescent university girlfriend had transformed into someone else. Amanda was not the fun-loving sorority girl he had fallen in love with. He was tired of her nagging, "Take out the trash, mow the lawn, burp the baby, clean the barbeque." On and on it went. His role as husband and father had become a grueling chore, and more than he had bargained for.

Brad grew up in a home with a mother who worked but also did everything around the house. His mom was fun and funny. She never complained and his dad seemingly did what he damn well pleased.

Needless to say, Brad loved leaving the house every morning and hated coming home in the evening. His after-work time at the neighbourhood pub had become therapeutic. The taste and effects of alcohol helped him relax, and his new friend Natasha, the female bartender, made him laugh.

Times had gotten tough for Amanda and Brad. Even though their lives had seemingly unfolded according to plan, their marriage was dissolving and neither had the desire or energy to repair it.

And then, just when things couldn't get any worse, their entire world came to a crashing halt.

Amanda knew that rarely did things go according to plan, but what she did not know was that their youngest daughter would be diagnosed with acute lymphocytic leukemia, the most common cancer in children and teens. It wasn't something she would wish upon her worst enemy, especially not another parent.

When her two-year-old daughter Branda collapsed on the playground at daycare and was rushed to the hospital, Amanda was urgently called away from her Grade 9 P.E. class. The devastating event changed the course of her life. Up until that terrible day, everything in her world was moving forward, despite the disappointments she thought she would be able to live with. Overnight, her world flipped upside down, and every day was a fresh new living hell.

When the invitation arrived in 1988, Amanda was on an open-ended leave of absence from her teaching job, tending to her daughter at MeadowBrook Memorial Hospital—sleeping on a cot, watching the nurses' every move, and researching alternative medicine from books and medical journals at the library.

In addition to her daughter's illness and the stress of a strained marriage, the sight of her husband getting ready for work filled her with a slow, bubbling jealousy. *Why does he get to carry on like nothing is wrong? Especially when everything is wrong!* she thought. Their finances were tight and getting tighter. The bills were mounting and getting higher.

Furthermore, her oldest son had become disobedient and unruly. He was recently caught stealing by Marvin at the Frugal Grocer. It was only a chocolate bar stuffed into his pocket while Amanda hurriedly dragged him through the aisles, but still, theft was theft. Bram would also not stop wetting his bed, no matter how much she scolded him, even though he was well past the diaper and potty-training stages.

Even though her marriage was rocky, Amanda remained generous and steady and was always there for her children. She had rarely left the bedside of her beautiful Branda, since she'd been admitted. Her daughter was so passive and sweet, an angel sent from heaven who was often referred to as Amanda's mini-me. She was also undoubtedly the favourite of her two children. Amanda repeatedly wondered and whispered to herself, "Why did Branda have to get sick and not Brad?"

Her heart, body, and mind carried a dull, persistent ache, and Amanda could not remember anymore what it was like to feel good.

"Everything else falls by the wayside when a child is sick," she wrote in her Precious Moments journal. Yet, the pouty faces and large mournful eyes of the cherubic characters on the cover of her diary never ceased to remind her that life is never what it seems.

MeadowBrook High School Ten-Year Reunion

Saturday, June 13th, 7 p.m. – midnight
Formal Dance, school gym
Sunday, June 14th, Farewell Brunch
11:00 a.m. - 3:00 p.m.

Cost: $25.00

RSVP ASAP
Tracy Hansworth
8722 Cherry Wood Drive
Meadow Brook
Canada

When the invitation had arrived a month earlier, Amanda stuck it to the refrigerator with a chicken-in-a-henhouse fridge magnet. The Fasp Farms had given them away at last year's country fair, along with a ten per cent discount on a dozen farm-fresh, free-range eggs. The expired coupon was next to the high school reunion reminder. Amanda asked herself, "If it's expired, then why is it even still there?"

Every morning before opening the refrigerator to pull out soy milk for the entire family's breakfast smoothie, Amanda would stare at the invitation. Some days, she would admire Tracy's beautiful handiwork on the graphics, and her mind would wander to Tracy's Capable Craft Club back in high school, making her smile. On other days, she would cringe and be repulsed at the very sight of the sickly-sweet pink invitation, looming and menacing.

Most times, however, she marvelled at where she had placed it on the fridge without thinking, right beside her wedding photo. All around the invitation were reminders of her past life, before her daughter's illness: her son's ribbon for winning the hotdog eating contest at the fair for his age group; an old shopping list; and the stupid Fasp Farms egg coupon, expired and curled at the edges.

Daily, the sight of the damned invitation brought on a massive sigh from Amanda, followed by combined feelings of annoyance and nostalgia.

She had adored everything about high school, from the clubs and academics to the sports and her many friends. Amanda knew she was the teacher's favourite in most of her classes and could clearly remember English essays, science experiments, and cafeteria lunches as if she had a photographic memory.

Amanda's emotions were discombobulated about attending the reunion. She was indecisive and continuously went back and forth in her thinking. On the one hand, as a teacher and employee of the school, she felt obligated to go. On the other hand, she was not enthralled with her husband at the moment and spent most of her days crying about her daughter.

Amanda wrote in her journal:

Living in the town where I grew up gives me constant reminders of my past. Every time I see Tracy in her pink event planning vehicle all over town, I smile. When I read Susan's column in the Gazette, *I laugh at her courage and moxie. And then Nelson, when he was at the Red & White Frugal Grocer, he was weird but kind to my children, especially when they were overflowing from the shopping cart, legs dangling and arms reaching. I sometimes wonder about*

Johnny and his weed, and if I should be using it to calm my nerves, and then I hope and pray he is still not dealing drugs at the high school. The world is picking up speed and I am losing gravity. I don't think I can hang on much longer. When did life become so hard?

Amanda was barely coping. Her family of four was fragmented, the shattered pieces dropping off like dried-up manure in a farmer's field. It was a shit storm, and she could not control any of it.

What she needed was a new yearbook prediction. Was her youngest child going to live or die? Was her marriage at the end of the road, taking a hairpin turn or crashing into the guard rail, and what did the future hold for Bram?

Amanda wrote, *"Life is a shooting match, and I am on the losing side. I want to stop dodging the bullets. Nobody seems to care that I am under fire."*

Chapter Four

Staying Home

"If a home is where the heart is, then my heart will be safe here."

—Susan Jillian

Grade 9 marked two occurrences that impacted Dakota's life. First, he began to notice that his status among his peers seemed to have shifted, and he started to feel admired by almost everyone at MeadowBrook High. Dakota felt like he had been raised onto a pedestal and had become popular, even though he never wanted it. It was apparent to the entire school.

Secondly, over the years, Dakota had grown to admire a girl he had known since Grade 1, and then eight years later in Grade 9, he fell in love with her.

Prior to these changes that occurred when Dakota turned fourteen, he had always struggled to fit in, and never felt comfortable with his fellow students in the predominantly white school. Dakota referred to it as a "white bread and butter school," which to him meant bland, boring, and flavourless. Darcie was the butter that made it all worthwhile.

He was much more comfortable at home with family, engaging with his culture, history, and stories that his father, mother, uncles, aunties, and elders had told him. He hung on to every word about the universe, the seasons, and the animals. The lessons of respect, appreciation, and gratitude were embedded deep into his being, staying with Dakota for all of his life.

He had not always felt that way. There was a time when Dakota was embarrassed by his family and often tuned them out, which led to thoughts of wondering how he ended up at MeadowBrook High School and why he was so different from the other children. He walked with his head down and appeared aloof and distant.

To find peace of mind, Dakota tried to get lost, but repeatedly found his way home. Physically and metaphorically. During his times of turning inward, he wandered the meadows, streams, and outlying forested areas. There he discovered the beauty of nature, the changing seasons, and the infamous wild horses that were talked about but rarely seen. Everything about the outdoors became cathartic to him.

The sunshine gave him clarity and the stars guided his way. The rain and winter storms made him pause and appreciate their power. The horses became his only friends. By gaining their free-spirited trust, Dakota learned from them to see life with his heart and not just his brain. He learned that what was essential was sometimes invisible to the eye.

Even though he was different from the other students due to his upbringing, the colour of his skin, and his Indigenous heritage, he came into his own when he turned fourteen. It was then that Dakota knew his love for the land, family, and community gave him an inherited sense of belonging that defined his happiness and gave him satisfaction. That gave him inspiration, as did his soul mate, Darcie Richmond.

More specifically, he was not who others perceived him to be. In contrast, his thinking was far more profound. His compassion and kindness encapsulated what his father had told him since birth, "You are destined to be a great leader, my son. Stay true to yourself and never waver from who you were born to be. When you achieve that, life will unfold as purposed."

His father was never wrong with his predictions.

Dakota was conscious that his relationship with Darcie was more than a chance meeting, teenage crush, or a match made in the white man's heaven. Instead, Dakota romanticized their love which, in his mind, surpassed the stars and far-reaching galaxies. It was a flame that would never be extinguished even after death, and the dust of the earth became their everlasting home.

Most days, Dakota left school early to catch a ride home with his uncle, just to avoid the old school bus that the younger children used. It stuck out like a sore thumb, with flaking light blue paint, and it belched black smoke as it rumbled along the backcountry roads. It was often late for school or late getting home due to mechanical breakdowns.

On the day he reconnected with the most intriguing girl in the universe, he did not want to go home at all.

Dakota was sitting at a table in the school library, watching the clock and waiting for the block to end. When he looked across the table and noticed his childhood friend Darcie, he was reminded of how they had played together on Saturdays and prayed together in Sunday school. And then they went a long time without seeing each other. That was that.

They had grown apart, and then at the beginning of Grade 9 in 1974, just before the end of class, there she was, her wide doe-like eyes staring at him from across the same table as if she was about to say something. Mesmerized, he noticed her tanned skin, soft and touchable. When she spoke, he was pulled in hook, line, and sinker.

At that moment, Dakota felt born-again and irrevocably in love.

Darcie spoke with her head slightly bowed and tilted to one side, shy but quizzical. In contrast to her mannerisms, her voice was confident and pleasing to the ear, a voice that made people pause to see where it was coming from. More specifically, to Dakota's senses, it was like the sound of nature, comparable to a warm summer breeze floating high above the trees, swirling, swooping, and gathering him up into its gentle vortex.

What she said next would be forever etched in his mind: "Hey, your name is Dakota, right? I remember you from elementary school. We were friends back then. Wow, you sure are all grown up now!" She laughed at her own observation. Darcie often did that, laughed at herself and the oddities in life.

He responded, smiling and more sure of himself than he usually was when talking to a girl, "Yes, I guess you could say I'm all grown up. How come you didn't get up and go when your friends left the library just now?"

Darcie smiled, lifted her chin, and responded with conviction, "I didn't go because I would much rather sit here with you." Dakota sensed that Darcie felt the same way about him as he felt about her. They talked well after the 3:00 p.m. bell, until the librarian told them to go home. Dakota asked Darcie about the music she liked, her interests outside of school, and why she dressed so differently. She cheerfully said her favourite bands were Fleetwood Mac and Led Zeppelin. And then, she quietly stated that her mom was single and she didn't have a dad. Darcie added off-handedly that she didn't care because her mom was all she needed and neither of them even knew who he was anyway.

Darcie looked down at what she was wearing, a denim jean jacket and a pair of hipster bell bottoms with frayed cuffs that were long enough to cover her black boots. Then she smiled and looked Dakota directly in the eyes, saying, "And I love to sew and reuse used clothing. See this jacket? It used to be blue, so I dyed it black, and these jeans used to be my mom's back in the hippie days!" Laughing, she boldly confessed, "Honestly, I hate Barney's department store. Everything in it lacks originality and looks like clothes a paper doll cut-out would wear."

Dakota laughed at her clever visual. Darcie explained how she wanted to stay true to her free spirit and often went to the next town to purchase fabric or second-hand clothing to rework. For example, she once created a whole outfit from an old 1950s housedress. She finished her brief description of herself by saying sincerely, "One day I just might become a famous artist and fashion designer. There has got to be more to life than this town, don't you think?" Without giving him a chance to answer, she said, "What about you, Dakota Hillsman, what makes you tick?"

Dakota became quiet, looked down at his folded hands and then lifted his head again, unsure what to say. When he saw the warm compassion in her eyes, Dakota instantly felt at ease, so he spoke softly and shared from his heart. "I don't like school so much, even though I get good grades. My family means more to me, and I would choose them over school anytime."

Dakota described his younger siblings and how he often entertained them. He talked about nature and how he found peace in it, because it filled his need to be alone. He told her that he rode horses in the spring and summer and roamed around on snowshoes in the winter by himself. He felt he was his true self outside, alone with Mother Nature, wandering around and exploring. Lastly, he said, "I actually have no desire to leave. This is my home, and MeadowBrook needs me as much as I need MeadowBrook."

After sharing, they sat in silence. Dakota knew they must be soul mates, and destiny had connected them that afternoon. Darcie felt powerless over her attraction toward him, and she knew their instant love was beyond their control.

They kept their friendship and budding relationship quiet and to themselves. From that point on, Dakota's time spent with Darcie was sparse, but intense and magical when it happened. They had their favourite meeting spots.

Wild mustangs still roamed the low-lying hills and windswept plains behind MeadowBrook, and Dakota knew them all well. Glistening thick coats, strong swishing tails and tangled manes were a sight to behold and treasure. He took Darcie out to see them many times and taught her how to get close. They brought the horses apples and carrots from the Dumpster behind the Frugal Grocer, as well as bits of grain and remnants from the floors of the outlying chicken barns. Sometimes late at night with the light of the moon to guide them, they went on treat-gathering expeditions for the horses. Holding hands and meandering through the shadows, alleyways and closed-up barns, they felt like secret agents on a mission to save humanity. Darcie enjoyed rebelling against the fearmongers who repeated the oft-told stories of unknown murderers stalking MeadowBrook, while Dakota enjoyed their time together as boyfriend and girlfriend with the dark night and vacant streets as their backdrop.

The couple marveled at the animals' high-spirited mannerisms and sense of knowing they were not in harm's way. Darcie and Dakota were accepted by the magnificent wild beasts like they all belonged in a secret club and had become one with the animals. Together they gave them all names. The horse they named Boots was Darcie's favourite, a chestnut mare with four matching white legs that reminded her of the 1960s go-go boots. Salt & Pepper was a speckled appaloosa, and Hi-Ho-Silver was pure white, just like the Lone Ranger's horse.

Nature was Darcie's and Dakota's playground, where their relationship grew and was galvanized.

In the spring and summer, they would sit for entire afternoons by an out-of-the-way creek, hidden under a weeping willow tree, whose graceful branches swept into an arch that created a round canopy over the water. There they contemplated life and talked about their futures, and the many hopes and dreams they dared not share with anyone else. Darcie sketched and wrote poetry, and they took turns playing her guitar.

With the bulging roots beneath them and branches above them, Dakota shared his knowledge and softly described their surroundings. "The willow is the fastest-growing plant anywhere in the world. It can absorb large quantities of water because of its deep, strong, and broad base of roots." Darcie was enthralled by his storytelling voice and wanted him to keep going, so he continued. "It's actually a symbol of fertility and new life, and its ability to grow and survive is symbolic, showing humans they too can thrive even in challenging conditions."

Dakota reflected on his desire to have many children. He would teach them the ways of the land and about their ancestors. Darcie closed her eyes and imagined she would have Dakota's babies and they would live happily ever after. Dakota felt encouraged by her open heart and willingness to listen.

With only her mother as her family, she asked Dakota about his. Even though she loved Johnny's family, she always found them to be abrupt and cold. Darcie longed for the closeness she felt Dakota had with his. He paused, not sure how much he felt like sharing, but again he spoke quietly. "Ever since I was old enough to think and notice the world around me, I have sensed that the elders in my community have known hardship. I feel great sadness coming from them. I know there are secrets and skeletons in the closet, but I don't know where the closet door is or how to unlock it if I ever find it."

He explained his need to stay close to his community, to listen and remain watchful. After expressing his inner thoughts, Dakota stopped talking but felt a deep connection to the bohemian girl sitting inches away from him.

Be that as it may, Dakota did not share everything—that prevailing darkness that loomed in his community, with no known origin, at least to him. So instead, Dakota kept to himself about the alcohol. He assumed they drained the bottles to forget, like a solvent used to rub out dirt and grime, only their wounds and undisclosed past hurts always resurfaced the next day. The torment and anguish in his father's eyes grieved him.

Dakota's time spent with Darcie gradually moved from a budding romance to a deep meaningful connection.

When they got older, and Darcie worked at the A&W, Dakota would bring his little sisters, brothers, nieces, and nephews in the back of his uncle's truck for root beer. Darcie would sneak them large orders of French fries and enjoyed watching their eyes light up when she approached.

Dakota knew Darcie enjoyed having them there, like her own personal cheer team while she worked. He could see her love for his family. He cherished this part of her.

They both felt secure and unbreakable in each other's company, and love became an addictive drug reminding Dakota of the song "Love Potion Number Nine" by The Searchers, except that Darcie was not his number nine but rather his one and only.

However, by Grade 12, something had shifted. The two teenagers were more serious about life and felt the pressure from teachers at school and their parents at home.

It was the onset of plans and figuring out what would happen next. They both knew time was ticking and non-renewable. They had gone from fourteen to eighteen in the blink of an eye, and no matter what they did, they could not win it back again.

On the night of the Grade 12 graduation, there was unrest in Dakota's family, and things were not well. So, even though he wanted to be at the ceremony, if only to see Darcie, he chose not to go. He stood her up, and regrettably, Dakota never got the chance to explain why. Instead, he sat outside on his doorstep under the summer night sky. He imagined Darcie would be the most heart-stopping girl at the dance. From the distance, he sensed her disappointment because of his absence.

But, in the true essence of the saying, "Home is where the heart is," Dakota stayed home on the night of graduation because he felt unsettled. His instincts were correct, as there had been a tragic suicide that afternoon in his community. People were mourning the loss of a loved one's life cut short. There was heartbreak and confusion, and an ending that seemed wrong and out of place.

Dakota wanted to explain his pain to Darcie, but he did not know how.

First thing the next morning, he knew his lack of communication with her had been a mistake, but he felt pretty sure she would understand. So, he went to "their" tree at the crack of dawn and planned on waiting as long as it took for her to get there.

The warmer-than-usual early summer had affected the brook, which was once a fast-flowing body of water. Almost overnight it had turned stagnant and sluggish. As Dakota pondered his surroundings, he could not help but feel the correlation of his love for Darcie to that of the receding water. He hoped the lifeless remnants of sand and sludge were not a representation of his future with a girl he could not imagine living without.

Dakota stayed until the stars appeared and the cool night air beckoned him to return home. The ache in his heart was insurmountable. He did not understand his actions in the moment, of not picking up the telephone or ringing her apartment buzzer.

***

The days and weeks passed, and neither of them reached out to the other. Finally, summer turned to fall, and fall turned to winter.

December was unusually bitter that year and brought an abundance of ice and freezing wind. With the starless nights came an overwhelming sadness, and Dakota felt grave loneliness. He did not know how to fix the desertion of joy within himself and his community, so Dakota did what came naturally. He cooked, cleaned, and played with the youngsters.

Many people in Dakota's community ran out of firewood that winter. It had been a dismal fall, and sadly, many families were unprepared. Dakota's father was withdrawn, and unbeknownst to Dakota, fearful. To help his father the only way he knew how, he took on his dad's usual duties and chopped wood until he thought his back would break. He took wheelbarrow loads up and down the street, and his brothers and sisters all pitched in.

Dakota worried a lot about his community.

By mid-December, the overabundance of cold pelting rain and dense fog, combined with the absence of streetlights in Dakota's neighbourhood, made for poor visibility. The clouds and dense fog blocked out the moon and stars which created an ominous foreboding.

Dakota and some of the elders had petitioned City Hall to install better lighting in their territory, even though all of MeadowBrook rested on their land. So, the question was, why were they being left out of upgrades and proper lighting? The politics and bureaucracy were notably unfair and Dakota was appalled at the injustice.

Later, when he thought back to that grievous season and the year he lacked hope and purpose, Dakota speculated that what happened next was inevitable. Yet, regrettably, he had not seen it coming because he failed to read the signs.

On his way home from town one night, Dakota's father's truck was hit by a train.

Sound carried. When the train's whistle repeatedly blew, the townspeople froze in a position of dread while they waited. Everyone instinctively knew what was coming next—a sickly loud screech, metal on metal, followed by a hard thud and smashing glass—pushing, pulling, and dragging. Then nothing but deafening silence.

It was the winter solstice, December 21st, the day with the shortest period of daylight and the longest night of the year. And now, it was also the day Dakota's father left them.

For thousands of years, his ancestors told stories and legends of the seasons and how the cycles should be acknowledged and celebrated through ceremonies. In the earth's period of darkness during the winter solstice, they were taught to look inward with deep intention, to look after loved ones and family and to prepare for the days ahead.

However, in 1978, on the night of the deadly crash, families were distracted and struggling, the need to find warmth overriding the need for spiritual self-care. Worry, past hurts, and trauma overrode ancestral memory of belief, desire and trust, if only for a time.

After Darcie had failed to show up the day after graduation, it became Dakota's main purpose to shift his priorities and look after his mother and siblings. In the days following his father's death, he vowed to save his community.

Ironically, after his father's death, it was the community who saved him. Dakota's extended family and neighbours reached out and the elders took him under their wing. They gathered and practiced traditional teachings about death and looked for guidance from the universe to deepen their spiritual connection.

They solemnly cooked and shared meals, reflected on the past year, and gave thanks for all their blessings. Afterward, as directed by the elders, each family went home and cleaned to honour their living space, and they held personal moments of prayers of appreciation. The teachings continued well into the new year.

To help him cope, Dakota assumed his father's death was a sign and the catalyst to get back to what was necessary. He spent the years after graduation taking care of his family and emulating joy to the best of his ability. Eventually, he went to university and got his teaching degree, and then stayed in MeadowBrook to teach at the high school.

Dakota spent his spare time putting together soccer and street hockey games in the summer. During the winter, he pulled neighbourhood kids on sleds and arranged ice hockey games on a few local frozen ponds. As time went on, he got permission to open the school gymnasium for his community. There they played floor hockey. Finally, he reached out to an event planning business to organize a Christmas carnival and food drive for the town of MeadowBrook, specifically those who went without many of life's necessities.

Dakota never lost hope that Darcie would eventually return to him, and his instincts were rarely wrong. However, Johnny was always on his radar. He steered clear of any dealings with the local drug dealer, and avoided the pond and outlying areas near the Fasp family farm. If spotted, Dakota would offer an occasional nod or tip of his hat, but his sure-footed stride indicated he would not be stopping to chat. He could not help but wonder if Johnny had remained friends with Darcie and knew that it would have been easy to just ask, but he did not.

When he was hired at MeadowBrook High, the school became his second community. He gradually opened up to other teachers about his beliefs and some became his friends. However, it was the reluctant learners and the students who were on the path of slipping through the cracks for whom Dakota had a heart.

In the spring of 1988, after teaching school one afternoon, Dakota's spirits were lifted from within. Winter had turned to spring, birds and blossoms had come to life, and Dakota felt happy. He chose not to drive the short distance into town to do errands, so he left his truck in the school parking lot. When he walked down Main Street, a warm breeze swirled around him and carried with it a sense of hopefulness. His expectancy grew as the MeadowBrook wind whispered in his ears, "*Everything is going to be okay.*"

Dakota had checked the post office the day before and usually only went for the mail once a week, but on this bright, cheerful afternoon, he decided to look again. After inserting the small silver key, he opened the hinged cubby door and caught sight of a light pink envelope.

He saw that it was from Tracy, but waited until he returned to the school and got into his bright red new 1987 Ford Pickup before he opened it.

He smiled when he saw Tracy's invitation and then nodded, sighed, and looked out of his open window to the warming spring sky. Dakota let out a small cheer and fist-pumped the heavens.

MeadowBrook High School Ten-Year Reunion

Saturday, June 13th, Formal Dance 7
p.m. to midnight, school gym
Sunday, June 14th, Farewell Brunch 11:00
a.m. to 3:00 p.m. picnic at the pond

Cost: $25.00

RSVP ASAP
Tracy Hansworth
8722 Cherry Wood Drive
MeadowBrook
Canada

Driving home to his three-bedroom rancher, he admired his pristine vehicle and gave gratitude for his teaching job. The truck was the first large purchase he ever made. With the rest of his money and free time, he helped others.

His father taught him early on not only about his culture and the universe around him, but also the importance of getting an education and giving back.

***

On the evening following graduation, Susan went to Lovers' Lane with a decent boy, so she knew he was not entirely to blame for her predicament.

Before leaving for the ceremony, Susan had climbed up on the kitchen counter at home and in one of the higher cupboards she found some small one-ounce bottles of liquid courage in the form of vodka. She stuffed four into her new push-up bra, and two under each breast, with the intention of smuggling them into the dance. Once at the school, she downed them one after the other, coughing and choking in the process. The contents warmed her, and Susan began scouting her surroundings for a rendezvous partner, knowing soon she would be warming someone else with her body.

Susan thought that losing her virginity would be like a rite of passage commemorating the end of an era, something to lead her into adulthood. Therefore, she was determined to have sex on the night of her high school graduation.

Susan had been a cheerleader since Grade 9 and still didn't understand basketball jargon. But she did profess to understand athletic boys and that none of them would ever turn down her advances. Susan eventually chose Dwayne and whispered in his ear on the dance floor, "Meet me at the back doors. I want to go for a drive because I have something I want to show you." Susan smiled wryly as she walked away from the awestruck teen, who gaped after her with his mouth hanging open and his heart racing.

Soon the power forward of the basketball team would be sexually satisfied in the backseat of his mother's car.

In a slurred voice, Susan stated, "Dwayne, I don't understand your position on the team because you're not powerful or forward, as your title indicates." Letting out an overly loud shriek of laughter, she followed up with, "Come on, cowboy, let's giddy up and get this show on the road!" More laughter ensued and without hesitation, Dwayne complied with Susan's advances.

Needless to say, on the night of graduation in his parents' car, on the outskirts of town, Dwayne happily and unexpectedly lost his virginity. Later, Susan wrote in her journal, "*What red-blooded boy would refuse what I was offering?*" She then went on to describe how uncomfortable the whole act was and not at all what *Cosmopolitan* said it would be like. Her final entry for the day stated, "*I suppose I could learn to like it even though it was not very fun or pleasurable at all.*"

Neither of them had thought to bring any form of protection, even though their health class had gone over the importance of contraception for the last five years of their lives.

It should therefore not have been a surprise when, shortly after Susan and Dwayne participated in the mutually agreed upon act, she missed her period.

Susan kept it a secret for a few weeks and then broke down one night after an episode of *Happy Days*. It irked her how the popular television show put so much emphasis on making out, necking and canoodling with the opposite sex. She blamed her whole circumstance on the behaviour of Arthur Fonzarelli. Susan had grown up idolizing his bad boy image and desperately wanted to be Pinky Tuscadero or one of the other bevy of girlfriends the Fonz played homage to.

She found out the hard way that life was not a sitcom and she was not Pinky Tuscadero. She came to regret her stereotypical fast-girl persona, and then wished she had been more inclined to be in Tracy Hansworth's Capable Crafters Club.

Eventually, Susan mustered up as much courage as she could and braced herself for the impact of her mother's expected response. When she entered the kitchen, her mother was right in the middle of mopping the floor. She stood for a moment in the doorway and was transfixed by the twirling strands at the end of the mop handle, like tendrils of dirty hair. Susan speculated her mother would be wiping the floor with her next.

Without mincing words, she came right out with the matter-of-fact predicament she and Dwayne were in. "Mom, I have some bad news. I think I might be pregnant." Susan's words were straight to the point.

The rest of their dialogue was one-sided in favour of Susan's disappointed and furious mother. Her voice came out in an angry whisper, "You stupid little twerp! How is it that the first time you have sex, you go and get yourself pregnant? What was the rush? Honestly, Susan, I thought I raised you better! You should know to never trust a man! Every woman knows that men are useless when it comes to womanly matters. It's our job to make sure these kinds of things don't happen. They are all wolves in sheep's clothing, I tell ya!!!"

On and on, she lamented. Finally, she said, "Do not expect your father and me to help you out of your hornet's nest! Because I will be the one to get stung—this whole town will be gossiping soon enough and you can bet the day you were born that I will be the talk of the town! You made your bed, now you can lie in it!"

From the minute Susan woke up in the morning until she went to sleep at night, she was belittled and shamed, and felt she had nowhere to turn. The night after she shared her situation with her mother was when she decided a drastic option was the only solution.

Susan spent the first part of the summer after graduation reflecting on how she had always tried to please her parents. She babysat her little sisters, cooked and cleaned. She diligently did her homework, even though her grades were average. She attended church, visited her relatives and got a part-time job as a clerk at Barney's.

She wondered why most townspeople thought her to be a tramp when all she ever did was try to make everyone happy. *I don't have the time to be screwing around while trying to please all of you people*! she thought.

Her reputation at school was just as bad. From as far back as she could remember, Susan had been nicknamed Suzi-Q, labelled as the dumb blonde, and always a fast girl. The titles, lewd comments, and advances from boys inspired mixed emotions in her. Susan liked the attention and yet loathed the assumptions that went with the judgment.

For most of her high school years, Susan planned and plotted how she would lose her virginity. She decided early on that in no uncertain terms was she going to remain a virgin until after graduation as her mother had done! "Save yourself for marriage" was something Susan had heard since she was old enough to understand what she was saving herself from or for.

At seventeen, pregnant, and newly graduated from high school, Susan was not as devastated as most would expect. Instead, she was excited, optimistic, and wondered, '*What next*?' She secretly wanted to get knocked up as her first outward statement of rebellion, and a creative way to get out from under her parents' wrath.

When the hush-hush incident was revealed, her mother, whom Susan thought was holier than thou, suggested an abortion.

At her mother's declaration, Susan erupted into a state of fury and spit out words she had never uttered before. "You hypocritical monster! Do you think your god would approve, Mother? How about the neighbours? I know! Why don't I take out an ad in the newspaper and tell the whole town what you're willing to do? I will not allow anyone to cut my love child out of my body and throw it in the trash. No way!!!" screamed Susan.

She thought to herself, *Mother, Dwayne's mother, and Pastor Herman can shove their consequences where the sun doesn't shine!*

Susan's and Dwayne's drastic decision was to tie the knot on September 21st, 1978, three months after graduation. Her three sisters were bridesmaids, crafty Tracy and her talented mother made all the dresses and decorated the hall, and the ladies' auxiliary from the church pulled a quick reception together, with ham, lasagna, potato salad and lots of devilled eggs. Even though MeadowBrook was acclaimed for its laying hens, Susan thought it a little slanderous to have so many deviled eggs when the whole town suggested she was no angel.

To sum it up, Susan and Dwayne's wedding was anything but perfect, but as Susan would tell it, it was "Good enough." They played Susan's favourite song by Earth, Wind & Fire, "September." Immediately after the song, as a romantic gesture, Dwayne had arranged for Elton John's song "Crocodile Rock" to play, because it reminded him of Susan and the night they first hooked up. As soon as the needle hit the vinyl, Dwayne extended his hand to Susan in the most gentlemanly of ways and led her out to the dance floor. As they twisted and gyrated Dwayne leaned in and whispered to Susan, "My feet just can't keep still when I'm around you! I will never forget that tight red dress you wore on our first night together."

They danced and laughed. Susan thought that just maybe she could fall in love with Dwayne if she didn't think too long and hard about it.

They pulled it off and their life began. Never once did they refer to their daughter as a mistake. Instead, they decided that nothing was predestined, and the obstacle of their past became a gateway to a new beginning.

Dwayne said to Susan one afternoon when they were pushing their baby through town in a stroller, "Some people know the right things to do, whereas others need to figure it out by doing the wrong things first." Susan reached over to his hand on the baby buggy and gently placed hers on top. Dwayne looked at her, then stopped and turned toward her, kissing her tenderly on the cheek.

The only previous work experience Dwayne had was flipping burgers at the A&W during high school. As Susan put it, "He was a clean slate and ready to learn." They had heard that Fasp Farm needed workers at their chicken farm, so he applied and was hired. He went to work before dawn and came home at dusk.

Dwayne was never without scrapes, scratches, and bloody fingers from making wire cages. He regularly smelled of manure and his body ached from top to bottom. Susan tended to his wounds, washed his clothes and massaged his aching body.

Dwayne started at the bottom and within a year he knew everything there was to know about laying hens, egg production, marketing, and farming. He was promoted from cage maker to tending to the chickens, then egg production, and eventually marketing. He became the Fasps' foreman and right-hand man.

Soon enough, Dwayne was not an awkward teenager anymore. He had grown up, and by his early twenties stood six feet four inches tall. He was strong, muscular and handsome. Ultimately, his looks, work ethic, and morals caused Susan to fall head over heels in love with him, knowingly in the wrong order of traditional courtship and marriage, but it didn't matter to either of them.

They became a typical country bumpkin family, and both were professedly happy.

Regardless of how it all turned out, Susan was still considered a blemish on her parents' reputation, and they remained embarrassed about the scandalous event that occurred because they had much higher expectations for their seventeen-year-old daughter.

Over the years, Susan became outspoken and confident and could be heard saying on many occasions, "I don't give a rat's ass what anybody thinks!" Since the incident at Lover's Lane and the race to the altar, Susan always made a point to speak her mind. Shortly after her first child was born, she got a job writing a column for the local newspaper called, "Sarcastic Susan—What Will She Say Next?" Susan's column was the topic of the day and grist for the gossip mill on print day, along with "Astrid Ann's Horoscope Predictions."

She made it her duty to discuss politics, religion, current events, sexism, and her all-time favourite topics—male chauvinists and religious fanatics. When the royal wedding of Lady Diana to Prince Charles took place, Susan asked, "Why are YOU Obsessed with the Royal Family?" She was quoted as saying, "If more women were in power, there would be fewer wars because what mother wants to see her child brutally murdered?" Some wanted her column banned and others reveled in it. Her most recent column spoke about stereotypes. Titled, "How Dare You," Susan asked, "Are we our stereotype, or does our stereotype make us who we are?"

Susan's personal favourite article was, "Am I a dumb blonde? I dare you to say it!" She gave a basic history lesson at the beginning of the column: "Okay I am guilty of telling a few dumb blonde jokes myself, so don't think I am all high and mighty. But that was before, this is now. So, to set the record straight, 'Blonde jokes' that employ the stereotype, overlap with other jokes that portray the subject of the joke as promiscuous and stupid. Many of these jokes are variants of ethnic jokes about other identifiable groups dating back to the seventeenth century. The new and not-funny-to-everyone jokes about being blonde are overwhelmingly female-specific and undeniably sexist…"

Nearly ten years after high school, it still made Susan's blood boil to think about the labels and treatment she endured throughout her entire education. It was like she had a Rolodex filing device in her brain and could summon all the past hurts, mean words, and derogatory comments she had accumulated over the years. "*If you smiled more you would be much prettier…It's okay if you are bad at math; you're a girl so don't worry about it…She's only good for one thing...She was asking for it...*" Words and statements were rudely directed at a woman's anatomy, looks, and personality.

Everybody in MeadowBrook read Susan's column, even though some said her outspoken views were hogwash and balderdash. The ladies' church auxiliary skipped over her outspoken articles and her parents never left the house on a print day out of sheer embarrassment.

Susan was still the talk of the town, but she now felt worthy of the reasons why.

To help deal with her anger, Susan started jogging. It surprised her how good it made her feel. All year round, before the sun rose and her children woke up, Susan would run throughout neighbourhoods and on back country roads. With every stride and foot slamming down on the pavement, she knew she was stamping out the demons from her past. Even though her outdoor private therapy sessions felt healing, Dwayne did not like her out running alone and often pleaded with her not to go. Susan was headstrong and fearlessly responded, "I dare anyone to mess with me!" He loved this side of his wife but hoped it would not one day get her into trouble.

Eventually, Susan jumped on the fitness bandwagon and became an aerobics instructor. Once again she was in the limelight and somewhat of a celebrity, complete with a thong leotard, leg warmers, headband, scrunchies in her ponytail, high-top running shoes, and cassette tapes for her music. She also sported a trendy gym bag slung over her shoulder, with the word SWEAT decorating the sides.

Ten years of marriage and three kids later, Dwayne still adored Susan and continued to call her his little Suzy-Q. Likewise, Susan's adoration for Dwayne grew, even though she was against the whole idea of a knight in shining armour rescuing a damsel in distress. But she knew there was a storybook romance in all of it. Besides, she often joked, "It only makes sense for the head cheerleader and the power forward on the basketball team to get hitched and live happily ever after." After her analogy, Susan always winked as part of her sarcasm.

Susan loved her three children and quaint four-bedroom brick house with yellow shutters on the windows and yellow daffodils in the window boxes. She enjoyed country living and all the conveniences a chicken farmer employee could offer. Even though as a columnist and fitness instructor she made more money than her husband, she never brought it up and neither did Dwayne.

The invitation for the ten-year grad reunion did not come as a surprise to Susan. Even though they weren't friends back in school, Tracy and Susan became friends while preparing for Susan and Dwayne's quick-fix wedding. Their bond started with Susan's race to the altar, and their friendship developed shortly afterward. They got in the habit of daily phone conversations and then became jogging partners. Eventually, they attended fitness classes together and had lunch dates. While sharing their highs and lows and supporting each other through thick and thin, both women came to the conclusion that although they wanted to change the world, they needed to first change themselves.

Susan and Tracy based their friendship around their similarities and allowed their differences to complement one another.

Tracy got Susan's opinion on everything for the reunion, from choosing the invitations to picking out the date, the venue, and the food to be served. And with Susan's connections at the newspaper, she helped Tracy find all of the addresses for the MeadowBrook graduating class of 1978.

Early on in their friendship, Susan had made Tracy Hansworth not only her best friend, but also her top priority. She was determined to find Tracy a mate, and if she had anything to say about it, it would *not* be Kent Gordon, the man Tracy wanted.

MeadowBrook High School Ten-Year Reunion

Saturday, June 13th, 7 p.m. – midnight
Formal Dance, school gym
Sunday, June 14th Farewell Brunch 11:00
a.m. - 3:00 p.m. picnic at the pond
Cost $25.00

RSVP ASAP
Tracy Hansworth
8722 Cherry Wood Drive
Meadow Brook
Canada

***

Tracy Hansworth had a way of looking at life from the perspective of before and after, and rarely lived in the moment, as her brain was a whirling dervish of ideas, plans and events.

The morning after grad, all Tracy could think about was that everything had gone wrong, and it was not the night she had hoped and planned for. The week after graduation, Tracy's obsession with what she perceived as a failure caused her to be mortified that she had prepared for the entire year for that one night to be perfect, and she had not achieved her goal.

As she reviewed the events of grad night, Tracy repeatedly went over the debacles in her mind. She was tormented that her fellow grads disliked her decision to kick off the dance with a Karen Carpenter song and had not held back in telling her so. She could not understand how the balloon archway collapsed, and she was embarrassed that the ladies' auxiliary served dry and tasteless chicken. Summing up the night in its entirety, Tracy felt deflated and heartbroken that of all the things that went wrong, her greatest regret was that she did not see Kent leave or get a chance to say goodbye.

Tracy spent a lot of time that summer evaluating her past and being confused about the future. In doing so, she had flashbacks of a busy, happy childhood; a loving, kind father, an overly attached mother, and a sister who was the complete opposite of her.

Tracy recalled that as supportive as her mom Eunice was, she could never figure out why she would not allow her to date, or discouraged her from having any boys around, even just as friends. Especially since her mother was an attractive older woman and was flirtatious with half the men in town, a trait of her mother's that humiliated Tracy. She speculated that her father disapproved, as well.

However, there were many qualities her mom possessed that Tracy admired. She hoped to one day be as appealing as her mother, and to eventually snag a boy like Kent. Not only was Eunice Hansworth beautiful on the outside, but she had an endearing quality on the inside, too. Even though some folk referred to her as nosy, Tracy saw her mother as deeply caring and concerned for all of humanity. They were both sticklers for organization, agreeing that everything had a place. This trait also enabled them to compartmentalize their family, friends, and tasks.

Most importantly in Tracy's eyes, she learned all of her crafting skills from her mom, and she was proud that they called themselves the Suzy Homemaker Twins, even though her best friend Susan cringed every time Tracy said it.

With little to no dating experience, the boy she had a crush on was gone, with no warning, proper goodbye, or forwarding address. The only telltale sign of Kent Gordon's departure was his smashed-up sports car abandoned in a farmer's field. He had disappeared without a trace. While some conspiracy theorists from the UFO Science Club speculated extra-terrestrials had abducted him, Tracy knew this to be ridiculous.

Then a couple of months after graduation, Tracy had a vision. It came to her in a flash, like a lightning bolt of the most essential kind, an epiphany of what to do for the rest of her life.

It was a regular Sunday morning after church when Tracy opened the *Gazette* from the past Wednesday. Thumbing through, she flipped straight to her horoscope, her usual routine. Then, the first line of Astrid Ann's predictions for her sign caused Tracy to pause, catch her breath and whisper, "Of course!"

It stated, "Libra, you cannot start the next chapter if you keep re-reading the last one."

Even though Tracy said her nightly prayers and put her faith in God, she also read her weekly horoscope and hoped the astrological readings would guide her. Kind of like a backup plan or a safety net for what God had in store for her.

On that warm August morning, Tracy's zodiac sign had given her the advice she longed for. Right then and there, Tracy decided to move out of her parents' house… but first, she needed to find a job, and to take it one step further, a successful career. Pondering her many strengths, Tracy knew she was gifted at arts and crafts, had keen organizational skills, and was a stickler for detail. Additionally, she liked people and always wanted to help them. She reasoned that being an entrepreneur would be the life for her.

Tracy Hansworth came from a long line of family members born and raised in MeadowBrook, so naturally she had no desire to leave. She loved small-town living and was proud to know everyone from the butcher to the baker and candlestick maker.

Shortly after her revelation, Tracy showered, got dressed in skinny stirrup jeans, an oversized Cotton Ginny floral sweatshirt and her favourite sneakers, and walked into town, hoping to find some inspiration along the way. Minutes into her stroll, she spotted Susan sitting on a park bench. Tracy got a clue that something was wrong, so she meandered over and sat down beside her in an authentic meddlesome manner, all the while telling herself that her curiosity was inspired by care and compassion for her fellow classmate.

Looking up, Susan's eyes met Tracy's, and she instantly burst into tears. Everything came spilling out. Susan described grad night, what happened in the car afterward with Dwayne, and her mother's reaction, with baby makes three being the eventual outcome.

Tracy listened, thought, and listened some more. Then, after Susan's heartfelt unraveling of events, Tracy blurted out a common-sense plan in her signature, no-nonsense way of speaking. First, she soothed her, validated her, and said how proud she was that Susan took a stand against both her mother and Dwayne's mother, neither one of whom wanted her to keep the baby.

Then Tracy shared her idea and her new career path all in one fell swoop.

She took Susan's hands in hers and looked sincerely into her teary blue eyes. Then she said, "Okay, here's the plan. Let me arrange your entire wedding because it just happens to be my new business. You get married, have the baby, and voilà! All your problems will go away!" Both women felt a gust of ambition that spoke louder than the MeadowBrook wind brushing over the fields and through the town. It was as if all negative thoughts had been whisked away and their minds filled with fresh new ideas.

Directly after solving Susan's problem, Tracy went to the library and researched how to start a small business. She created a name, Events by Tracy, with the tagline, "*Let me be in charge, so you won't have to.*" On Monday morning she went to the courthouse and applied for a business license. Tracy's first client also became her new best friend.

After Susan's wedding and reception, Tracy was booked up for the following year with events ranging from a two-year-old's birthday party, to more extravagant affairs like the refurbishing of the giant MeadowBrook egg statue that greeted those who entered the bustling little town, and the farewell egg, that said, "Thank you! Come again!" when people left. Anniversaries, weddings, store openings, and the sixty-five-year anniversary of the Frugal

Grocer became some of the many milestones celebrated with the help of Tracy's business.

Eventually, neighbouring towns heard about her company and wanted to hire her event planning services, so she expanded and hired staff. As a result, only one year after creating her company and operating at full throttle, she had branded herself, was doing local television commercials, could be found in the Yellow Pages, had a downtown office, and had vehicles emblazoned with her face and logo. Going into her second year, Tracy wrote an *Events by Tracy* manual, sold three franchises, gave workshops, and took twenty per cent from each of her franchised locations.

Tracy adored being in charge. She thrived at dishing out orders and knew she had found her true calling. Everything was going better than Tracy could have imagined, until her nineteenth birthday, sixteen months after graduation and fourteen months after starting her event planning business, when her outer shell would crack and her heart would break like that of a Fasp farm fresh egg when accidentally dropped.

Tracy and her mother had a seemingly irreparable falling out.

It had been her mother's idea to treat Tracy to dinner at Robinson's Diner and her first cocktail as a legal drinker. Just the two of them. Tracy adored the idea. She had never dabbled in drinking alcohol, although she had always wanted to. She had heard about hangovers and how expensive it could be to drink, and both consequences had kept her from ever partaking.

Nevertheless, Eunice convinced Tracy that turning nineteen was a monumental time, and toasting the occasion was imperative. So, mother and daughter got dressed up, walked into town, and sat in their favourite booth at the back of Robinson's. Champagne was ordered first. Tracy laughed at the bubbles and then decided she liked the sparkly feel on the back of her throat and the taste of crisp apple and melon on her palate. Eventually, she noticed a slight numbness in her legs, heat on her face, and a carefree effect on her brain.

When Tracy was finished with her first glass of champagne and was ready to order dinner, her mother said, "Now just hold on, sweetie, there is more to celebrating your birth and turning the legal drinking age than just having one drink!" They both laughed wholeheartedly. Eunice then ordered a bottle of her favourite white wine, a local pinot grigio called *Windy Meadows.*

By the time dinner was ordered, both women were carrying on, giggling and freely reminiscing.

They talked about the good old days of bake sales, craft tables, and arts and crafts birthday parties. Tracy boldly stated in yet another toast, with a loud clinking of their glasses, "THANK YOU, MOTHER, FOR THE BEST CHILDHOOD EVER!"

Following Tracy's praise, she asked her mother, "By the way, how did you spend your nineteenth birthday, Mom?"

Eunice said matter-of-factly, "Well, I got laid of course!" After a brief pause, Tracy let out a loud cackle that sprayed alcohol across the table, which caused them both to laugh until tears streamed from their eyes.

Feeling encouraged by her daughter's response and inebriated by the booze, Eunice continued, "Actually, darling, since we're here, just the two of us, and you're all grown up now, I do have so many things about life I can share with you…"

Tracy had no idea where her mother was going with the conversation but she was intrigued, so she said, "Oh, really? Well, carry on, Mother. I would love some motherly wisdom and advice."

Leaning in toward Tracy from across the table, Eunice slurred, "Well, since you asked, I must say that your mother—me—has not been a very good girl over the years…"

Before Eunice could continue, Tracy panicked. She didn't like the path her mother was on. She asked her to please stop. She covered her ears and said, in a slightly worried and curt voice, "Um, too much information, Mother! Some things are better left unsaid."

Eunice just waved off her daughter's objection and said, "Oh, don't be silly. We're all grown-ups here, and I just want you to know, that boy Kent Gordon…well, a few years back, we had a little fling…"

Eunice didn't get a chance to finish. Tracy leapt up and out of the booth, staring at her mother, speechless, as visions of the movie *The Graduate,* flooded her mind. Her mother was Anne Bancroft and Kent was Dustin Hoffman, an older woman seducing a younger man and ruining his life. All Tracy could muster to say was, "MOTHER! HOW COULD YOU?"

She then stomped out the door, with her mother hollering after her, "Don't be so dramatic! It was a mutual affair, you silly goose!"

Sitting alone in the booth at the diner, Eunice reached across the table, grabbed Tracy's half-finished glass of wine and poured it into her own. Within seconds, two plates of food arrived. Robinson's evening special steamed from both dishes: tender roast beef, creamy garlic mashed potatoes, buttery sweet corn, and golden-brown Yorkshire pudding, all smothered in rich dark gravy.

Eunice looked at the server and pointed to Tracy's empty seat, saying, "She'll take hers to go, and I'll have another drink, but make it a Scotch this time."

Tracy stopped taking her mother's calls and made arrangements to visit her sister in Milan, who was still there modelling. She thought that because her sister was older and had known their mother longer, she would understand how difficult their mother was and help her through the traumatic event of losing the only man she ever loved—to their mother.

Without saying goodbye to Eunice, Tracy stopped by her father's automotive shop on the way to the Hillsprings Airport. Pulling up to the garage, Tracy felt nostalgic. Seeing the old Model-T Ford out front made her smile. The smell of car grease and rubber tires was like a heady perfume, and seeing her dad in his mechanic jumpsuit chatting with a few old-timers reminded Tracy that growing old is mandatory and growing up is optional. She then thought of Kent and whispered, "Where are you?"

Her dad greeted her with open arms and a large gregarious smile. It wasn't until Tracy told her father she was flying to Milan to see Lisa that his beaming face stiffened and the once inviting expression turned into a grimace. He begged her not to go, even though Tracy had spent weeks making her decision to leave. They both knew she was fleeing and running away from the harsh reality of her mother's behaviour. The hidden truth had been divulged and Tracy hated it.

She had researched the city of Milan and remembered from her geography class that it was in Italy. The difficult part about going away was finding coverage and hiring a right-hand helper for her business. Temporarily off all men, she made sure it was a woman.

Her sister Lisa had been gone for almost five years, working as a model, and the periodic postcards she sent revealed she was doing well. Feeling the time crunch of getting to the airport, Tracy quickly summed up by saying, "Oh Daddy, this will be good. I can give you an update on Lisa, and don't you want your daughters to be close?" Before he could respond, Tracy added, "Besides, Mom and I had that big fight, and this trip will help me figure things out."

Tracy's dad nodded. Very rarely did he speak negatively about Eunice, but he forced out the words, "I'm not very pleased with your mother right now. I love her dearly, but why does she have to be so gull-darned flirtatious? It embarrasses me to no end!"

On that note, Tracy reached up to her father, hugged him around the neck, kissed him on the cheek and said, "'Bye, Daddy. I'll call you here at the shop when I get there!"

Tracy had never wanted to travel, but unlikely things kept happening, so she threw all caution to the wind, especially since "Astrid Anne's" most recent horoscope said, "Libra, understanding requires compassion, patience, and a willingness to believe that good hearts sometimes make poor choices." Tracy was utterly unwilling to show mercy, grace, or understanding to her ever-increasingly distant, obtrusive and flirtatious mother.

Climbing aboard the elite 747 jet, Tracy was alarmingly uncomfortable. She could not fathom how on earth the massive aircraft carrier would get off the ground, and she didn't like the idea of having her life in someone else's hands. She knew nothing of the pilot and hoped and prayed he was not a lunatic, and that the silver bullet she entered would not be her coffin headed for a watery grave. As she settled into her seat, she crossed her fingers, prayed, and then tightly closed her eyes.

Once in the air, she felt herself relax, until the food cart arrived and an overly friendly stewardess said, "Coffee, tea, or me?" With her mouth open in shock, Tracy shook her head to erase what she imagined the flight attendant was saying, and then slammed her mouth shut and smiled weakly. Accepting the food, she muttered under her breath, "I would never be caught dead serving this grey mass of undetectable cuisine at any of my events." Looking from side to side, she noticed everyone else was digging into their food trays like they hadn't eaten in weeks. Her appetite had been left behind on the tarmac, so she popped some Wrigley's spearmint chewing gum into her mouth instead, covered up the Chicken á la King with a napkin, closed her eyes, and tucked her nose into her fluffy pink angora turtleneck, leaving the food untouched.

When the plane landed, Tracy was surprised to see a grey fog over the city. Disembarking, she felt the sticky, humid weather weighing down on her like a foreboding sign in a mystery novel. Immediately she wanted to turn back around and go home. Tracy said to herself, "Oh my goodness, what have I done?" She had become wholly disappointed with the entire trip before it even began.

Lisa picked her up at the airport and immediately Tracy was taken aback by her sister's physical appearance. She could have been a body double to their mother. Both Eunice and Lisa were tall, thin, and strikingly beautiful. Tracy was the opposite, petite and not the least bit elegant. Some even referred to her as annoyingly cute. Tracy had not noticed the similarities before, when Lisa was still at home, and first impressions indicated that Lisa and Eunice were cut from the same cloth. Tracy quickly learned that both women ostensibly had a way with both men and alcohol.

Lisa's apartment was artistically beautiful. Whitewashed walls, high curved windows, and blue-tiled floors graced the space. Tracy appreciated how aesthetically pleasing it was, but wondered why there was no shag carpeting and thick drapes covering the expansive windows. She felt the apartment was stark and not the least bit cozy.

During the taxi ride to her home, Lisa had attempted to show her little sister the sights, but Tracy was uninterested and only wanted to talk. The conversation was strained from the very start, and when Tracy tried to explain their mother's roving eye, Lisa acted like she was being childish and overreacting in regard to their mother's salacious ways. Her dismal attempt at counselling Tracy was to say, "Oh Tracy, grow up! You know what your problem is?" Without giving Tracy a chance to respond, Lisa said, "All you need to do is meet a man, get drunk, lose your virginity, and not be so uptight!" She finished with, "Live a little, sister! In fact, let me show you how!"

Tracy's only response was to roll her eyes and dread the upcoming evening. On their first night out, Lisa wore white spandex pants, a red sequined halter top, and sparkly red stiletto heels. Tracy, on the other hand, got dressed in denim capris, Birkenstock sandals and a pink Minnie Mouse sweatshirt.

Lisa laughed out loud at the sight of her little sister and said, "They will never let you into the club looking like that!" She then tried to convince Tracy to put on some of her clothes, but Lisa's pants were too tight and the tops were too big. She insisted Tracy at least wear a pair of her heels and went through her bag until she found a simple white blouse. Lisa unbuttoned it to Tracy's naval and tied it in a knot at the bottom. She backcombed Tracy's hair and put red lipstick and false eyelashes on her.

Tracy felt small and meek and knew she looked uncomfortable and like a fish out of water. Glancing at herself in the mirror on their way out, Tracy felt like a wild-haired troll doll without the gemstone in her naval.

The taxi arrived and Tracy hobbled out of the apartment, fearful she would break her ankle on the cobblestone street. Lisa strode gracefully with confidence as if she were on the runway at Fashion Week.

Once at the club, Tracy admired the decor and mentally jotted down ideas for a possible event back at home. She then sneakily dumped her strong drink, pineapples and all, in a nearby potted plant. Looking around the darkened, mirrored discotheque, the men all appeared wolf-like, and Tracy knew they thought of her as an innocent lamb in need of slaughtering or teaching a lesson. When she got tired of warding off the hungry animals and being prey to their plunder, she ordered a taxi, went back to her sister's apartment and changed her airline ticket to go home the next day.

Lisa never did come home that night, so in the morning, in her best penmanship, Tracy left her older sister a cordial note that said,

Dearest sister,

Thank you for trying, but I am quite happy with who I am, living in the small hick town you so despise. I wish you well, and if you ever decide to come home, I will treat you to a cup of coffee and peach pie at Robinson's Diner.

Love,
Tracy xo

P.S. To give you a better visual, if we were animals, I would be a teacup Chihuahua and you a prestigious Australian shepherd.

P.S.S. Please be careful!

Arriving home to MeadowBrook, Tracy never felt so happy to be on familiar ground in the familiar small town amongst familiar people. She was thrilled to return to the food she loved, her seven-day work week, and her 9:00 p.m. bedtime.

As soon as she set foot in the door of her bright, sunny apartment, the first person she called was Susan. They made arrangements to meet the following day for lunch, so Tracy could fill her in on the foreign country she had come from, complete with the horrible flight experience, lewd men at the disco, her floozy sister, and how lucky they were to live in MeadowBrook.

Happy and grateful to be home, Tracy picked up right where she left off. She delved into her work with passion, drive, and determination, and each event was more successful than the last.

In 1987, Tracy made the cover of *Women in Business* magazine, along with forty-nine other successful women worldwide. She was nominated anonymously because of a 1986 spread in an acclaimed regional publication, which had put MeadowBrook on the map, due to the extensive event she had planned and executed for Mayor Gordon's sixty-fifth birthday party.

The extravagant celebration had been an outdoor affair. The highlight was twenty-five colourful hot-air balloons. Events By Tracy added individual wicker picnic baskets filled with champagne, chocolate-covered strawberries, caviar, and gifts for each guest. The cost was astronomical, but the mayor, Kent's father, had money to burn and said, "Money is no object. Let's put this town on the map!" So, she did.

Tracy had hoped Kent would attend but was equally relieved when he was a no-show.

Then, nine years after graduation, Tracy put all her eggs in one basket, in true MeadowBrook fashion, in a grandiose plan to see Kent again. As part of her *Bring Kent into My Arms* campaign, Tracy and Susan decided to throw the greatest reunion party of all time. Susan had softened to the idea of Kent Gordon and her best friend Tracy Hansworth becoming a couple, for the sole reason that she was worried her friend would remain a virgin for the rest of her life.

After a few years of dissociation, Tracy forgave her mother and gave her an office manager position at her company, with only one stipulation—she was not allowed to sleep with any of the staff or clients. Eunice sheepishly agreed.

In the spring of 1988, the most magnificent celebration imaginable was about to go down. Tracy was sure it would be remembered as the greatest high school reunion of all time. She decorated the gym with a farm theme, checkered tablecloths, bales of hay, and miniature white picket fences. The classrooms were turned into multimedia party rooms. In one classroom, a DJ with a disco ball would be turning out tunes from the 1970s. In another room there would be a live rock band, and in a third room, carnival games complete with a dunk tank, ring toss and a cake walk.

On the matter of Kent, Susan was Tracy's go-to woman when it came to advice and relationship tips. They both decided that first, Tracy needed to find him, and then figure out how, when, and where she would share her true feelings.

MeadowBrook High School Ten-Year Reunion

Saturday, June 13th, Formal Dance 7
p.m. to midnight, school gym
Sunday, June 14th, Farewell Brunch 11:00
a.m. to 3:00 p.m. picnic at the pond

Cost: $25.00

RSVP ASAP
Tracy Hansworth
8722 Cherry Wood Drive
MeadowBrook
Canada

Chapter Five

The Disappearance of William Farnsworth

"Fortunate are those who find love at any age—happy, lasting, and true. A love that deepens over time. A love that survives the unknown currents of a long life in a cold, deep void. Or a love cut short, as nothing lasts forever until death does us part."

—Founder of MeadowBrook,
William Farnsworth

MeadowBrook was described as a small rural town smack dab in the middle of nowhere. Its residents experienced hot, sticky summers and bitter cold, freezing winters and complained about all the seasons.

The town's notoriety came from their laying hens and Fasp farm fresh eggs. A giant egg constructed in 1912 by the founder, William Farnsworth, was situated on Exit 88 at the highway off-ramp heading into town. Their slogan was, "*Welcome to MeadowBrook! We hope you have an EGG of a time.*" Ironically, most teenagers only ever thought of leaving, and very few ever said they *had an egg of a time* while there.

Since 1953, the locals had told the tragic tale of William Farnsworth. The disappearance and unsolved murder of the revered well-to-do businessman forever haunted the town's residents and all who passed through.

He was an early settler arriving in MeadowBrook in 1911 when it was only a pimple on the prairie. William immediately began work claiming land, opening a general store, and starting the first chicken farm. Eventually, he incorporated the small thriving town, because William had a hunch the picturesque village surrounded by undulating hills, crystal clear brooks and pristine countryside would be a success, and the peaceful ambiance would be the main selling feature.

In 1911, William Farnsworth was twenty-six years old, and until then, he had lived a meagre and poor existence. He had been told by his father that his mother died in childbirth while delivering his youngest sibling, so William, being the eldest, was forced to raise his seven brothers and sisters almost entirely by himself. In addition, his father was a heavy drinker, not a caregiver at all, and in William's mind, not a father. Later, his father fell victim to sclerosis of the liver and died bedridden of pneumonia.

However, William's only parent had been keeping a huge secret, later revealed in his last will and testament. Assuming that mental disorders can be the result of both genetic and environmental factors, it was ironic that William developed a fascination with the stigma and discrimination faced by those unfortunate individuals who were locked up in padded rooms because he had no idea how closely connected he was to the criminally insane. His father failed to tell him that his mother had not died while birthing his youngest sibling. She had instead been imprisoned for *murdering* his youngest sibling. Public knowledge of the incident had been suppressed.

Unbeknownst to everyone, William's father was wealthy and yet lived the life of a pauper. Therefore, he put his seven children through unnecessary and extreme hardship. He bequeathed $267,000 to his oldest son, William Jr., with a brief note: *Thank you, son, for all you have done. Please be a good person and spend this money wisely.*

Following his father's death, William became bitter. So, he packed up—lock, stock and barrel—to create a new life elsewhere. Before he left, William divided the money he inherited among his siblings and fled. After stumbling upon what eventually became MeadowBrook, William never looked back and never saw his brothers and sisters again.

Moving forward, William Farnsworth vowed to be generous with his money.

William's wife Gladys was only nineteen when they married, and twenty when their son Marvin was born. Twenty years later, she had utterly lost touch with her aging husband and rarely knew where he was or what he was doing. Their initial meeting was somewhat scandalous to the small town, followed closely by scrutinizing townspeople. Nevertheless, community members considered William Farnsworth their saviour and the next best thing to royalty.

In the 1930s, with only a Grade 7 education, Gladys was known for her beauty, but not her brains. People referred to her as a little bit of a thing, standing five feet two inches and weighing only ninety-eight pounds. Her most distinguishing features were her strawberry blond hair which she wore in pigtail braids, and her rosebud lips shaped in a perpetual pout as if she was greatly disappointed.

Gladys worked at her father's cherry orchard, and in 1932, at the start of cherry-picking season, William pulled up to her family's roadside fruit stand and purchased everything she was selling that day. Then he said with a wink and a smile, "Since all your fruit is sold out, I reckon you don't have anything else to do today, so how about going on a picnic with me?"

Gladys wondered what the noticeably older man would do with the flats of cherries and was worried they would all spoil. So instead of saying yes to William's offer, in a barely audible whisper and with poor grammar, she said, "Whatcha gonna do with all them cherries, mister?"

William confidently responded, "Well, I suppose I will make eighteen cherry pies to represent every year since the day the blessed angels put you here on this earth!"

William was forty-eight years old, thirty years older than Gladys.

Without saying anything else, Gladys loaded the cherries into the back of William's car and made her way over to the passenger side of the customized four-door Cadillac limousine, complete with sideboards, sun visor, and chrome wheel coverings.

Gladys had never seen such wealth and elegance. She climbed into the spic-and-span automobile with trepidation. William could see she was timid, so he jumped to the occasion to set her at ease. In an informative, bellowing voice, as if making a declaration, William said, "Dear, sweet Gladys. Even though the Great Depression has hit hard, I have lived by my motto and have come out completely unscathed!" He followed with one of his many slogans, "Instead of investing in the stock market, I invest in people. You are safe with me, sweetheart."

Gladys still said nothing, but inwardly felt the stirrings of excitement mixed with her usual insecurities about her intelligence.

As they drove the dusty backcountry roads, Gladys reflected inwardly on her home life. She wondered why her parents had focused so much on telling her what to do: "Do this, Gladys! Do that, Gladys! And hurry up while you're at it!" She had never been asked a direct question about her thoughts or her opinions. Sitting next to William, she was pensive. She felt like her brain was empty, like a blank page in a notebook.

Meanwhile, William was a keen talker and disliked being at a loss for words. He interrupted Gladys's thoughts and said, "So tell me your story."

Gladys was stunned by his question, but responded in the best way she could, "Well, mister, I live with my ma and pa, and they got an orchard and five kids, so I do what I's bin told."

William quickly realized that Gladys had no idea who he was or anything about the beautiful farming community he had founded. So, he launched in with a history lesson. "Well, little lady, you happen to be driving in a car with the founder of this town. I started the first chicken farm, and now MeadowBrook is famous for its eggs. Have you ever seen the highway off-ramp?"

Gladys paused and meekly responded, "Um, I dunno, maybe I have."

As if she hadn't said anything at all, William continued, "It was my idea to construct a giant egg welcoming all those who pass through, with the slogan, '*Welcome to MeadowBrook. We hope you have an EGG of a time.*'" William laughed, and Gladys was bemused.

From that day forward, Gladys never worked again. No longer would her small hands be stained with purple cherry juice or her legs ache from standing in the plywood fruit stand in the heat of the noon-day sun. Instead, she was groomed by William to become his wife.

There was no romantic proposal. It felt much like a business deal to Gladys, a mutual agreement between William and her parents—her father the seller, and William the buyer. Gladys decided the arrangement made sense because she was dirt poor, uneducated and had no other immediate plans.

She never told William about the realities of her life, growing up in a one-room shack with her father. He was an evil and violent man, frequently backhanding her on whatever part of her body was available. His sharp tongue often sliced through her gentle nature like a butcher's knife to a slab of beef. The onslaught of abuse caused her to bury the pain and suffer it all in silence, blocking it from her memory. Her mother never stood up in her defence, as she was also a victim of the abuse herself. In essence, when Gladys was picked up at the cherry stand, she was escaping the wrath of an abusive father and fleeing into the arms of a man who was old enough to be her father—a man she knew nothing about.

Gladys was moved into a guest cottage on William's estate, which was bigger than the family home where she grew up. Her dowdy boyish clothing was thrown in the incinerator immediately, and a new wardrobe was purchased. It was made-to-order garments only for Gladys, even though mass factory-produced ready-to-wear clothing was the going trend. Her frayed checkered shorts and worn sneakers were replaced with modern high-waisted sailor pants and shiny buckle-up T-strap high-heeled shoes.

All the new apparel was made with silk or rayon crepe, not cotton, with puff sleeves, belted waists, and large yoked collars. Gladys's evening gowns (even though there were few places to wear them) came in chiffon, silk, and satin. When metallic lamé came into fashion, her dresses were cut low in the back, with a train that swept the floor, just like the movie star Marlena Dietrich's.

Her assortment of mink stoles and fur coats became the talk of the town, even though Gladys abhorred them. She did not like the idea of wearing a dead animal and complained that the fur itched around her neck.

By 1933, despite the hard times of the depression era, makeup and cosmetics sales doubled in North America, and Gladys Farnsworth was at the front of the line. She was given makeup application lessons and began reading every Hollywood movie magazine she could get her hands on. She tried to emulate Greta Garbo, Joan Crawford, and Hedy Lamar.

Gone were her pigtail braids, to be replaced with a chignon bun pinned tightly to her head. Next, Gladys tried romantic waves, soft curls, and a centre part. Finally, she settled on a new asymmetrical blunt hairstyle from *Vogue* magazine. William was stunned by the futuristic look.

He hired a speech coach, history professor, and handwriting specialist and sent Gladys away to an etiquette school in England.

William was pleased with his handiwork and was proud of Gladys's visual image, even though he knew she was only superficially attractive and entertaining, and somewhat lacking intellectually. Despite all of that, he felt her appearance showcased his success.

Shortly after her transformation, Gladys Farnsworth became a regular topic of the day, and she loved the attention. Gladys had become privileged and well-to-do seemingly overnight. Every night when she settled down in her soft quilted bedding, she included in her prayers how thankful she was. As she drifted off to sleep, Gladys knew she had won the lottery and would someday acquire a great fortune.

A year after their courtship began, an elaborate wedding was held, and the whole town was invited. It was a memorable outdoor ceremony and went down as the event of the century.

In the 1930s, the going trend for the bride was hats instead of veils, and reusable dresses instead of elaborate gowns. The depression made wedding dresses a luxury, and they were rarely worn. However, William insisted Gladys wear a full-on ensemble that would have been more suitable for royalty. Even though Gladys had grown opposed to outdated fashion, William held the reins and Gladys plodded along.

William wore a top hat and tails, and Gladys was adorned in a beaded and embroidered, streamlined gown hailing back to the 1920s flapper era. Her headdress resembled a large white fan with lace and fabric that covered her head like a crown. William imported white diamonds from Australia to be sewn into the fabric. Gladys was given an oversized bouquet of tiger lilies, long shafts of wheatgrass and baby's breath, a decadent yet local floral arrangement designed by William.

Gladys had no say in the matter.

The wedding ceremony and celebration was an all-day event that included an exchange of vows and photographs—indoor and outdoor—for the newspaper, followed by an elaborate four-course dinner, dance, and fireworks. Above all else, it was a community event that involved neighbours, friends, and family. Being the town's founder, William insisted all businesses were closed for the day so shopkeepers could attend. There was even talk of making the wedding date a local holiday.

The guests whispered to each other that the whole wing-ding was too gaudy and outlandish. Some called it a "hideous display"; others were sure it was some kind of cover-up. Many had grown suspicious of where William's great wealth was coming from. The skeptics said, "The truth is elusive because it knows where to hide." However, nothing stopped the guests, interlopers and cynics from gobbling up the food and imbibing the alcohol. The party-goers arrived hungry and thirsty and left full and drunk.

***

Exactly nine months after the nuptials, William and Gladys welcomed a baby boy. They named him Marvin, after Glady's favourite rockabilly singer and songwriter Marvin Rainwater from Wichita, Kansas. Strangely enough, William agreed to the name.

However, due to William's poverty-stricken upbringing and raising his seven younger siblings, he refused to impregnate his young bride more than once. Therefore, shortly after Marvin's birth, William Farnsworth took on a mistress and kept Gladys as a devoted mother to the son he barely had the time of day for. This resulted in their marriage being in danger of demise, only one year after being established. Gladys had thought that a baby would make all things fresh and new, but she did not understand the concept of history repeating itself.

Staff first began documenting the bickering when Gladys outwardly refused to speak in the proper English dialect she was taught at the finishing school. She stopped saying "please" or "thank you" and replaced them with "gimme this" or "gimme that."

Gladys abhorred perfume, body lotions, and taking a bath, but she loved swimming. She could often be heard saying, "A swim and a bath ain't much different, and if I have to get wet at all, it will be in the cement pond you'z done put in!" If she didn't hear what someone was saying, she said "Huh?" instead of "I beg your pardon?"

Sometimes as a joke, she would say, "I beg yer huh?" mostly to taunt William.

Everything Gladys had learned in etiquette class dissolved completely, and she resorted to her old way of speaking. On more than one occasion, she told William, "I ain't gonna be no phony baloney and speak like a rich duchess with her high falutin' nose in the air!"

Over time Gladys's grammar got worse and was magnified when she was annoyed. Her earlier dialect, filled with slang and backcountry lingo, exploded into each sentence, much to William's disdain and embarrassment. When this occurred, he turned his back and walked out the door, into his paramour's arms.

The walls recorded everything, through the ears of cooks, housekeepers, groundskeepers, and nannies. Some would smirk and laugh, while others would immediately hand in their resignation upon hearing, "You'z a damn ole coot! Keep yer stinkin' paws to yerself and go down yonder and git yerself a hussy, fer all I care!"

In spite of William's dedication to transforming Gladys, he realized that part of the problem was that they were complete opposites from the beginning.

By the 1950s, Gladys paid no mind to William's disapproval. She was far too busy and enthralled with all the modern conveniences money could buy. She preferred store-bought cake mixes and cookies from a package, TV dinners from Swanson's instead of homemade, and canned meatballs. In contrast, William wanted a wife who prepared home-cooked meals from scratch. As a result, her homemaking, or lack thereof, became a bone of contention and left him in a state of fury.

William considered it a woman's duty to shop smart and look smart by wearing the latest fashions, and a wife was considered a good steward of her husband's money if she could feed and dress her family on a dime.

Gladys had no qualms about spending William's money. Making matters worse, she rejected her husband's expectations and would call him "'diculous" instead of "ridiculous," which only annoyed him further.

She hired more than enough staff and took lavish holidays abroad. Gladys shopped in the larger town of Hillsprings to her heart's content and ordered from catalogues the minute they arrived on the doorstep.

William soon determined that he did not believe in the age-old theory that opposites attract. It only made sense for like-minded people to unite, conquer, and succeed. Therefore, William deduced that his union with Gladys was a sham and a foolish mistake he could not take back.

"You are not the wife I wanted, and our son is a huge disappointment. I do not belong here. I might as well be dead."

(William Farnsworth, in a birthday card to Gladys)

In contrast to being a controversial wife, many referred to Gladys as a devoted mother, even though William could be seen rolling his eyes and erupting into outrage at her nontraditional relationship with their son Marvin. He complained that Gladys behaved more like a sister than a mother. William felt she coddled Marvin, and he repeatedly tried to undo her tender, indulgent pampering.

And yet Gladys could be heard saying on more than one occasion, "What Daddy don't know won't hurt him!" She told numerous people she would one day write a book and call it *Don't Tell Daddy*. This was always followed by an eruption of laughter at William's expense.

She relished riding bicycles around town, swinging on the swings, and playing tennis with their son. They swam in the pool together, played tag and card games, and painted scenery, using easels and dressing the part with smocks and French berets. The Farnsworth estate became a playground for children of all ages. Gladys offered swimming lessons and dance classes and hired artists to come in and give workshops. After Marvin got his driver's licence, he became her personal chauffeur, and heads would turn every time he held the door open for his mother.

Meanwhile, Marvin and most of his friends adored Gladys and had nothing nice to say about William. Even though Marvin adored his mother's childlike ways, she would often slip into deep, dark, brooding moods. Her icy demeanour could make summer feel like winter, and her moods would come at him like a snowball at the back of the neck—shocking and painful, but quickly dissipated.

Eventually, William no longer ruled the roost and gave up on his son and wife altogether. By 1953 he had become a stodgy, cantankerous, alcoholic man just like his father. He had tried everything in his power not to be like him, but as the old saying goes, "The nut doesn't fall far from the tree."

Gladys was not tight-lipped in the least, and enjoyed gossiping and telling others about William's neglect and lousy behaviour. She could be heard saying to whoever was in earshot, "Honestly, that man may be rich and generous on the outside, but if people only knew what went on behind closed doors, they would drop him like a hot potato!" And then, in proper Gladys form, she would throw her head back and laugh.

Whether or not William was interested, Gladys Farnsworth entertained regularly and held extravagant galas and costume parties. She was always in the limelight with both positive and negative gossip.

Aside from her outlandish behaviour, Gladys did have some successful projects. The opening of the Starlight movie theatre on Main Street was all her idea. Her most loved movies were about star-crossed lovers. She particularly liked the 1950s film *Sunset Boulevard* with William Holden as Joe Gillis, and Gloria Swanson as Norma Desmond, a former silent-film star who drew him into her demented fantasy world. Gladys would often introduce each movie in person and give a play-by-play of the Hollywood gossip about whomever the actors were. She recited right from the tabloids before each Saturday matinee. Her voice was animated and fun, with facial expressions and actions to match.

Gladys was also instrumental in putting a fountain, a gazebo, and a tree-lined park setting in the centre of town. However, her popularity ended abruptly after William disappeared.

***

May 1953 was warmer than usual, and most residents kept their doors and windows open. The only reprieve was in the evening when the breeze that stirred up in the surrounding weeping willow trees picked up speed and cooled down the town and its inhabitants, making it feel like the start of a new season.

Like all the other homes in town, the large estate where William, Gladys and Marvin lived was unlocked and wide open. And because William had built the monstrous mansion in the early 1900s, it was situated practically in the centre of town. Passersby frequently stopped on the sidewalk to admire the manicured gardens, swimming pool, tennis courts, and massive Tudor-style home, unfenced and ungated.

Even though Gladys complained about her estranged husband, she appreciated where her bread was buttered from, so it was commonplace for her to cheerfully go about her business, whether he was home or not. As per usual on the night in question, Gladys had the cooks prepare and put supper on the table at 5:00 p.m.

Due to her husband's independence and philandering, when he did not come home, Gladys assumed he was out with his cronies playing poker and tying one on. She turned a blind eye to his many affairs. As a result, she decided to give it a day before she reported William officially missing.

Yet outside in the dark, hidden in clever disguise, death cruised by in a 1953 Pontiac Parisienne. Was it looking for the man everyone seemingly loved and admired? Or was it just a coincidence that on the same night William Farnsworth went missing, the pristine automobile was spotted slowly driving past his estate, never to be seen again? It had disappeared without a trace, just like the man who built and established the small farming community.

Out of curiosity, Gladys called William's friends and a few local business owners, yet no one had seen him. When she did pick up the telephone to finally call the precinct, twenty-four hours after William failed to return home, witnesses said her demeanour was calm, relaxed, and collected as she dialed. However, the second the officer picked up the phone, Gladys instantly became hysterical. The house staff whispered to one another that she cried crocodile tears—no moisture came from her eyes and not one tissue was used to blow her nose which failed to run.

On May 19th, 1953, at 1:00 p.m., just after lunch, the MeadowBrook Police Department received a worried call from forty-year-old Gladys Farnsworth. Her words were indistinguishable, and when she finally became coherent, the officer on the desk made out that William Farnsworth, the notable businessman and Gladys Farnsworth's husband of twenty years, had not come home the night before from a short business trip.

Without taking a breath, Gladys yelled into the receiver, "Lordy, Lordy, git here on the double! My husband ain't nowhere's! He's done got hisself kidnapped, or sumpin' worse, brutally murdered! Dear God, what will I ever do!"

William was expected home for supper and never arrived. He had left on a business trip two days prior and had rented a hotel room in the town of Hillsprings, three hours away. William was looking to purchase a dry cleaner to turn into a chain of stores he would name William's Brite Rite Cleaners.

When her husband was reported missing, the common knowledge that her marriage had a long history of not being what William or Gladys had expected, did not work in her favour. It was a known fact the couple had not been getting along for quite some time and slept in separate bedrooms—he at one end of the house and she at the other.

So, shortly after her call, two police officers went to speak with Gladys, at the house situated only a stone's throw from the police station. Officer Malone was a big, broad-shouldered, slow-talking detective with a poker face and a thick head of dark hair, while his partner, Officer Brown, was a fast talker who was a bit thinner, with a shaved head and a fixed sardonic smile. They greeted Gladys like she was a celebrity.

Gladys welcomed them in, and when she offered them lemonade, she commented how opposite they were from each other. She said, "You boys ain't nothin' alike, kinda like William and me is."

Her observation was odd but went unquestioned. The two police officers politely accepted the ice-cold beverage. Seconds later, the wait staff brought a selection of *Dad's* original Scotch oatmeal cookies on a paper plate, still wrapped in their cellophane wrapper.

The detectives sipped their beverages and crunched their cookies while admiring Gladys's state-of-the-art hi-fi stereo and black-and-white television. Neither took notes, brushed for fingerprints, walked the property, or looked for foul play. Instead, they checked their watches, thanked Gladys profusely and went home for the day. There did not appear to be any urgency, and their questions lacked competence.

When the townspeople were interviewed, most repeated the same mantra, "William Farnsworth was generous, hardworking, helpful, and an honest businessman." Many thought him to not have an enemy in the world. Others were afraid to comment or say anything negative, being suspicious that the law might be corrupt and perhaps they could be next to wind up missing, or worse.

Each person questioned by the police followed up with, "Gladys, on the other hand, has a few screws loose!"

Many wondered if William Farnsworth had deliberately gone into hiding. Others speculated the founder of MeadowBrook was leading a double life, and perhaps greed had gotten the better of him. Or maybe his wife and son had done something sinister. Written in the back of the detectives' minds was the question, *Did someone do the unthinkable? And if so, who wanted the acclaimed town founder and well-to-do businessman dead?*

Following the disappearance, children from town were made to believe Gladys Farnsworth told fibs, and their parents disallowed them to go anywhere near her. Consequently, songs and rhymes were quickly made up about Gladys. Kids of all ages took to standing on the edge of the sidewalk lining the property, singing little ditties, "Crazy Gladys Farnsworth, sold fruit on the road. Liar, liar pants on fire like a croaky old fat toad!"

Gladys took it upon herself to run down the long winding driveway to stick out her tongue at the rude children, and once it was reported that she held up her middle finger to the scallywags and scamps. Then, as they ran away squealing with delight, Gladys would holler mockingly, "Yer all a chip off the old block, and you can tell yer folks I say so!"

The gossip around town was slanderous and not supportive or kind toward Gladys. Some people said, "It's all an act. Gladys Farnsworth is harmless!" Others would comment how she loved the attention. And most parents would warn, "Stay away from the old battle-axe, or you might be next!" as they motioned with an invisible knife slitting their own throat.

All gatherings, parties, and visits from the local children ended. No longer did kids from miles around have free reign on the property, swimming, playing tennis, climbing trees, and playing Nicky-Nicky-Nine-Doors.

Many were saddened that the once free-for-all estate was no longer open to the general public. But many were also relieved the home of the missing man was under investigation.

Marvin adored his mother and would disagree with the rumours and gossip mill on all accounts. And his boyhood friends, John Fasp, Brian Gordon, and Chuck Barnes, concurred, as they had enjoyed Mrs. Farnsworth's childlike ways and witnessed Mr. Farnsworth mistreating them. Hence, Marvin and his pals all agreed that his wealthy millionaire father and founder of MeadowBrook was a tyrant—a mean, nasty shyster.

Soon the press got wind of the haphazard investigation, and the gossip and speculations started spinning out of control. Finally, with no leads coming in, a statement was issued. The small local news station announced to the public, "William Farnsworth, our founder and loved by all, has been listed as a missing person. Foul play is suspected, with no known reason for him to flee or go into hiding. After deep digging, we have many people of interest. Please report anything suspicious to the police. And lastly, lock all your doors and windows!"

The entire town became fearful and divided. From that day forward, what used to be a safe and peaceful community turned paranoid and distrustful. Residents locked their doors, closed their blinds, and suspiciously watched for anything amiss.

Later, the blame would rest on the police department. It was said they handled the disappearance most unprofessionally, and what could have been used as evidence was missed or destroyed. As a result, the entire case had become a sham and a mockery of the justice system.

Footprints leading out to the street were trampled on, and the citizen who spotted the car initially was not brought in for questioning. The housekeeping staff had been let go, due to a lack of funds on Gladys's part to pay them, so they moved to neighbouring towns and were never interviewed or heard from again. Additionally, witnesses close to the Farnsworth family had either changed their story or left with no return address. Whether it was hearsay or not, it was speculated that they were forced out, or fled out of fear.

It was later unveiled that Gladys and Marvin were not immediately brought in for cross-examination. There were other suspicious suspects—mistresses, and the business owner of the laundromat William was trying to purchase. However, they too were not hauled in for questioning.

Fortunately or unfortunately, in the small town of MeadowBrook, enemies became friends, and friends became enemies. It was a very confusing time. To make matters worse, the police chief's wife was a friend of Gladys's and begged her husband to let the beautiful and eccentric socialite grieve.

At one point, the police were overheard referring to the public as "a community of tight-lipped nitwits."

"We might as well wash our hands of the whole case, as this town is full of dummies and losers."

It later came out in a statement that with all things considered, "The MeadowBrook Police Department was inexperienced and slow to the starting gate in their investigation of the William Farnsworth case." With so many things having gone without question, a headline in the *Gazette* stated, "The MeadowBrook Police Department Is an Embarrassment."

To make matters worse, when finally asked for a statement, and with no lawyer present, Gladys willingly went down to the station to be interviewed. Unfortunately, even though she had an alibi, parts of it were foggy, and Gladys had difficulty staying on track and recalling the entire night in question.

Her patchwork account, in her own words, was hard to decipher when describing what she did before and after William was reported missing. Gladys said, "Well, let me see. I 'member going to William's grocery store, as they had some discounted pork loin I wanted. Then my son—you know he's such a lovely, sweet boy—drove me to the library to return some books. I've read *The Great Gatsby* four times, and I do recommend it. Oh, then I picked up some corn and eggs at the Fasp Farms roadside stand. Now there's a strange man, and perhaps you should interview him? Anyways, after we got home, the cooks made a beautiful meal, and I 'member bein' irritated that William was not there to enjoy it! After dinner, I watched *I Love Lucy*. Oh yes, it was damn funny...you see, Lucy and Ethel had gotten jobs in a chocolate factory, and when they sped up the conveyor belt, Lucy couldna' keep up, so she started eatin' them chocolates and shoving some down her bosom..."

The detectives sat speechless, listening, taking notes, and coming to the conclusion that Gladys was off her rocker.

When the detective said, "You certainly don't seem very distraught over your missing husband," Gladys responded indignantly, "Oh come on, boys, don't be 'diculous. He was an obnoxious, philanderin' louse. Still, he paid the damn bills, and I'm not gonna look a gift horse in the mouth. And just what er you implyin'? Do you'z think I killed him?" Before they could respond, Gladys said, "Besides, what would I have done with his body? I'm five feet two inches tall, and William was busting out of his newly tailored business suits, so in other words, he was a fatso. I couldn't budge him, precisely why we moved into separate bedrooms years ago!"

She then belly laughed and sent a spray of spittle into the faces of the officers while slapping her knee at her own humour. Suddenly, Gladys started crying uncontrollably, and the detectives noted that her tears appeared forced.

Both detectives noted: *goes back and forth between a hillbilly accent and a prestigious proper dialect*, followed by, *emotions rising and falling*, and *this broad is seemingly off her rocker*. Lastly, *Gladys Farnsworth is undeniably a person of interest who should be watched closely*.

After gathering herself, she could not remember when she went to bed on the night in question but did remember she was out of toothpaste. And then Gladys recalled phoning a few of William's old geezer friends in the morning. She described her morning ritual of stretching exercises and feeding the fish in the pond, and later that morning, getting her hair professionally dyed and cut short like Audrey Hepburn, stating that she no longer wanted to have red hair like Lucille Ball. Gladys went on to say how annoyed she was that she, as the owner of the Starlight movie theatre, could not obtain the movie *Roman Holiday* with Gregory Peck and Audrey Hepburn. Finally, after her nonsensical monologue, she said, "This town sucks!"

The detectives questioned Gladys for most of their eight-hour shift, with no lawyers present, and when they left her alone in the interrogation room, she took out her knitting and took off her shoes. When they returned, she asked for a cup of tea with a wedge of lemon and wondered if they could accompany it with a biscuit, then added, "Not homemade, it has to be store-bought, or I won't be able to git 'er down!"

Marvin's interview was similar, except the detectives noticed his body language was tighter and more rigid than his mother's. In addition, he had a habit of scratching behind his ear and shifting in his seat. This appeared suspicious, and his awkward behaviour was noted.

Marvin explained he had driven his mother to the grocery store and the library. Like a dutiful son, he waited in the car while his mother ran errands. Once home, while Gladys watched the cooks make dinner, Marvin said he sat outside on the lawn. After dinner, two friends came over and they played a Monopoly game in the basement. Of course, Marvin's friends, Brian Gordon and Chuck Barnes, were interviewed next, and they both corroborated his story.

Even though there was very little evidence, eventually Gladys became the number one suspect, and by week two, they were no closer to finding William's killer than week one.

Shortly after the press release came out, detectives Malone and Brown both agreed to be interviewed by the *Gazette*. Their intention was to instill fear into the guilty party, and hopefully evoke curiosity in the citizens of MeadowBrook.

Malone stated, "All murders take place because one of three things. The first is love—they love someone else and want their current wife or husband out of the way. The second reason is money. Killers think if they get rid of the person, then they get that inheritance payout a little sooner. Or maybe they're being sued. You know what the Bible says, 'Money is the root of all evil.' And the third reason is pride, especially in couples. They don't like the way their partner is looking at them. They feel disrespected. Or maybe they know they're on the verge of being dumped."

The second-to-last paragraph of the article was a statement by Detective Brown. He said, "I may be the new kid on the block, but it is my theory that once we figure out a motive, it will help us determine who the killer is. This is a stubborn mystery because we know that the people or person of interest is simultaneously so close, and yet seemingly so far."

The article concluded with a line that put in question the detectives' investigative skills: "WELL, MEADOWBROOK, IT LOOKS LIKE THE POLICE

NEED YOUR HELP, SO PUT ON YOUR THINKING CAPS AND LET'S GET TO THE BOTTOM OF THIS!"

The unsolved mystery would keep the citizens of MeadowBrook on edge for years.

Even though the police detectives appeared stumped, new leads would come in every day—scribbled notes left under windshield wipers, letters mailed in to the detachment, phone calls placed to the detectives themselves, and letters sent to the newspaper. But all the hearsay and speculation were not helpful and only blurred the lines. Malone and Brown were infuriated with the unsolicited advice they were getting on a daily basis from armchair sleuths. Finally, a substantial lead came in and they hoped it would break the case wide open. Neither of the homicide detectives believed in coincidences.

There had been a second sighting of the 1953 Pontiac Parisienne. This came in as late-breaking news from two cherry pickers working in an orchard adjacent to the highway. They both told the same story because they remembered talking about it when they had crept out of their tents on the moonlit night in question. The pickers had set up their pup tents right in the middle of the orchard. As they relieved themselves under the light of the moon, they heard and saw a vehicle neither had ever seen before. Both stopped to comment what a groovy car it was. This happened only hours after the automobile was spotted slowly driving by the Farnsworth estate, except this time it was headed out of town toward the Highway 88 on-ramp, and it was no longer moving slowly.

The detectives had a hunch others knew more.

***

Unbeknownst to anyone, Marvin had a secret he planned to take to his grave. It was a clear vision of seeing his father get into a luxurious car in the middle of the night. Marvin had gotten out of bed for a drink of water, when he heard the front door quietly close, followed by the sound of his father whistling a happy tune while walking down the long driveway. It was a peculiar, shrill sound in the otherwise lifeless night air. "Five foot two, eyes of blue, has anybody seen my gal…" Marvin ran to the front room window to see his father get in the passenger side of an unfamiliar vehicle.

He kept his observation to himself because he was trying to protect his mother. Even though he knew his father was a good-for-nothing grifter, his mother was the complete antithesis of his father, and Marvin wanted to protect her. At the time, he was twenty years old and had no idea about relationships and the importance of revealing certain information at the right place and time. When the local small-town mystery turned into a nationwide sensation, Marvin became a fearful, secretive man.

***

One year after William Farnsworth's disappearance, there hadn't been any arrests, even though the police had many people of interest. The founder of MeadowBrook was still considered a missing person, and a death certificate had not yet been issued. Therefore, his money and estate were tied up in probate.

The police and the two detectives were working on a mystery with very few clues.

Even though many people could be quoted as saying, "Gladys Farnsworth is as dumb as a brick," she was not. Early in the marriage, Gladys began to hide money under her mattress because she didn't trust her husband, the bank, or the men who ran it. Women were not allowed to have their own bank accounts back then, so she held money back from the allowance William gave her. Gladys also stretched the truth about various bills and the cost of groceries. Therefore, she had enough money stashed away to last her for quite some time, just in case anything might happen. At the time, Gladys did not know why she would need a safety net, but she could only imagine.

Gladys had always had two sides to her personality, both light and dark. Many saw her as being either a real live wire, or the opposite, gloomy and bleak…but always unpredictable. In the months after the scandal, her once entertaining moods seemed to be magnified under the microscope where many had placed her. Family, friends, and law enforcement insisted her actions were not those of a grieving widow, but of a guilty, scorned wife.

Speculations abounded that Gladys had become bored, or that her loneliness had gotten the better of her. In reality, the persecution she felt saddened her. As she struggled through her blue funk, Gladys felt comforted by throwing herself into the renovation of the mansion her supposed late husband had built. However, when it was completed, she changed her mind and refurbished it back to its original state.

Rumours circulated around the community, tales of Gladys digging in the yard on a moonlit night, then being seen pouring concrete in the heat of the midday sun the following day, filling up the holes from the night before. Nothing made sense to the staff, or onlookers who might stroll past the property on any given day or night.

If asked what she was doing, Gladys had various responses: "My life, my business!" Or "Go look in your own backyard and stay out of mine!" And her most frequent, "Clean up your own mess before you try to make my mess worse!"

The gossip mill spoke of outlandish behaviour coupled with the question, "Where is she getting the money to live off?" The most repeated story in the first few years following William's disappearance was that William's body was hidden or buried somewhere on the sprawling property, and that mother and son were in cahoots.

Sadly, the swimming pool was eventually drained, weeds began growing up through cracks in the tennis court, and the overall lack of upkeep reduced the home to shambles. If there could be a positive side to the culmination of events, the Frugal Grocer had never been busier. All the nosy busybodies and looky-loos who came in to snoop, ended up purchasing something.

Eventually, Gladys, tired of being judged, felt the need to clear her name. So, on the second anniversary of her estranged husband's departure, she took out a full-page ad in the local newspaper, even though her lawyer—or rather a high school student who wanted to be a lawyer—advised her against it.

Her motive was to state her innocence. More specifically, she wanted the world to know she had nothing to do with her husband's disappearance. Gladys was anxious to move on and needed closure.

The headline in the *MeadowBrook Gazette* read: "William Would Have Wanted It This Way." The story described the couple's rocky marriage, complete with photographs, and details as to how the late, great founder of the town had wronged her. At the bottom of the page, Gladys added, "Let us celebrate the life of a man we all owe our livelihood, homes, businesses, and futures to! I cordially invite the entire town of MeadowBrook to one last gala event at my estate to eat, drink, and be merry. Let this event go down in history as 'William Farnsworth Day!' William would have wanted this. So please join me in wishing him well. And who knows, maybe he will show up out of nowhere and grace us with his presence?"

Gladys had also partnered with Astrid Ann, the newly hired newspaper astrologist, who would be at the event to offer readings.

The extravagant affair would be a catered event with advertised pony rides, a merry-go-round, a dance, bluegrass music, and fireworks in the evening. In addition, there would be parting gifts for the adults and goody bags for the children.

Unfortunately, the full-page newspaper submission had the opposite effect and only made Gladys seem more unbalanced and guilty. However, no one would turn down a free meal, and most townspeople were intrigued by the idea of a gala. As a consequence, most planned on attending, from shop owners and local politicians to the police and armchair detectives.

On May 18, 1955, two years after William went missing, the case was still wide open and the police planned to attend the celebration of life in full force. Plainclothes officers were brought in from the neighbouring town as undercover detectives to mingle with the crowd. They were expected to be on high alert and sift through all the idle chit-chat, meaningless prattle and hearsay for much-needed clues to the ongoing mystery.

Meanwhile, Marvin would not have the support of his childhood friends at the gala event, because Chuck Barnes and Brian Gordon were away at university. Chuck was getting his law degree, and Brian had hopes of going into politics with a combined degree in political science and business. Both had high hopes of returning to MeadowBrook after they graduated, with careers and beautiful wives to share in their success.

When Marvin's pals left for school, Marvin chose to stay behind, as he had taken over the Red & White Frugal Grocer upon his father's departure.

Concurrently, Chuck and Brian had hatched a plan and decided to skip out of school and sneak back to MeadowBrook while the entire town would be living it up at the Farnsworth estate. The two students had discussed at length how to do a little sticky finger shopping. In other words, they planned to burglarize stores and steal whatever they could get their hands on. They knew that none of the residents would ever suspect them of a thing.

The event turned out to be a complete disappointment for the town and an embarrassment for Marvin.

The demise of the Farnsworth Estate was unveiled as the guests began arriving. The lush, well-maintained gardens were an overgrown disaster, and the swimming pool had two feet of sludge in place of water. The publicized merry-go-round was merely a rusty swing set, and the pony rides were only one stubborn donkey. The hoped-for extravagant food consisted of overcooked hotdogs and stale potato chips. The entire promised gala event was nothing more than a strange display of a woman gone mad. The parting goody bags were brown paper sacks filled with stones that Gladys had spent countless hours painting. It was noted that her designs were well done, but other than that, the guests were wholly disappointed.

When William went missing for no known cause or reason, he left behind a wife, an adult son, and an unsolved mystery. This resulted in a cold case of suspected murder that essentially stayed cold indefinitely, begging the question, 'Who killed the founder of MeadowBrook, and where on earth was his body?'

The entire town feared a killer was on the loose, lurking in the shadows and lingering on back country roads, leaving them worried that they would be next. An unexpected result from the investigation was the exposure of corruption and payoffs, extortion, tax evasion, and mishandling of information due to the police department being under the thumb of politicians, and under the thumb of William himself.

Those aware of his misconduct were paid to keep their mouths shut. At the same time, others were paid to spread worthy praise. Few agreed with Gladys's opinion of William, placing him on an undeserving pedestal.

***

As the seasons change and the circle of life continues, events from history are bound to repeat themselves in some manner. Marvin had enough rationality to understand this. He told Diane shortly after she became pregnant, "It's all a setup, a profound ripple effect. The pebble has been dropped in the pond, and none of us on the shoreline are safe." He dreaded the birth of his son Nelson. As he watched his son grow and turn into a detached boy, a lonely and secluded teenager, and ultimately a friendless unattached man, Marvin did not regret choosing work over everything and everyone. His earlier intuition proved to be a valuable instruction manual for what was to come.

Often, when there is not enough illumination, people lose sight of the truth in the darkness that results, and evil hides there, morose and waiting. People can grow old and sometimes pass on without ever knowing the truth of their past.

***

By 1978 MeadowBrook had grown into a bustling city. The changes occurred slowly, much like the tiny bubbles in a pot of boiling water. At first, they were barely noticeable, just wisps of steam rising, but suddenly it was like a brilliant sunrise bursting over the horizon. Still, everyone in Meadowbrook knew everyone else. Many were related somehow. The hamlet had become a town, and then a city, and was self-contained and thriving, as the residents worked hard to increase their businesses and raise families. Even though the gossip mill regarding William Farnsworth had settled, and many had forgotten about the case completely, there were some who still lived under the foreboding spell of imminent danger. Their only recourse was to wait and see what came of it all.

It had become a trend for young people to leave the town in search of a new beginning somewhere else. Thus, many students left after the 1978 graduation ceremony, while, at the same time, many new families arrived. The mysteries and sins of the past remained an undercurrent shrouded in darkness, much like the moon hidden behind a turbulent cloud cover. Nevertheless, the town's shops and businesses continued to prosper, and many more sprouted up. With all of the new infrastructure and refurbishing, there remained a core group of townspeople who were disgruntled and reluctant to embrace the changes, worried about what the future might look like. They preferred the memories and simpler ways of the past.

For example, Barney's department store expanded. The store had been for many years the only establishment in town for clothing, accessories, household items, hardware, and sundries. They had completed a previous renovation and modernization in the early 1970s. The owners had retained the rusty red brick exterior to blend with existing businesses, but had replaced worn hardwood floors with sleek marble tile, old countertops with glass, and had installed a new state-of-the-art elevator with smooth chrome doors that inspired in children's minds the idea of climbing aboard a sleek rocket ship as they ascended to the 5th floor toy department.

The previous elevator had been a loud, clanking metal contraption that creaked and heaved its way upward, causing children to cry in fear. The accordion doors squealed as they opened and closed, and the friendly elevator attendant assisted the shoppers in and out of the antiquated device, as they selected the departments they wanted to shop in.

Despite the improvements, the same complaint remained about the lack of fashionable inventory. Because everyone shopped there, many townspeople would be caught wearing the same outfit. When this happened, people laughed and shrugged it off, or walked in the opposite direction, wholly mortified and vowing to never wear that outfit again.

This new expansion added yet another floor, this time with a buffet-style restaurant.

On November 17, 1978, the front-page headline in the *Gazette* read: "Out with the Old and in with the New!" The article went on to say, "Join Clive Barney and his family for coffee, donuts, and 10% off, to celebrate the unveiling of MeadowBrook's new and improved Barney's Department Store Buffet Restaurant!"

The announcement caused a flurry of excitement in the community, and families lined up around the building as they waited to get into the new restaurant.

Marvin Farnsworth, Nelson's father and the town founder's only heir, continued to operate the Red & White Frugal Grocer, and he proudly held the title of unbeatable prices. However, rumour had it never to trust the expiry dates, and to cook your meat until it was well done.

Marvin added a new dynamic to the store. Even though drinking alcohol was frowned upon in the straight-laced and somewhat narrow-minded township, there was a new demand, and Marvin fulfilled it. He built a distillery behind his grocery where he made dandelion wine, potato vodka, moonshine, and malt liquor. He rented a billboard on the outskirts of town that stated, *"Alcohol may not be your cup of tea, but allow my spirits to change your mind—Marvin Farnsworth, Red & White Frugal Grocer."*

Providing an escape to Egyptian pyramids, Mediterranean seas, dusty cowpokes, and gun-blazing gangsters, The Starlight Movie Theatre remained open, even though it was on the verge of bankruptcy due to poor management. Diane, Marvin's wife, had a grand idea, and took over Gladys's passion project, adding another element. Movies were screened on the weekends, and the theatre was transformed into a flower shop during the week. The scent of floral arrangements and popcorn was nauseating for some but oddly refreshing for others.

The comfort of simmering stews, fluffy biscuits, and dark rich gravy remained the backbone of country living. Farm life continued, and families relished the down-home cooking, potluck suppers, barbecues, and picnics at the local swimming hole. People rarely dined out. However, the three original restaurants remained. As the town expanded, so did the competition for people's cravings. Donna Wong's Chinese Food, A&W, and Robinson's Diner, home of the best BLTs, had to compete against new steak houses, a muffin chain, numerous coffee shops, and bars with happy hour and five-cent wings.

Special occasions—first dates, anniversaries and divorces, business lunches, and family visiting from out of town—were all cause for celebration. So, dining out was a great luxury, and all the restaurants were always busy.

Al's Automotive and Repair Shop was a popular place for retirees to hang out. Al, Tracy's father, installed benches back in the '60s and purchased a Melita coffee maker. He could often be heard saying, "Every town needs a place to shoot the breeze and a mechanic to go along with it." Al's great-grandfather had opened the shop in the 1920s, and his original Model-T Ford was the focal point parked in the front and a great conversation piece.

By the 1970s, Al was known as a pioneer. His fingernails gripped oil like a monkey gripping a banana, and he held just as tightly to the past and his title of being the original grease monkey. Like everyone else, Al Hansworth had aged, his daughters had moved out, and his wife remained a mystery, a riddle he sifted through like gravel. He spent most of his time at the shop, sharing his wide smile with all who passed by, and turning a blind eye to Eunice.

The MeadowBrook Community Church was a place where all faiths were welcomed. It continued to be a mainstay. Their slogan was *"Bringing the Heavens closer to Earth, with angels rejoicing on high."* The doors opened at 9:00 a.m. every Sunday for coffee and fellowship, and the service began at 10:00 a.m. for a sermon of fire and brimstone, delivered just before communion was served, with grape juice and stale bread torn into bite-sized pieces.

By the early 1970s, the church doors were opened to the community. They hosted many groups in the facility, and all of them experienced a great deal of growth. They had a fully operating daycare, weekly choir practices, youth group gatherings, Overeaters Anonymous, and AA and Alateen meetings. The Jazzercise classes in the basement every Monday and Wednesday night, for a two-dollar drop-in fee, had become the talk of the town.

They were proud of the youth gatherings every Thursday night, even though some of the teens gathered at A&W instead, if they could all pile into someone's car for the carhop service. However, MeadowBrook also had its fair share of atheists and agnostics—certainly, the religious fanatics must be out to get their money or fill their children's heads with myths and tall tales! And yet, parents of teens who rebelled or chose the A&W over attending youth group were sure their young people were going straight to hell in a handbasket.

As the '70s turned into the '80s, church attendance dwindled, but the women's church auxiliary was steadfast and strong, always available to prepare food for weddings, baby showers, and funerals. Included with the array of finger sandwiches, casseroles, and Jell-O molds with extra whipped topping, was a dollop of gossip to spice things up.

The library was renamed after MeadowBrook's founder William Farnsworth. Engraved on a plaque at the front of the building was one of his acclaimed quotes, *"Literacy is a bridge from boredom and ignorance to liveliness and intelligence."* The William Farnsworth Memorial Library was also home to the 4-H Club, Quality Quilters, Knitting Needles by Nelly, The Rotary Club, and the very controversial UFO Science Club.

The Meadow Brook Memorial Hospital offered upstanding health care, including an emergency department, a pediatric ward, and two fully outfitted operating rooms. In 1966, an annex for the veterinary clinic and assisted living for senior citizens was added.

Naturally, the police station and courthouse were in the same building. Unfortunately, those employed in these departments were stuck in the outdated "men's club" mentality, habitually marginalizing women and other groups. Gladys and her son Marvin remained on the radar, never far from sight. They were referred to as the "Dynamic Duo" by the police detectives, the mayor, and the only judge in town.

Aside from the Farnsworth murder investigation, MeadowBrook law enforcement had little going on.

Handing out traffic tickets and parking fines, and responding to the occasional domestic disturbance or drunken brawl was about as exciting as it got. They nicknamed the jail "Andy's Drunk Tank" after the 1950s television show *Andy Griffin*. Be that as it may, the men's group that ran the town was incomparable to Barney Fife, Andy, Aunt Bea, and Opie.

Standing six feet four inches tall, Mayor Gordon, Kent's father, had chiselled good looks and a rigid demeanour. He was feared and respected, and the men's club around him referred to him as their mighty leader. The city council, police detectives, and even the chief of police, bowed down to the man. He freely told off-colour jokes and felt the world revolved around him. His exotic vacations, endless games of golf, and yearly celebratory birthday parties—all at the city's expense—were never questioned or challenged. Be that as it may, the voluntary town council frowned upon Mayor Gordon's after-hours card games and the scantily clad women traipsing in and out of the mayor's office. Despite the awareness that there were wrongdoings going on in his office, he maintained an open-door policy.

As a new day dawns, it brings with it the expectation of a fresh start, crisp and clear. The MeadowBrook Funeral Home had the opposite impact. It was dark and gloomy, built in the 1920s, and the only changes were those brought about by the markings of time. By the late 1970s, the lush gardens were overgrown, with tangled weeds strangling the once pristine flower beds like a boa constrictor in a murderous attempt at a slow death.

The funeral parlour had a slogan since the 1930s that was a running joke no longer funny: *"If you want people to attend your funeral, make sure you go to theirs."*

It had seen better days. The delicately carved mahogany front door was weather-beaten and creaked when opened. Furnishings were drab and dusty, and the burgundy velvet draperies hung ragged and threadbare. The air was thick with the aroma of embalming fluid and lilies, assaulting the nostrils and conjuring visions of the deceased.

For years already, the director of the facility had seemed old, even back when he was relatively young. Now in the '70s, his appearance was hauntingly severe. His rigid bones poked through his moth-eaten sweaters, and his once-tailored pants slouched well below his crotch, reeking of mildew and other indecipherable odours too alarming even to discuss. He wore his white hair shoulder-length, and the scraggly tendrils appeared more like wire than hair.

There were many tales told of Fred Ferguson, and his deceased wife and three children who died during an influenza outbreak in the great depression. Folklore abounded and warned of black nights with silver moonlight casting claw-like shadows on the foreboding front lawn. The wild shrubs were turned into fanciful animal carcasses, leafless trees were trapped spirits of the dead, and faceless rosebushes became lost souls seeking refuge in unsuspecting people passing by in the wee hours of the night.

Some people claimed to have seen the spirit of William Farnsworth late at night in the adjacent cemetery. It was common for dares and bets among the teens to be made during the witching hour when supernatural events were said to take place and witches, ghosts, and demons would appear. Some even tried to take photographs as proof of wispy shapes, bodiless spirits, or low-lying mist that travelled over the graves like a silent killer.

In the years leading up to William Farnsworth's disappearance, he had developed a plan offering to help businesses with low-interest loans or grants of tax-free money. Very few businesses refused the offer, so many shops were refurbished, renovated, or upgraded. The town began to look like a movie set, enviable and enticing to any cinematographer or movie critic.

The problem was that many people failed to read the fine print on the document. They were elated by the opportunity, not realizing that there were strings attached to the agreement. William had ulterior motives, and with a stroke of the pen and a quick signature, he was given ten per cent of the profits. MeadowBrook, built from his inheritance and a determination to not turn out like his father, had quickly changed William into a replica of his mean-spirited dad.

Ferguson's Funeral Home was the only business that refused any assistance. No matter how much William pestered, hounded, or threatened him, Fred would not comply. William finally backed off when, days before he went missing, Old Man Ferguson drove downtown in the hearse, and screeched to a halt outside of William's office. Bursting through the doors, he marched inside and dumped his late wife's ashes in the middle of the founder's desk. The dust cloud rose up from William's pristine Maplewood desk like a volcanic eruption, while he sat in disbelief and horror until with clenched fists, he stood up in a fiery rage.

Before he could say anything, Fred shouted while pointing at the mound of ashes, "If you don't back off and leave me alone, this will be you next!" He turned abruptly to leave, but as he walked out the door, he turned and spat out, "I mean it, Farnsworth. I have a fifty-gauge shotgun and a cremation oven that gets hotter than hell, and I ain't afraid to use either one!"

The funeral director was questioned three days after the town founder went missing. Fred refused to speak without a lawyer. William was never seen again, and some townspeople began taking their dearly departed to Clement's Crematorium in the neighbouring town.

The local newspaper had been established in 1912. Although the typesetting had changed over the years, the name had not. The *MeadowBrook Gazette* came out every Wednesday and promised local news along with a long list of regular columns by local contributors. There were the usual want ads, the bi-weekly obituary column, enlightening horoscope predictions, incoming movies, book reviews, buy and sell items, and upcoming community events. And of course, much venting by way of letters to the editor, ostensibly meant to be a cathartic release for the sender.

Barney's Barber Shop and Helga's Hair Salon shared the same facility. However, neither of the shopkeepers outwardly got along. Barney's father owned and operated the department store, and Helga's father was a dairy farmer. Their families had been feuding as far back as the early 1900s. Little did anyone know that in the early 1970s, Barney and Helga became infatuated with each other, but they kept up the charade of squabbling in honour of their ancestors.

Winters were cold and windy, spring times were fresh, summers were sweltering, and fall brought gorgeous red sunsets over faded cornfields. Every year since MeadowBrook was incorporated, in every season, it had offered family-oriented community events. The Winter Ball was attended by wide-eyed children on ice skates, devouring hot cocoa and Christmas cookies. The Grand Easter Egg Festival in the spring brought out festive bonnets, Easter egg painting stations, and a rabbit mascot costume worn by Mr. Marples, hopping through town to deliver chocolate eggs and stuffed bunnies. The country fair in the summer was planned months in advance, complete with a Ferris wheel, kissing booth, and corn-on-the-cob eating contest. The fall pumpkin patch was at the corn maze, with expectations of Halloween candy, ghosts and goblins, carved pumpkins, scarecrows, and hay rides.

On the day that Manfred Marples graduated from teacher's college, neither of his parents were present for the ceremony because both were disappointed that he would not be taking over their taxidermy business.

Manfred had always been put off by his parents' creations of deceased animals stuffed for display. The science of mounting a dead animal's skin to make it look lifelike was frightening to him, although he was happy the critters showed up already dead and were not also butchered by his parents. He thought a proper burial or service was more appropriate for their demise. He concluded that the practice of taxidermy was too sinister and disturbing, so he avoided it at all costs.

When thinking about his childhood, Manfred would recoil emotionally, trying to block out memories of his unconventional upbringing. He had often heard the hushed murmurs of his parents as they discussed their son. "For heaven's sake, why is that child such an outcast? I doubt he will ever amount to anything. He behaves so strangely, and he sure ain't no looker!" They criticized him mercilessly with no regard for his feelings.

Unfortunately, the walls were thin, and Manfred heard everything. It was quite natural that he would develop a grudge toward his parents, with seething anger just below the surface. His plan was to one day get back at them for his reclusive, sad existence.

Throughout Manfred's early childhood, he never experienced bedtime stories, frothy steamed milk, or warm cuddles at bedtime. Instead, on most nights, he would rock himself to sleep while covering his ears to the sound of sculpting, woodworking, sewing and carpentry as it echoed up from the basement and permeated the floorboards of his bedroom. As he hummed himself to sleep in his meagre room with no toys, books, puzzles, or games, he would escape reality and make up stories of damsels in distress and fire-breathing dragons with thorny wings. Feisty trolls with wild hair were hiding under bridges and barbaric boars were gnashing their teeth, ready to attack at a moment's notice.

Manfred grew up knowing he was not well-liked or considered handsome. He had an enormous forehead that his father referred to as a five-head, and a nose so pointy his mother said he could slice bread with it. In addition, he grew tall, with long, gangly legs that seemed to take up most of his height. Common hurtful nicknames for him in his early years were "String Bean" and "Thermometer." The running joke was that Manfred came into the world with only legs attached to an absurdly large head, which encouraged another label: "Freakazoid."

By the time Manfred turned thirteen, he had developed an extraordinary imagination from all the years of loneliness. This is how he came across the concept of puppetry, out of sheer boredom and a natural tendency toward artistic virtuosity.

It all began one early spring when the world was thawing and blossoms were bursting. Manfred had discovered a single wool sock peeking out from under his bed. He had no idea where its partner had gone, so after he had shaken off the dust, he slipped his hand into the dirty, itchy sock and named it Floyd. He used his ingenuity and his parents' taxidermy needles and thread, and sewed on an opaque white button for a nose from a collection of buttons kept under the sink in an old Mason jar. He then fashioned a tongue from a strip of his father's discarded flannel shirt, and after whispering "Ta-da!" Manfred had a friend. The lonely sock reminded Manfred of himself, and he compared its toe hole to the hole in his torn heart.

He continued to amuse himself through puppet play and began creating a whole cast of characters from his parents' discarded material. Bird feathers were hair, wire was bent and shaped into arms and legs, leftover fabric became clothing, wooden stands were dismantled and used for midsections, and shoes were cleverly crafted from various scraps.

During his teen years, Manfred studied hard, graduated high school at sixteen, and finished university at twenty years old. While at university, Manfred found happiness and respect. He had managed to create a positive spin on the damage his parents had inflicted. Manfred's childhood memories no longer had a foothold in his psyche because he had turned neglect into a means to create something for the greater good of humanity.

Manfred manufactured an entire collection of marionettes to entertain the student body with. His first acclaimed puppet show carried a political message representing the civil rights movement. He included racist police violence, fascist stormtroopers, and a grand finale celebrating equal opportunity, freedom, and democracy for the people. His show brought a standing ovation.

No longer was he teased for his gangly limbs and great height. Instead, his new nickname became "The Puppet Master." Professors and students alike highly regarded Manfred Marples as a trendsetter who believed in justice for all. If anyone suggested he looked like one of his puppets, he took it as a compliment, smiling and tipping his well-worn top hat, "Why, thank you very much!"

As soon as he was able to, Manfred moved far away from his already distant parents and vowed never to return. Instead, he settled in MeadowBrook and found spirituality in the landscapes and peaceful beauty of nature.

Within days of his arrival, he was hired as the primary teacher in the one-room schoolhouse. Unfortunately, within two months of him settling in at the school, his parents fell ill and died. They were not discovered for nearly six weeks, and when they were, their appearance was somewhat reminiscent of the subjects of their occupation. From that point on, Manfred chose to call MeadowBrook his home, and his marionettes his family.

In the beginning, he was welcomed as a unique, creative educator. His reputation took a different turn as he began creating look-alike characters for the mayor, the police chief, and William Farnsworth, the town founder. His puppet shows began publicizing a corrupt political realm, misogynistic men, and a town that refused to recycle.

William Farnsworth sent a cease-and-desist order to stop Manfred from using his educational puppetry to expose the corruption, but the townsfolk rebutted and rebuked his efforts. Finally, the school board rallied and demanded that the well-loved teacher be left alone. The Parent-Teacher Advisory Council stated that "Manfred Marples is the salt of the earth, and our children adore him. His entertaining social injustice lessons through his marionettes are valuable to our children's development."

Nonetheless, a silent feud between William and Manfred ensued. Neither trusted the other, and they developed a mutual seething hatred. After William went missing, Manfred was brought in for interrogation. Adding to the intrigue, it was discovered that his parents may have met with foul play, yet there was no evidence to prove it. When questioned about his deceased parents, Manfred dryly and solemnly responded, "I have no idea how they died. Maybe they were attacked in the night by their mummified birds and stuffed animals?"

Every account of the vehement arguments between the two men was considered and recorded. It did not help that Mr. Marples lived alone in a bungalow full of wooden puppet faces and handcrafted dolls, all hanging spookily throughout the rooms, in dark closets and folded into bins, waiting for their next show.

Some townspeople passing by his home swore they could hear strange voices coming from the rooms, others heard loud weeping and heart-wrenching sobs. It was speculated that he was only practicing for his next performance but there were some who added grist to the gossip mill by suggesting that Vice Principal Marples had come clean off his rocker. Therefore, he was never ruled out as a suspect in the missing persons case of William Farnsworth.

MeadowBrook High School was initially a one-room schoolhouse for grades one through seven. There was no secondary school in the early days, as most students were expected to work the farms after seventh grade. However, everything changed when William Farnsworth bequeathed half of his estate toward constructing a modern school that would take children through to Grade 12. The other half went to Gladys and Marvin, who also remained the number one and number two suspects in William's disappearance. Even though Marvin managed the store and did quite well for himself, his mother squandered every last penny of her late husband's money.

A cult-like following developed over the years, and Gladys and Marvin became celebrities, almost as recognized as Bonnie and Clyde in their day. Aside from the stain of the reported marital dysfunction and Gladys losing her mind, it was petitioned to have a statue erected and placed in the park near the gazebo, with a quote from William emblazoned on a plaque: *"A man can always work the farm, but an educated man can buy the farm"—William Farnsworth 1888 -1953 RIP.*

Chapter Six

You Can't Hurry Love

"True love is my new goal and more satisfying than any business deal."

—Kent Gordon

Tim boarded the plane to Hillsprings and planned to take the Greyhound bus home to MeadowBrook for the reunion. He told no one he was coming, except in his RSVP to Tracy, and he had no idea where he would stay.

He was on a brief hiatus from the musical production of *Fame* and had never been happier, making friends with like-minded people and working his ass off. Tim adored everything about his physically grueling career. He knew he was on the road to stardom.

Tim's confidence had soared from finally being noticed and valued. However, with the plane almost ready to touch down, he became overwhelmed with mixed emotions of apprehension and self-doubt. He worried that his old self would re-emerge the minute he saw the landscape, the second he smelled old manure and fresh wheatfields. As he felt the bump and jostle of rubber thumping the runway, he instantly craved a drink.

Walking across the tarmac and through the glass doors of the airport, Tim squinted at the change in lighting. All at once he was confused at the sight of a young woman frantically waving at him. Tim looked behind himself and hoped the pretty lady was waving at someone else.

Freezing in his footsteps, he was faced with an unexpected reality. He saw the absence of her braces, thick-lensed glasses, knobby knees, and stringy brown hair. Instead he took in straight white teeth, pale blue eyes, a petite fit frame, and wispy short blond hair. The familiar yet foreign young woman ran toward him. As she threw her arms around his rigid body, he did not hug her back.

She pulled away from Tim and exclaimed, "Hey it's me, your little sister!"

Tim immediately said, "Oh my god! I can't believe it's you! You are absolutely stunning. What happened to you, and why are you here?"

Marnie confidently beamed like a cat who had eaten the canary, and said, "Well, I guess you could say I was an ugly duckling who turned into a swam, or you could say, I've been transformed because Tracy Hansworth took me under her wing and single-handedly helped me grow up. But wait a minute, will ya look at you? You've changed, too! How'd you get to be so buff and handsome?" They both let out a stress-relieving laugh. Marnie followed up with, "I'm here to pick you up and take you back to MeadowBrook."

She then began a monologue that reminded Tim of every audition he had ever tried out for, except hers was faster and more enthusiastic.

"I thought you might be surprised to see me. I just had to come. I work for Tracy Hansworth now—you know, Events by Tracy? Anyway, as her number one employee, I have been helping her plan the reunion, so I was privy to your RSVP and knew you were coming. When I shared with Tracy my idea of picking you up, she said I should do it and make it a surprise. And since you and dad don't see eye to eye because of your homosexuality, I thought you could stay with me. I have my own apartment now!" She clapped her hands repeatedly and squealed with delight.

Tim stood dumbfounded. All he heard from her speech was "homosexuality." A wave of irritation washed over him and then his street smarts and brotherly love kicked in and he was able to see who she really was.

Without addressing her comment, Tim had the need to apologize because his only connection with his little sister up until then had been treating her like a spoiled brat. He knew he had been a self-centred, mixed-up teenager, and had carried on to become a self-loathing twenty-year-old before finally learning to be comfortable with who he was.

He responded, "Thank you for coming, Mar-Mar!" But before Tim could say anything further, Marnie interrupted him.

"Oh my goodness, I am so embarrassed! People do not call me 'Mar-Mar' anymore, and while I'm sharing, I simply have to apologize. I am so sorry I was such an annoying brat. I really am not like that anymore!" She then paused and turned toward the rotating conveyor belt and quickly said, "Come on, let's get your bags before they get sent back!" Laughing, she suggested they collect his things and get to her car, reminding him of the three-hour drive ahead of them.

After grabbing his suitcase, Tim slung his arm around Marnie's shoulder as they walked out to the parking lot, and she willingly wrapped her arm around her big brother's waist.

The air was typical for the late June day, fresh and warm. Tim found himself breathing more deeply than usual from his increased heart rate, and then he became aware of the way Marnie nestled into him while they walked the short distance to her red Chevy Chevette. He as the big brother, and she as the little sister.

Once in the car, they sat quietly. The silence was awkward for Tim but after Marnie pulled out of the airport parking lot, she instantly began speaking and used the time to recall the words she had practiced for the last year.

She cleared her throat and told her brother the story of her life.

Marnie shared like a person reading a self-help manual. Her tone was even and kind, without any accusation. She described the years of bullying at school, the many hours spent alone, and the endless gifts their parents bought her to keep her company in her perfect ballerina pink bedroom—Barbie dolls and baby strollers, Easy-Bake ovens and Etch-a-Sketches, board games she played by herself with soulless, mute dolls as opponents. She finished with descriptions of disinterested housekeepers and nannies paid to be her friend.

Tim's little sister gripped the steering wheel with petite hands, while her memories and past hurts continued to spill out. This was all a narrative Tim knew nothing about.

While Marnie spoke, Tim looked at her china-doll complexion, fine features and long eyelashes, and tears welled in his eyes. Guilt consumed him and he turned to look out the window so Marnie wouldn't see the feelings of regret slip from his eyes and roll down his cheeks.

He continued to listen as she went on to describe tap dancing lessons, scraped knees and sprained ankles, swimming lessons that brought on severe ear infections, and figure skating classes she cried all the way through.

As she spoke, Tim tried to come to terms with their very different childhoods. Growing up, he had experienced physical and verbal abuse, while Marnie was raised in a household of emotional neglect coupled with financial privilege. Neither was aware of the other's struggles.

When she stopped speaking, Tim expressed how sorry he was that he wasn't the big brother he should have been. He chose not to speak of his own childhood trauma. At least not yet.

Staring at the road ahead, Tim had flashbacks of getting cuffed in the head for missing a fly ball on the baseball field; fumbling the basketball and getting told off on the sidelines; losing to an opponent on the wrestling mat that brought hours of extra practice sessions. Each harsh word and bit of ridicule shaped him and created his hatred toward their father. The emotional and physical abuse felt like layer after layer of tightly wrapped hockey tape around his heart, constricting the life out of him.

Marnie eventually stopped speaking and then quickly concluded in a sing-song tone, "Oh well, that's all in the past now. We have the rest of our lives to be the brother and sister we both always wanted. Besides, I don't think Mom and Dad had bad intentions."

Tim was taken aback at Marnie's dismissal of their parents' guilt, but he chose not to comment on her casual tone of voice and choice of words about her evidently dysfunctional childhood. Instead, with his mouth agape, he said, "Holy shit, will you look at all the new stores! What the hell? Is that a new hotel?"

Marnie laughed and exhaled. She was pleased to talk about something else and happily responded to Tim's shock, "Yup, MeadowBrook is not a small town anymore. We even have a mall now. See? My ears are pierced, and I might even get a tattoo! Nothing gross, like maybe a tiny butterfly or something."

Tim let out a genuine, heartfelt laugh. He felt it all over his body and he liked the sensation.

"Hey, I have another question. Did anything ever become of that cold case? You know, the one about the founder, William Farnsworth, who disappeared?"

"Not really, but they still talk about it. There has been a cult following too. People come from all over the place trying to solve it. They look like a bunch of kooks walking up and down Main Street."

As they drove down Main Street, Tim tried to stay positive, but he struggled to control the voices that took him back to the person he never was—the mistakes, upheavals and phoniness.

Marnie put her signal on and pulled into a large brand-new apartment complex. When she parked in her reserved spot, Tim interrupted the silence and said, "Hey, is Robinson's Diner still around? I'm famished, but first I need a shower."

It was Marnie's turn to laugh, and then she responded yes to the diner and yes to Tim using her shower.

***

Before there was any mention of a funeral for Grandma Fasp, or any time for Johnny to call his father out on his lies and infidelity, he decided to get out of Dodge.

Always an avid reader, Johnny devoured books on travel and any books by Jack Kerouac, Garry Trudeau, and Tom Robbins. He had read *On the Road* like a bible, laughed at *Doonesbury* when he was high, and could not put down *Jitterbug Perfume*. He considered himself to be a hippie, even though the Beat Generation movement had long since passed. Johnny advocated nonviolence and love, and had a bumper sticker to prove it. "Make Love Not War" was displayed in yellow and orange for all to see on the back of his GMC pickup truck.

Nonetheless, his feelings of anger toward his father did not match his 1960s mantra. Johnny decided he needed to leave before he did something he might regret.

Moreover, there was a price tag on his head and the bounty hunters were out in full force. So, in no uncertain terms was he going to stick around. Not only was he done with his entire family, but he had heard through the grapevine that the MeadowBrook Police Department had his number and they were ready to shut him down and haul him in.

The nearest travel agent was a three-hour drive to the town of Hillsprings, so without giving it any more thought, and still under the influence from numbing his feelings, Johnny jumped in his truck and drove recklessly over the speed limit. The only time he stopped was to fill up a gas can he kept in the back of his truck.

Johnny pulled up to the agency. From outside, he could see the travel posters through the window—exotic beaches, bikini-clad, sundrenched women, and swaying palm trees.

Early on in his teenage years, Johnny had been interested in travelling to San Francisco, and yet felt he had been born at the wrong time. Haight-Ashbury, the Summer of Love, and the counterculture movement encouraged artists, musicians and young people to "Turn on, tune in, and drop out." Johnny related to everything he read about San Francisco and how it was in 1969. It was a haven for revolutionaries and his favourite singers, who sang about social change, freedom, peace, love, religion, and politics. His record collection represented all of his mentors, including Bob Dylan, The Grateful Dead, Neil Young, and Janis Joplin.

But San Francisco was not far enough away, and by 1988, the hippie movement had not only faded but had also turned bitter. The effects of psychedelic drugs had caused mental illness to run rampant, and homelessness plagued the beaches and back alleys. Unless they had the wherewithal to get out, there were many drifters and disillusioned flower children with nowhere to go.

In contrast, during the 1970s, Johnny had also read about hippies travelling to Budapest, South America, and Morocco, all in search of peace, love, and happiness. Even though he had grown tired and mistrusting of bumper sticker wisdom, he still ultimately wanted a do-over to live life as a free spirit immersed in adventure.

Music had always motivated Johnny; he dissected song lyrics and looked for meaning in them. The harmony, poetic riffs and visuals of the song "Marrakesh Express" by Crosby, Stills & Nash created a desire in him to see far-off sunsets and experience firsthand the romantic Moroccan skies.

The decision was made, and Johnny handed a wad of cash to the travel agent and purchased a one-way plane ticket to Morocco, with the hope of finding himself in Marrakesh. He looked forward to riding the Marrakesh Express and witnessing a Moroccan sunset.

On his drive back to MeadowBrook, Johnny had sobered up some, but knew he looked like crap. He had been on a two-week bender and was feeling the aftereffects. Even though his body wanted to shut down, his mind was cracked wide open. The sunlight hurt and memories of his grandmother and her confession were screaming at him.

He was on a mission.

Johnny had an adrenaline rush that led from his heart to his hands on the steering wheel, and right on down his leg to the gas pedal. He put his foot down hard and steady and felt a sense of renewal. Pulling up to his parents' property, he jumped out of his truck, and once inside the house, he ran up the stairs taking two at a time.

He was still angry, but was pleased that his anger was propelling him.

He grabbed a duffel bag and stuffed in his sandals, cut-off denim shorts, a few old concert T-shirts, his journal and his signature poncho. He paused to see if he missed anything, and while scanning his room, he saw his guitar and was transported back to high school and serenading the many teenage girls all vying for his attention. Johnny reached for his guitar at the last minute as an afterthought.

Running back downstairs, he momentarily noticed the stench of empty liquor bottles, overflowing ashtrays, and a stale life he no longer wanted. He carried on outside and threw his bag, guitar, and bundle of money into the cab of his truck. And then Johnny opened the tailgate and reached for the full gas can in the back.

He walked briskly in behind his house, with only the sound of his purposeful footsteps and the sloshing gasoline, past the trees and rose bushes toward the full-blooming marijuana plants neatly contained in a substantial rectangular greenhouse. Johnny stopped, and taking in a deep breath, he filled his lungs with what seemed like a lifetime of false relationships. Upon his exhale he got busy, and without any anguish, he walked the perimeter of his grow-op and doused it with gasoline.

Stepping back, he lit a match and threw it. Within seconds, smoke replaced the warmth of the sun, and the melting plastic and crackling wood frame exploded like a neutron bomb. Johnny apologized under his breath to his grandmother, "Sorry, Grandma, it was good for a time, but now it's over. I'll see you on the other side."

The pyrotechnic combustion lit up the sky like a Canada Day celebration, and then the forked flames divided and united like a threatening dance daring anyone to partake.

Johnny knew it was the beginning of the end.

Quickly, the infernal blaze was noticed by his family. Their chaotic voices and incoherent shouting were barely audible above the roar of flames as they brought buckets overflowing with water from the rain barrels, and garden hoses that hardly reached. The confusion on his brothers' faces matched the devastation. Johnny felt his parents' eyes bore a hole right through him. Combined with the heat of the fire, both were unstoppable.

Johnny turned to his father as he made his way toward his truck and yelled over the crackling, burning plants and polyurethane greenhouse walls, "I may have caused the external fires but now it's your turn to put out the fires you have created within! You made your bed, now lie in it, and I hope you go straight to hell!" Johnny turned his back so his dad couldn't see his tears of rage. His pain spilled out of his tired eyes, and his wounded heart revealed to him that he had made the right decision.

As he climbed into his truck, he could hear his father hollering, pleading after him, "Wait, John, come back! I can explain everything! Please, don't go!"

Johnny straightened at hearing his father refer to him as John, and not the little boy version of his name he had grown up with. Pausing, he momentarily felt satisfied. Then, turning to look over his shoulder before peeling out of the driveway, he saw his mother's face, or rather, the face of the woman who had raised him. Johnny detected a look of pleasure and briefly wondered if it was an expression of "*good riddance*" or "*good for you to be getting out of this godforsaken place.*"

Johnny chose not to look back at his father. With disdain, he thought, *how could someone so smart be so dumb?*

John Sr. had only one thought: *If you think my infidelity was bad, just wait until you find out about my many other sins.* The aging father of seven sons and a secret daughter—with two of those children being born of affairs—walked pridefully into the house to let his family clean up and douse the flames.

***

With his hands steady on the wheel, Johnny felt his body slacken as he drove past the infamous egg on Exit 88. The town had erected a matching plaster egg monument for people leaving MeadowBrook, so they would not only be welcomed into town but they would be told to "*Please Come Again*" when leaving. Johnny said out loud as he gunned past the monstrosity, "Misery, your company is here!"

Finally arriving at the airport, he was exhausted. His flight was not until the following day, so he hunkered down in his vehicle and slept soundly. Awakening at the crack of dawn, he ripped out a blank page from his journal and scribbled on the torn piece of paper, "*FREE for the taking. Drive safely!*" Placing the note on the windshield of his truck and leaving the keys in the ignition, he grabbed his duffel bag and guitar. Walking across the parking lot in the crisp early morning air, Johnny wondered if the bar at the airport would be open, as he was craving a drink.

From looking at a world map in the travel agency, Johnny learned that Morocco was about the same size as California, and was located in the northwest corner of Africa. The terrain was mostly mountainous, and the country was bordered by the Atlantic Ocean and the Mediterranean Sea.

Taking the train from the airport to Marrakesh, the gateway to the grand Sahara Desert, was just what Johnny needed. Thinking about where he had come from, he visualized the small town he could drive through with his eyes closed and knew he had made the right decision. However, his nausea from the alcohol and lack of sleep had given him a foggy brain. He felt unprepared for the beauty of the red city. Having never spent much time outside of MeadowBrook and the town of Hillsprings, with the exception of a few alcohol-infused trips to New York, Johnny was mesmerized by the dusty red roads, crimson-tiled rooftops and historical monuments.

He remembered reading somewhere that Marrakesh was known as the Pearl of Morocco, but before he could investigate further, there were two pressing thoughts on his mind—he needed to either sober up and get clean, or find the nearest drinking establishment for a beer and a shot of whiskey.

Walking into the youth hostel, Johnny's greenish-grey complexion told the front desk worker that the unmistakably laid-back dude in front of him needed a shower and a bed. He speculated he was looking at just another weary traveller who had consumed one too many sangrias with not enough shut-eye.

Johnny threw some bills on the counter and in a barely audible voice he asked if he could lie down somewhere. He flopped down on a single bed in the six-bed room. Every bed had a nightstand, and a few open-air windows sent a warm aromatic breeze throughout the space.

Without saying a word, Johnny fell into a fitful sleep. He spent the next three days detoxing, perspiring, and having nightmares. Eventually upon waking, his body odour caused the bile to rise in his throat, and before he could run to the nearest bathroom, he noticed a bucket had been placed beside his bed.

He threw up until dry heaves caused his stomach muscles to burn from overuse.

On day four Johnny bolted into an upright position from the bed that had become a part of him. Instantly he felt a warm breeze across his wet sticky brow. And then he heard a sweet, angelic voice. At first, he wondered if he had died.

"Good morning, sleepy head. I thought I was going to have to call a doctor. I'm glad you are alive."

Before responding, Johnny looked across the room at the source of the voice—a girl, or a teenager, in a white eyelet sundress, with her tanned legs crossed and a map stretched out across her bed.

She continued talking, to Johnny's amusement, in an accent he could not detect, "Oh, please forgive me. My name is Margarita. May I ask what your name is?"

When he heard her name, Johnny thought of the frosty tequila lime drink of the same name, and then he remembered his manners and hurriedly spoke, so as not to appear rude, “Oh yeah, my apologies. My name is John. It’s nice to meet you!”

She told him not to apologize and then she asked if he would like to go with her to get an espresso. Johnny mustered up as much enthusiasm as he could and said yes, even though he had no idea what an espresso was. But first, he asked where the nearest shower was.

Johnny didn’t know what time it was, and he didn’t care. Stepping outside the youth hostel, he was impacted by bright sunlight, chickens clucking, and shopkeepers selling their wares in what appeared to be an overall bustling community. He relished the smells foreign to him and the kind, friendly faces that seemed strangely familiar, as if he already belonged.

The small ceramic cup with hot bitter contents tasted magical, and was surely the most delicious drink Johnny had ever had. He commented enthusiastically, “Wow, this espresso shit is pretty damned good!” And then he remembered the refreshing taste of an ice-cold beer.

Margarita tilted her head at Johnny’s use of foul language and smiled. She opened up the conversation and told Johnny how her best friend and travelling companion had abandoned her and taken off with a Dutch man she had met. She went on to explain she was from a small town in Argentina named San Rafael. She missed her family, but was curious about the world and determined to see it.

Johnny was spellbound by his new friend. He was surprised to learn she was twenty-two and not a teenager at all. And then in just a few languid, romantic days, he wondered if he might be falling in love with her.

The farmland, windswept hills, and dark soil back home was all Johnny had known and was a huge contrast to the terrain of Marrakesh. The warm powdery earth comforted Johnny's bare feet, and the heat of the sun embraced him from the inside out. He was enticed by the city and the girl, and was compelled to learn as much as he could about both.

Johnny repeatedly made a point to cancel out thoughts of anything to do with his past, even though he couldn't help but wonder what Darcie would think of such a place. In the course of a very short time, Johnny found that all he could see was Margarita. The distance and unique surroundings had taken him far away from everything he had ever known, and not just in miles. His mind and spirit were connecting with a woman from whom he had become inseparable.

The days turned into weeks and Johnny shared as little about himself as possible. It was evident to both of them that he was learning more about his new girlfriend than she was about him.

He was enamoured with her thick, dark curls that tousled around her freckled round face. He felt pulled into her massive brown eyes that were filled with curiosity and wonderment. When she spoke in her Spanish accent, all he wanted was to crawl inside of her soul and never leave.

Johnny visualized her life back home and was captivated by her stories.

Margarita's parents met as tango dancers in the streets of Buenos Aires. A man named Astor Pantaleon Piazzolla was an Argentine tango composer and had led a troupe of dancers around the country. Her parents fell in love when they were paired up as dance partners. Months later, they married, settled down and continued dancing until their first *nino* was born. They joyously instilled dance, musical instruments, and delicious *asados* into their family rituals. Margarita explained that an *asado* was like a barbecue. The grilled beef, pork, chicken, or chorizo sausage were accompanied by salads and red wine.

Margarita taught Johnny how to dance under the black velvet sky while a million stars shone down on them. She emphasized the importance of their connection in the walking tango embrace, with straight backs, elbows raised, and the precise and intimate navigation of the fluid movements. She taught him how to lead, even though he fell under her spell and wanted her to be the dominant partner.

They referred to each other by pet names—she called him her hippie boyfriend, and he referred to her as his tango princess. He felt dopey and clumsy to her poised and balanced beauty.

Their days began to follow a routine of espresso, exploring, and napping in the afternoon. Johnny played his guitar in the evenings while they waited for the sun to set. As he strummed and softly sang the poetic melodies of Bob Dylan, Joni Mitchell, and Neil Young, Margarita would endearingly close her eyes to listen. And just when he least expected it, she would snatch the guitar away, giggling, to take a turn and strum out the rhythms of the Gypsy Kings, while Johnny played the bongos on his thighs.

Johnny tried to explain what the word counterculture meant. He said, "Margarita, I know that I am different from other guys you may have dated, and there is so much I want to tell you about myself. There are things you might not like about me."

Before he could finish, Margarita interrupted and said, "But I love everything about you! What is this 'counterculture'? Is it something bad?"

Johnny smiled and realized he wasn't making sense, so he got back on track and finished his original thought, speaking lightly and yet informatively, "No, sorry, the meaning of counterculture is the opposite to how I was raised. It stands for people who reject the dominant values and behaviour of mainstream society." He talked about the effects of pollution and the negativity and corruption of capitalism.

She smiled and proudly jutted out her chin when Johnny explained feminism and then they both laughed when she said, "So, in other words, it's okay if I lead while we are dancing?"

Margarita shared recipes her grandmother had taught her. She explained the ingredients in empanadas and how to make the pastry light and crispy around the edges. She described the hours spent in the kitchen preparing food and sitting around the dinner table, laughing and telling stories. Johnny was especially taken by the part about how after dinner every night, her whole family gathered to dance, sing and play music together.

The loving descriptions she told of her family made Johnny think about the deceit and coldness of his own.

As the orange-and-pink setting sun dropped behind the city, a day did not go past that Johnny didn't think about the alcohol and marijuana he had come to rely on. The night shadows only increased his anxiety, and when the anguish rose up, his cravings were unbearable. He made up an excuse and told Margarita he needed to move on from Marrakesh. He was desperate to find the ocean and swim. But not without her. So, Johnny invited Margarita to go with him.

As they left Marrakesh, both knew they would someday return, because it was the birthplace of their love. Johnny quoted Plato over breakfast the day they were set to leave, "*The beginning is the most important part of the work.*"Then, adding his own words, he said, "I set out to run from my past, but in the process, I stumbled onto you, or was it you that found me?"

Margarita smiled, and as the morning sun rose on their familiar place for espresso and pastries, she said wistfully, "I believe we found each other, as if the stars were aligned, and our union was meant to be. Besides, our beginning was not hard work, so this Plato person certainly did not know us!"

During their conversation, Johnny knew it was part of his journey to dig deeper, so he shared how the small town he grew up in had stifled his creativity. But then he stopped talking, because he still couldn't share his family's burdens. He gazed into the eyes of the woman who ignited a fire of desire within him like no other, and said, "I don't want to turn you off, but I come from a long line of industrious, insensitive men, and I don't want to be like them."

Margarita didn't understand the magnitude of Johnny's past hurts, so she soothed him by patting his hand and said, "Cheer up, baby. I am sure your family misses you, and everything will be better when you go home."

Johnny smiled at her sweet, innocent response and knew she was not ready to hear his ugly truth.

They decided on Casablanca, located on the Atlantic coast of the Chaouia Plains. Johnny wanted to experience a bustling city and swim in the salty ocean. At the same time, Margarita romanticized Humphrey Bogart and Ingrid Bergman from the Hollywood movie *Casablanca*. She was greatly disappointed when Johnny told her the film was shot entirely at Warner Brothers Studios in Burbank, California. With teasing in her eyes, Margarita responded, "Hmph, I don't care, Johnny Fasp, because it's the symbolism of their love that matters most!"

Then Johnny explained the movie's plot and said, smirking, "Well, it's actually quite a sad story, as the guy doesn't get the girl in the end."

They both laughed, and Margarita said, "Okay, bad comparison. Let's just say we are about to go to one of the most romantic cities to change the outcome of the flawed characters, Rick Blaine and Ilsa Lund."

With that, Johnny was reminded of why he adored her.

During the bus ride, Margarita thought it would be fun if they each made a list of what they wanted to do once there. She wrote, *"See as many palaces as possible and kiss Johnny underneath each archway."* He wrote, *"Play my guitar and serenade Margarita on the sandy beach of La Corniche."*

When they first arrived, it felt significantly different from other Moroccan villages they had already visited. Johnny assumed it was due to the busier city vibe, but something else had shifted from within, and he couldn't place his change in mood.

When they discovered there were no youth hostels, they settled on the cheapest hotel as close to the beach as they could find. Johnny knew Margarita was low on funds, but he had enough money for both of them. He chose not to tell her that because he didn't want to explain why he had so much money, or interrupt their routine of splitting everything fifty-fifty.

Once they were settled and set out to wander, they both admired the European flair, modern architecture, and crumbling colonial-style buildings of Casablanca.

Their hunger tugged at them and propelled them to stop at the nearest outdoor café they could find. Johnny had become accustomed to the once-unfamiliar smells of turmeric, ginger, saffron, and cinnamon. He craved the comforting and satisfying traditional stew known as *tagine,* accompanied by flaky and crispy *M'semen* flatbread.

As they sat across from each other at the tiny wrought iron table, Johnny wondered how many other travellers had sat there before them. Margarita only noticed her boyfriend, sitting across from her. His sandy blond hair streaked naturally, and his skin was now copper-coloured from the sun. She liked how his forehead wrinkled when he was lost deep in thought, always looking like he was about to say something philosophical and meaningful, which he often did, though he rarely talked about his family and home life.

They looked up from their bowls, savouring every mouthful, and spoke simultaneously, laughing at themselves. They had begun to have the same thought at the same time and both commented to each other how they must learn to make the flavourful stew they had come to love. Johnny thought of Darcie, from what seemed a million years ago, and how they, too, used to finish each other's sentences. He wondered if the two women would ever meet and if they would like each other.

Johnny and Margarita had begun a new morning ritual, sleeping later and packing a picnic for the beach. He had forgotten how much he liked to swim and recalled the many hours and endless summers spent with Darcie at the pond back home. Johnny had almost forgotten how much he missed her. And now instead of jumping into fresh water with his best friend, he was jumping into the ocean with someone new.

While Johnny headed toward the water, Margarita stayed on the shore busying herself with her journal and at the same time keeping her eyes on Johnny. Wading out into the powerful surf, Johnny decided the swimming hole back home was incomparable to this body of water that was much more vast and warm. He breathed in the tangy salt air and enjoyed the feel of the hard sand beneath his feet. The ocean waves and their shifting shades of aqua blue acquainted Johnny with the soothing, rippling effect as it caressed his body. Diving downward, he ascertained the gentle sighs of the water could be both Zen-like and merciless at a moment's notice.

It was in the briny deep water that Johnny regained his natural balance. During the oceanic experience, his mind drifted back and looped around with thoughts of Mary Jane, Jack Daniels, and Captain Morgan all entangled in the perfumed essence of Southern Comfort. With each stroke of his arms and kick of his legs, Johnny's longing for the poisons of his past slightly diminished. He had begun to notice a transformation and hoped he was making progress.

Eventually, Nancy, his real mother's name, came to his mind. Then he saw her looking so much like his sister and wondered what part of his biological mother was in him.

Johnny's mind unraveled the lies that felt like a noose around his neck, a tightly wound rope that got tighter every time he thought of his cheating father. When the secret was first revealed it had encapsulated him like quicksand, and the stifling town had swallowed him. He now understood why he needed to leave the leg-hold trap with its vice-like grip that strangled his heart.

He questioned the meaning of life and wondered if things happened for a reason. If not for his father's unfaithfulness, would he have still met Margarita?

Johnny cried. He wept for missed opportunities and what could have been. He screamed underwater at the loss of his grandmother, and he feverishly kicked his legs at the thought of never returning to MeadowBrook. Johnny wanted a clear mind but repeated memories rushed in like a kaleidoscope of images. Grandma Fasp, Darcie, and his family, all jumbled and unforgettable. His pent-up fear and pain kept them current.

Sometimes while swimming, Johnny laughed at the irony of the blue surf being his form of Alcoholics Anonymous, or therapy sessions. Then he would stop and tread water, in awe of how the extensive salty sea meshed with the abundance of his own salty tears. The ocean had become his pathway to healing. He swam to heal.

His body became dark-tanned, sinewy and muscular and the saltwater purified his mind and stung his eyes. He welcomed the discomfort that complemented the beauty.

Soon his natural high from the ocean had replaced the addictions that behaved like imposters for his happiness. Things gradually started to make sense.

His connection with Darcie had been a mistaken attraction for the twin he had known in the womb before his thought process had formed. Johnny's mood lightened when he whispered the word *sister,* and then he had a strong urge for closure or openness or something he was not yet sure of.

He felt a deeper glimmer of happiness and new beginnings. Johnny remembered a Kurt Vonnegut quote, *"I urge you to please notice when you are happy, and exclaim or murmur or think at some point, if this isn't nice, I don't know what is."*

Only two months into his union with Margarita, and two months clean and sober, a deviation from Johnny's healing occurred when his nightmares began.

Margarita and Johnny had gotten used to sleeping in the same bed, both wanting to get closer than they already were, clinging to the other like a life source. Sleep always came quickly for Margarita. She was exhausted at the end of each day and often shared with Johnny how safe she felt nestled in his arms. Unfortunately, when it was time to go to bed, Johnny's sleep took a long time. As he cradled Margarita in his arms, she reminded him of one of the barn cats back home, curled up, purring and oblivious to the harsh outside world. When he did eventually doze off, he found his unsettled rest more exhausting than being awake.

One night, after he was sure she was soundly snoozing, Johnny inched away from Margarita's loving embrace. He needed to fidget and didn't want to disturb her. At some point just before sunrise, while Johnny tossed and turned, he cried out incoherently, waking Margarita. She heard him screaming people's names that she had never heard of and saw sweat glistening on his forehead. She was initially frightened, and then as she attentively watched over him, she prayed, "Please God, help me to understand this man." Margarita hoped Johnny would talk in the morning about the ghosts that haunted him.

When morning broke after that fitful night's sleep, Johnny woke to Margarita staring down at him while she perched up on one of her elbows. He made out her whispered prayers, noticing that some dark tendrils of her hair had fallen from behind her ear. Johnny's breath caught at her natural beauty. He immediately asked her what was wrong, and before she spoke, Johnny said, "I am so sorry, babe. I slept like shit last night. I hope I didn't disturb you, but I should probably talk to you about a few things."

Walking hand in hand to the beach at sunup, Johnny was exceptionally subdued and quiet, and then he knew it was time. He wanted to come clean, but not fully. Decidedly he only felt comfortable sharing certain parts of his past and home life. He delved into the death of his grandmother and the mother and sister he had been deprived of; his distant father and how his family had camouflaged their love for one another with superficial jokes, sarcastic jabs, and fake camaraderie.

Johnny talked and talked until he lost his voice and then he continued on in a raspy whisper.

During his recollections to Margarita, Johnny left out the part about his past vices for fear of losing her. Especially since he saw her as white as snow, and deep down inside he knew he was the prince of darkness and there were demons he had yet to reveal—two unnamed beasts called booze and pot. In his mind, Margarita was pure and perfect, untarnished and faultless. He felt poisoned from substance abuse and he did not feel safe enough to divulge that side of himself.

Yet.

Margarita listened attentively, nodded and tried her very best to understand. She couldn't help but think of her family comparatively, and the only disagreements they had were what to barbecue or whose turn it was to do the dishes.

Johnny paused, exhaled, and with pleading eyes, he took Margarita's face in his hands and said, "I need to go home, back to MeadowBrook. Will you please go with me?"

She reached up and wrapped her arms around his neck, pressing her body into his, and said wholeheartedly, "Yes! How soon can we go?"

Johnny smiled and said, "Thank you! Now please let me treat you to breakfast and a plane ride to meet my messy family."

Three months after fleeing MeadowBrook, Johnny boarded an airplane back home, with the woman who had become his destiny and a power source he had come to rely on.

Johnny was hopeful and at the same time scared to death, a paradox he was getting used to. Meanwhile, Margarita had a secret of her own. It started with her suddenly being repulsed by coffee, which soon led to morning sickness, and then the realization she had missed her period.

After they boarded the plane and sat back in their seats, Johnny squeezed Margarita's hand and told her about the ten-year high school reunion and that he wanted to take her. She smiled and nodded and said nothing about her condition.

***

Before work one morning, while waiting for his wheatgrass smoothie, Kent spotted a copy of *Women in Business* at a newsstand. The face on the cover was none other than Tracy Hansworth.

Kent stood admiring her business suit, stern facial expression, and the caption that read, *"Ten powerful women you wish you knew. Meet Tracy Hansworth, owner and operator of Events by Tracy."*

He immediately bought a copy, placed it in his briefcase, and the minute he got to work, Kent told his secretary to hold all of his calls. He locked his office door, sat down and read the entire article, devouring it like a proud papa reading about his next of kin. And then he read it again.

The two-page article introduced Tracy and her successful business, her no-nonsense approach, and her common-sense attitude. The magazine story went on to showcase a fleet of pink vehicles, plastered with Tracy's face and logo—*"Let me plan your next event so you don't have to!"* On the adjacent page were dozens of colourful hot air balloons, with the caption, "Travel Up, Up, and Away with the Mayor of MeadowBrook as he Turns 65."

Kent remembered having been invited to his dad's birthday party and not going, due to a big golf tournament he was hosting for some important clients.

His thoughts then shifted to high school and he could not help but smile. Kent had always admired Tracy's work ethic and how she was always up to something. He could still see her petite frame making her way from group to group, clique to clique, checking in with the jocks, potheads, preppies, and brainiacs. She even chatted with him on occasion, but regrettably, he rarely gave her the time of day, and when he did, he only teased her.

"Hey Tracy, whatcha doing? Knitting a scarf for a street urchin?" Or "Hey Tracy, why don't you make me a necklace out of hundred-dollar bills? I'll pay you fifty cents for it!" And then he would laugh at her annoyance and how she responded to his clever quips, "Kent you can just shove it where the sun don't shine!" as she stomped off in the other direction. He would get a kick out of their badgering banter and a sense of shared camaraderie. But sometimes he was not quite sure if it was mutual.

When Kent thought more intently about the cute girl from his past, he remembered being on the debate team with her. He recalled how unexpectedly smart Tracy was, and laughed at her insistence that they all wear her berets that she had knitted in her spare time. He recalled her always arriving early with homemade brownies or decorated sugar cookies. He smiled at the thought of her high-fiving each teammate for every correct answer and demanding they thank the opposing team when their team beat them. Once when they travelled to a neighbouring town for a debate competition, Kent refused to take the school bus and asked Tracy to ride with him. When she turned him down, Kent took it as an indication he should back off. So he did. Later he saw the disappointment in Tracy's eyes when he started dating a girl in a different grade two years younger than them.

Seeing her highlighted on the front cover of a reputable magazine brought on wistfulness for a girl he hardly knew and a town he thought he could live without.

The year following Kent's transformation and new lease on life, his mind had cleared, and with it came an aversion to his old persona. He hoped the wrecking ball of good health and clean living had demolished his narcissistic patterns and cruel behaviour.

Tracy's invitation was the perfect excuse for Kent to go home. He was instantly consumed with the need to pay back all the citizens of MeadowBrook, whom he had at one time taken to the cleaners; the people he scammed and those who had fallen for a certain rate of return that was only put into his pocket. Even though it was only chump change, Kent was determined to right his wrongs.

Since starting his mindful yoga classes and therapy sessions, and quitting the nightclub scene, Kent had known without a shadow of a doubt that all his past victims deserved an apology. He would make amends, and in the process earn Tracy's love and respect.

***

Three weeks before the reunion, Kent hired a light aircraft, complete with a pilot, for his personal use. He also contacted a MeadowBrook farmer who allowed small single-engine planes to land on his farm and makeshift runway.

Next, he shopped. Kent's intention was to buy back some of his old friendships and fellow students with designer watches and expensive wines, and eventually to win Tracy's hand in marriage.

Two weeks before the reunion, Kent arrived at the airport with four suitcases and three dozen long-stemmed pink roses. Dressed in a brown leather jacket, with slicked-back hair and Ray-Ban aviator sunglasses, he checked in and made his way outside to the airstrip. Then he touched the tarmac for good luck, and greeted his pilot with a firm handshake, asking him to take his photo next to the plane with his brand-new Nikon camera.

Buckling up in the seat next to the pilot, Kent looked forward to the new experience of being airborne in a light aircraft. He anticipated seeing Tracy again. As the plane taxied down the runway, his adrenal glands began to surge, which reminded Kent of how he relished the pure excitement his body and mind went through when trying something new. He liked to think of himself as a daredevil, and as the plane left the runway, he made a mental note to try skydiving.

When the plane lifted off, Kent glanced down at the ant-like figures, tiny model cars, and the exquisite view. As they flew over land and water with cotton candy clouds above them, Kent imagined his own plane and Tracy sitting at his side in the cockpit. His brain instantly calculated the prospect of getting his pilot's licence.

Kent's mind was buzzing, and whispering to himself, he said, "Where there's a will, there's a way."

His thoughts often shifted, and Kent knew his rapidly calculating brain attributed to his success. So with the excitement of the day, Kent remembered a recent form of adrenaline, one that brought on a fight-or-flight mentality and could have gone terribly wrong. A few days before leaving for MeadowBrook, an unlikely person paid Kent a visit, and what transpired was straight out of a psychological thriller, with elements of mental illness and a dissolving sense of reality.

Nelson Farnsworth showed up at Kent's office without an appointment, and because their fathers had been friends back in the day, and Kent knew him from school, he welcomed Nelson into his luxurious corner suite office.

Besides, Kent knew he owed Nelson an apology or two. He was sure the nerdy kid had been the brunt of a joke or two on his part—an elbow to the ribs, an extended foot to cause the poor sap to trip, or a request across the cafeteria tables as to what romance novel Nelson was reading.

Kent could read a room and size up a situation like nobody's business, so when the school brainiac stood before him with a blank expression, not speaking, Kent sensed that he needed to speak first, so he said, "Whoa, hey buddy, long time no see!" Getting up to shake his hand, Kent strode toward Nelson and said, "What can I do for you?"

Immediately Nelson's face turned crimson, and Kent detected perspiration on his forehead and upper lip. When they shook hands, Nelson's hand was cold, wet, and clammy. Kent could not help but wipe his hand on his pant leg afterward. Speaking in a whiny voice,

Nelson sounded odd, revealing his lack of confidence. Kent realized they had never conversed before.

"Well, I don't know if you remember me, but I used to have bad acne, and now I don't, because I invented some cream, and yeah, I need you to invest in my product."

Kent knew that Nelson was an academic whiz, but other than their fathers being friends, he had no idea who he was. Face to face, Nelson appeared conspicuously insecure, and Kent could not make any sense of his request or why he was asking for a handout.

Kent responded as he would to any other individual wanting his money, especially one with seemingly no business sense at all. Feeling slightly put out, Kent said in an agitated tone, "Well, you see, Nelson, it's not that easy. I need more facts and documentation to convince me that your invention is viable and could be lucrative. Do you have anything you could leave with me?"

At the finishing of his sentence, Kent could see that Nelson's persona changed. His eyes turned black, his body became rigid, his arms tensed and his fists clenched.

Kent's mind switched to high alert, and adrenaline instantaneously surged through his body. As if he was being threatened, he instinctively braced himself for a possible attack. With his mind racing, he quickly evaluated his options, knowing from years of working out and being a foot taller, that he could defend himself from Nelson

Farnsworth with one hand tied behind his back. However, Kent thought he might be face-to-face with a deranged sociopath, so he waited in balance for Nelson's response.

Nelson just stood before Kent like a boiling pot ready to explode. As if trying to summon the right words, Nelson began stamping his feet and hollering at the top of his lungs, "Noooo!!!" in a long, extended yell. "Dammit, I have documents, but I forgot them at my hotel, and then I missed the bus. And I haven't eaten all day. This town sucks. I hate it here!"

Just then, Kent's secretary burst through the door to see if everything was okay.

Kent said, "It's all right, Becky, but could you please call security?" Then he calmly said to Nelson, "Whoa, buddy., It's just protocol, no need to blow a gasket…" Before Kent could say anything else, Nelson ran out of Kent's high-rise office without even noticing the spectacular view of New York City. He then frantically pressed the elevator button half a dozen times, as if it would make it come faster. When the doors slid open, Nelson got on and paced the circumference of the small metal box until it whisked him down to the main floor. Outside on the street, Nelson gasped for air and began walking back to his hotel, defeated and confused.

And that was that.

The makeshift runway on the farmer's field was not conducive to a smooth landing. The aircraft shook, bounced, and rattled. When it finally stopped, Kent let out a "Yahoo!" followed with, "Whoa, that was so cool! Thanks, buddy!"

The pilot smiled, sighed and said, "You are very welcome!"

Kent had made arrangements earlier for his mother to pick him up, and just before disembarking, he quickly asked the pilot if he needed a ride into town. The aviator enthusiastically said, "Thanks, but no need, man. The farmer and his wife offered to give me lunch before I take off again." He then added, "They sure are a friendly couple; people would never be so welcoming where I come from!"

Kent smiled and said, "Yup, that's MeadowBrook for ya! I used to think everyone here was a loser! But I was undeniably wrong."

Kent walked toward the farmhouse and heard the sound of his mother's Porsche in the distance. He visualized her taking the windy roads and corners over the speed limit. In the past, he would have been proud and elated. Instead, the newer version of his old self was embarrassed and mortified as he thought about his family's wealth, privilege, and arrogance.

It was then he realized how much he had changed.

Kent had always admired his mother for her beauty, grace, and style. She had a presence and was hard to miss at five feet ten inches tall. However, she was the antithesis of a typical mother, as she did not bake, cook, or clean. He and his sister had rarely been hugged and were always instructed to keep a stiff upper lip in times of stress or struggles. But, when all was said and done, Kent knew their mother loved them, and if nothing else, she was proud of him and his sister's good looks and stature. She tried to be there for her children, provided she was available and not travelling the world or helping his father with his political career.

By the time Kent approached the farmhouse, his mother, Anita Gordon, was leaning against the $80,000 vehicle. Kent stopped, smiled, and walked toward her.

He noticed her jet-black hair had been cut short and was possibly dyed. He also knew his mother's navy-blue tailored dress and high-heeled, knee-high boots were Calvin Klein, valued well into the thousands. And then he thought of Tracy Hansworth and wondered if the two women would like each other. He grimaced slightly, feeling disconcerted at the very thought of them meeting.

Kent momentarily put his thoughts of introducing the two women he deeply admired to the back of his mind, and gave his mother an expected air kiss on both cheeks.

Looking at her son delightedly, Anita said, "Hey there, stranger, what's new?"

Without mincing words, Kent took his mother's hands and sincerely said, "Hi Mom. Well, since you asked what's new, I am here to tell you I'm a different person! You are now looking at the new and improved Kent Gordon!"

Kent's mother put her head back and laughed, a loud boisterous sound that took charge of every space she occupied. Even though she didn't understand what Kent meant, she adored his cocky, self-assured response.

Stepping back and walking around to the passenger side of the vehicle, Anita threw her son the car keys and said, "Here, catch! I thought you might like to drive!"

Aside from Kent's efforts to change his narcissistic ways and advantaged outlook, he still loved a beautiful car and nice things. He outwardly smiled and inwardly thought to himself that some things never changed. Catching the keys above his head, Kent knew that no other car could stir his soul like the unique-handling and heavy-gripping rear end of the Porsche. He remembered the day his father brought the sporty white car home in 1968, when he was only eight years old. It was tied with a big red bow, as a birthday present for his mother. The look on her face changed from astonishment, to joy, and then to anger. Kent was confused, but over the years, he speculated the expensive gift was a bribe to fix something his father had done.

Behind the wheel, Kent felt free. The horse logo on the vehicle was fitting, as Kent often said to his mom, "Any wild mustang got nothing on your new car, Mommy." Later, he learned the meaning behind the horse was a nod to the car's birthplace, Stuttgart, Germany. The headquarters was built atop a horse-breeding farm.

Kent sped out of the long driveway with gravel flying and dust following them like the poof of a magic trick. He had to refrain from going over the speed limit, as the last thing he wanted to do was get in trouble with the law, mainly because his central focus, besides "getting the girl," was to fix all his wrongdoings, not create more.

He looked at the bright green rolling hills, ancient weeping willow trees and brooks that lined the back country roads as if he had never seen them before. When a sudden influx of moisture threatened his vision, Kent chalked it up to the wind coming in from the wide-open windows.

Breaking the silence, he said to his mom, "Hey, would you mind if we don't go directly home? I have a delivery to make." Anita had noticed the enormous bouquet of pink roses and thought they might be for her. Feeling slightly disappointed, she realized they were for someone else.

Clearing her throat and quickly getting over her disappointment, she said, "Actually, darling, why don't you drop me off at home and you take the car, go see some friends, and get reacquainted with the town."

Kent wanted to say, "What friends?" but changed his mind. Which only reminded him of all the damage he wanted to undo and the amends he wanted to make. As they approached the big black wrought iron gate, which was almost always left open, Kent noticed that his parents had done some landscaping and upgraded their swimming pool since he had left. He remembered there was a massive inheritance for everyone in the family when his grandfather died. Kent had his money locked up, but was planning to use some of it for a set of matching diamond wedding rings.

His mother had one stipulation as she climbed out of the car. She spoke kindly but with conviction. "Please be back by 7:00 p.m., as Dad and I have a function to go to, and we do not want to take the truck. It's a black-tie event."

Kent winked. "Yes, absolutely no problem, my beautiful mother!" As he turned up the radio and sped out of the driveway, ironically, the song playing was Billy Ocean's latest hit, "Get Outta My Dreams, Get Into My Car." Kent smirked at where he was going and who he was about to invite into his car. He hummed along to the radio and was shocked by the town's expansion. His business sense and calculating mind wondered who was funding the progress and recent infrastructure. Keeping a running tally, he counted three new gas stations, an entire mall, three apartment buildings, two townhouse complexes, and two high-rise office buildings, all constructed in the quaint brick theme that MeadowBrook was known for. Kent smiled and nodded approvingly.

Near the end of Main Street, he saw pink helium balloons and a life-size cardboard cut-out of Tracy. Kent laughed out loud and said to himself, 'That's so awesome, Trace!'

***

Darcie boarded the plane with her headset on and a Walkman playing her new mixed tape with songs from her past. She felt it appropriate to walk down memory lane as she was about to take flight toward a nostalgic past.

She had packed light, taking only a canvas backpack with her onto the plane, but had paid extra money to transport most of her belongings in the plane's cargo hold. Even though she was planning to stay for an indefinite time, she had still found someone to rent her garden apartment in Kitsilano as a safety net, just in case she wanted or needed to return.

Darcie had become an environmental minimalist and felt like a traitor, as she was highly against air travel. She had recently read how the emissions from commercial planes had a potent impact, triggering chemical reactions and atmospheric effects that heated the planet. She knew her beliefs and the topic of global warming were controversial, but she put a lot of faith in her idol David Suzuki's ideology. So, naturally, she felt guilty flying home and contributing to the problem.

She was also a vegetarian, even though she spent her teenage years working at the A&W fast-food chain and came from a town of chicken farmers. The thought of her orange-and-brown uniform with the change pouch around her waist caused her to instantly smile. Everything about MeadowBrook reminded her of Dakota.

Darcie nestled into her window seat, popped some cinnamon chewing gum in her mouth, and turned up the volume on her portable device. Her ears were flooded with the heartfelt melody of Joni Mitchell's song "The Circle Game." She closed her eyes and visualized painted ponies on a carousel, herself as a little girl going 'round and 'round. She wondered if for all those years, she had been held hostage to time, as if the ticking of the clock was holding her back from returning—metaphorically being held captive on the carousel of time.

Darcie marveled at the aspect of time. It had been ten years since she had walked through the town of MeadowBrook. Ten years since she swam in the pond and got high with her best friend Johnny, and ten years since she had been with Dakota, the teenager who took her breath away.

Over time, Darcie had concluded that she did not want someone who took her breath away. She needed her breath in order to survive. And that was part of the reason she fled. But she never stopped loving Dakota and often felt perplexed at how it was still possible to feel out of breath at the mere thought of him.

Darcie knew in 1978 that she was running away, but why she'd done it didn't occur to her until ten years later. She had not forgotten the sleepy little uneventful town and missed everything about small-town living, from the slow, lazy days of summer to the crisp winter snowfalls. She remembered her first time snowshoeing with Dakota out past the edge of town, along the northern hilly ridge of MeadowBrook. The beauty of nature was heart-stopping, but the serenity and peacefulness unnerved her. Even though the scenery and company were perfect, Darcie had felt scared on that day. She knew it was all her mother's fault that she always felt a little on edge.

Darcie's mom told her about the William Farnsworth murder case throughout her entire childhood. Therefore, when she was growing up, she had been instilled with fear. "Don't be out past dark…never get in a car with a stranger…never go anywhere alone…you know they haven't found the killer yet…if you have to go out, always go with Johnny." Her imagination ran wild. Darcie visualized predators around every corner and speculated that most men were evil. Sometimes she wondered if her mother chose not to speak about her biological father by virtue of his being an unsavoury character—or worse, perhaps the dad she never knew was actually the guy who killed the town's founder. Even after she moved away, her mother would periodically send her newspaper clippings in the mail of the ongoing investigation of the William Farnsworth murder. Darcie would often not read them and just throw the redundant articles in the trash.

Snapping back to the present time while waiting for the plane to take off, Darcie felt an anxious warmth stirring in her belly that moved rapidly to her heart; it was the same feeling she had as a little girl on Christmas Eve, or just before a meet-up with her teenage boyfriend Dakota many years earlier. "*Puppy love,*" her mother called it, and "*butterflies.*" Darcie smiled and said in her mind, *Hey Mom, the puppies are jumping and the butterflies are fluttering again in full force!*

When she finally leaned back in her seat to get comfortable, she let out a deep sigh and looked out the small oval-shaped window at the mild Vancouver drizzle, and thought she might never return. She was by no means a city slicker and the ocean had been her saving grace. She would miss the ocean.

When she first arrived in the city, young and alone, the smell of the ocean—salt, and sand combined—drew her into her new home. The Pacific Ocean was the welcoming committee, and the continuous Vancouver rain was the backdrop. She thought it odd that the locals seemed to take the beach for granted and didn't notice the aroma. Darcie swore she could taste the dry seaweed bits and tiny baby crabs every time she breathed in deeply or swallowed. From anywhere in the city, the ocean was always inviting, and yet somehow it felt ominous. Darcie learned quickly there was a heaviness to the sea, unlike the lightness of the lakes and ponds she had grown up with back home.

Sometimes when feeling heavy-hearted, she would try to dissect her mood, but most times Darcie expressed her sad thoughts through her art, without using any words. She purchased a camera with some of the money her mother gave her, and took a few photography classes at a community college. Darcie plastered her walls with nature photographs and built a portfolio. A few times over the course of her last ten years in the city, her shots of wildlife and early morning sunrises were published, from individual submissions to more significant layouts.

Her favourite part about Vancouver was the coastline in the mornings. The sparsely populated beaches devoid of people made her wonder where everyone was. Seagulls swooped and dived for their breakfast or scavenged from the garbage cans for leftover French fries. She delighted in their play and how they taunted her, almost like they were saying, "Hey lady, take my picture, feed me, play with, notice me…!"

The photo opportunities proved to be endless.

Just before the beaches became busy with cyclists and joggers, Darcie would prop herself against one of the many logs the tide had brought in. They appeared to be scattered about but were actually placed in organized rows. She thought of the history behind each stranded tree, like aging artifacts intended for sunbathers, picnickers and loners like herself. As she sat down with the smooth cedar at her back, she rested. While there, she drew, or read, and more recently, wrote poetry.

Placid, harmonious and tranquil, or tumultuous, hostile and fierce—Darcie loved how the ocean was full of emotions—it helped her write and create prose that became her friend. A voiceless confidant. Darcie enjoyed the melancholy of being alone, to the point where her mother worried about her and people would look at her strangely, like an unapproachable drifter. In due course, she mistook her loneliness for finding herself, discovering the meaning of life, being settled and established. But deep down inside she knew that to be untrue.

Darcie also expressed herself through dance. Her classes were always booked up before any other instructors at the dance studio where she taught. She grew to adore the children but was bothered by the bickering parents in line at the start of every dance season, and she told the studio owner she would not be in on registration day for those reasons.

Boredom was not a part of Darcie's thinking. She would often be heard stating to her dance students, "Boredom is the opposite of being curious; let's be curious together!" At that precise moment, she would cue the music, and they would break out into abstract movement and freestyle dance.

When the engines revved in preparation for takeoff, Darcie was startled. The sound of the plane made her thoughts take a turn and she cringed at the state of the world: pollution and poverty, unrest and upheaval. When the plane finally picked up speed, she felt her body pressing back from the force of lift-off. Darcie noticed a woman a few rows up and across the aisle who looked familiar. She stared for a moment trying to place her, and could not put her finger on who she might be. Eventually, she assumed it was a mistaken identity because at no time could Darcie remember knowing a suntanned, athletic, bleach-bottle blonde. She closed her eyes and speculated that perhaps the woman was a model or an actress.

Chapter Seven

I Was Made for Loving You

"Being in love with someone who does not feel the same way in return can be heartbreaking, but is not the end."

—Amanda Marsthrop

If Nelson could have described what was going on in his brain after his mother abruptly left, he would have said he heard a snapping sound, like the cracking of a whip or the breaking of a twig.

At the moment Diane Farnsworth came upon her son's secret shrine to Darcie Richmond in his dormitory room, fear gripped her, and she immediately thought of

Nelson's notorious grandmother Gladys, and the infamous disappearance of his grandfather William Farnsworth. She then wondered if Nelson would end up the same way—a murderer, or institutionalized for stalking and being downright crazy.

Diane Farnsworth was unprepared for what appeared to be madness in her son and fled back to MeadowBrook without asking any questions or investigating her son's strange behaviour any further.

Nelson in turn felt betrayed at a time when he was flying high. He was financially, academically, and romantically on the threshold of great success. He could not understand his mother's reaction and reason for leaving. So, he decided to ignore it and move forward with his end-of-term thesis project and life-changing invention. Without concern, and a simple shrug of his shoulders, Nelson came to the conclusion that anyone who did not support him one hundred percent could go straight to hell.

Nelson had spent countless hours researching oral medications, scrubs, masks, and topical creams for acne. He discovered that diet and hormones did not always trigger outbreaks. And after his experimental data was completed, the procedure supported his hypothesis.

"Science is never wrong, and variables never lie," became Nelson's motto.

His discoveries indicated the cause, effect, and logical analysis of his namesake product, Nelzema, which reduced blemishes, promoted skin renewal, and stimulated the skin's collagen production within one week of twice daily applications to the face.

With the right measurements of benzoyl peroxide, salicylic acid, tea-tree oil, and Vitamin A, the entire world would soon be free from the debilitating effects of pimples and acne scars forever. Provided they purchased and used Nelzema religiously.

Nelson had perceived the MeadowBrook High School yearbook prediction for himself would be accurate and his notable achievement of fame. He had memorized the Grade 12 prophecy: Nelson Farnsworth, voted "*most likely to invent the latest, greatest pimple cream and become a millionaire,*" and he was looking forward to making a mockery of their so-called joke, by proving the statement true.

Early in his university education, for experimental purposes, Nelson took out an ad in the school newspaper that read:

I am a second-year business and science student with breakthrough data looking for human subjects who suffer from the debilitating effects of acne. All subjects will be safeguarded from unethical research and will be in good hands with guaranteed results. Please contact Nelson Farnsworth in Dormitory B, Room 312, if you fall into the category of desperately looking for a solution to meddlesome blackheads, embarrassing pimples and ugly scars.

Within twenty minutes of the ad coming out, Nelson had an extensive group of pimple-faced students lining up in the hallway outside his room.

Thus began a four-year-long case study, complete with deductive methods and Nelson's full understanding of his observations and data. By applying various solutions to the skin of his volunteers, he would formulate his hypothesis with a one hundred per cent claim and prediction that Nelzema would reduce and diminish acne with no known side effects.

He kept their names anonymous. Subject #1 was an eighteen-year-old teenager bullied for her blemishes; #2 was a twenty-year-old man who could never get a date because of insecurity due to acne; #3 was a thirty-five-year-old single mother getting a degree, embarrassed by her monthly outbreaks; and the list went on, totalling sixty participants, all with similar stories of the same or greater magnitude.

When everyone became free from acne, as expected their self-confidence, self-esteem, and self-worth drastically improved. Ironically and unexpectedly, almost all the subjects became Nelson's friends. The conclusion was outstanding. Nelson became an idol to some and a scientific genius to others.

Nelson's claim-to-fame product came with triumphant testimonials, which then became a part of his data, and the accounts were included in his thesis. It was then turned into a portfolio for eventual shareholders and venture capitalists. All that was left was FDA approval, a patent, and investors. He had heard rumours that Kent Gordon, the narcissistic jerk he had graduated with, was a bigwig at the New York Stock Exchange. Nelson had full intentions to pay him a visit. And once he had Kent as an investor, Nelson would make his debut at the 1988 grad reunion.

When Nelson finally completed his thesis and was ready to hand it in, his mother showed up. Nelson was overjoyed to see her and felt it a good omen that she would be the first person with whom he would share his joy and scientific discovery. Instead, she left before he had a chance to explain. And like all of the other doubters and naysayers in his life, Nelson ascertained she could rot in H-E double hockey sticks like the rest of them. All except his human guinea pigs and his utmost supporters.

Meanwhile, back in MeadowBrook, Marvin and Diane Farnsworth changed the locks on their doors, installed bars on their windows, filed a police report against their son and bought a gun. They had been paranoid for years, Marvin since his father went missing, and Diane from the continuous stories her husband shared of a very strange childhood, complete with a dead-beat dad, eccentric mother, and an eventual missing persons criminal investigation. So, when Diane explained to Marvin about their son's behaviour, memories of the year 1953 and his mother Gladys came flooding to the forefront of his mind.

Over the years it had been determined that since the disappearance of his father, Marvin suffered from PTSD, long before there was such an acronym and diagnosis of Post-Traumatic Stress Disorder. Instead of getting treatment or counsel, Marvin became a workaholic and gained financial success from working seven days a week and marketing the Red & White Frugal Grocer, and later on, his liquor store.

Subsequently, it had been speculated but not proven that his mother had been responsible for the disappearance of his father, which grieved Marvin considerably. In turn, he wondered if all the times he drove his mother around as her personal chauffeur, his father's dead body had been in the trunk of the car.

Now, thirty-five years later, the sleepless nights and nightmares still plagued Marvin. A few nights a week he would wake up trembling in a cold sweat from visions of his mother roaming the property in a white cotton nightgown, while the moon illuminated her unkempt hair and magnified her increasingly stark expression. Marvin had never gone forward with what he saw on the night the brand-spanking-new 1953 Pontiac Parisienne pulled up in front of his house. He had gotten up to go to the bathroom and later wondered if the slamming front door had awakened him. Or maybe it was how his father was cheerfully whistling as he walked down the path to the awaiting car. It was out of character to see any form of joy coming from the man Marvin had feared.

What he saw and heard remained a secret. It had been so long since his father left that sometimes Marvin thought he had created the memory, and made it up in hopes that his mother was not a killer. However, after she was carted away and locked up in the looney bin, Marvin had a sense of relief. He decided to never utter a word about his observation, or his speculation that perhaps his father had left willingly.

Through all his reasoning, he ignored how the information might have taken the presumption of guilt away from his mother and given her a sense of balance and sanity. If he had spoken up, her mental state might not have taken a turn for the worse.

The weeks, months, and years that followed William Farnsworth's disappearance had gotten to Gladys. After seven years, when William was finally pronounced dead, Marvin was twenty-seven, running the store quite successfully, and Gladys was a mere shell of who she used to be.

Over the course of time, she had spent all of her husband's money, let the house go to ruin, and took to peeking in people's windows. Late at night, Gladys would go looking for her missing husband. She would run through neighbourhoods and frantically call out William's name. On many occasions, she could be heard singing in a shrill voice, "Wee Willy Winky, runs through the town, upstairs and downstairs in his nightgown, tapping at the window, crying at the lock. Are the children in their bed, for it is past ten o'clock?" She would finish up the little ditty with, "William…come out, come out, wherever you are!" Her laughter would follow until she manically began to cry.

Marvin would be called to pick up his mother, and eventually, the annoyance in the policeman's voice became more easily detected, "Hey Marvin, your mom's up to her old tricks again. You better come get her." Or "Hello Marv, Peeping Gladys is on the loose again. You gotta do something about her, buddy!" And worst of all, "Marvin this is ridiculous! The entire town is in an uproar. COME

GET YER DAMN MOTHER BEFORE WE LOCK HER UP AND THROW AWAY THE KEY!" If he could not be reached, the paddy wagon would come and take her away. It got to be frightening for young and old alike. The police complained about the cost and time management of the whole ordeal, so needless to say, something had to be done.

Marvin, being the sole heir and only living relative, made the decision to send his mother away. He hated to do it and had very fond memories of her and all the fun he had growing up. But he was not equipped emotionally, mentally, physically, or financially to keep rescuing his mother, making excuses, and paying off the police department.

He donated the mansion to the art society and sent his mother to a sanitarium. In the next town over, a mental institution had been built at the turn of the century. For a time it had been used as a home for unwed mothers and later turned into a place for the criminally insane. Shortly after Gladys had been admitted, there was a devastating fire, and then it lay empty and on the verge of ruin. Some private practice naturopathy and yoga gurus had a vision in the 1970s to compile their knowledge and create a place of healing and refuge. Extensive renovations had taken place.

After the fire, Gladys was transferred to the new wing of the MeadowBrook Hospital in the geriatric ward. Marvin visited her every Sunday with a bowl of chicken stew—the exact recipe he and Diane made for their son Nelson.

However, the vanishing of his father was still considered a cold case. Gladys had never been charged or arrested due to a lack of evidence, compounded by the blunders of the police. Therefore, the investigation was still open thirty-five years later.

Meanwhile, Marvin and Diane were worried the nut had not fallen far from the tree and their only son was crashing down and had lost his mind.

Nelson was planning his return to MeadowBrook for the sole purpose of proposing marriage to Darcie, and to show everyone what a tour de force he had become. His invention and subsequent confidence propelled him forward. He was breaking free from his awkward, stereotypical nerd image and he was ready to show the world. His acne and scars had wholly disappeared, he had purchased a diamond ring from his early inheritance, and soon he would be purchasing a whole new wardrobe. There was no stopping him. He would often whisper to himself in a mantra, "Just watch me now!"

***

Patty hated flying. She blamed it on her obsession with the news and world disasters.

What made matters worse and added to her stress, was that Patty had to change planes on her flight back to MeadowBrook. L.A. to Vancouver, Vancouver to Hillsprings. When she arrived, both parents and, more specifically, her newly sober mother would be picking her up.

She shuddered at the thought of seeing her mother and was not looking forward to her recent sober transformation, only because she had seen it before and it rarely lasted.

As the plane prepared to take off, so did Patty. She ensured her seatbelt was fastened correctly and snuggly wrapped around her lower abdomen. Then she pulled out and studied the cardboard information booklet that she found in the pocket of the seat in front of her. She read what to do in case of a plane crash and was pleased the stewardess went over all the instructions again. Her bag was safely stored underneath her, the tray was upright, and after she spotted the two exits, she gripped both armrests tightly until her knuckles turned white.

When the plane picked up speed, Patty clenched her jaw, shut her eyes tight, and recalled why she had taken the bus to California ten years earlier instead of flying. It was because of a plane crash that greatly impacted her life.

On April 4th, 1975, at fifteen years old, Patty had planted herself on the sofa in the downstairs recreation room with Ruskin at her side. Her mother had been on a two-week bender, and neither Patty nor her father knew where she was. Consequently, she was happy eating macaroni and cheese right out of the pot and was excited about the pan of brownies cooling upstairs in the kitchen.

As far back as Patty could remember, she was fascinated with true crime and plane crashes. She never shared this aspect of herself with anyone, but for some reason, a visceral fear inside of her told her to never fly—as in, birds fly, not humans. So, the thought of something going wrong up in the sky was particularly unsettling, and yet thoroughly fascinating. As Patty watched the late-breaking announcement of the plane crash, she was fascinated. The newscaster called it "Operation Babylift."

The war in Vietnam was coming to an end, and the U.S. government had announced a plan to get thousands of displaced Vietnamese children out of the country. Twelve minutes into takeoff, there was what seemed to be an explosion, as the lower rear fuselage was torn apart. A rapid decompression occurred, and two of the four hydraulic systems went out. It skidded for one-quarter of a mile and then was airborne for half a mile. Finally touching down in a rice paddy, the airplane slammed into a dike. It broke into four parts, some of which caught fire.

One hundred and seventy-six people survived. However, 138 were killed. Seventy-eight were children and thirty-five were Defence Office Saigon personnel.

Not only did the story horrify Patty, but she thought it a bad omen that the plane crashed in a rice "*paddy*"! That word sounded too much like her name!

She had never forgotten sitting in her basement alone, enthralled by the news story. Patty could repeat the tragic event verbatim in the years to follow, and since this was her first time on a plane, the memory was front and centre in her mind.

After the plane had reached cruising altitude and the seatbelt sign blinked off, Patty kept hers on. When the stewardess began to make her way down the aisle with the food cart, Patty turned to look over her shoulder, mainly to see the progress, and hoped at that very moment the beverage cart would not hit her when it squeezed past. Thinking more in-depth, Patty decided that being killed by a flying food cart would be a good thing because she would die instantly and not notice the flames, burning flesh, and mangled bodies of an actual crash.

In the process of fretting, Patty caught sight of a passenger she knew. Someone she had been jealous of her entire life, and also the girl she had always competed with for Nelson's attention. What annoyed Patty further was that Darcie Richmond had no idea that Nelson

Farnsworth existed. And she knew without a shadow of a doubt that Darcie did not know she existed either.

Patty felt her breath catch at how beautiful Darcie had become. She tried not to stare but had a hard time looking away. She thought how easy it was for onlookers to stare and ogle when anything out of the ordinary came to their awareness, whether it was a devastating plane crash or someone they hadn't seen for ten years. You just didn't want to get caught in mid-gaze. Darcie Richmond was certainly something out of the ordinary.

Reflecting on Darcie's natural beauty, Patty's confidence had risen to where she knew she was pretty, too. Yet she realized that comparing herself to the woman a few rows back stirred up past hurts and jealousy from when they were both teenagers. She marvelled at Darcie's makeup-free face, rosy lips, straight white teeth, thick dark eyelashes, and gorgeous mane of lustrous black hair. Patty's self-esteem plummeted because she knew her own beauty was not natural and had been purchased with thousands of dollars—braces, diet gimmicks, exercise gyms, tanning beds, and hair colour from a bottle. She looked down at her bright yellow hoodie, unzipped to showcase her hot pink pushup bra, and felt the constriction from her tight white pants. Her feet ached from the points in her stiletto heels, and she worried about her hair drooping from the stale dry air, even though she had just poofed and sprayed it.

After her own personal assessment, Darcie appeared like an uncultivated natural garden, like the Garden of Eden. In contrast, Patty thought of herself as the Mojave Desert, bone-dry and parched, with tumbleweeds for hair and the cracked dry sand her complexion. And then, Patty's self-deprecating thoughts halted because, for a fleeting moment, she was acutely aware that she and Darcie had made eye contact. But Darcie looked away, peacefully closed her eyes, and showed no sign of recognition. Patty stared a little longer at the familiar young woman a few rows back, another person from her past she had never spoken to when she used to be invisible. Then she folded her arms across her chest and tried to stop seething.

To distract herself from thinking of Darcie, Patty's mind made a transition smoothly to comforting thoughts of Nelson. She had practiced their conversation in the mirror hundreds of times since receiving Tracy's invitation to the reunion. Patty once again played through the hoped-for dialogue in her head.

Nelson would say, *"Is that you, Patty? I barely recognized you, you have changed so much, and for the better! You are gorgeous. Where have you been all my life, and why have I been obsessing over Darcie Richmond?"*

Patty would respond, *"Oh, don't be silly, Nelson. Thank you for the compliments, but I've been under your nose the whole time. By the way, I go by Patricia now, and I live in California where I work for a local news station."*

Nelson would then quip, *"That's so cool! I am so impressed. You have achieved so much in the last ten years!"*

They would then hear the strains of her favourite song, "Heartbreaker" by Pat Benatar, followed by Nelson saying, "Hey, this song reminds me of you! C'mon, let's dance!"

Patty let out a slight giggle and then whispered, willing the lyrics to be true, *"Don't you mess around with me, Nelson Farnsworth, or I just might have to be a heartbreaker AND a dream taker!"* Again Patty giggled and smiled with confidence.

Her smile quickly turned to a grimace when she remembered that Nelson had never given her the time of day.

When the seat belt sign dinged back on, Patty reached overhead and pressed the call button for the stewardess. She was worried and wanted to know why the warning had appeared. When the flight attendant failed to come, Patty's heart rate increased, her palms became sweaty, and a dry, parched cough itched to burst out of her throat.

While waiting, she breathed in through her nose and out through her mouth like her recent edition of *Shape* magazine instructed for curing anxiety. Patty slowly began to relax.

She thought of her parents. She looked forward to seeing her father but was annoyed by his obsession with her mother's recovery, especially since his wife of thirty years had hurt them both emphatically.

Patty knew she was not ready to forgive and forget, as all she could ever do was relive and regret everything. Her childhood and teenage years were gone, and she hoped her adulthood would be different. She felt that she had already made significant attempts to change the narrative.

***

Even with all of Amanda's years of competitive sports, she did not describe herself as a competitive person. She liked to think of herself as driven. After reflecting in her journal, it had recently come to Amanda's attention that she had been driven to graduate high school, driven to become a P.E. teacher, driven to help others, driven to get married, driven to have children, driven to heal her daughter, and driven to save her marriage. And most importantly, driven to have a happily ever after.

Yet, Amanda and Brad were not speaking, and each expected the other to start the conversation with an apology. They were truly stuck. Nevertheless, they went about their duties. Amanda grocery-shopped, cooked, cleaned, drove Bram to sporting events, and spent most of her days at the hospital. There she would pay close attention to Branda's treatment and scrutinize her condition. She missed teaching her P.E. classes but didn't know how to fit work in with her other duties. She wrote in her journal, *"Work does not agree with my motherly and wifely duties!"* Then she underlined it with a red Jiffy marker.

Meanwhile, Brad's duties consisted of teaching P.E. classes, Grade 9 English, and occasionally mowing the lawn at home. He loved his family, but he was restless and bored. He worried about his daughter, but in his mind, he was convinced his wife was better suited to take care of her. Brad had become complacent with his job and his marriage.

Therefore, when a group of teachers headed out to a new pub one Friday after school, Brad was the first to arrive. As the various MeadowBrook High School faculty members made their way into the bright, airy establishment, Brad had already finished his first beer and ordered tequila shots for the rest of his coworkers. Everyone cheered, clinked their glasses and toasted Brad.

Shortly after the teachers' first pub night, Brad became the designated happy-hour organizer. Amanda never participated and fumed at all the teachers who did. She often told Brad how she thought they were all alcoholics. She wondered how Brad could shift gears in what seemed like a blink of the eye, from being a non-drinker and making popcorn on family fun night, to a man whooping it up, behaving like an unruly teenager.

For her part, Amanda juggled too many things and wished she would accidentally drop one and it would break into a million pieces. Then the particles would disintegrate into dust and blow away, leaving her with one less responsibility. On her bad days, she dreamed about Brad dying in a fiery car crash and wondered if she would be better off if she were a single mom. On her good days, Branda inspired her to take back her wish of something breaking off or an untimely death occurring. She longed to grow old with Brad, retire, travel the world, and look back on a well-lived life. The reality was that most days, she was too busy to even notice Brad, and when she did, he only irritated her.

A month before the reunion, Brad observed a new teacher at an after-school staff meeting. Amanda was not there because of her leave of absence, and Brad felt confident and independent in Amanda's absence. *Besides,* he thought to himself, *what harm could come from being friendly? My wife no longer seems to care, and she has a million other things to do. Looks like I'm on my own to welcome this new staff member.*

Just out of teacher training, Virginia Harrington was a sight for sore eyes. At first glance, one could tell she was in the arts. Everything about her was unique and different, from her messy bun with chopsticks holding it together, to her rolled-up faded blue jeans, men's dress shoes, and oversized men's denim shirt on her slim frame. She neither smiled nor frowned but had a pleasant, approachable look.

Brad couldn't help but stare and hoped she did not notice. He was enthralled by her keen, fresh attitude and thought he might be of some assistance to her. Brad remembered being the new kid on the block and wished he would have had a mentor when he was a new teacher.

After being introduced as MeadowBrook High's new art teacher, Brad noticeably leapt up off his chair to shake Virginia's hand. He enthusiastically said, "On behalf of all the staff at MeadowBrook, please let me be the first to welcome you. We are a friendly, all-inclusive school, and I would be honoured to be your personal tour guide." He then took the opportunity to invite her to the next afternoon's pub night. When Virginia spoke to thank him, Brad was blown away by her sweet-sounding voice and southern accent.

A few other teachers shifted in their seats and thought Brad's behaviour to be over the top friendly and embarrassingly awkward. Brad's performance toward

Virginia became the new topic of conversation and gossip at MeadowBrook High among staff and students alike.

That evening, over a dinner of creamed corn, instant scalloped potatoes and an overly cooked pork chops, Brad waited for Amanda to ask about his day. She did not. Instead, she scolded Bram for spilling his milk, complained about the lab technician at the hospital, and asked Brad to please take their son to his baseball practice after school on Friday.

When Brad heard Amanda say 'Friday' he jumped to attention. As if not hearing anything else, he pleaded. "Gee, sorry, sport. I have a school event that I can't miss. Maybe Uncle Dakota can take you?"

Amanda rolled her eyes and released an exasperated "Grrr," and Bram proceeded to "accidentally" spill his second glass of milk.

Amanda blurted out, "Well, I'm outta here. Branda needs me at the hospital! And I expect the two of you to clean this kitchen, as it will not clean itself!"

After she left, slamming the door on her way out, Brad turned to Bram and said, "Sorry about that sport. Mom's a bit tired. Why don't you go outside and play? I'll take care of the mess in here."

Brad's guilt about choosing pub night over his son's baseball practice was the catalyst for his doing the dishes, sweeping the floor, and mowing the overgrown lawn.

After completing the chores, he pictured himself wrapped up in Virginia's arms instead of being wrapped up in remorse. Then he decided to take a cold shower.

At the hospital, Amanda unexpectedly ran into Dakota. She spotted him before he saw her and she could not help but notice how strikingly handsome he was. When they made eye contact, a red flush of embarrassment spread over Amanda's pale complexion, which was instantly followed by a fumbled attempt to say, "Hey Dakota, fancy seeing you here. Whatcha doin'?" Walking toward her, Dakota gave Amanda a gentle "just friends" hug and then sincerely asked how she was doing.

The minute Dakota offered a kind look of concern with his inquiry, Amanda burst into tears. She shared how frustrated she was with Brad, and how she thought Bram and Branda were being neglected in the process. Amanda added bluntly, "Is there any chance you could take Bram to his baseball practice tomorrow after school?"

The following day, in preparation for pub night, Brad had left school early to use the tanning bed at the new hair salon. Then he popped into Barney's department store to purchase some new clothes. Coincidentally, he ran into Tracy Hansworth there. Brad remembered initially meeting her at the mayor's birthday party. On first impression, he hadn't liked her much and thought her too assertive and bossy.

In a rush to get his shopping done, Brad hurriedly said a quick hello, his arms full of clothes to try on. Tracy smiled rather sweetly and cordially said hello back, with a puzzled look on her face as she went on her way. Brad made his way into the men's changing room with a pair of acid-washed jeans, pleather pants, high-top running shoes, and a few Run DMC T-shirts—a complete change from his rugby pants and polo shirts.

Once at the pub, Brad used his brand-new credit card to purchase B-52 shooters for all the staff who had signed up, and then he eagerly waited for Virginia.

With one eye on the door and the other on his coworkers, Brad drank his liquid courage, and by 5:15, the new art teacher appeared to be a no-show. Brad felt stirrings of disappointment. By 5:30, he was ticked off, and at 5:45, some teachers had started to leave.

When he was just about to knock back his last Harvey Wallbanger, Brad spotted her, and his adrenaline rush made him feel eighteen years old again. Virginia was flustered and apologetic and even though Brad had grown irritable waiting for her, he acted as if he hardly noticed she was late.

"Oh my goodness, please forgive me for my tardiness!" Virginia charmingly stated. Before Brad could respond, he noted the word *tardiness* and could not help but smile. He then noticed she had changed out of her artistic school clothing into a short skirt and short-waisted red jacket with shoulder pads and brass buttons. He almost laughed out loud, thinking she looked like a cadet in a marching band.

Finally, acting surprised to see her, he said, "Oh, hi Virginia. I'm so glad you could make it. What can I get you?"

The following two weeks flew by for Brad. He was up early, cheerful and helpful around the house. Just when Amanda thought she was getting her old Brad back, she got the sinking sensation that her husband's turnaround was not intended for her.

She wrote in her journal, "*If Brad is having an affair, I will kill him, or her, or perhaps both of them will meet their demise in one fell swoop!*" Then she erased it.

Meanwhile, in the late afternoon on the reunion day, Amanda and Brad silently got ready for the upcoming event. They went through the motions, lost in their own thoughts, even though neither one of them wanted to attend.

Brad reached into the back of his closet and pulled out the only suit and tie he owned. Amanda said, "You're not going to wear that, are you?" Brad responded, "Why the hell not?"

Instead of explaining how handsome she thought he looked in the white dress shirt and black Calvin Klein dress pants she had bought him, Amanda said, "Because it's outdated, too small, and you look like a used car salesman!" Brad shrugged and went downstairs in his boxer shorts to crack open a beer.

Stepping into her black cocktail dress with the slit up the side, Amanda released an exasperated sigh, followed by a growl when she couldn't pull her dress up over her hips. She stepped out of it and threw it on the unmade bed with disdain.

Neither of them was in the moment. Amanda's thoughts were on Branda, tiny and forlorn, fighting for her life, while Brad thought about the new art teacher at school and how he could hardly wait for Monday morning.

Just before leaving for the reunion, Amanda found a skirt with a stretchy waistband and a blouse with enough pleats to cover herself up quite nicely. Meanwhile, Brad was irritable because earlier in the day, he thought he spotted Virginia with a possible boyfriend. Not only that, but his coworkers had taken to teasing him about his new wardrobe, and Amanda asked if he was rehearsing for a school play, as she mistook one of his new outfits for a costume in a performance about teenagers.

As they climbed in the car, Brad wondered if they should take separate vehicles. His mind drifted to Virginia again. He still thought he might be able to eventually woo her and win her over.

Chapter Eight

Still Standing

"If you are fuelled by purpose, there will always be a solution."

—Tracy Hansworth

Dakota's purpose in life was to help others; in doing so, he found happiness. He wanted to make a difference and believed that being useful could fill others, as well as himself, with hope.

However, at night, in the calm stillness of the evening, Dakota thought of Darcie and he often felt hopeless. He had questions that plagued him. Why did she not say goodbye? What had he done to make her flee, and would he ever see her again?

By the morning light, Dakota would start the day fresh and new. The best antidote for his worry was his work. The best cure for his loneliness were his kind gestures and looking out for other people.

Dakota's days began before dawn with tending to his animals. The horses, dogs, cats, chickens, a goat with one eye, and a three-legged sheep all gave him unconditional love, and he loved them back. He had recently been given a donkey delivered without a voice, which he named Eeyore, and Dakota admired his quiet, sweet personality, not at all like the stereotypical "hee-haw," stubborn nature most people expected from such an animal.

Dakota had a menagerie and it seemed to be growing. He could not seem to turn down a runt or a disabled beast to add to his group of misfits. Dakota loved them all.

On his way to work, he made two deliveries regularly, both of which complied with the two philosophies that he lived by. The first philosophy was passed down to him from generation to generation—*Our food should be our medicine and our medicine should be our food.* The second one he developed over time, as it became relevant to so much suffering in the world—*Our body is our temple. Fill it with pure goodness for our soul to reside in.* For his friend and fellow teacher Amanda, and her little daughter in the hospital, Dakota brought two fresh fruit-and-vegetable smoothies almost daily. He researched alternative healing forms and found nutrition and meditation at the top of the list. He was not prescribing anything or interfering with the doctors, but he knew the earth had so much to offer. He always felt led to share whatever he could to make others more comfortable.

Arriving at MeadowBrook High, where Dakota was a teacher, he set up for the breakfast club he had implemented years earlier. His research indicated a full stomach made for a satisfied, healthy, and happy learner. Even though there were parent volunteers for this, he liked to check in, say hello and show his appreciation. On his way out the door, he always said, "Thank you all so much. It takes a village, and all your efforts do not go unnoticed."

Afterward, Dakota went to the gymnasium to check on the early-morning floor hockey kids. He made a point to grab a hockey stick and jump into each game to score a few goals for each side. Collectively, the players cheered for their favourite teacher, Mr. Hillsman. He usually only had time to play for a few minutes, but the kids all anticipated him stopping by. They would plead for him to stay, but when he left, his parting words were the same every day, "Play fair, be safe, and most importantly, have fun!"

His next stop would be the teacher's lounge to brew a fresh pot of coffee for himself and his coworkers. The smell of dark roasted beans and a sprinkling of cinnamon regularly brought everyone to the staff room. The teachers counted on a hot cup of Joe and Dakota's cheerful disposition to start their day on a positive note.

Dakota was a learning support teacher. His belief was that diversity made the world go 'round, so he tried to find wisdom in every child's thinking. He believed there was no wrong answer and that everyone was a straight-A student—it just looked different for each person. For the kids on the spectrum, Dakota liked to bring as many teenagers as he could to his hobby farm after school and on the weekends. His animals looked forward to the pats, nuzzles, and cuddles. The teens delighted in the array of farm animals that nobody else wanted. Dakota referred to it as a win-win, for each needed the other. His reasoning rang true for anyone who visited his farm. *Looking into the eyes of any animal, one will feel no criticism. They ask no questions, tell no lies, and are only agreeable friends. They always give back more than they receive.*

Needless to say, Dakota went full throttle every day until late into the evenings. When dusk fell, he made a point to be still, to reflect and be grateful. Dakota sat on his wrap-around porch in the semi-darkness before sleep beckoned, and looked out at all he had created.

He had worked alongside the contractors to build a spacious three-bedroom home on his three acres of land, with large bay windows to bring in light, and high ceilings for air to circulate. Each room was creatively painted a different shade. Dakota believed the right use of paint could be powerful and mood-altering. He used the world around him as an example to feel the impact each colour brought. Vibrancy was the key.

Dakota painted the front door and window frames on the outside of his house red to emphasize power and love. He had always liked the theme of bricks throughout the town. So he used the trees from the land as lumber and red bricks for their history and durability.

Inside the home, he painted the living room a light yellow as a reminder of happy times, summer, and the sun. He felt it gave energy and a positive vibe. His favourite colour was green to represent the environment and the outdoors. Dakota thought it gave the feel of nature and had an organic quality. Therefore, he painted the wide hallways green as they led from room to room, offering balance and an air of stability. Last were the outbuildings. The barns were painted blue inside and out. Blue was the colour of trust. It brought forth calm and serenity and inspired security and a feeling of safety for his wide range of animals and all those who entered.

He hoped that Darcie would one day see his handiwork and understand his intentions and the meaning behind everything. Two weeks before the reunion, Dakota had a visitor come to his classroom, which was filled with couches, artwork, and a kitchen at the back for teaching life skills. Knocking on the door frame of his open door was an older man in a crumpled, oversized, and outdated suit. Before the man spoke, Dakota took note of his appearance. His whisker stubble, hunched shoulders and hesitation gave the older gentleman an aura of defeat.

Dakota smiled and signaled for the man to enter his classroom. The students had left just after the 3:00 p.m. school bell, and Dakota was anxious to leave too. He had offered to read to Amanda's daughter Branda, and he did not want to be late.

The man introduced himself and spoke in a raspy tone. Dakota instinctively knew he was depressed, and a heavy smoker from the sound of his voice.

Stumbling over his words, Mr. Krakatoya said, "Hello…Dakota, right?" Dakota nodded and tilted his head to the side.

"My sincere apologies, but someone said that you often give out favours, and I desperately need one. You see, my daughter—you went to school with her, but she was a bit of a wallflower, so you might not have known her—Patty Krakatoya." When Dakota didn't show any reaction, the man hesitated, cleared his throat and tried to speak a little more loudly and confidently. "Well, I was supposed to pick her up at the Hillsprings airport next weekend. She's flying in for the reunion, you see, and her mother and me…well, I can't go now. My wife, Patty's mother, has suffered a setback, and she can't go with me or be left alone…"

Even though Dakota always put action behind his beliefs, and was a helper to all, a wave of irritation washed over him after hearing the stranger's request. Before responding, Dakota invited Mr. Krakatoya to sit down.

He responded, "I don't recall knowing your daughter when I was in school, but teenagers can be rather self-centred." Dakota chuckled, adding, "Back in the '70s, I had a lot going on with my family. Anyway, I'm sorry to hear about your wife, and coincidently, I offered to help Tracy Hansworth, our fellow student who organized the whole event. Maybe I'll reach out to her and see if there is anyone else coming into the airport that might need a lift. So my answer is yes, I'll pick up your daughter Patty."

Patty's father profusely thanked Dakota, gave him the flight information and left in a hurry.

Afterward, Dakota wondered what kind of "setback" the stranger's wife could be dealing with. Nevertheless, he added to his to-do list—*»Stop by Tracy's office after reading to Branda."*

Dakota's thoughts shifted to Darcie on his way out the door. Again a wave of irritation hit him like a ton of bricks. This time it was directed at his long-ago girlfriend, the one he could never quite shake from his mind. He always had only a sense of softness toward her, but after a busy day of giving to everyone around him, Dakota felt spent, and his tank was on low.

Not being one to fret for long, Dakota decided to pay a visit to Nancy, Darcie's mother.

Once outside the school, Dakota turned back and looked up at the place he used to call an asylum when he was a teenager. He often referred to the stylish brick building as an institution that forced itself on those who entered. Back then, he professed that schools took away all ambition and yet Dakota liked to quote Henry Wadsworth Longfellow, who said, *"Youth comes but once in a lifetime,"* and then he would add his own words, "So why are we wasting it here?"

The thoughts of his past made him smirk and reminded him how he felt seeing Darcie in the hallways, sneaking a kiss or holding her hand and being next to her when no one was looking. He was sometimes mad at how she needed to keep everything from Johnny, when Dakota wanted to shout from the mountain tops his love for her. Regretfully he brooded like a typical teenage boy when he felt she was not returning his sentiments, all the while knowing she was his only reason to attend school in the first place.

He shook his head, sighed and climbed into his truck. He saw a book on the passenger seat that he had taken out of the library, called *Goodnight Moon* by Margaret Wise Brown. He decided to finish all his errands, and then go to the hospital to read Branda a bedtime story.

Since thinking of Nancy earlier in the day, feelings of anguish had risen, so Dakota made her apartment his first stop. Dakota knew he could have made more of an attempt, but felt there was no time like the present. So, right after school, he headed straight to Nancy's place. He knew the route well, and as he parked, he remembered the first time he had met Darcie, how nervous he was, and how easy Nancy had made his visit.

He felt guilty and remorseful that he had rarely thought of her over the years, even though they occasionally bumped into one another in town. But now as he pressed the intercom to Apartment 304, it was as if no time had passed. When Nancy answered, Dakota immediately sensed something was wrong.

Nancy had always been warm and friendly to him, and he remembered her whimsical ways, beliefs in astrology, and love for the earth, moon, and stars. The flatness in her voice was foreign to him when she said, "Hello, who is it? Can I help you?"

Dakota paused briefly and then said, "Hi Nancy, it's Dakota. You were on my mind…long time, no see! I just wanted to stop by and say hi."

Nancy also paused, and without saying a word, pressed the buzzer, indicating she wanted him to enter and come upstairs. Once inside the outdated mirrored lobby, Dakota was hit with the familiar smell of closed-in apartment cooking. The hum of the elevator gave Dakota flashbacks. He briefly wanted a do-over and smiled at the thought of being teleported back in time.

Dakota shuddered and held back his emotions as he knocked on Nancy's apartment door. When it slowly opened, he saw the hesitation on Nancy's face. Dakota hardly recognized the woman who stood before him, and instantly knew she was not well.

Regardless, Nancy smiled sweetly and greeted him with a weak hug. Dakota maintained a more prolonged embrace than usual, and before he spoke, he looked past her shoulder and took in the surroundings.

Nothing had changed. It was as if time had frozen. Dakota remembered fourteen years earlier, the first time he had gone to the apartment. Macrame plant hangers were overflowing with spider plants and ferns, wooden orange crates were draped in scarves, and beaded room dividers hung in the doorways. Tiny Christmas lights framed the windows, and around the room were empty wine bottles with candles wedged in the neck and hardened wax that had once romantically dripped down the sides in an array of textures and colours.

The entire room was decorated in a bohemian style that still seemed as chic and avant-garde as it had years earlier. Dakota smiled when he remembered the fondue dinners—how awkward he initially felt and how delicious the melted, dripping cheese was. Darcie held his hand under the kitchen table while they dipped chunks of French bread into the warm cheesy goodness, sopping up the top layer of oil and digging deeper for the full-bodied cheddar richness.

Dakota wondered if Darcie's bedroom had remained the same as well. Her mattress on the floor, with hand-knitted blankets and homemade quilts, was brought to mind; rock and roll posters on the walls and how she liked to put newsprint on her windows to block out the summer's light and the winter's freezing temperatures.

The lump in his throat rose at the lingering smell of patchouli oil and the memory of mother and daughter dropping the earthy-scented essence onto the light bulbs under red-fringed lampshades.

Pulling apart from the young man who towered over her, Nancy interrupted his private recollections and asked if he would like a beverage. Dakota replied that he would love a cup of tea.

As Nancy went into the small kitchen, Dakota noticed the record player still in the corner. No longer did he hear the sound of Jimmy Hendrix's electric guitar, Janis Joplin's raspy pleading voice, or Led Zeppelin's crooning and long instrumental riffs. In their place were the peaceful strains of Yanni. Yiannis Chryssomallis was known for his blend of jazz, classical, soft rock, and world music. His instrumental works were said to reflect his encounters with cultures around the world and embody his philosophy of "one world, one people."

Upon hearing the mystical strains, Dakota instinctively knew that Nancy was in a place of mourning and loss. Sitting opposite her at the Melmac kitchen table with chrome legs, Dakota slid onto his chair covered in light yellow vinyl.

Nancy slowly poured the herbal tea concoction into large pottery mugs and simultaneously began to pour her heart out to Dakota. He quickly gathered from her first sentence that he should settle in and forget about his other errands.

What began as a low-spirited monologue, quickly picked up speed and came bubbling out like a fast-flowing waterfall, a dam Nancy had been waiting to burst for years.

"Dakota, did I ever tell you they tried to pin the murder of that Farnsworth man—you know the founder of our town—on my father?"

Taken aback, Dakota responded with interest. "No, I did not know that, Nancy. Please go on."

Thus began the story of Nancy's life, including more insight into Darcie than Dakota could have ever imagined.

"Oh, yes. I was only ten years old, and my mother had just died. I still don't know what she died of. Nothing was ever discussed or explained back then, but my father worked as a groundskeeper for Mr. Farnsworth and his wife. Sometimes my dad would take me to work with him, and his wife would let me swim in the pool. Her son Marvin would be all gaga over me, even though I was not interested in him in the least. You see, he was a mama's boy and a geek all rolled into one. Oh, I'm sorry, I'm all over the map these days..."

As Nancy continued, Dakota took in her long wavy hair that had turned salt and pepper, but still appeared thick and soft. He smiled at her hoop earrings and thick grey men's sweater. The contrast was nothing less than beautiful and artistically eccentric. Her petite frame reminded him so much of Darcie, and he briefly longed to grow old with the girl that used to be his soul mate.

Nancy continued, "He was interrogated and accused of helping Gladys Farnsworth bury the body. Of course, that was ridiculous because that old battle-axe had gone downright crazy. She was always so kind to me, but for some reason, she thought someone else had buried her husband's body somewhere on their expansive lawn. So, she had my father spend days digging, looking for the possible dead corpse. So you see, he was just being a devoted employee and following orders. He had nothing to do with the missing man after all.

"Anyway, shortly after that whole fiasco, I got a job washing dishes at Robinson's Diner. My dad was friends with the family that owned it, and they must have felt sorry for us, so they gave me a job. By age fifteen, I was waiting tables and making pretty good tips. But here is where my story gets a bit creepy, and probably the reason why my daughter and I became feminists!"

Dakota noticed a change in Nancy's tone. A rosy hue had come over her face, and she suddenly appeared more youthful and vivacious. She walked over to the record player while still speaking, changed the album from Yanni to Carly Simon, and giggled when she put the needle down on the song, "You're So Vain."

Switching to a contemptuous voice, Nancy sang along with the singer known for her 1970s pop song hits. During the interval, Dakota speculated the lyrics were referring to Darcie's mysterious father, or as she called him, her deadbeat dad.

It only made sense, as the contempt and sarcasm in the singer's voice indicated the narcissistic creep she was describing strategically dressed to attract the opposite sex and was more interested in looking at himself in the mirror than the woman he was trying to entangle.

As her singing trailed off, she smirked, and Dakota felt her warmth and saw the twinkling in her eyes, reminding him of when he first met his girlfriend's mother when he was a teenager. This was the Nancy he remembered.

Nancy continued smiling, and then she became sombre. "Forgive me, I digress. You see, Dakota, back in those days, most women had no voice, and I was one of them. There used to be a group of men that came into the diner, not much older than you are right now. After supper, they would leave their homes, farms, and families to let the wives put their children to bed. They would make up stories about going for coffee, meetings, or card games. They would actually come into Robinson's for beers and flirt with the waitresses. Me being one of them."

Taking a few sips of tea, Nancy asked if Dakota would like something a little stronger. Dakota kindly refused her offer and said, "No, thank you. I rarely drink alcohol, but I'm intrigued by your story, Nancy. Please, continue."

Nancy smiled at him. "I appreciate you listening. I've been holding on to this secret for twenty-eight years, and it has been such a burden. I need to let it out and start speaking my truth."

She then added, "I need to practice because I have to tell all of this to Darcie next week when she gets here for the reunion. She has a right to know everything."

Just hearing Darcie's name made Dakota feel surprisingly annoyed. He wondered where his random moments of agitation were coming from, especially since he knew he loved her.

"John Fasp was not like the other men. He was quiet, slow to speak, and never dared to pat my bottom when I walked by. He reminded me of the movie actor Clint Eastwood. John was very handsome. He looked straight into my eyes when speaking to me, like he was trying to climb right into my soul and stay there. Anyway, maybe he was sincere, maybe he thought of me as a daughter, but he asked if he could drive me home one night, and it just became a habit. He said he was worried about me walking. And quite frankly, I was worried about walking home alone too!

"On his usual nightly visit to the restaurant, on my eighteenth birthday, he gave me the cutest little stuffed animal chicken and a piece of peach pie." She shook her head at the memory.

"Now, here's where the story changes. As soon as I turned eighteen, we began going for drives in the countryside instead of him taking me directly home. By then, I was in love with a man almost the same age as my father."

Nancy paused, and with tears in her eyes, she went on.

"I came to know that every evening when my shift ended, we would go for a drive. I assumed it was kind of like a date. So, I would bring a change of clothes. My dad and I were quite poor, and I only had one pair of pants. To make them pretty, I would embroider flowers on them. We called them hipster bell bottoms back then." Nancy laughed and took a moment to ponder the visual. When she got back to her story, her voice had changed and taken a joyful lilt.

"Every time I came out of the bathroom in my 'driving around town' outfit, John would smile. He had a gorgeous smile, and I loved seeing it. Every morning before work, I would stitch a new flower on my pants. Each night before getting in his truck, he would make me twirl until he spotted my latest handiwork. When he did, he would laugh, pick me up and hold me tight, as if his life depended on it. And that was that, then we would go driving. Sometimes he drove me around town, but mostly we would go out on the backroads. While John drove, he would talk and I would sing to the radio when he grew silent. He told me his hopes and dreams and how much he loved farming. But never did he speak of his wife or children. When he was all done speaking, he would let me turn the volume up on his truck's radio, and I would sing all those old '60s songs, 'Chantilly Lace,' 'Rock Around the Clock,' 'Sixteen Candles' and so on…"

Dakota detected the delight in Nancy's voice, but he already knew there would not be a delightful ending.

When Nancy continued, her gaze shifted, and bowing her head ever so slightly, she looked down to the worn, chipped kitchen table and softened her voice. "Meanwhile, three months after my eighteenth birthday, we had sex. I didn't want to, but by then, I loved him so much, and he seemed to want me so badly…"

With more conviction, Nancy said, "Dakota, I have gone over that night a million times in my head, and I adore Darcie more than life itself. So I can't say I regret anything. Yet I do. After that night, everything changed. My romantic drives home turned into lusty sex romps in his pickup truck. No longer did he tell me stories or let me sing. In fact, after that first time, he refused to turn the radio on at all! Mrs. Fasp, John's wife, finally figured out John was screwing around. It was inevitable she'd find out. All his buddies knew, as did anyone who saw us at the diner. So here is where my story gets dramatic, like an episode of *Dallas*, or *Dynasty*. You see, from that first sexual encounter with John, I got pregnant, and when I started to show, Mrs. Fasp decided to pay me a little visit."

Dakota desperately wanted to look at his watch, but he did not dare. Even though he had animals to feed and a sick little girl he wanted to read to, he knew he could not take his attention away from Nancy. Nor could he leave just yet.

Nancy didn't notice Dakota shifting in his seat, or the detour of his attention from her story, so she continued.

"I kept working at Robinson's Diner, and like any foolish teenager, I thought John might marry me or leave his family for me. Of course, I was wrong.

"I will never forget going into my third trimester. I woke up to the sound of my apartment buzzer going off. Confused and feeling the weight of my expanding body, I lumbered out of bed, and when I pressed the intercom, it was none other than John's wife. She said I needed to let her up or come downstairs to talk to her immediately. So, I buzzed her in, panicked, and wished I hadn't. I was mortified at how my place looked. It was messy, and worse. I knew I looked like a flaky hippie girl. I can still remember what I was wearing—a large, oversized men's purple T-shirt. It stretched over my expectant belly, making me look large and cumbersome. While waiting for her to get out of the elevator, I put the kettle on, thinking we would sit down and have a nice chat. I was so naive and ignorant! And then I opened the door to a beautiful woman with long blond pigtail braids. She was wearing a red plaid shirt, faded blue jeans and scuffed-up cowboy boots. Mrs. Fasp was alarmingly beautiful. I was completely intimidated—she looked so wise and strong, and her tanned skin was fresh, but weathered, as if she had just been cutting firewood or mending fences. I said nothing. I was speechless, and remember Dakota, I was only eighteen."

Dakota felt like he was sitting on the edge of his seat, and he noticed the sun had dimmed outside, but he was transfixed by Nancy's sad tale.

Taking a breath and finishing her cup of tea, Nancy continued, "Was she ever mad! She spoke so harshly to me that spit was gathering in the corners of her mouth. She stood very close and had her finger pointing in my face. Anyway, I remember it so clearly, like it was yesterday. She said, 'What's done is done. The whole town knows you're a tramp, and no way in hell will you steal my husband. He will never leave our children or me, you got that!?'"

"I was trembling, Dakota, and I thought I might lose the baby right then and there out of pure and utter fear. Rebecca Fasp said, 'Now here's what we're gonna do. I will pay your rent and food. And you will quit working and never leave this apartment! My older son will bring you groceries, and when the baby is born, if it's a boy, you will give him to me. If it's a girl, you can keep her!'"

"And that was that. I did exactly what she said."

Dakota reached over and put his hand on Nancy's firmly clasped hands, no longer resting peacefully in her lap. With tears in her eyes and a voice lacking any vibrancy, Nancy continued.

"Halfway through my ninth month, when my water broke. I called the Fasp farm, and she came over and took me to the hospital. None of us knew I was having twins. And long story short, the Fasps took my baby boy, Darcie's twin brother. And the worst part is that I never fought to get him back. Yeah, they included Darcie in family functions, and they let me come too, and to keep the peace, I went. John avoided me at all costs, and I spent many years with a broken heart. Mostly over my naivety in loving the wrong man and my weakness in not fighting for my son. But as you know, the Fasps are a powerful family and practically own this town."

When Nancy finished and Dakota was getting up to leave, he said regretfully, "I am so sorry, Nancy, for the years that have passed, the missed opportunities for us to be friends. I should have reached out to you sooner. But I know, and the whole town knows, you were always a good mother. You raised a beautiful, kind, conscientious daughter who adores you."

He could see she had become tired and had started to cry. They were not delicate tears, but deep heartfelt sobs of pain. Dakota hugged her like she was his own mother, inspiring flashbacks of when his father died, and his whole family was devastated and heartbroken. Dakota thought of Nancy and the young girl she used to be. She had suffered a tremendous loss of innocence, resulting in a wide-eyed eighteen-year-old single mother, a fatherless child, and two siblings torn apart without an explanation.

Through her tears, Nancy said, "Thank you, Dakota, for listening and letting me speak my truth." Nancy then straightened up, wiped her tears on the sleeve of her sweater, and gave him a fragile half-smile. She concluded, "And the worst part of this long, drawn-out story is that I am very sick. I've been getting cancer treatment for the last three months."

Dakota had suspected there was more to Nancy's decision to come clean about her past. But he also knew she had become his new priority, and he would do whatever he could do to help her, and he told her so.

"I am so sorry, Nancy, but if it gives you peace of mind, I want to help. I can bring you meals and do errands, and you may have already noticed that I am a great listener." Dakota winked and smiled.

On his way out the door, Nancy sheepishly said, "Well, there is one favour you could do for me..." Pausing, she looked him directly in his eyes and said, "Could you please pick up Darcie at the airport next weekend?"

Dakota responded simply, "Yes, I would be happy to do that for you, Nancy."

Taking the stairs instead of the elevator, exhaustion washed over Dakota. As he walked out to his truck, he gathered his thoughts. Once sitting in the driver's seat, he quickly summarized and said to himself, *Go home, feed the animals, grab one of the puppies, take it to Branda, read to her, go home, make dinner and hit the hay.*

Dakota shuddered at the thought of the following weekend when he had two women to pick up at the airport, one he did not know, and another he wanted to get to know again.

***

As Susan walked out to the aerobics floor and onto the small stage at the front of the room, the first thing she did was check her makeup in the mirror, pull her scrunchie tighter in her ponytail, and make sure her thong leotard was evenly placed on her backside. Not only was Susan known for her intricate routines and patterns, but she was also admired for her many matching fitness outfits.

Tracy and Susan shopped together and sewed together. Or rather, Tracy did the sewing, and Susan picked out the stretch Lycra fabric for her outfits and polyester wool for her leg warmers. From paisley, stripes, and flowers, to ruffles, plunging necklines, and one-piece body suits, all of Susan's exercise clothes came in an array of fabrics and colours: orange and green neon, pastel pink, red pleather, and gold lamé sequins. To pull all her outfits together, Susan spent a small fortune on running shoes, Nike, Reebok, and her favourite, New Balance. All were purchased in Hillsprings.

She always made her own mixtapes and chose upbeat music from the '70s and '80s. Tracy kept Susan abreast of the fitness trends and cut out articles and fitness routines from various magazines. More recently, a video store had just opened up in town, so Tracy would take out exercise videos to keep her best friend and favourite aerobics instructor in the loop.

Tracy and Susan had gab sessions and seamstress parties, early-morning muffins and coffee dates, and evenings with wine for Susan and herbal tea for Tracy. All the while, Tracy kept busy sewing and knitting, while Susan managed her children. They talked about relationships with family, friends, and townsfolk, current events, music, movies, and Tracy's non-existent love life.

Many of Susan's followers and avid fitness participants begged her to open a fitness-themed store, selling exercise clothes and accessories. But Susan loved motherhood too much to forsake being there for her children. Besides, she was busy enough as it was.

So, Susan's clients crowned her the best dressed, fittest, and most well-loved instructor in the continuously growing town of MeadowBrook. She had the most well-attended classes, and could not walk down the street without getting noticed. Dwayne would often tease her that she was the next best thing to a movie star, and he was proud to be her behind-the-scenes husband.

Three weeks before the reunion, Susan made a hair appointment. She was dismayed with the few grey hairs that were already coming in and wanted her blond locks back, determined to showcase how she had hardly aged in the ten years since graduation. Besides, she was proud of her fitness instructor figure, newspaper columnist brain, and happy ending story to her rocky beginning with Dwayne.

Two weeks before the reunion, Susan was in town doing her usual Saturday morning errands after her Buns and Bellies class. She dropped one child off at Karate lessons and another at ballet class. She felt pleased knowing her two other children, the oldest and youngest, were in good hands with their dad. Dwayne had taken their ten-year-old son to his soccer game and brought their toddler with him.

Susan adored how Dwayne cared for her and their four children. She noted how he prepared the baby's sippy cup, poured Cheerios in a small Tupperware container, and filled the diaper bag with everything needed to ensure a happy little one. She watched him meticulously cut two dozen oranges for their son's soccer team and then wink and whisper to her upon leaving, "Don't forget, you get one of my specialty massages tonight. I hope you'll be ready!"

Susan laughed and gave Dwayne a gentle shove, purring like a cat, "Ooh, you better believe I'll be ready. Bring it on, my great big stud muffin!"

Saying goodbye and kissing him on the lips, Susan's heart swelled, and she felt like the luckiest working wife and mother in the world.

After returning books to the library and dropping off the dry cleaning, Susan made her way back to their new Ford Escort. Before getting in, she spotted a familiar man walking toward her. Stopping in her tracks, she could hardly contain her smile and desire to holler out his name. She watched and waited excitedly for eye contact. As soon as he saw her, he picked up his pace and smiled from ear to ear. When he was two feet in front of her, he reached out and took both her hands in his. Tim said in a warm, happy tone, "Oh my god, Susan Jillian! How the hell are you?"

Before responding, Susan realized she was relieved that Tim had never been her boyfriend. She had always suspected he was not into girls, at least not like the rest of the basketball team. It always appeared odd that he often had a girlfriend but never seemed into them. Now being older, wiser, and more worldly, Susan could see he was the best dressed and most perfectly coiffed man she had ever seen. Then she wondered if he was finally confident and out in the open about who he was.

When she took a closer look, Susan admired Tim's slim, fit physique, eye-popping yellow Hawaiian shirt, rolled-up faded blue jeans, and huarache sandals. He looked completely out of place on Main Street, and the newspaper columnist in her loved the strange looks he was getting from people walking past. Consequently, Sarcastically Susan had another story brewing. Susan felt slightly breathless standing only inches away from the once-loved MeadowBrook High basketball star.

Feeling Tim's hands firmly grip hers, Susan let out a shriek of gladness, "TIM! How great to see you! When I saw you walking toward me, I couldn't help but feel relieved that we never hooked up!" They both laughed wholeheartedly and then hugged.

Susan knew she had thirty minutes before she needed to pick up her kids, and she had planned to go for a tan at the salon. Instead, she suggested they go for a coffee.

Tim said he had just been at Robinson's Diner the night before with his little sister, so Susan suggested a new café near the ballet studio.

She insisted on treating him, and Tim accepted, comforted to be saving the money he didn't have. Not yet a successful actor, his cash flow was still a little tight. He felt so at ease with Susan that he ordered a piece of cherry pie with his coffee and was ready to confide in her.

Sitting across from the gorgeous man from her past, Susan delved into her story first. She spoke about getting pregnant, foolishly attempting to break free from her parents, and the early years of her marriage, struggling with a new baby and a man she hardly knew. She spent time venting about the stereotypical high school persona she felt was inflicted upon her. She finished by describing her transformation into a fitness instructor, newspaper columnist, and women's rights activist, and then said, "And here I am ten years and four kids later, and I can honestly say I am content and happy! Now, what about you?"

Before Tim could chime in, Susan looked at her watch, and in a hurried, dismayed voice, she said, "Oh no, I've taken up all of our time. It's so good to see you, but I am so sorry Tim, I have to go and pick up my kids. Could we please do this again?"

Tim felt a combination of disappointment and benevolence. He had wanted to share everything about himself with Susan. Instead, not showing how displeased he was, Tim covered up by saying, "Oh yes, of course, I totally understand. But before you go, I must tell you that I am an actor now, and I'm performing in the hit stage production of *Fame* in Florida next month!"

Susan felt horrible that she had used up all their time talking about herself and yet was elated to hear Tim's exciting announcement. As she was getting up to leave, she said pleadingly, "Please come for dinner at my place one night soon, will you? Dwayne has to go away on a farm equipment-buying trip. How does Tuesday night sound? I live near your sister's apartment building in a little yellow house on Callaghan Avenue. You can't miss it. What do you say…six p.m. next Tuesday?"

Tim said, "Yes, I would love to. I'll bring the wine—red or white?"

Clapping her hands as if it was the happiest news she had ever heard, Susan said, "Oh, wonderful! White, of course. It's much fresher and nicer in this warm weather." On that note, Susan waved goodbye as she stepped into the ballet studio next door. Instantly her little pink ballerina daughter jumped into her arms.

She greeted her daughter with a cuddle and laughter and then wondered if her old school chum would let her interview him, thinking how controversial a potential coming-out story would be for the narrow-minded town of MeadowBrook. When Susan thought more in-depth about composing a story around Tim, she remembered how she had to fight to get her job and work even harder to keep it.

She and Tracy often discussed how the1980s brought a slew of influential women, from Madonna to Margaret Thatcher, and how feminist activists created impactful public campaigns addressing sexism in music and art. They brought to the surface in-depth conversations on racism and classism. Susan felt that the early 1980s was when women everywhere were getting things done, and she was honoured to be a part of a new revolution. She decided her next article would be titled, "Change Can Be Happy and Exciting, as Well as Messy and Complicated."

Susan felt nostalgic and remembered her first write-up after being hired at the *Gazette,* titled, "It's Not Just About Side Ponytails and Shoulder Pads." She remembered delving into the significance of the movie *9 to 5*, about an unlikely trio of secretaries played by Dolly Parton, Jane Fonda, and Lily Tomlin. She stated, "Few films can address a serious issue with such humour. However, justice is rarely served in real life as it is in *9 to 5* when all three women join forces to give their pig of a boss a taste of his own medicine. This movie remains a feminist victory for telling the stories of the women who rarely get heard."

Her readers wrote letters to the editor praising Susan's bravery and candor. Many townspeople petitioned to have the Starlight movie theatre bring in the film *9 to 5,* and the new local art gallery hosted an exhibit of male nudes.

Dwayne took it upon himself to cut out every story Susan wrote and place them in photo albums. He often told her how proud he was of her, and local residents got tired of how he endlessly bragged about her many accomplishments. Even his coworkers, who were all men at Fasp Farms, often whispered to one another to never bring up the topic of wives, as Dwayne would never shut up about his.

In retrospect, Susan and Dwayne did have their fair share of struggles, especially early on. Neither knew very much about babies, late-night feedings, housework, and meal preparation. Then came a mortgage, house repairs, and keeping up the yard.

But Susan often shared with Tracy that she felt her marriage had a shooting chance because Dwayne had been raised by a single mother. He saw how hard his mother worked and consequently helped with the chores and anything else he could do around the house to make life easier. Dwayne's mother, in turn, taught him how to cook easy meals, how to treat a woman, and how to manage his money from his A&W job where he flipped burgers.

All of which prompted another controversial topic written by Sarcastic Susan. Her article began with two questions to get her readers' attention, "Is family structure an essential correlate of a boy's behavioural deficit?" followed by "Is it true, if boys are raised outside of a traditional family, they fare poorly?" Susan went on to say, "Get your mind out of the 'Father Knows Best' mentality, people!"

Susan had spent hours researching case studies and learned that single mothers spent no less time caring for their children. They did, however, do less housework than the moms with husbands, and got more leisure time and sleep. What made Susan's article the most contentious were her suggestions that performing as a wife in the kitchen and the bedroom took up a lot of time and that single mothers had no need to put on such a show.

Susan concluded the article with her own personal experiences, stating, "Having married a man who was raised by a single mother, I can honestly say that my husband can cook, clean, coach soccer, and bring home the bacon! And he does very nicely behind closed doors, too. So, hats off to all the single mothers out there!"

Needless to say, Susan's parents were aghast, and Dwayne's mother was flattered and appreciated the pat on the back. Therefore, over the years, Susan gravitated to her husband's mother, aunts and uncles, cousins and grandparents, rather than her own.

That night, after running into Tim, Susan shared the events of her day with Dwayne. She first talked about the kids and their activities, and that the dry cleaners had raised their prices. Then she said in a teasing manner, "You will never guess who I bumped into today." Dwayne was stumped, so Susan continued, "Well, he just happened to be the best-looking jock in our grad class." Still without a clue, Susan exclaimed, "Dwayne! You know him! Does the name Tim Barnes ring a bell? And boy has he ever changed!"

Dwayne said, "Oh, that's really neat, Suzie, but how has he changed? What, did he gain a bunch of weight? Lose all his hair?" In response, Susan just rolled her eyes and smiled.

At first, Dwayne doubted Susan's speculation regarding Tim's lifestyle. But he did wholeheartedly agree that Susan should have him over for dinner to learn more while he was away on the farm equipment-buying trip. As she slathered her corn with extra butter, Susan admiringly reflected on her husband's easy-going persona and loved how he seemingly did not have a jealous bone in his body.

The following week while Dwayne was away, Susan taught her fitness classes, planned her next newspaper story, took care of the kids, and had Tim over for dinner.

To give them more privacy, Susan asked Tracy if she could look after her oldest, and then asked Dwayne's mom if she could take the younger three.

Tracy was happy for the distraction from all the reunion plans and setup, so she happily took Susan and Dwayne's oldest son to the movie *Big* with Tom Hanks. Even though the storyline sounded suitable, Tracy was mortified when the main character, Josh Baskin, played by Tom Hanks, developed a love interest. She almost walked right out of the theatre, but instead, she covered the eyes of ten-year-old Dwayne Jr. during the racier parts.

Meanwhile, Tracy wished she could be a fly on the wall and could hardly wait for Susan's late-night follow-up phone call after her dinner with Tim.

By the time Tim arrived, Susan was exhausted. She had taught an early morning aerobics class, and because it was the summer holidays, she'd had all four children underfoot for most of the day. *Thank god for outdoor sprinklers and water guns,* she thought.

Tim brought flowers, Pinot Grigio, and a magazine layout of when the whole theatre company for the Florida production of *Fame* was interviewed by *People* magazine.

Over a glass of the crisp white wine, Tim began to unravel his story. He delved deep into his relationship with his father, the physical abuse he experienced as a child and verbal abuse as a teenager. Susan listened intently, nodding her head at all the appropriate moments and welling up with tears when visualizing the little boy that Tim used to be.

Over a simple dinner of spinach salad and garlic toast, Tim shared his years as a bartender and the endless hours of struggling as a movie extra. Susan delighted in his stories of Hollywood Boulevard, Universal Studios, and Venice Beach. But just when Susan thought Tim was going to get to the unpretentious heart of the matter, her three youngest children came bursting through the doors. When Susan looked at the dining room clock, she gasped and said, "Geez, where did all the time go?"

Apologizing to Tim, Susan said, "I'm so sorry, hon, I have to get these young'uns to bed, or there'll be hell to pay tomorrow."

Tim understood, and as he was putting on his running shoes to leave, Tracy arrived at the door with Dwayne Jr. She was thrilled to see Tim and gushed over how handsome he had become.

Waving goodbye, Tim said, "I look forward to seeing you both this Saturday night at the reunion!"

Later that week, a few days before the reunion, a knock came on Susan's door, and it just happened to be her mother. Taken aback, Susan asked what she wanted. With her head tilted upward and nose in the air, Susan's mother said, "I'll have you know the whole town's talking about you and that Tim Barnes fella! Half of MeadowBrook saw you fawning all over him in that new overpriced coffee shop!"

Susan responded, "First of all, Mother, where do you get off on not calling first? Secondly, you should know by now that I do not give a rat's ass about what anyone thinks in this town, so you can go shove your small-town gossip where the sun don't shine!"

Just before she slammed the door in her mother's face, she finished with, "So why don't you go tell all your busy bodies that I'm sleeping with the entire basketball team and I can hardly wait for the reunion? It sure will be a great workout hooking up with all those luscious men from my sordid past!"

As Susan's mother stomped off, her disgruntled daughter—mother of four and feminist—ran to the telephone to gleefully tell her dearest friend Tracy how she told her mom to back off.

***

Tracy always got up early and worked late, especially since the reunion was just around the corner.

Her typical day started with attending her best friend Susan's 7:00 a.m. high-impact fitness class, followed by a quick shower at the gym. Her grooming consisted of pulling her wet hair up in a high ponytail; a thick application of her favourite lipstick, Sugar and Spice; and a light coat of brown mascara.

On most work days, Tracy dressed in a simple skirt and sweater set, and on the weekends, stirrup pants and a cozy sweatshirt. Her favourite stores were Cotton Ginny and the Eaton's department store, both in the next town over, but she rarely shopped because she rarely had the time.

Tracy preferred to walk everywhere, and after her early morning routine, she would pick up a banana-chocolate chip muffin from the Edelweiss Bakery. Upon arriving at work, she always brewed a fresh pot of coffee with cinnamon, for herself, customers, friends, and anyone wanting a place to chat. Her well-used Betty Boop coffee mug, a gift from one of her long-standing clients, was always filled with black coffee and Splenda. It often went cold, so Tracy perpetually heated it up in the microwave she had in the back room.

She fondly and frequently thought of her father's automotive shop. He had purchased a Melita coffee maker back in the 1960s and brought in benches for all the old fogeys of MeadowBrook to sit a spell and shoot the breeze.

She wondered, *If a child grows up similar to their parents, both in behaviour and physical characteristics, will they also make the same mistakes?* She hoped to be more like her father than her mother, even though everyone said Eunice and Tracy were two peas in a pod. Tracy was determined not to follow in her mother's footsteps with her blatant infidelity and disregard for her husband.

After the coffee brewed, Tracy regularly put out a plate of cookies from the Edelweiss Bakery. Her routine never changed. She had a specific order and never faltered or mixed anything up.

After clicking the coffee ON switch, she turned on the radio next, tuned to a local station of mostly 1960s music and the local news. She opened the blinds and put the doorstop under the heavy glass door—a large rock painted with pink cherry blossoms, and also a gift from a client. Tracy liked to keep the door open as a marketing tactic, winter, spring, summer and fall. She believed it to be welcoming and friendly. Plus, she knew the smell of coffee could lure people inside. Her favourite quote by John Barrymore was written in calligraphy on a pink sign above the door, *"Happiness often sneaks in through a door you didn't know you left open."*

Completing her opening routine, Tracy would drag the life-size cardboard cutout of herself onto the sidewalk. This had been a parting gift when she was highlighted in a women's business magazine. It was a replica of her appearance on the cover. All five feet two inches, arms folded, head tilted to the side, smiling warmly, with her well-known catchphrase, *"Events by Tracy— 'Let me plan your next event, so you don't have to!'»*

After checking her daily calendar and familiarizing herself with upcoming events, she dished out the orders. Events by Tracy employed sixteen staff members—four full-time, and twelve part-time high school students for the many catered events. However, with thirteen franchise locations, Tracy had a full plate.

She loved every aspect of her business—opening the doors in the morning, making her shop comfy, creating unique and diverse events, and visiting all her franchise locations to ensure quality and consistency, and to collect franchise fees.

Two weeks before the high school reunion, she had the worst and best day of her life, all rolled into one extremely hectic day.

Tracy woke up early like any other day and grabbed the bag she had packed the night before to walk to the fitness studio. The first thing to go wrong was that Susan was absent and had a substitute teaching her class. The fill-in instructor could not get the stereo working, was far too bubbly and messed up on all her choreographed routines. She was ultimately off on her timing and had improper form for her squats. Tracy had half a mind to walk right off the exercise floor, but thought twice about it, as she did not want to be labelled rude.

After the class, Tracy had a cold shower because the hot water was not working. And then, when she was about to do her face, her favourite lipstick broke off and rolled on the floor underneath the sink. When she retrieved it, it was covered in dirt, dust, and, undoubtedly, horrendous germs undetectable to the naked eye. She threw it in the garbage with such force that she pulled something on her shoulder and screamed out loud, "OUCH, dang it!"

Making do with shampoo that would not lather due to the cold water and then no lipstick, Tracy dressed and made her way to the bakery. To her dismay, her chocolate chip banana muffins were completely devoid of chocolate. It was explained to her that the owner forgot to replenish their stock of chocolate chips.

This blunder appalled Tracy, as she could not fathom doing such a thing in her own business. She was a diligent, organized business owner and knew that a mishap like that would reflect poorly on her company. She could lose a client, and clients were money. Satisfied, happy people would spread the word and become repeat customers. Unsatisfied clients would not. Tracy made sure her mission statement—"*The key to a successful business is to prioritize your service and to service your priorities*"—was clearly stated in her franchise manuals and part of her training program.

Once at the shop, Tracy quickly discovered there was no power; the electricity had gone out and had not yet been restored. Consequently, she could not prepare coffee or turn the radio on. Both offered a welcoming appeal to her business and were greatly missed as part of her morning routine.

Summarizing how her day was shaping up, Tracy decided to go home, something she had never done before. Considering that she needed a moment to regroup, calm her nerves, and hope the afternoon would be better if she had a do-over, she closed the blinds, brought in her life-size sign, and before leaving, wrote a note in her eloquent handwriting: "*Hello, I have briefly stepped out and will be back at 2:00 p.m. Please come back or call my pager.*"

Fortunately or unfortunately, depending on how one looked at it, since the day was Friday, no staff members were there because, to keep everyone happy, she gave them one day off a week.

Tracy walked home, annoyed with everything and everyone. As soon as she entered the door of her well-kept, sunny apartment, she phoned Susan to see if she was okay, asking why she didn't teach her exercise class that morning. Susan enthusiastically responded, "Oh yes, I am more than okay! Dwayne wanted to spend the morning in bed with me, and you know, hubba-hubba ding dong!"

Tracy replied, "Eww, way too much information, Sue!" With that, she curtly said goodbye and hung up.

Still exasperated, Tracy made her way to her exquisitely decorated bathroom and admired the pink fluffy towels, sparkling clean appliances, and shower curtain with pink geraniums on it. She exhaled, feeling considerably better, and turned on a piping hot shower. While letting the pulsating hot water beat down on her shoulders, Tracy repeated her feel-good mantra, "Tracy, you are beautifully and wonderfully made. Don't sweat the small stuff! Tracy, you are beautifully and wonderfully made. Don't sweat the small stuff! Tracy, you are beautifully and wonderfully made. Don't sweat the small stuff..."

Drying off and slathering on Jergens body lotion, she put on a new outfit, a light grey pleated knee-length skirt, crisp white blouse, her favourite penny loafers and white knee socks. She then applied fresh mascara and found a pastel pink scrunchie for her high ponytail.

After tidying up her bathroom, she felt ready to face the day and just about anything that may come her way. Tracy left and walked down the three flights, after rechecking three times that she carefully locked her door.

Taking a slight detour on her way back to work, she walked into Barney's department store and purchased a brand-new lipstick. To make herself feel even better, she also purchased a pink sweater—a soft, pastel pink button-up cardigan with cream-coloured pearly buttons. After paying for it with cash, she wore it right out the door.

Just before leaving, she bumped into Brad, Amanda's husband. Saying a quick hello, Tracy wondered what Amanda saw in him, as she thought he was a bit of a louse, and the cute high school athlete nicknamed "Spot" could have done much better.

Walking back to her office, Tracy felt one hundred percent better and proud of herself for making a complete turnaround. She finally felt like she could breathe, and with each step, Tracy noticed and appreciated her surroundings. The day had gotten warmer. She was reminded that June was her favourite month. Almost every flower was in bloom, and the varying trees that lined Main Street were full. MeadowBrook was alive.

Tracy enjoyed hearing tidbits of conversations as she walked past various townspeople: "Oh yes, he became terribly ill. We think it was the outdated meat from the Frugal…Well, honestly, if she doesn't graduate, there will be hell to pay…My goodness, Rochelle! You look pretty as a picture today." Tracy revelled in the energy of others.

Decidedly, she had become her old self again and picked up her pace to prove it. The bad morning was over. The new leaf she turned over made her determined to have a beautiful, productive afternoon. Consequently, her demeanour and no-nonsense way of thinking had been restored. Tracy knew that nothing stayed the same. A moment, an hour, or a day could continually be reshaped or turned on its axis.

She had decided that when she returned to the office, she would head straight to the blackboard at the back, and in pink chalk, she would write, *"If the day is grey, a colourful horizon is behind the next cloud. Sometimes we just need a do-over."*

Tracy had a habit of talking to herself. Not out loud, just a quiet murmur that helped her sort through her thoughts. She made lists in her head, practiced conversations, and went over plans and projects. Sometimes she wondered if her lips were moving; other times, she did not care what anyone thought.

Just a few doors away from her shop, lost in her thoughts and quiet murmurs, with her head down and a sure-footed stride, Tracy was taken aback when she heard someone holler, "Hey, good looking, whatcha got cookin'?!"

Momentarily bewildered, the out-of-context appearance of Kent in a fancy sports car stopped Tracy in her steps. Then completely out of character, Tracy squealed in excitement, "Oh my gosh! Kent Gordon, is that really you?!"

Responding in his usual confident style, he said, "You better believe it's me, sweetheart. Now hop in and let's go!"

Usually, Tracy's better judgment would say she had to work, but on this warm June afternoon, Tracy unexpectedly threw all caution to the wind and opened the passenger side of Kent's mother's Porsche. With enthusiasm, she said, "Let's go to Robinson's for a coffee. We need to talk!"

Getting in the car, they did not embrace but smiled warmly. Both wondered what the other was thinking and hoped they were thinking the same thing.

Kent revved the engine as he hit the gas pedal, while Tracy loosened her ponytail to allow her long brown hair to blow freely. The gusts of warm, early summer air swept in and around the car from the open sunroof, and Tracy had never felt so free and daring. Kent glanced over at her, gunned the car and yelled, "YIPPEE-KI YAY!!" Tracy laughed and whispered a silent prayer, "*Thank you, God.*"

***

Dakota held up two signs while standing at the baggage claim area of the Hillsprings airport. One said "DARCIE RICHMOND" and the other said "PATTY KRAKATOYA."

He was still miffed that Mr. Krakatoya had asked for a favour. Dakota had always had a hard time saying no, and he just wanted to pick up Darcie and only Darcie. He felt they needed time alone since they had the past ten years to talk about. On the other hand, Dakota thought that Patty might be a sound interference to keep things between him and Darcie light.

Within minutes of his arrival, a tall, suntanned, blond woman approached. He quickly looked behind himself and then realized it must be Patty Krakatoya. He had no memory of her from school, but she seemed to recognize him, plus her name was on his sign.

Dakota then noticed her trepidation, so he spoke quickly with a friendly tone. "Hey Patty, it's me, Dakota Hillsman. Your dad stopped by my work, as he knew I was picking up Darcie Richmond at the airport. He asked me to give you a ride back to MeadowBrook too."

Bewildered and disappointed, Patty responded, "But wait, where's my mom and dad? My dad said they'd be here."

Dakota could see that she was upset, so he tried to calm her, but while speaking, his voice slowed because he spotted Darcie. He was instantly in awe of her casual beauty. Her hair was longer. The khaki army-style jacket she was wearing made her eyes seem greener. He almost started laughing, while bursting with joy at the very sight of her, and then remembered he was in mid-sentence with Patty, "Well, yeah, I'm not exactly sure why they couldn't be here, but something came up with your mom and..." He stopped speaking.

Darcie saw him, gasped, smiled and then laughed.

She had no idea Dakota was coming, and it scared her at first, as she thought his appearance meant something may have happened to her mother. She started running toward him—just dropped everything and ran. He instinctively held his arms open.

At that moment, Patty noticed what was going on and became annoyed. She said loudly, "Oh, that's just great!"

She remembered them all being seventeen, ten years earlier and thought about Janis Ian singing about beauty queens and clear-skinned smiles, ravaged faces lacking social graces. Patty was instantly lost in the past memories of all the valentines that never came...

Neither Dakota nor Darcie gave any mind to Patty. They were enthralled with one another. Dakota placed his hands on the sides of Darcie's face, and she reciprocated. They stared and smiled, rocking back and forth. Then they embraced as if the world had come to an end and they were the last two humans standing.

Patty had enough and blurted out, "Get a room already!" And then she followed up with, "Um yeah, can we get going?!"

Patty's tone and close presence interrupted the homecoming, and in unison, Dakota and Darcie apologized. They both laughed and then Darcie started to cry, only for Patty to say, "Oh my god, is this really happening?!"

Finally, Dakota looked at Patty and said, "Oh my goodness, so sorry, Patty. It's just that we have missed each other so much, and well, it's been a long time, and…"

Patty could not stand it anymore. She needed and wanted Dakota to stop talking. She was worried about her parents and equally envious of the couple before her. She said, "Never mind, just forget about it. Can we please get going? And for the record, my name is not Patty anymore, it's Patricia!"

With that, Dakota grabbed Patty's bags in one hand and Darcie's hand in the other. She only had a backpack and a guitar but said they would need to pick up her trunks at the cargo desk, as she had brought all of her belongings. Darcie added, "I'm home for good." Then it was Dakota's turn to cry.

Patty fell in behind the two lovebirds. She had difficulty being mad as she observed how in love they were and they were undoubtedly the kindest people she had ever met.

After picking up Darcie's trunks, the three became silent. The Hillsprings airport was still relatively small, so Dakota had pulled his vehicle up front. Making their way out to his truck and watching while Dakota single-handedly hoisted Darcie's belongings into the back, the two women stood as if waiting to board a ride at the fair. Patty reluctantly, and Darcie eagerly.

As they all piled into Dakota's truck for the three-hour drive to MeadowBrook, Patty knew her place would be as close to the window on the passenger side as she could get. She prepared herself to sit in silence while the obvious couple canoodled. She worried they might get into a head-on collision from the pure and utter distraction of the driver.

The warmth of the afternoon matched the mood as everyone settled in for the long drive, each going over separate thoughts. Dakota was at a loss for words, Darcie wanted to savour the moment, and Patty was conflicted. She knew her mother had messed up again, and yet she was excited to show MeadowBrook,. and a certain someone, her new self. She pondered changing her last name in preparation for becoming a famous news reporter.

Patty only knew Darcie and Dakota from their popular high school image, so it was odd to be in the same vehicle with them ten years after the fact. She then thought of her own hopes to find fame as a TV personality, so in the stillness of strangers, Patty went on privately practicing in her head a more prestigious name for herself.

She sampled *Patricia Dakota* and *Patricia Darcie* and then smiled inwardly at the silliness of it all.

In the course of time, Darcie broke the silence and unexpectedly asked Patty what she had been up to all these years. Instantly, Patty wished the couple beside her would just leave her alone; she was totally up for being ignored. But out of sheer politeness, surprising even herself, Patty launched into her story about leaving MeadowBrook, going to broadcasting school and meeting Albert. As her story took shape, so did her self-confidence.

Both Darcie and Dakota were a receptive audience, nodding at all the right times, smiling and acting like they were truly interested and impressed.

The picture that Patty painted left out her transformation from a socially awkward, unfashionable school geek, and went straight to being a California beachball champion and soon-to-be popular news anchor.

By the time they pulled up to her parents' home, Patty had relaxed and decided that maybe she had just made some unlikely new friends. Pleased with herself, she thanked Dakota for the ride, and as she walked up the small, curved path to her childhood home, she stopped for a moment and realized she did not reciprocate the interest in either one of their lives.

***

Since Dakota had picked Darcie up at the airport, they'd become inseparable. They couldn't get enough of each other and took on the role of being the only ones in the room. Walking down Main Street, they held hands. Sitting at Robinson's, they stared into each other's eyes, and driving around town, Dakota rested his hand on Darcie's knee.

Neither one of them really wanted to attend the reunion, although, in some ways, they both felt obligated. Dakota because he worked at the school, and Darcie because she hoped Johnny would be there.

Meanwhile, they felt complete; each had found the other and could not think of anyone else they wanted to spend the rest of their lives with.

They spent hours talking, unfolding the past and extracting what went wrong. High school now seemed like it had been a small insignificant window of time, a time of beginnings, falling in love, and a sad goodbye, even though farewells were never spoken.

As Darcie and Dakota spoke well into the night, she reminisced and said, "Grade 9 until Grade 12 will be etched in my heart forever."

Dakota agreed and added, "Yeah, but am I ever glad I grew up!"

They both laughed, and Darcie concurred, "We are so much more mature, and I'm pretty sure we know what we want by now." She then apologized for leaving him. He said he was sorry for never trying to find her.

Being reunited, and more seasoned in life, Darcie and Dakota simultaneously decided they were ready to settle down. It was almost as if no time had passed and yet they were aware that maybe they had missed out on ten valuable years of togetherness.

Shifting gears from their love story, it still pained Darcie that Johnny was off galivanting around the world. When her mother shared the story of how she came to be and that Johnny was her brother, she realized she had many emotions wrapped around the Fasp family. When she thought of the father she never knew as a daddy, Darcie reacted with a tugging at her heart. The pulling and twisting sensation came with a heated feeling of betrayal and an agonizing sense of missed opportunities. Darcie could only visualize John Fasp as a coward, disguised as a successful man about town—a highly acclaimed chicken farmer, dominant and pig-headed. The Fasp family farm brought reminders of Christmas presents, peach pie and tractor rides.

Darcie's thoughts flipped back and forth from her biological father to the best friend she could finally call her brother. She hoped Johnny was coming home for the reunion but doubted it. From the sound of things, he was very angry when he left, so she speculated *"Why would he?"*

***

Riding the bus from Hillsprings to MeadowBrook, Johnny slept, while Margarita held his hand and sat as close to him as she could. She would have climbed on top of him, like a little girl sitting on her grandfather's lap for warmth, security, and protection, but thought better of it.

Instead, she snuggled in close and felt him sleep. Except that Johnny's slow and steady, rhythmic breathing did not soothe her like it usually did back in Morocco. Margarita had no interest in looking out the window at the unchanging wheat fields and rolling hills. Instead, she looked at the back of the bus seat in front of her while her legs twitched, reminiscent of the long flight. Margarita's empty belly reminded her of the distasteful airplane food she could not get down as she increasingly became more nauseous. No matter how tightly she tried to hang on to Johnny, she felt like she was slipping.

The closer they travelled to his past, the more fragile her future became.

Margarita decided to comfort herself with daydreams. She thought back to the morning they first met in the youth hostel and how she had watched Johnny sleep from across the room, admiring his shaggy long blond hair, whiskers, and wrinkled clothing. She wondered if he was sick or hungover, noting how she wanted to take care of him. Margarita knew while sitting on that bed a short distance from Johnny, that he was a good, kind person, even before they officially met. When he woke up, his smile was wide, and his blue eyes drew her in like a mesmerizing spell on her heart. Margarita felt happy and giddy when Johnny spoke, and she took it to be love at first sight.

Now three months later, Margarita had grown weary of travelling on an air-conditioned bus through the middle of nowhere. Unexpectantly, Johnny had grown quiet and unapproachable. Her three months of joy had been replaced with fear; lightness had turned to longing and confidence to insecurity.

Margarita wondered if there was such a thing as kismet, and if so, hers had a hidden agenda. If her heart was the moon, Johnny's new behaviour was an eclipse.

When the bus driver's voice came over the intercom, Margarita nudged Johnny awake and softly said, "Hey, wake up sleepy head. You slept the whole way. I think we are here now." Johnny was initially confused, and when her sweet open face and tousled curls came into focus, he kissed her familiar freckles on the bridge of her nose, smiled and pulled her close. Margarita exhaled like she had been holding her breath, and then she smiled up at Johnny and received his kisses willingly.

"MeadowBrook—next stop, and the last stop. Please take all your belongings, including your garbage and any mess you made. I'm not your mother!!"

It was like a rude awakening and a smack in the face, with the harsh reality of what would come next. Johnny felt sick to his stomach. He stood up too briskly, bumped his head on the overhead rack, and then said abruptly, "C'mon, we're here. Get out, get out, go!"

Never before had Johnny spoken so sternly to Margarita. She became flustered and then frantic. It seemed she could not get out of his way fast enough, so she fell down in the aisle. Tears stung her eyes as he pushed past her. She immediately thought of their baby inside of her.

Once off the bus, Johnny ran to the closest garbage can and threw up.

A stranger helped Margarita up and then muttered under his breath, "What a jerk!" She realized the other passenger didn't know she and Johnny were together.

Margarita found Johnny and asked if he was okay. He could only nod, then Johnny started hating himself. He was sorry they came and even sorrier that he brought her.

"I am so sorry, babe. I'm just so effing stupid." Johnny couldn't bring himself to swear in front of Margarita.

She was too beautiful, like a porcelain doll, pure and perfect. He thought of his brothers and farm life and how swearing was their family's common language. Even his mother swore. He used to think it was cool. Now he was embarrassed at the thought of it.

Johnny said nothing, and neither did Margarita. Instead, he took her hand and thought it felt like a child's, tiny and soft. Instantly her fingers curled around his like a clamp, and he instinctively knew she was scared, which only validated his feelings of remorse.

Johnny led her to a pay phone and called his oldest brother, the one he was closest to. After a few rings, Michael picked up, and Johnny said, "Hey, it's me. Can you come get me? I mean, come get us?"

Johnny's brother Michael had been the first to get married, build a house and have two kids. He was also the only one in the family Johnny trusted, especially since his grandmother had died, which reminded him of how he had fled without saying goodbye. The day was now just a memory in his rearview mirror, a burning grow-op and the disappointed face of the father he now despised; the jumbled voices of his family all hollering at the same time and then his mindset to split and go AWOL.

Michael was initially surprised to hear Johnny's voice, then happy. He yelled to his wife, "Hey, Johnny's back in town! I gotta run into town and get him. He's got some girl with him, so don't say anything to Pa yet. Be back in twenty minutes—and they might be hungry!"

Turning his attention back to Johnny, Michael said, "Hang tight. I'll be there in ten minutes. Go stand by the city bus loop."

Replacing the receiver, Johnny let out a sigh of relief and turned to Margarita and apologized. He pleaded with her to forgive him, and then paused, as he knew things would be worsening soon.

Right then and there, Johnny decided that once home, he would get Margarita settled in his house, run her a bubble bath, and go speak to his father alone.

However, Johnny's plans to shield Margarita from his father's wrath were all for naught, because it was not just his dad she needed protecting from. After embracing his brother and introducing him to Margarita, he learned his brother was a racist just by the way he looked her up and down and then said nothing, completely disregarding her.

Meanwhile, Margarita sat in the middle of the two men, Johnny's hand on her leg and his brother sitting as close to the driver's side door as he could. Staring straight ahead, she failed to notice the pristine countryside and vast farmland. Instead, she was heartbroken that Johnny's family seemed to have so many problems. She had never experienced secrets, infidelity, or lies in her family, which only made her miss them even more.

In contrast, Margarita's family would have received Johnny with open arms. They would have embraced him, fed him, and insisted he play his guitar. She smiled at the thought of her grandmother coaxing him to dance with her.

Margarita adored her family's values and strong faith in God. But more than anything, they respected each other and would do anything to keep their family safe and united.

The Fasps were the opposite of everything her family stood for. She hoped Johnny was an exception.

The conversation in the truck on the way to the farm was heated. Michael was happy to see his brother but mad at how he had left. He took no notice of Margarita and only spoke directly to Johnny.

"First off, where the hell have you been? Ma has been worried sick about you! We had a funeral for Granny; we all spoke, Pa gave the eulogy, and practically the whole town came out! Besides, you were always her favourite! What the fuck is wrong with you?"

For the duration of his brother's rant, Johnny was embarrassed by Michael's swearing even though they had grown up with foul language laced into every conversation. He looked down at Margarita's hand and noticed that his grip had become tighter.

As they pulled into the Fasp Farm's main gates, the crunching gravel underneath the heavy 4 X 4 pickup sounded thunderous. When Michael turned the ignition off, the dead silence was ominous. Before getting out of the truck, Johnny said, "Hey Mike, you know Dad was a two-timing bastard, right? I didn't get a chance to be a proper brother to my sister Darcie. And what about Nancy? You do realize she's my biological mother. His secrets and lies messed me up, man! I thought you would be on my side, but from what you're saying, I guess you've become like the others!"

Margarita slid out of the seat and followed behind Johnny. She felt small and insignificant. Turning around, Johnny looked back at his brother and said more calmly, "I'll talk to ya later."

Michael loved his younger brother but was equally annoyed with him. He wanted him to grow up and cut the crap, be a man, and he wondered who the floozy was that he brought home, and why. He thought she looked like a twelve-year-old. He was bewildered as to what nationality she was, and then with a shrug of his shoulders, he decided not to think about it any further.

Johnny's front porch had not been swept in months. The dust gathered in the entranceway, and when he opened the front door, it swirled up as if to greet them, filthy and menacing.

Before Johnny could give Margarita a tour of the home he had built with his brothers and father, he pulled her close and asked her if she wanted to leave. He suggested they fly to Argentina asap and forget everyone—MeadowBrook, the reunion, his sister, and especially his family.

As she was just about to respond with a *"Yes, please, let's go now!"* the front door flung open, and his father stood eyeing up the two of them.

Seeing his son, whom he loved and favoured the most, and his doe-eyed, dark-haired girlfriend, John Sr. was taken aback. His secret romance with Nancy flooded his mind. John Fasp's heart skipped a beat; all he wanted to do was embrace his son. He wanted to advise them both to leave. He thought of paying their way for them to live their lives as freely and romantically as possible.

Instead, his stern expression, weathered face, and slightly rounded shoulders displayed a defeated man—a father filled with trepidation that quickly changed gears into anger.

"What the hell, Johnny? Thanks for saying goodbye, thanks for missing your only grandmother's memorial, and thanks for nothing! I thought I raised you better than this. Your mother has been worried sick about you! And while I'm at it, who the hell is this?" As he looked toward Margarita, she immediately bowed her head, bit the inside of her cheek and held back tears.

If Johnny was unsure if he loved Margarita, his father's disdain made him adore her. She represented everything he wanted and reminded him what was wrong with his family. In the heat of the moment, Johnny's anger boiled up, and he blurted out words that would stay with him for the rest of his life.

"Screw you man! What right do you have bursting into MY house and disrespecting MY wife? Furthermore, thank you for not telling me I had a sister!"

Johnny had lied about being married, and yet Margarita stood a little taller at the prospect of him being her husband. She instantly straightened her shoulders, jutted out her chin and looked toward Johnny like he was the knight in shining armour who had just ridden in on the white horse to save the day. Her entire being felt like one big, happy heart, bursting with love and pride for him.

Johnny's dad was at a loss for words and turning on his heel, stomped out the door and slammed it behind him.

After the dust settled, literally and metaphorically, Margarita said, "I love you, Johnny." He picked her up two feet off the ground and said, "I love you too, sweetheart, more than you will ever know!"

She suggested he go inside the main house and try to make amends. Johnny reluctantly agreed, and said, "Wait here, I'll be right back. You're right, he can't just walk out on us like that."

Margarita was antsy, her legs ached, and she had forgotten her hunger. She needed air and a moment to collect her thoughts. She instinctively rubbed her belly. As she circled her hand around the not-yet-noticeable protrusion, she whispered, *"Todo ester bien, bebe,"* all the while praying that everything would truly be fine.

She opened the front door, stood on the porch and saw a massive barn not far away. Just breathing in the country air relaxed her, and finding the cooped-up chickens grounded her. Moving from one outback building to the next, she found solace in the farm animals, the rustle of hay with its dusty sweet smell, and the creaking boards as she heard horses moving in their stalls. When her eyes adjusted to the dim light, she saw a rusty pitchfork and shuddered.

Margarita took note of the elaborate setup and state-of-the-art farm equipment. She noted how clean everything was, and then decided, *clean on the outside and dirty on the inside,* referring to the people who inhabited the homestead. Margarita whispered in Spanish, "Too many secrets and so much anger."

She knew she loved Johnny, but pondering the situation, she felt victimized and remembered something her father had said to her before she left to travel. *"Gitta,*

Estás a solo una opción de cambiar tu vida, elegir sabiamente." Margarita made a mental note that she would tell Johnny her father's wise and kind words. "Johnny, you are only one choice away from changing your life. Please choose wisely." And then she would say, "Those are my father's words, not mine."

Tears welled in her eyes. Before she erupted into laughter, Margarita decided that MeadowBrook sounded too lovely and charming for the disharmony she had so far experienced, so from then on, she decided to call it MeadowDitch.

As the baby inside her grew, Margarita was determined to pass down loving and happy thoughts, but with the roller coaster ride of emotions she had gone through in the last twenty-four hours, she was worried. To make matters worse, she was afraid to tell Johnny she was pregnant, especially after seeing his behaviour toward his brother and father. She had an imminent fear that cruel patterns and a mean temperament had been passed down to Johnny.

Margarita did not want to wander too far around the unknown territory, so she returned to the swing on Johnny's front porch, where she sat down. She felt comforted and soothed by the gentle swaying, and as she squinted out toward the setting sun and vast fields, she longed for the beach. There were no crashing waves or hot sandy shorelines here, or the sweet sound of Johnny's voice and folksy guitar music. Margarita cried out for her Casablanca romance and hippie boyfriend to return.

She thought of her home and ached for her mother's embrace and father's healthy laugh. She visualized her parents dancing and her brothers and sisters cheering them on. The Argentinian sunsets and heavy, warm evenings were incomparable to the dusty, windswept prairie and the blunt, discourteous people who lived here.

Margarita decided the minute Johnny returned from his parent's house, she would tell him about the baby. She assumed he might still be upset, but hoped he would have ironed out their differences. Perhaps finding out he was going to be a father would be the Band-Aid to make everything right.

Margarita prayed aloud, "Hi God, I know it's been a while. Please help Johnny with his family, and help me tell him about our baby. I know it happened out of wedlock, but I'm sure it will all be okay if I can just have Your blessing."

When Johnny came up the front steps, he brushed past Margarita without saying a word. She got off the swing as her happy thoughts dissolved and followed Johnny inside. She watched him open a small carved wooden box on the mantel above the stone fireplace and take out an already rolled joint.

Johnny sweetly said, "Sorry, babe, but I need this right now."

So far, coming home was nothing like Johnny had imagined. It had been far worse. In less than an hour of being back, he was outwardly smoking weed, and ready to pour a drink. He figured it was his only way to manage. Even though his secret habits had been carelessly revealed, he was glad his minor vices were finally out in the open.

Now it was Margarita's turn to brush past Johnny and say nothing. She climbed the stairs to his sparsely decorated and cold bedroom, and still fully clothed, climbed into bed. Margarita was filled with melancholy, the kind that comes with feeling left out.

Before she drifted off to sleep, her optimism suggested that maybe Johnny's pot smoking was a one-time thing. With that, Margarita felt a glimmer of hope.

Johnny stayed up sipping and puffing long after Margarita had gone to sleep. The deep drags from his joint relaxed him, and the alcohol blurred his mind and burned his throat. Finally, he wearily climbed the stairs and fell into bed. He chose not to spoon and cuddle Margarita for fear of waking her.

***

Kent was flying high. He was making amends with everyone he could think of, and he was pleased that after he shared his true feelings with Tracy, she reciprocated.

During his two-week visit, Kent created a routine, one that was mindful and could keep him on task for continued positive growth. He meditated in the beautifully manicured flower garden outside his family's majestic home. He worked out in his parents' home gym and swam in their pool. He practiced positive affirmation every morning in the bathroom mirror and remained sober.

When harsh thoughts and bad memories appeared, he wrote them down and willfully expelled the negativity. He helped his mom, even though she had house staff, and tried to reach out to his father by asking him questions about when he was a boy.

Kent tried to make connections with both his parents. His mother was open to his new and improved self, but his father thought his son's transformation was hogwash, unnecessary and possibly a result of brainwashing. Mayor Gordon, whom many thought to be corrupt, kept quiet but was ready to dismantle any cult he thought his son might be a part of.

As part of his method to right all his wrongs, Kent arranged coffee dates, hiking dates, and even games of tennis with those he had taken advantage of. He had calculated how much he owed everyone, with interest, paid them back, and let them pick an apology gift of red wine or a wristwatch.

Many were leery and still did not trust Kent, yet some were forgiving and grateful.

Kent referred to his acts of kindness as the Kent Gordon Twelve-Step Program. Except he narrowed it down to five steps:

1. Admitted I was powerless over greed;
2. Came to believe that the power of a therapist could restore me to sanity
3. Made a decision to turn my life over to health, fitness, and abstinence from alcohol;
4. Made a list of all the people I have harmed;
5. Made amends with all the people I have duped.

One of Kent's therapists told him, "Some of the healthiest people in the world are the ones who work the hardest on themselves. The key is to find a balance." So, when not busying himself with himself, he was trying to find a balance between remaining financially successful, being kind, and winning Tracy's hand in marriage, even while taking it slow. Kent wanted to prove to everyone, especially Tracy, that he had changed.

***

Tim had no qualms about not seeing his parents. His little sister Marnie had given him the sense of family he had always dreamed of, and his career was finally taking off. After meeting up with Susan in town and being invited to her house for dinner, Tim felt like he had a good friend.

Susan had convinced Tim to perform a song and dance routine from *Fame* at the reunion. He had just finished rehearsals before his week-long trip home and since being reunited with a forgotten sister and having dinner at Susan's cute little country home, his respect toward his true self had increased. Tim felt ready for the reveal but he couldn't help wondering how his basketball buddies and the entire class of '78 would react. He could only speculate they would be shocked and might disown him, or worse, mock him. Especially because he was not living under the ideal social and cultural mores of the narrow-minded town where he grew up.

***

Immediately after Nelson's bus rolled into town, he took a taxi over to the geriatric wing of the hospital. He went there only because he was not sure where else to go.

He gathered that his parents were mad at him about something or other because they were not answering their telephone, and they had made it known he was not welcome at home. So, the only other family member for Nelson to get help from was his wealthy grandmother, the notorious Gladys Farnsworth.

By the time Nelson arrived at the hospital, visiting hours had ended and since he was desperate and had a hard time taking no for an answer, Nelson assessed the outside of the hospital building and tried scaling the wall. He saw an open window on the third floor, but unfortunately, his climb ended almost as soon as it began. The hospital security had been notified by a passerby and the police had been called.

Marvin and Diane's earlier police report about their son immediately came up in the system, and because of this, Nelson was arrested. He was taken in for trespassing and causing a disturbance. The bail was set at $10,000, and his parents were contacted.

Nelson paced the small cell at the MeadowBrook police station, and as time went on, he became more agitated and felt a frantic need to get out. With only forty-eight hours before the reunion, he needed help.

He didn't want his misdeeds to get out, especially to Darcie. So, he began hollering to anyone who might be in earshot, "I demand a lawyer! This is a travesty. I am innocent, I tell you. Innocent!"

No one responded.

Giving up, Nelson sighed, sat down on the floor, and tried to devise a plan. He pictured Darcie, his raven-haired beauty, and it gave him the hope to keep moving forward. She had always gotten him through his frustrating, bleak periods, even if she was unaware he existed. Besides, Nelson knew his arrest was a complete misunderstanding.

As he sat and pondered his predicament, Nelson thought back to last week before arriving in MeadowBrook, when his product, Nelzema, had finally passed FDA approval. Three days before the reunion, Nelson packed up everything. He filled two enormous suitcases with his latest and greatest pimple cream, locked the door on his warehouse space, and took the bus home to MeadowBrook.

Upon entering the city limits, Nelson was amazed at his town's growth and noted the new mall. He marvelled at all the businesses and shops that had popped up in the short time since he left.

After Nelson's reflection, a calmer state of mind took over and he came up with an idea, combined with the stirrings of success. He said out loud to himself, "First get out of jail, next secure an investor, and lastly, get Nelzema on the shelves."

Nelson decided that a little smooth talking to his parents was in order, and if all else failed, he would make his grandma pay to get him released, and then give Kent another shot at investing, even though it went terribly wrong the first time they met.

As the clock ticked past midnight, Nelson was wide awake, his energy coming directly from his nerves. While passing the time in his jail cell, Nelson composed a letter.

Dear Mom and Dad,

I am completely confused why you have seemingly disowned me. There must have been a misunderstanding because I am doing very well. I was only trying to visit Granny, and how was I to know climbing the side of a building is not acceptable? Especially since Spiderman has been doing it for eons. Can you please bail me out? I promise not to do anything illegal again.

From your one and only son,
Nelson

As much as Nelson was desperate to be released, he also had ulterior motives. He knew his parents had money, and even though his meeting with Kent Gordon was a bust, Nelson planned on hitting him up again at the reunion. He was optimistic that someone would invest in his product. He just hoped it would be soon.

Shortly after 1:00 in the morning, Nelson heard murmurings from down the hall. Standing up abruptly in hopes he was being set free, he was thrilled to see the worried look of his mother and the agitated face of his father.

Nelson said, "Finally! What took you so long?" As they made their way to the bailiff's desk, Nelson shoved his composed letter into his mother's hand and said, "I'm starving! Whatta you got to eat at home?"

***

On the other side of town, Patty rehearsed the speech she had written for Nelson. She felt strongly that if he could see her transformation and hear what she had to say, he would be hers forever.

All over the small town, families were reuniting with the returning grads who were anticipating rekindled relationships, and many who were hoping to see the one who got away. On the day of the reunion, the MeadowBrook grads of 1978 were looking forward to the night's events.

Although some were filled with trepidation, many knew the reunion would be cathartic.

Chapter Nine

Reunited

"In the end, you always return to the people who were with you at the beginning."

—Dakota Hillsman

The sign above the front doors of MeadowBrook High School said, "Welcome Back Graduating Class of 1978."

After receiving Tracy Hansworth's enticing pink invitation, the selling points for most of those returning were proving they were not the stereotype they were labelled with back in high school, and boldly expressing who they had become.

Without their knowing it, the ten-year grad reunion would be significantly life-changing for Dakota, Tracy, Johnny, Amanda, and Kent. However, for Susan, Nelson, Patty, Tim, and Darcie, it would be a second chance to break free from their high school image and finally represent who they always were inside. They had changed and were no longer intimidated about showing it.

In just under four hours, friends and strangers would be reunited. Most anticipated an evening of laughs, warm hugs, and shared memories. But in some cases, unbeknownst to the partygoers, past hurts and destructive memories would pour down like rain on the cold, windswept prairie.

Tracy was a nervous wreck and was thankful Kent would be at her side to keep her in balance. The thought instantly calmed her and filled her with hopeful anticipation. Even though everyone saw her as a confident businesswoman, and she was no longer the nervous Nellie she was as a little girl, Tracy still secretly had anxiety before each event, no matter how many she did or how successful she became. Tracy knew she was not alone because Susan often shared that before teaching every fitness class, she felt like throwing up, even though no one ever suspected it. Both friends understood where the other was coming from, which proved to be supportive and therapeutic.

Since Kent's arrival, the two of them had spent every day together. Tracy still went to work, but Kent drove her, picked her up for lunch, or made her one of his healthy salads with oil and vinegar dressing. Every night they walked and talked. He shared his misgivings, and she shared her future hopes and dreams.

They both had dug deep into Kent's sordid past, and he promised Tracy he was a changed man. He shared about his counselling sessions, yoga meditation, and abstinence from sex and alcohol. He apologized many times over for his dishonest behaviour and unruly past. Together they cried and laughed until they were crying again.

On the topic of sex, Tracy felt vulnerable but was pleased they were getting to know each other slowly, especially since Kent had displayed patience and put no pressure on her to be intimate. She in turn shared that she was "white as snow," in other words, still a virgin and that she had never dated, not even so much as going on a walk or having coffee with someone of the opposite sex.

Tracy wanted to get through the reunion before any physical union was to occur. Even though they had taken to sharing the same bed, Kent restrained himself and Tracy appreciated his respect in honouring her wishes to take it slow. They had developed a routine, almost like an old married couple; after they brushed and flossed their teeth, they read before turning out the lights and cuddling.

The night before the reunion, Tracy could not get to sleep. Every time she tossed and turned, Kent's loving, vice-like grip reminded her she was not alone. Sometimes though, she wished she was.

Tracy had never had so much togetherness with another human being in her entire life and was glad she had already set some boundaries. She was adamant they save their lovemaking until she had a ring on her finger and a wedding date on the calendar. And she avoided talking about the elephant in her room—her mother—and what had happened back in Grade 10 between Eunice and Kent.

Kent was not aware that Tracy knew about what had happened between him and her mother twelve years earlier. Kent also did not know that one of Tracy's biggest fears was that he might still be pining for her mother, or worse, using her to get to Eunice. It sickened Tracy to think about it for too long. She chose to savour the fact that she had what she had always fantasized about, a soul mate and significant other.

While Kent was out jogging, she thought back to the Kent she knew in high school. Tracy could easily summon his face, cheeky grin, and fit body, making her shiver.

Even though he teased and complained about her, she had always liked him.

The past two weeks had been a whirlwind, from the moment he pulled up in a sports car and whisked her away, to their discussions of marriage, setting up a home, and keeping his apartment in New York. It all seemed so crazy and dream-like, and Tracy hoped it was the real deal. She caught herself smiling until her cheeks hurt and felt a warmth fill her body like a luxurious warm bath she never wanted to emerge from.

Tracy thought of how much Kent had changed. Yet there were parts of him that remained the same. His charismatic ways and determination to succeed in some ways matched her personality perfectly.

On the morning of the reunion, as she finished up her breakfast, the perpetual thoughts of Kent carried Tracy through doing the dishes, showering, applying her makeup, and getting dressed. As she pulled on her favourite pink stirrup pants, sneakers, and oversized pink hoodie, her mind shifted gears to the upcoming event. She was anxious to touch base with the decorating committee and catering staff to ensure everything was running smoothly for the event that night.

In the interim, she left Kent a note: *"Hey, good lookin', whatcha got cookin'? I'll be back at 4:00 to get ready. Help yourself to anything you want XOX."* She signed her name and left a perfect lipstick kiss.

The doors were set to open at 6:00 p.m., but Tracy and Kent arrived early to ensure the ice sculpture and movie projector were set up correctly and everything was good to go. Individually, they looked around the expansive gymnasium. Kent was impressed with the elaborate setup and beamed with pride at Tracy's obvious labour of love. Tracy let out a sigh of satisfied accomplishment.

The long tables were clad with white linen tablecloths and balloon centrepieces in traditional school colours. Each place setting had a Kodak Instamatic camera and a keepsake 1978 grad photo in a silver frame. Engraved on the bottom of each frame was the word, *Reunited.* Tracy had hired a professional DJ complete with disco ball, turntable, and mixtapes. She had made a special request for all the music to be from the 1960s and '70s, with an emphasis on crowd favourites like "The Chicken Dance," "YMCA," "The Bunny Hop," "Disco Duck," and the "Don't Look, Ethel" streaking song to be played later in the evening once everyone had downed a few cocktails and would be more courageous.

Everything from the $2 bar drinks to the swag bag parting gifts had been planned months in advance. Tracy was determined that nothing would or could go wrong.

Smiling and letting out a little cheer, Tracy and Kent held hands while they delightedly walked around straightening tablecloths, wineglasses, and balloon arrangements. Kent made sure there were no cords visible that anyone could trip over, and Tracy admired his attention to detail.

Tracy wanted to pinch herself because she could hardly believe she was with the man of her dreams. However, she knew many other grads would not feel the same due to Kent's earlier high school behaviour. She braced herself for controversy and a possible backlash in regard to him being there, and so did Kent.

Staying true to her business sense and persona, Tracy had memorized every RSVP, and she knew some of the women Kent had gone around with in high school would be at the reunion. Months earlier, she was rattled by this, but not anymore. Tracy felt confident that Kent only had eyes for her.

Every once in a while Tracy caught herself comparing herself to the women Kent had dated in the past. She had spent hours discussing this with Susan. Over coffee and bran muffins, Tracy would whine, "Not only do I look and dress conservatively, but I am also a virgin. How on earth will I cope with Kent's past?" Susan's wise words came back to her, "Trace, he must see something in you or he wouldn't have looked for you and confided in you.

Besides, you may be conservative, but at least you have a brain in your head, so Kent is obviously attracted to your intelligence and strong work ethic. Besides, he has only ever dated bimbos, so honestly, you must be a refreshing change!"

Tracy always felt better after hearing Susan's firm and sensible view on things.

In addition to Tracy's raised self-esteem, she felt good about refusing her mother's involvement in the reunion. She could not shake the incident that happened twelve years earlier between her mom and sixteen-year-old Kent. Meanwhile, she did not breathe a word of it to Kent, even though it still plagued her. Tracy was afraid to rock the boat since everything was going so well.

Tracy believed her dress to be eye-catching and sexy. She had spent hours sewing it, using fabric in her signature pink, a hue known for sweetness. She laughed out loud, recalling how months earlier, she and Susan had concocted the whole reunion plan to lure Kent Gordon back to MeadowBrook. Tracy never in a million years expected to have already snagged him by the time the reunion took place.

Susan's aerobics classes, combined with walking to work, had narrowed Tracy's waistline and improved her self-confidence, and her evening gown was made to complement both. The gown was a full-length style, off the shoulder on one side, with a puffy short sleeve on the other. The waistline was fitted, and a small ruffle trimmed the neckline. Her bare shoulder was slathered in Avon's Sweet Honesty body lotion, a gift from Susan.

Tracy's hairstyle had been a dilemma that only a best friend could solve. She loved her trademark ponytail and bangs, but wanted to look modern and glamorous. Tracy had thought of booking an appointment at Helga's Hair Salon, but Susan cautioned her not to and said in a whisper, "With Helga's failing eyesight, she has developed a reputation for cutting women's bangs too short, and it's been reported that she has snipped a few ears in the process."

So that afternoon, before getting ready and meeting up with Kent, Tracy sat in Susan's kitchen for some backcombing, teasing, and frizzing. Doused in hair spray, Tracy felt like a rooster making its debut in the henhouse. When she balked at Susan's handiwork, she was told, "Look at it this way, Trace, the 1980s is all about big hair, just like all men want a big you-know-what!" Needless to say, Susan advised Tracy to "go big or go home."

Tracy disliked Susan's raunchy side but found her remark unusually funny for some reason.

***

The proof was in the pudding when Kent's eyes popped out of his head like a cartoon character first laying eyes on an attractive female, as he loudly exclaimed, *"FOXY MAMA!"*

Meanwhile, Kent had done his due diligence. After baring his soul and confiding in Tracy, he decided to make good use of his time while home in MeadowBrook. So, every day after he dropped her off at work, he made his way throughout the town and tried to rectify all the wrongs he had committed when he was a foolish, money-hungry teenager. With a chequebook in hand, his plan was to apologize and pay back the people he had swindled. Kent found most people to be receptive, forgiving, and kind. He only came across two that told him he could go straight to hell.

Unbeknownst to Tracy, while she was getting ready for the night's event, Kent also met up with Eunice for coffee and swore her to secrecy.

When Eunice answered the telephone, the sound of Kent's voice caused her to break out in a sweat. She could feel perspiration droplets on her temples, and the phone receiver in her hand became slippery. She wondered if she was having a menopausal hot flash. Regardless of her physical reaction, when Kent asked if they could meet up, she chose to dress as seductively as she could. Just in case.

Instead of meeting at Robinson's Diner, the usual meeting spot for townspeople, Kent suggested to-go coffees at the park. He told Eunice he would bring the coffee and be waiting at the statue of William Farnsworth.

The day was unusually hot, with a limited breeze. The oppressive air, combined with the heaviness of Kent's heart, reminded him of all the hot water he used to get into, with the same nervous energy that followed every bad deal or breakup. In the interim, while waiting for his girlfriend's mother, he questioned if he was doing the right thing.

Kent did not hug Eunice upon her arrival and immediately started in. He spoke in a firm business-like tone, "Mrs. Hansworth, in no uncertain terms will I ever sleep with you again, and quite frankly, even though I was a willing participant twelve years ago, it was wrong and distasteful for you to have made advances in the first place. Furthermore, I love your daughter and hope to marry her someday."

After hearing Kent's admission of love for her youngest daughter, Eunice didn't hide her disappointment and felt embarrassed at her own assumption that she and Kent were about to take a roll in the hay. Eunice just stared at him without responding. She grasped at the plunging neckline of her silk blouse, and with mournful eyes, just nodded.

In a regretful tone, Eunice promised she would not make a play for Kent ever again, and she apologized for her predatory behaviour many years earlier.

Before Kent got up to leave, engulfed in shame, Eunice felt the need to hurt him, so she divulged the information that Tracy already knew about her many other infidelities and their one-night stand. She then added that since her admission of scandalous behaviour to Tracy, her once special mother-daughter bond had been forever scarred. Kent was derailed and deflated by her admittance. He was initially angry that Tracy had not said something to him. Then his anger turned back toward Eunice and he got up, threw his coffee cup and its bitter contents on the ground, and abruptly left.

Eunice stayed behind, looking down into a full paper cup of coffee while clutching her low-cut blouse to cover up her ample cleavage. After an abundance of time had passed, she got up to leave. Eunice glanced up at the statue of town founder William Farnsworth and thought it looked like he was winking at her.

Armed with a wad of cash, Kent immediately visited the only jewellery store in town. After he found what he was looking for, he looked both ways before leaving, like a robber making his getaway. Kent then plunged the newly purchased burgundy velvet box into his pocket and went to his parents' home to get ready for the party.

***

At 5:45 p.m., Kent and Tracy opened the big gray doors to the school gymnasium to let people in. No one was there yet, so Kent grabbed Tracy's hand and pulled her into the equipment room.

Tracy laughed and said, "Oh my gosh, Kent, what on earth are you doing?" She had flashbacks to the Capable Craft Club, and how Kent had often outwardly mocked her. It now seemed ironic that deep down inside, he had always loved her.

Amongst the volleyball cart, wooden bowling pins and orange pylons, Kent bent down on one knee and took Tracy's hands in his. Her hands began to tremble, and her knees became weak as Kent began his speech…

"My dearest Tracy. These past two weeks have been phenomenal. But I have loved you from afar since Grade 4. I am so sorry I have been a narcissistic shit head all these years. If you could forgive me, I would like to make you my wife and live together in wedded bliss until death does us part. In other words, will you marry me?"

At that precise moment, they heard a faint voice in the distance say, "Hello? Is anybody here?"

Even though duty called, Tracy felt that Kent's question was far too important and that everything else could wait.

Looking down into Kent's hopeful face and chiseled features, she responded in her usual no-nonsense fashion.

"Kent, I am honoured and flattered, but you must know that I am a career woman and I am not going to become anything for anyone." Just as Kent began to lower his gaze, Tracy continued, "You see, I know about you and my mother. You, unfortunately, have years under your belt as a dishonest person, and even though I am unequivocally in love with you too, I'm not sure that the last two weeks is enough time to decide if we're right for each other."

Meanwhile, Tracy's heart soared with Kent's proposal and the possibility of spending the rest of her life with him.

The voice they had heard earlier became louder and seemingly more assertive so that both Kent and Tracy were distracted by it, and then Kent mouthed the words, "Is that Nelson Farnsworth?"

Tracy whispered back, "Yes, I think so."

Before either of them could say anything else, Nelson burst through the equipment room doors and said in a frantic tone, "Tracy, I need to speak to you immediately!" followed by, "Kent Gordon, is that you? Good, I'm glad because I need to speak with both of you!"

Kent leapt up off the floor, brushed off the knees of his tuxedo pants and was momentarily relieved, as he was not ready to be turned down by a tiny woman in a cloyingly sweet pink dress, smelling like a grandmother. He smiled at the thought of how adorable Tracy was.

Nevertheless, Kent put his arm around Tracy's bare shoulder in a territorial kind of way, and then he thought twice and instantly lowered it to her waist.

Once he had both of their attention, Nelson blurted out, "I'm going to need a microphone as soon as everyone arrives, as I am proposing marriage to someone!"

Nelson's words hung in the air like the lingering smell of used sports equipment, and without responding, both Kent and Tracy burst out laughing. This sent Nelson into a tailspin. He was reminded of the many times he was teased behind his back or called "The Frugal Weirdo" to his face.

Tracy instantly regretted their outburst. She realized that Nelson didn't know that just seconds before, Kent had proposed to her. Not wanting to explain, she calmed the waters by apologizing and kindly said, "Yes, I remembered your request, and I have already added it to the agenda. So, after I give the welcome greeting and opening remarks, we will all toast the event, and before Tim Barnes performs a dance number, you can come forward. Can I ask to whom you're proposing? Is it someone we know?"

***

Some wished they had never accepted the invitation, yet most of the returning '78 grads were happy and excited to be walking through the gymnasium doors of their youth.

The smell of sweat, old leather volleyballs, and running shoes flooded Darcie with memories of how much she disliked P.E. She smiled and shook her head at the thought. In retrospect, she concluded that she would have done quite well at sports if she had not been so intimidated by the athletic girls who dominated the volleyball court and ran circles around everyone in floor hockey. She made a mental note to speak to Dakota about MeadowBrook High offering yoga classes that she could volunteer to teach.

Darcie hated arriving alone but was reassured that Dakota would not be far behind her. She had done so many things by herself over the last ten years that she was not going to let her old insecurities get in the way of having a good time now that she was home.

Without looking around the gym first, Darcie found a table, sat down, and let her mind wander to the afternoon when she'd first arrived back in MeadowBrook. Entering the Hillsprings airport and seeing Dakota had been unexpected and disconcerting. Darcie wasn't sure she was ready. But their initial embrace and sitting next to him in the pickup with their thighs touching had been reaffirming. It was as if she had never left. She was unequivocally happy to be home and had no regrets about being there. Even if she felt some remorse over not doing it sooner, Darcie wasn't about to sing the blues when she believed that everything happened for a reason.

Her thoughts then shifted to Patty. Even though they had gone through school together, they were worlds apart back then, and meeting Patty for the first time ten years later had been a revelation. Both women wondered why they had never spoken before and concurred with how ridiculous cliques and stereotypes were.

After Dakota had dropped Darcie off at her mother's apartment, which used to be her apartment, too, Darcie felt nostalgic and melancholy. Walking through the door and greeting her mother, Darcie couldn't help but question if she had made a terrible mistake leaving ten years earlier.

She embraced her mother and was taken aback by her tiny frame and bones that protruded beneath her fuzzy yellow bathrobe. The contrast was alarming. Darcie said nothing about her mother's skin tone and wispy grey hair, but she couldn't not comment on how frail Nancy had become.

In a pleading tone, Darcie said, "Mom you've always been petite, but I have never seen you this small before! Are you eating enough?"

Skirting the question, Nancy recalled the day Darcie and Johnny had been born. Instead of answering, she began to tell the story of Darcie's birth, and that Johnny was her twin. Darcie was dumbfounded, but then all the pieces began to fall into place as to why she and Johnny had always experienced such a profound connectedness. Nancy continued, "It has been my lifelong regret giving your brother away. I cannot believe how meek I was. How could I have just signed him away? I can't imagine what he must think of me. You know, Darcie, I felt powerless back then."

Darcie knew her mother did her best with what she had, but she still felt torn and conflicted between being mad and sad. The question haunted her: It was one thing to give away her twin, but why not tell her she had a sibling?

Under different circumstances, she could see herself disowning her mother or at least not talking to her for a while. But she knew in her heart that Nancy's days might be numbered, so what was the point? Darcie chose to say nothing and let her mother continue.

In a gentle, calming voice, Nancy described her own difficult childhood and how everything changed after her mother died and William Farnsworth disappeared. She had no one to turn to when she got pregnant at eighteen. She described how in some ways, the Fasp family had helped her out of a tough situation.

What caught Darcie off-guard was how kindly her mom spoke about the Fasps. The more her mother's recollections unraveled, the more Darcie felt irritated with the wealthy, privileged family that practically owned the town. Like water boiling, her anger first simmered and then started bubbling up. Just before it exploded, the apartment buzzer sounded.

Darcie was bewildered about who it might be and relieved by the distraction. She said, "Who is it, Mom? Are you expecting someone?" Despite her confusion, Darcie sensed her mother knew exactly who it was, like a planned guest on *The Merv Griffin Show*: "Up next we have..."

When Nancy didn't answer her daughter's question, and immediately went to the intercom, Darcie walked into her old bedroom. She felt miffed and needed a moment to cool down. Once there, she gasped at how much it had changed. Most noticeable were her missing posters and mattress on the floor that had been replaced with a brand-new futon couch.

She marveled that all traces of her childhood had disappeared, almost like she had never existed. Darcie's bedroom had morphed into a Zen-like setting for meditation. Filling her old space were plants, yoga mats, candles, incense, and homemade quilts that looked warm and inviting.

She dropped to her knees and spread her hands onto the bamboo floor mat, thinking it ironic that she had gone into the Child's Pose, especially since she was not a child, no longer had a home, and her only parent was preparing to leave the earth. As Darcie rested her forehead on the bristly texture, she turned her head to one side and caught sight of a bookcase filled with books. Sitting up to get a better look, she observed titles on healing, meditation, becoming a vegan, and vitamin supplements. And then a book that stood out instantly panicked Darcie, *How to Tell Your Children You Are Dying.*

Darcie got a clearer picture of her mother's state of mind, and her spirit momentarily warmed. Suddenly her breath caught mid-exhale when it was interrupted by a familiar voice.

"Hey Nancy, did you tell her we were coming?"

Sitting up cross-legged, Darcie knew the visitor was Johnny. She waited for him to make his entrance. And then she whispered to herself, "WE?" and wondered whom he had brought with him.

Tears welled in Darcie's eyes as she looked up toward the doorway, and there was Johnny. In conjunction with her mixed emotions that switched between joy and sorrow, all she could do was smile. They both smiled.

Johnny reached down to Darcie's hand to help her up.

They didn't embrace, but with no trepidation, Darcie cheerfully said, "Hey dude, what happened to my hippie pothead friend, the skinny boy with the white Colgate smile? You're all 'growed' up!"

Margarita came around the corner and shyly peeked into the room where the twins were standing, with Nancy hovering behind her. When all four of them were just a few feet from each other, Nancy clasped her hands together and exclaimed, "Gee, a few minutes ago I had one daughter, and now all of a sudden I have two daughters and a son! My, oh my, the world sure works in mysterious ways." The four of them laughed and cried with relief.

Darcie shifted her thoughts from the memory of the day she was reunited with Johnny back to the high school reunion. She looked around the decorated gym and felt admiration for Tracy, a girl she hardly knew, who was known back in school for her crafting abilities and who Darcie knew had organized this whole event.

Darcie jumped when she heard a chair being pulled out and scraped along the gym floor. Patty said, "Hey, how's it going? Do you mind if I sit at your table?"

Darcie replied, "Yes, of course, please do!" She couldn't help but notice how different they were from one another. Complete opposites. Patty stood out like a runway model with her California sun-kissed flair. Her ensemble consisted of an all-white silk jumpsuit with a silver belt and matching silver stiletto heels. Her hair was big and bleached blond, adding at least two inches to her six-foot, sinewy frame. Darcie smiled at her new friend and noted the contrast between Patty's outfit and her own simple black dress, flat shoes, and hoop earrings. She still wore her hair layered, but natural with no chemical enhancements.

Darcie asked Patty if she would like some punch, to which Patty responded, "Yes, I would love some, provided it's not spiked. I had a bad experience in this gym ten years ago!" Both women laughed. Darcie responded, "Oh my gosh, girl, you must tell me! And then I'll tell you a few of my own stories!"

As Patty sat down next to her new friend, she thought how she adored how eccentric and eclectic Darcie was. Both were thrilled to finally get to know each other.

***

Before going into the reunion, Johnny held Margarita's hand in the truck parked outside the school. He knew his family had upset her, so he said, "Please don't be sad. Have a drink, smoke a joint with me, kiss me…do something to make yourself happy."

At that moment, before going inside to relive Johnny's high school memories with him, Margarita had enough. She turned to Johnny and said emphatically, "You are correct. Your family did upset me, and I will not have a drink or smoke a joint or fake being happy…because…" Her voice softened as she looked up into Johnny's face and continued, "Because, I am already happy and I am pregnant, you dummy!"

It did not come out the way she wanted it to, and her delivery only made her burst out crying. Before Johnny could respond, Margarita said through tears, "And furthermore, your family is horrible. They are mean, uptight bullies, and I do not want my baby raised here around these people!"

Johnny was ecstatic. He pulled her close and declared, "I may not be a religious person, but praise the Lord and hallelujah! Why did you wait so long to tell me?" Before Margarita could answer, Johnny said, "C'mon, let's go inside and tell my sister"—Johnny liked saying that—"and tomorrow we'll tell my family, or not, whatever you want, my love. Afterward, we'll fly to Argentina to live under the Argentinian sun, dance to our hearts' content, and raise our babies with love and empanadas! After tonight we'll kiss MeadowBrook goodbye, never to return!"

Overjoyed with Johnny's reaction, Margarita couldn't help but laugh at his enthusiasm and boyish charm. But before she agreed, Margarita became silent, and when she found the courage and her voice, she meekly said, "But what about your drinking and pot smoking?"

Johnny said nothing. They exited the truck and walked through the familiar gym doors, holding hands, with Johnny in the lead. They spotted Darcie and strolled over to her table.

***

Tim, Susan, and Dwayne all arrived at the same time, followed by Amanda and Brad. They all greeted one another and laughed. Tim said, "Hey, what's this? Alphabetical order again?"

From the outside looking in, everyone seemed happy. However, undetected by the others, Brad and Amanda were at odds with each other. On the car ride over, Amanda said to Brad, "I wish they had a word for being happy and sad at the same time, because that's what I feel every time I am with you." Brad couldn't help but feel some warmth toward his wife of eight years. She rarely said anything nice to him, so he took her comment as moving in the right direction to fix what felt broken. His emotions then shifted to guilt.

Darcie kept looking to the door for Dakota, and when she spotted Nelson, she had an instant unsettled feeling, keeping her eyes on him standing at the back of the gym. Nelson awkwardly shifted from one foot to the next, as if in waiting for something or someone. Tracy took to the stage, tapped the microphone to ensure it was on, and said, “Testing, testing.” Darcie looked away from Nelson and spotted Kent standing near the stage against the wall, proudly giving Tracy the thumbs-up. Seeing the exchange, she blinked and whispered to Patty, “How odd. Why is Kent looking at Tracy like that?”

She saw Patty noticing the same thing, and she whispered back, “Yeah, that's weird. What the heck?” Both women laughed in unison, and Patty could hardly believe how much they had in common, even though they appeared to be complete opposites.

After Tracy took her place behind the podium, she took a deep breath, and on her equally deep exhale, she proudly gazed out at the flurry of friends celebrating with laughter, hoots and hollers. She thought about how every single person had changed, and yet, in some ways, they had not changed at all.

Wow, they all look so great! she thought.

Breaking her thought bubble, Tracy leaned into the microphone, cleared her throat and spoke in a clear, professional voice, “Welcome back, Grads of ’78! How the heck are ya?” Without missing a beat, the gym erupted into cheers, whistles, and applause. Kent winked at Tracy as she continued.

“Well, we made it! It's been ten years since most of us graced the doors of our alma mater, so thank you all for coming. I would first like to acknowledge our principal, Mr. Marples. May he rest in peace. In honour of our favourite high school administrator, his famous marionettes will be on display in the library. Before we begin, I must go over some general housekeeping. Please do not wander aimlessly around the school, but feel free to enter any open classrooms. For your enjoyment, we have a carnival theme in the science lab. The music room has a rock and roll theme, and there is a disco theme in the cafeteria. Here in the gym, we have alcoholic and non-alcoholic beverages, but please be reminded not to drink and drive. And now, before the festivities begin, let us all raise our glasses to toast the graduating class of 1978!"

More hoots and hollers ensued, along with the clinking of red plastic cups and clear plastic wineglasses.

Tracy continued, "You will notice disposable cameras at each table setting. Please take photographs, as many or as few as you want. All I ask is that you leave your camera in the big basket by the doors. I will develop the film and create a keepsake book of memories for anyone who wants one. The estimated cost will be twelve dollars. Dinner will be served at 7 p.m. here in the gym, and dancing will start at 9 p.m. Now, let's begin by mingling and getting reacquainted!"

***

Meanwhile, at the hospital, Dakota was at his wits' end. He desperately wanted to be with Darcie and hated being late, especially since he'd missed the 1978 graduation altogether. Instead, he was with Branda, being a do-gooder and burden-bearer. He was there out of the goodness of his heart, but also because he wanted to give Amanda and Brad a break from the long arduous hours of worrying over their daughter's health. Dakota had put together a sign-up sheet so the entire faculty could help with meals, visiting, and anything else that was needed. It was not a secret that Amanda and Brad were struggling as a couple and even more so as a family. Everyone had sensed the tension in Amanda and Brad's marriage and their hearts broke for little Branda. It seemed Dakota would be arriving late to the reunion.

***

Seated at the table closest to the stage were Kent, Tim, Susan, Dwayne, Johnny, Margarita, Darcie, and Patty, while Tracy buzzed around to ensure everything was going as planned. In doing so, she noticed the entire graduating class had ostensibly forgotten about the high school cliques and stereotypical groupings from back in the '70s, as if the past had not mattered at all.

Tim shared with the group at the table about his rehearsals for *Fame*, and how different his life had become. Susan was enthralled with Tim's stories and pleased that Dwayne could take care of himself socially. Both men had been on the basketball team together and laughed about the belligerent coaches and fanatical parents. It was obvious to everyone that Tim and Dwayne were happy with who they had become.

Johnny got up from the table and moved closer to Darcie. He whispered for her to sit with Margarita, as she had something to tell her. Instantly Darcie knew. And before Margarita could say a word, Darcie leaned over and said, "I hope you're not having twins. I hear they can be quite a handful!" The three erupted into laughter until the whole table wanted in on the joke. And then Darcie said, "Gee, I've become a sister and an auntie all in one fell swoop!"

And then, without any warning, Nelson was ready to make his move. As Patty looked up to see him approaching their table, she did a double-take. There was something strikingly handsome about Nelson; he was different somehow. Patty wondered why he was walking with such purpose. She surmised that he had finally come to his senses, and her physical transformation had worked.

And then the news reporter in her became instinctively alarmed.

Patty looked to the others at the table, but no one had noticed a thing. Grabbing the microphone from the podium and jerking the long extension cord to move with it, Nelson made his way over to the table and assertively knelt down at Darcie's feet. Clearing his throat into the microphone, Nelson said, "Attention everyone, I have an announcement!"

Suddenly the table became quiet, and a hushed silence permeated the room. Bewilderment spread over the entire gym when in a loud voice, louder than necessary, Nelson spoke rapidly. "Darcie, I have loved you for the last twenty years..."

Darcie felt her face turn pale and her blood run cold.

"...and you, pretty lady, never gave me the time of day. But now I am a successful inventor businessman and want you to become my wife!"

Nelson's behaviour was brash and inappropriate. The whole auditorium sat without speaking, which created a paradox of awkward stillness.

Dakota had walked into the gym not two minutes before, having arrived just in time to hear Nelson's proclamation to Darcie. As soon as Johnny saw Nelson leaning into Darcie as if expecting a kiss, he jumped up out of his seat, spilling a red cup filled with pop. Kent was on high alert because of his run-in with Nelson a few weeks back, while Tim was oblivious to who Nelson was and didn't understand what the problem was.

For a split second, Patty was disheartened by Nelson's proclamation and baffled at the proposal. However, instead of being jealous, Patty's thoughts quickly turned to concern for her new friend Darcie.

Taken off guard, Darcie tried to find her voice and said, "Um, Nelson, I think you have me confused with someone else. We've never even spoken before, so I don't understand what you're referring to."

Nelson went from zero to one hundred within seconds of Darcie's response. He clenched his fists, tightened his jaw and started to yell, "What the hell is wrong with everyone in this town???"

Before things could go any further, Dakota strode over quickly, as he was unsure of what Nelson was capable of doing. Johnny tried to reason with Nelson and firmly said, "Whoa, buddy, settle down!" Kent came up behind Nelson and put him in a headlock, and even though he wasn't violent, he was strong and a perpetual leader, or so he liked to think. He tried to diffuse the situation by saying, "Hey bud, maybe we can talk business now. Why don't we just take it outside?" As if directly quoting his therapist, Kent finished by saying, "Don't let whatever is bothering you take over your true happiness."

Meanwhile, Tracy could not believe the mayhem at *her* event. She ran over and said, "I demand these shenanigans stop this instant or I will call the police!" And then, in a little girl's whiny voice, she cried, "You're wrecking the whole thing!"

As her long pink dress swished and her big hair itched, Tracy sanctioned the DJ to begin playing the music, even though it was two hours too early, which reminded her of the musicians striking up a tune when the Titanic went down. For some reason, the DJ started with the first dance song Tracy had picked as a joke, "We've Only Just Begun," by The Carpenters, a cheeky nod to the 1978 graduation ceremony when everyone bemoaned her choice. She had thought it would be comical and nostalgic.

Susan and Dwayne didn't want to get involved, so they moved away from the table, and Dwayne whispered to Susan that she'd better call the police. Instead, Susan started snapping photos of the debacle with one of the Kodak Instamatic cameras. Nelson screamed incoherently while in Kent's headlock. Johnny tried to separate the wrestling men, while Dakota, as unlikely as it was and entirely out of character, wound up for a punch.

Meanwhile, Susan thought it would make a great newspaper story, with the headline, "Hey MeadowBrook, Look What the Returning Grads Got Up To!"

Patty thought the whole incident to be rather ironic. There she was, having worked on herself for years so Nelson would notice her. Concurrently, Darcie, who she used to despise back in high school, had just been proposed to by Patty's hoped-for man. In a very short time, Patty had grown to like Darcie and no longer considered her an opponent, or someone she wanted to beat in beach volleyball.

Darcie was in the middle of it all, and as she looked up to Dakota with pleading eyes, his protective spirit imploded, causing him to act with his heart and not his brain. While Kent had Nelson in a full nelson, Dakota passionately punched the guy whom nobody remembered, square in the middle of Nelson's nose.

At the exact instant his angry fist slammed into Nelson's seemingly innocent face, the previously shell-shocked room erupted into chaos. After his first blow, Dakota wondered why physical power felt so good.

Patty grabbed Darcie's hand, yanked her out of her chair, and pulled her over to the side of the gymnasium, like a referee sending an unwilling player to the penalty box.

At the same time, the two new friends looked over at the catastrophe as sirens from outside interrupted the simulated bar-room brawl. Within minutes, the MeadowBrook P.D. had barged in. Tables were overturned, centrepieces went flying, and two roaring lion sculptures made of ice went crashing to the floor, causing the lion heads to split down the middle while ice shards splintered onto the well-used gym floor.

Tracy stood with her hand frozen over her gaping mouth, unsure of what to do next. Usually fast on her feet, she felt annoyed and unusually flustered.

The class of '78 waited for the outcome.

The unexpected blowout occurred before the serving of the 7:00 p.m. dinner and Tim's performance of his part in the musical *Fame*. Meanwhile, all five men—Nelson, Dakota, Johnny, Kent and Tim—who behaved like unruly primary students, were carted off to the MeadowBrook jail.

Law enforcement felt they had valid cause for bringing each of them in.

First and foremost was Nelson Farnsworth, for instigating a disturbance, and based on his criminal record, he was considered a threat. Dakota was brought in because he threw the first punch. Johnny Fasp, as the town's well-known pot supplier, even though he was no longer dealing, was still on law enforcement's radar; Kent Gordon was detained for holding Nelson down; and last but not least, Tim Barnes was taken in because he was guilty by association—and rumour suggested he was a homosexual, which was widely frowned upon, even though an unjust accusation and nothing to do with the whole fiasco.

All were handcuffed, read their Miranda rights, and loaded into the back of a police van, referred to as the town's paddy wagon. Everyone shuffled for a seat on the hard bench and flailed about as it screeched out of the parking lot with sirens blaring.

In the back of the police vehicle, Tim was the first to notice the extreme stench of liquor, old cigarettes, perspiration, and a general aura of criminal behaviour. At the same time, his four counterparts erupted into an argument for the sake of being heard. All in due course, they let off steam, rebuked the police, and shared their feelings of disappointment and the injustice of a wrongful arrest.

They spoke all at once and didn't stop to listen or hear one another.

Nelson: "Why the fuck did you tackle me, Kent!?"

Johnny: "What the hell, Nelson? Darcie doesn't even know you!"

Kent: "What's wrong with you, Nelson? My girlfriend has been working on this stupid event for a year, and you go and sabotage the whole thing!"

Tim: "Wait, what? You and Tracy are dating? Why am I even here? I'm supposed to be dancing right now!"

Dakota: "Okay, guys, we all need to settle down, breathe, and relax. Let's think about this for a minute!"

Nelson: "I was trying to have a meaningful romantic moment with my girlfriend, and then you idiots had to go and wreck it!"

Johnny: "For fucks sake, I just told you she's not your girlfriend. She didn't even know you existed!"

Kent: "Yeah, Dakota's right. We all just need to simmer down. I'll call my dad. He'll know what to do!"

Tim: "I hope we'll be back in time for me to perform!"

When they got to the police station, they were each allowed one phone call.

Nelson called the psychiatric ward of MeadowBrook Hospital to speak with his grandma. However, the receptionist would not put the call through and said to Nelson, "Our guests are not allowed phone calls unless they have been pre-arranged." Therefore, Gladys Farnsworth could not come to the phone or know that her grandson had called. This only infuriated Nelson further, causing him to slam down the receiver and yell, "DAGNAMITT!"

The rest rallied around Kent, and in unison said, "You gotta call your dad, Kent; he'll get us out of this!" Everyone knew that nobody messed with Mayor Gordon's son. Tim was not speaking with his father, so he hoped Mayor Gordon would contact his dad, as he was the best defence attorney, if the most corrupt. Even though Tim and his dad were not on speaking terms, he was willing to make an exception and allow his father to get them out of the group's predicament.

***

Meanwhile, back at the school, Amanda, Patty, Darcie, Susan, Dwayne, Brad and Tracy gathered behind the stage to figure out what they should do next. Since everything happened at their table, they all felt especially close to the situation.

Tracy exclaimed, "Oh my goodness, I can't believe this has happened. What is wrong with people? Does anyone know how hard I have worked for this event to be perfect?!"

Susan spoke to her husband and said, "Dwayne, I am so proud of you for not getting involved."

Amanda said, "Geez, Brad, why didn't you do something? You work here, for Pete's sake!"

Darcie apologized, "I am so sorry this has happened. I had no idea…"

Dwayne proclaimed, "Okay, so look, I know Johnny and his dad are not getting along right now, but Mr. Fasp and I get along pretty good 'cause I'm his number one employee. I'm sure I can get him to do something. You know he has a lot of power in this town."

Patty spoke up, "Look, I feel responsible. The proposal should have been for me. I should have communicated with Nelson all these years. I'm sure I could have influenced him somehow."

While cradling her tiny baby bump, Margarita moaned, "Oh dear, now what?"

Dwayne whispered to Susan while winking, "Hey Suzie, since we have a sitter, do you want to take off for a quickie?"

Susan just rolled her eyes, smiled and said, "Oh you! Don't be silly, not now. Tracy needs me. And I need you to contact your boss whom you speak so highly of."

Finally, in pure businesswoman form, Tracy stepped up to the microphone and announced. "Excuse me, everyone." After the room settled, Tracy cleared her throat and continued, "We have had a slight interruption, but everything will be okay. Thank you so much for your patience. Dinner will now proceed as planned. So, if everyone could please take their seats, the servers will be around with the first course."

Most people made their way to their tables, while some ran up to the bar to load up on more drinks, or went out to use the washroom to make more room for their four-course meal. Once the meal distribution was underway, Tracy, Susan, Margarita, Amanda, and Patty fled to the police station. Tracy left Tim's little sister in charge, and as she was going out the door, she said, "Here's your chance, Marnie, to show me what you're made of. You can do this! I promise to promote you and give you a raise if all goes well."

Menu
Fruit and cheese plate
Caesar salad

Roast Beef, mashed potatoes and gravy
OR
Salmon Wellington with Rice Pilaf

Sides—French-cut green beans, kernel corn, baby carrots, and a buttermilk biscuit.
Dessert—organic Peach Cobbler or Dark Chocolate Mousse

Meanwhile, Dwayne asked Brad if he had some school keys and could let him into the office to phone John Fasp.

Walking down the familiar hallways, Dwayne had flashbacks of school dances, assemblies, and all the girls he'd had crushes on but was always too shy to do anything about it. As they passed the wall with the past years of graduating photos, Dwayne slowed down and said to Brad, "Hey get a load of this..." Dwayne pointed to his 1978 grad photo, complete with feathered bangs, pimples, and an awkward smile. Both men laughed as Dwayne announced, "What a goof I was!" He made a point to find Susan's photo and then said, "Just imagine that guy hooking up with this beauty queen!" Eyeing up the photo, Dwayne went on to say, "Seriously, man, never in my wildest dreams did I ever imagine marrying someone as heart-stoppingly beautiful and intelligent as Susan Jillian."

Brad smiled, nodded, and then said, "Hey, can you help me find Amanda's photo?"

Dwayne mentioned that he and Amanda were both volleyball team captains and he once had a secret crush on her. In the sense of true team spirit, they supported each other and often went to tournaments together. He went on to say how cute Amanda was and how he couldn't think of one person who didn't like her back in high school, and that still, all these years later, people adored her.

Brad stood still and admired his wife's black-and-white graduating photo. He smiled at her pleasant demeanour, sparkly eyes, and charming dimples. He was immediately filled with remorse.

Before beating himself up for almost being unfaithful, he took Dwayne's suggestion to look into the next showcase at all the trophies the girls' volleyball team had won. There Brad saw more photos of Amanda with the whole team holding her up length-wise. In some pictures, Amanda's face was beaming, and in others, she was outwardly laughing. Brad wondered when the last time was that he saw Amanda smile, and then noticing her fit, athletic body, Brad gasped.

Dwayne added in a more sombre tone, "Hey, by the way, that sucks about your kid. I got four of my own, so I can't imagine how hard that must be." Staring down at the floor, Brad said nothing.

Dwayne broke the silence by saying, "C'mon, I gotta make that call and see if I can help those idiots!

Still captivated by seeing his wife in her school years before the weight of the world landed on her shoulders, Brad slowly turned away and said quietly to Dwayne, "Yeah, right, I'll show you to the phone."

Unlocking the office door, Brad wondered how he could have worked at the school for the last five years and never once tried to find Amanda's graduation photo. Let alone why he had not shown an interest in his wife's successes and past life, the life she led as a carefree, fit, popular jock before they dated. He then visualized how tired and sad she had become.

Brad heard a slight murmur from Dwayne speaking to someone on the phone, but could not make out the entire conversation because he was fixated on his marriage. Or lack thereof.

The jailhouse had been one of the first buildings William Farnsworth built when he founded the town. He intended for it to be purposeful and utilitarian. Therefore, the four cement walls were drab and barren. The hard benches were designed to be uncomfortable.

After the rowdy men had settled down and each was immersed in his own thoughts, the voices of the four most powerful men in MeadowBrook could be heard as they clamoured down the hallway toward the cell.

Through the bars, the five young men stood up and morphed into the little boys they once were, looking into the older faces that resembled their own; all except Dakota, as his dad was not there. Ironically even if his father were alive, he never would have come to the station, for fear his son would be treated even worse by his presence.

Dakota looked at the dads and how much they had aged. Some had worked harder than others, while all of them shared wealth, power, and a voice in the community. All were trusted and sometimes feared.

At that moment, Dakota held disdain for all of them.

Before anyone spoke, Nelson stood up, pointed to Dakota, and said, "He started it. I should have known; he always thought he was better than everyone else. I should have figured he would steal my girl!"

Everyone looked at Nelson in disbelief, as it was well known that Dakota was not self-serving and was probably the most upstanding and ethical person in all of MeadowBrook. Besides, Tim, Kent, and even Johnny knew that Darcie and Dakota had always been an item and the envy of the entire student body back in high school.

First to speak was Mayor Gordon, Kent's father. He had the gift of the gab, and was articulate and well-spoken, but could switch gears easily and become a crass man's man. "Okay now, Nelson, keep your panties on. There has been a misunderstanding with all you knuckleheads, and I'm sure it can be sorted out within minutes."

Next to speak was Tim's dad, lawyer Chuck Barnes, who looked past his own son and showed no sign of interest or pleasure in being there. "Hold on, everyone. As a lawyer, I must demand that none of you say a word. We need to determine if charges are being laid, and if so, who is being charged and for what. Remember, anything you say can be held against you, so, in other words, shut the fuck up!"

John Sr. leaned in toward Johnny and whispered, "Look, son, I'm sorry we got off to a bad start, but off the record, do you have any pot on you? If you do, just slip it through the bars right now, and I'll get rid of it."

Nelson's father, Marvin Farnsworth, was embarrassed that his son had somehow instigated something. He was overwhelmed and felt disoriented, not knowing what it was, so he stood meekly by the side, hoping the other fathers would sort the whole thing out.

The nine men—fathers and sons—turned toward the hallway when female voices were heard coming their way. Margarita was crying. Tracy was indignant, while Susan quietly and supportively held her friend's hand. Amanda craned her neck and looked feverishly for Dakota. She thought she could help defend him. She wanted to give back the kindness he had always shown her, especially since he was the only male friend she ever had. Patty and Darcie stood together tenuously, each looking and listening for clues about what would happen next.

Chaos erupted.

Finally, the three men with the most money and clout in MeadowBrook headed toward the bailiff to collectively bail everyone out.

Tim, Kent, Johnny, Nelson and Dakota were released, with dollar bills passed through hands and a pen stroke absolving the disturbance of the peace infraction. Money and power sorted the whole fiasco out.

The newly affiliated mob headed out into the summer night air, appreciating the freshness and freedom. The young adults went over the night's events as if they were describing an exciting movie.

Noticeably, Nelson had run off, to Patty's dismay. A few of the guys hollered after him, "Hey Nelson, where are you going?" Most annoyed was Kent, who said, "Thanks for nothing, Nelson," after which Tracy gently shoved Kent and whispered, "Be nice, hon. As annoyed as I am with him, I also feel kind of bad for the guy."

Kent spoke first. With Tracy at his side, he looked at the whole group and said, "Sorry, guys, but that bonehead just gets under my skin. Maybe we should just forgive and forget, though." Once again winking at Tracy for approval, Kent went on to say, "Tim, buddy! I heard you've made it to the big leagues. How about giving us a demonstration of what we missed at the reunion?" At first, everyone thought Kent had resorted back to his mean old sarcastic self, but the warm smile on his face changed their minds, and everyone broke into heartfelt laughter, Tim included

Tim turned toward Kent and the others, proceeded to take one giant step backwards, and performed the most remarkable pirouette, followed by a kick that was higher than anything anyone had ever seen.

As the group applauded, the four fathers walked down the courthouse steps. None of them were pleased with the gleeful sound of their sons' voices, and catching the tail end of Tim's dance move, Tim's dad turned on his heels and briskly walked in the other direction. Kent's dad exclaimed, "What the hell was that?" He called them all a bunch of morons and told them to stay out of trouble, and to thank him for setting the record straight. Johnny's dad was quiet and awkward. He shuffled from side to side, not knowing what to say or do. Then he looked toward Darcie with tears welling in his eyes and mouthed the words, "I'm sorry."

Darcie bowed her head, avoiding eye contact, and Johnny, Margarita, and Dakota moved in closer. Not knowing what else to say, John Fasp Sr. left the young people, got in his truck and drove home alone. Driving through town, he slowed down as he passed Nancy's apartment.

Amanda felt foolish for climbing into Tracy's pink vehicle and speeding off to the jail. Obviously, she was not needed, as Dakota had Darcie. She wondered if she was just trying to get away from Brad and the memories of her past—a time when she was popular and fun.

With everyone except Nelson still outside the courthouse, milling about, the three couples were all intertwined in one way or another. Kent had his arm slung over Tracy's shoulder, Dakota and Darcie held hands, and Johnny stood tall behind Margarita with his arms wrapped protectively around her waist. It was apparent they were all in love. Amanda longingly looked at their faces and tried to read their minds. She wanted what they had, but she was unsure of how to obtain it.

Patty just wanted a do-over of her whole high school experience. Suddenly, she felt ridiculous standing outside the courthouse, while couples cuddled and friends connected. She deliberately stood outside the circle to ponder why she was there and why she'd even returned to the town she owed nothing to. Patty tried to figure out Nelson's display of bizarre behaviour, but gave up.

All of it felt ironic to Patty. Since her feelings for Nelson had always been a secret, no mind was given to her in regard to his recent meltdown.

Out of the darkened night, Dwayne showed up. He had left the school after he called John Fasp, and to his delight, the five jailbirds were walking free. As he joined the group, he quickly spotted Susan, and after enveloping her in a huge embrace, he said, "Hey does anyone want to see photos of our kids?" Laughter ensued.

Tim and Amanda became quiet, and they too, like Patty, stood by, as if outsiders to the mix.

Tracy then announced that she needed to return to the school to assess the damage and begin the cleanup. Everyone agreed to join her. All except for Patty.

Before departing, someone said, "Hey, don't we have the picnic tomorrow?" Tracy chimed in and said, "Yes! And you better all be there!"

As Patty walked away, she visualized herself in her red bikini and decided she would attend. Looking over her shoulder, she asked what time, and they all yelled out different times and then collectively laughed. Tracy took charge and said, "People, get with the program. The invitation says 11:00 a.m!" Kent replied, "That's my girl. Don't you just love how bossy she is?" More laughter erupted as Patty nodded, smiled, and started walking home alone.

Tim ran after her and offered to walk with her, but she waved him off and said it wasn't far. Patty thought it interesting how not one person in the group knew where she lived, but she knew precisely where they had all grown up.

About a block from her parents' home, Patty saw a silhouette of someone sitting at the bus stop. She shivered briefly, pulled her purse in tighter to her body, and slipped off her high-heeled shoes. She considered walking back toward the courthouse but knew everyone would be gone, so she kept up with her confident stride and knew that with bare feet, she could run faster than most.

Keeping her eyes on the shadowy figure as if marking the distance, Patty saw her house come into sight and let out a quiet sigh of relief. Then, just as quickly as she felt free from danger, Patty froze at the sight of Nelson Farnsworth. His darkened frame sat motionless, illuminated by the street light. Expressionless, he slowly stood up, turned and looked Patty directly in the eyes.

***

Amanda wondered how Brad had fared at the reunion without her, especially since it was her get-together, not his. Her thoughts shifted to Branda, tiny and alone in her hospital bed, and then Amanda felt the pull to go see her.

She had been watching the four couples all evening and had grown tired of their outward displays of love and affection. It was almost as if they were in a competition. When the group walked past the street the hospital was on, she whispered to Dakota that she was not going back to the school with everyone else. Amanda asked if he could let Brad know she had decided to sleep at the hospital. Dakota assured her he would.

Before saying goodbye, Amanda took in the group and thought about how they looked like the cast from *St. Elmo's Fire*. It was one of her favourite movies, but she couldn't help thinking that she would have been cast as the sad, unpopular girl.

Nevertheless, she said goodbye as cheerfully as she could while everyone kissed and hugged her. They all vowed to watch her until she entered the building, and the last words she heard were, "See you at the pond tomorrow, Amanda! Be sure to bring your kids!" It felt instinctual to correct them, and even though she didn't, she wanted to say, "Oh, you mean *kid*. You see, I used to have two kids, but one is out of commission, the good one. The one *I like* is dying." Instead, Amanda waved and smiled and said, "Okay, will do! See you tomorrow!"

She knew they were watching her walk away, so she picked up speed and turned toward the nearest hospital entrance.

It was late, and the regular visiting hours were over. However, being the parent of a sick child is like having a free pass, or if it were a game of Snakes and Ladders, she would be shooting up to the next level. Parents always had priority.

When Amanda got off the elevator on Branda's floor, she checked in with the night nurse at the nursing station. The corridors were dimly lit, and the only sound was the beeping of the ventilators and heart monitors. The quiet hallway felt familiar, warm and welcoming. Only when Amanda thought of not being there did she feel its coldness, because it would mean the unthinkable if she wasn't needed at the hospital anymore.

Amanda was exhausted and ready to take off her shoes and curl up next to her baby girl. But when she entered her daughter's room, she was alarmed to see a human form sitting upright next to the hospital bed. She was initially frightened. Squinting her eyes until they adjusted to the darkness, Amanda finally made out who the person was.

She dropped her purse, moved over to the chair and knelt down on the floor next to Brad who was silently weeping. Amanda sat on the floor, put her head on her husband's lap and nestled into his legs while he stroked her hair.

***

The cleanup was almost finished when Tracy, Kent, Darcie, Dakota, Susan, Johnny, Margarita, and Tim returned to the gymnasium. Kent exclaimed how hungry he was and wondered if there were any leftovers, and when Marnie said everything had been eaten, the four couples decided to have a late-night supper at Robinson's.

Susan moved toward Dwayne's side and placed her arms around his waist. Nose to nose, she thanked him for calling John Sr. and holding down the fort with Marnie. She expressed how much she appreciated him and how happy she was that he did it all for her best friend Tracy.

Tracy profusely thanked Marnie and threw her the keys to lock up. At the same time, she said, "You just got yourself a raise, missy, and a new title, Project Manager. I think I may be travelling a little in the near future, so I'm going to need you!" Looking over at Kent, she winked, smiled, and finished with, "Even though I hate flying AND I hate big cities!"

Kent let out a hoot and exclaimed, "Yeah! That's what I'm talking about!"

Tim stayed behind to help his sister lock up, and after everyone had left, Marnie walked through the school halls with her older brother. They looked at the graduating class of 1978's photos and then found Marnie's graduating class of 1988. Tim apologized for being a no-show at his sister's grad ceremony. They stood for the longest time admiring the sports trophies in the case outside the gymnasium, all emblazoned with Tim's name. During this time, Tim opened up to his sister about how confusing his life had been. He speculated that their dad would never be able to see him for who he was, and yet how happy he was that they were getting to know each other, all because she reached out first and picked him up at the airport.

***

Leaving the gym, the four couples walked hand in hand down the middle of the empty street. Darcie couldn't get over how everything was within walking distance. She had forgotten how small the town was. Everyone laughed and called her *the big city slicker* for the rest of the evening.

Sitting in one of the largest booths at the back of Robinson's while they shared two plates of onion rings and French fries, with burgers on the way, the eight young adults went over the night's events.

Kent started the conversation by saying, "What the hell is wrong with that guy? Did I tell you he came to my office a few months ago and asked me to invest in some cream he had invented?"

Johnny added, "I just want to know where he gets off asking my sister to marry him. Like, what the hell? That is one unstable dude!"

Before anyone else could chime in, Tracy said she was disappointed that the night had been fun for many returning grads, but not for them, because they had missed almost everything. Susan said, "It's okay, hon. We can make up for it tomorrow at the picnic, and besides, you got what you set out to achieve." Tracy immediately kicked Susan under the table, and then they both laughed.

Kent said, "Hey, did I miss something?"

Dakota replied, "It was great, Tracy. I am so sorry the night turned out the way it did, and I really regret that I punched Nelson. I honestly don't know what came over me. I'll apologize to him tomorrow. But hey, this is fun!" And then he said with more enthusiasm, "I think we should all go around the table and share how much we appreciate something. I'll go first!"

Everyone laughed. Kent held up his hand as if to say, "Wait a minute." Johnny looked over at Margarita and put his hand on her belly. Susan and Dwayne rolled their eyes, and Darcie said, "No, let me go first!" And without missing a beat, she turned to Dakota and said, "I love you, Dakota Hillsman, and I appreciate how well you deal with people who are illogical and unreasonable, and I adore how you care for all the misfits of the world."

There was a smattering of laughter from the group, along with a few *awws*. And then Tracy said with a big smile, "I could have told you Dakota was like that years ago! They didn't call me the town busybody for nothing!" More laughter was had by all.

***

In the morning when Patty got up, her mother was at the kitchen table, already dressed, with a cup of coffee. Black, no sugar. Sighing heavily, Patty poured herself a coffee, chose not to add milk or sweetener, and then sat opposite her mom.

After saying good morning, both women sat quietly, sipping the rich dark goodness as if it was healing them. Staring at her mother, Patty noticed they held their mugs of coffee the same way, with both hands around the mug, gripping it like they never wanted to let go.

Patty thoughtfully looked at her mom and thought she was still an attractive woman—not quite as beautiful as she looked in her beauty pageant photos from long ago, but pretty for an older woman. She tipped her head to the side and decided her mom would look better if she cut her hair and stopped dyeing it jet black. Patty visualized her mom with a Lady Diana cut and then remembered her mom's addiction, knowing full well alcohol was a poison that robbed people of their looks, youth, and relationships.

Patty saw herself in a mirror above the kitchen hutch, and realized her own hair wasn't much better. She had coloured it for the past ten years and it looked very scraggly to her. She could use a trim and a hot oil treatment. She hoped she was not becoming like her mother and destined to be a dried-up wrinkly old drunk.

Maybelle Krakatoya looked up from what appeared to be deep thought and said, "How was the reunion?"

Patty typically would have shared the night's fiasco with her father and, in keeping with her journalistic flair, painted an elaborate picture. She would have described the food, what people were wearing, who she sat with, the look on everyone's face when Nelson proposed to Darcie, and how hurt she was that the proposal was not for her. Patty imagined her dad's eyes widening as she charismatically described the fight, the police arriving, and the horrific jail cell. Patty would have concluded her narration with seeing Nelson on the bus bench and how their eye contact unnerved her.

However, she recounted none of it to her mother, and before answering her simple question, Patty smiled, thinking about Nelson and how they had talked until the sun came up.

Bringing her attention back to the present, Patty could hear the flatness in her own voice when she said, "Oh, it was okay. It wasn't as much fun as I thought it would be."

Patty's mom responded with a smile, a nod, and no further inquiries. She said, "Oh, good. Well as for me, I'm taking it one day at a time and today is a brand-new day. Baby steps, dear."

Feeling exasperated, Patty guzzled her coffee, stood up and hurriedly said, "That's great, Mom. Well, I gotta get ready. There's a picnic at the pond today, so see you later. Good luck with your one-day-at-a-time thing."

Patty's mother was still sitting at the kitchen table when she breezed past with her beach bag. She decided to walk into town to see some of her old friends and then walk to the pond by herself for the picnic.

While she strolled, Patty thought of the day she flew into the Hillsprings airport and how disappointed she was that things were not as she had hoped. Her father had sounded so excited over the telephone and optimistic about her mother's recovery that Patty had almost believed it to be true. The sober woman he described was not the mother Patty had been raised by. She was the fairy-tale version, an image Patty had often dreamed of. Her childhood fantasy was to have a friendly, caring mother to wake up to in the morning, a capable parent throughout the day, and a truly attentive mom to put her to bed.

Patty's thoughts drifted back to the here and now. The sun was warm and gentle, but the neighbourhood and sidewalk were nostalgic, reminiscent of her childhood, which was cold and harsh.

The stirring up of past hurts had given Patty a headache. To lessen her misery and the tinge of pain in her temples, Patty stopped at a convenience store and bought a diet Pepsi—the same store she had walked to as a child to purchase Twinkies, Ding-Dongs, and her favourite ice cream sandwiches by the box. Once inside, Patty noticed how nothing had changed: the creaking hardwood floors, the shopkeeper behind the counter, the old-fashioned cash register, and the jingling bell when the door opened and closed were all exactly as she remembered. In contrast, Patty smiled at her own success when it came to transforming herself. Sipping the low-calorie sweetness, her mood shifted, and her spirits picked up when she thought of her new self and new friends back home in California.

As Patty made her way to Robinson's, she went over some positive things about being home. The three-hour drive from the airport with Darcie and Dakota had been fun, and more interesting than Patty imagined.

She recalled how the three of them had reminisced about high school. They had laughed about Principal Marples, with his marionettes at the school assemblies and how fun the basketball and volleyball games had been. Patty chimed in and said, "And will you look at us now, sharing all the hobbledehoy!" Darcie and Dakota smiled at Patty's choice of words, with Darcie asking while laughing, "What the heck is that supposed to mean?"

Patty smiled wryly and explained that as a journalist, she tried to use a variety of terms, and that "hobbledehoy" meant an awkward, ungainly youth. Her two counterparts nodded, and then Patty felt silly and wondered if she was showing off or just being creative and clever.

For part of the drive, Patty had opened up about all the years of feeling invisible. Darcie shared how she was not a partier like everyone thought, and Dakota told both women how he also felt unseen and greatly misunderstood back in high school.

As Darcie shared about her mom's cancer and Dakota talked about the death of his father, Patty knew that if she chose to, she could safely share about her alcoholic mother and how difficult her teenage years had been. Instead, she sat quietly and acted like a good listener.

Their stories surprised Patty because of her old habit of perceiving everyone else's life as better than hers. Growing up, she rarely felt content or happy in the moment and was always either pining for winter when it was stiflingly hot outside, or dreaming of the summer when the gloom and doom of winter became too much. However, her travelling companions' stories implied that they were all more or less in the same boat.

Deep down, Patty struggled to believe they were all on the same playing field, because to her, Darcie and Dakota still wore the high school titles of popular and attractive. She had never been either of those things, yet wanted to be both.

So even though she appreciated their openness, Patty held back while the couple she had always envied shared their true colours. She allowed the reunion of the teenage boyfriend and girlfriend to occur as if she were a fly on the wall.

Aside from being still, something had shifted for Patty. She felt calm, relaxed, and honoured to witness Darcie's and Dakota's process of unraveling their past. Staring straight ahead, Patty smiled and felt like a MeadowBrook cheerleader rooting for the team of two to make it, to be together and win the game of life.

As they pulled up in front of Patty's house, she thanked them for the ride and apologized for her initial rudeness. They all shared a collective sigh, as if they were exhaling the past and inhaling the future.

When she left the vehicle and her new friends, Patty felt light and optimistic, until the reality of her own family situation hit her like a ton of bricks.

Upon entering her childhood home, Patty had walked around the stark three-bedroom bungalow with judgmental eyes. It was dark and dismal and appeared as if she had never left. Everything had remained unchanged, from the brown sofa to the drab brown curtains in the living room, the dining room table that was never used for entertaining, and the kitchen where Patty's food addiction had comforted her loneliness. She laughed out loud in a sarcastic tone at the paradox of how she had bettered herself since leaving and while her mother was the same old drunk lying hungover in her same old bed, with crumpled bedding and frayed curtains. Maybelle Krakatoya, closed up tight like the dingy bedroom drapes, and Patricia Krakatoya open for all the world to see, like a rose on a spring day.

Patty asked her depressing dismal past, "Hey, where's my new and improved mother? Oh, I know, she's up to her old tricks again—disappointment and setbacks!"

On her first night back, as she battled the onset of a headache, Patty's dad exited the bedroom where her mother was held captive by the substance that controlled her. Mr. Krakatoya apologized. He said he was sorry for her mother's behaviour and explained how hard it was to quit an addiction. Patty had heard the familiar excuses one too many times, so, during her dad's admission, Patty was transported back to her old self and fell into her usual pattern of saying, "It's okay, Dad. It's not you, it's her. Besides, it's you I love."

Patty's father went on to explain how wonderful her sobriety had been. She had become her old self again, fun and funny. Then one week before Patty was to arrive home, her mother relapsed. He explained that she had experienced an unusually bad day. She'd run out of gas in the car, missed a hair appointment, and when she was walking home after leaving her car on the side of the road, someone she knew in a passing car yelled out their window, "Hey, you looking for a bar? C'mon, drinks are on me!" And that was it. She walked directly across the street to O'Leary's Bar and Grill and made a toast to her very bad day.

Patty became her twelve-year-old self again, too disheartened to pay her mother a visit. She went straight to her bedroom and plopped down on the bed with the same chenille bedspread from when she was a girl. Patty touched the fabric and remembered how the textured pile was rough and itchy, not soft and supple like the Eaton's catalogue had led one to believe. As a little girl, and later as a teenager, the rough thread with its blend of wool and cotton bothered her, so she would peel back the peach-coloured bed covering and sleep with just the sheet and blanket that had worn thin and threadbare.

Looking around her old room, she had felt sad and bleak. She knew right then and there that she would have to fight hard to remember who she had become in the ten years since leaving. Beautiful beach volleyball babe, Patricia Krakatoya. News anchor and soon-to-be investigative reporter—not the plain, unfit, dull girl the whole town talked about.

Crawling into bed, she had closed her eyes tight and visualized the sand and surf in California. Patty saw herself playing volleyball and laughing with all her coworkers and college pals. Curling up, she felt her body relax and pretended her high school past did not own her.

As she drifted off to sleep that night, Patty felt a glimmer of hope and slight stirrings of excitement when she thought about the upcoming grad reunion less than a week away. There she would make her mark and showcase her new persona, complete with the impressive job and toned body.

The morning after arriving, Patty took an hour to get ready. Without checking in on her mother and having not yet said hello to her, she left and walked into town. Even though her feet hurt in high heels, she stood tall and became Patricia. She was friendly to everyone she passed, and was surprised by how much the town had changed. She stopped by the department store and, for the fun of it, purchased a pair of her favourite white Keds. She refused to allow any flashbacks of her past to sneak into her thoughts, which forced Patricia to see her hometown with new, fresh eyes.

Later in the day, she had knocked on her mother's bedroom door and was told to "come in," but chose not to. She spent the next few days being kind and cordial to her mom, helping her dad around the house, sorting cupboards, cleaning, and suggesting her dad come and visit her after she returned to the Sunshine State.

Her new friend Darcie had met her for lunch at Robinson's. They were later joined by Dakota, and instead of laughing about the past, they each opened up about their struggles. When it was Patty's turn, she described her isolated childhood, reclusive family, and futile Alateen meetings.

Their lunch date lasted the entire afternoon, and the new friends listened raptly to Patty's story of leaving MeadowBrook with her cat Ruskin and her transformation in California. By the end of the conversation, Patty had invited them both to visit her and Albert in the fall.

The whole week had been cathartic.

On the day of the reunion, Patty was nervous, but not anxious; she had discovered there was a difference. In the past, and for most of her life, she had struggled with mental distress or uneasiness, always feeling as if she was headed for great danger, or that misfortune was waiting around the next corner. After moving away, Patty had grown, her views had changed, and her self-esteem skyrocketed. It was not until going back to MeadowBrook that Patty was able to make the correlation.

Decidedly, she preferred nerves over anxiety.

Getting ready for the reunion was easy. Arriving at the school and finding Darcie seated at a table went smoothly. However, what happened in the first thirty minutes of the much-anticipated event was difficult and troublesome for her to deal with.

After the grad reunion, which was nothing like Patty had expected, she thought the evening would go down in the history books of her soul as the most emotionally charged night of her life. She wondered if it was humanly possible for any one person to collectively feel joy, sorrow, fear, hate, love, and agitation in the course of one night.

When Nelson had walked over to her table and bent down on one knee in front of Darcie to propose marriage, the clock on the gymnasium wall stopped ticking, along with Patty's heart. The stillness had been broken by flying fists and exploding profanities.

Then it was over, and now on the following day, while she walked into town, Patty looked forward to seeing her old best friend Jan, who had once supported her, straightened her hair, and told her everything was going to be okay. However, when Patty entered the restaurant she was not warmly greeted. Instead, the look on her friends' faces was of surprise, followed by dismay. Instead of being happy for her, they behaved uncomfortably, as if Patty were a stranger.

Over scrambled eggs at the familiar diner, the conversation was strained, and as much as Patty wanted to talk about her college years, living near the beach, and her newsroom job, she held back. Most of her old friends had either gotten married or worked at Barney's department store or the local bank. To Patty, their lives seemed small and uneventful. Most of their light chit-chat over the breakfast table consisted of the newest books the MeadowBrook library had brought in, recent episodes of

Dallas, and which developmental stage each of their babies was currently at.

Patty noted that she had become an outsider among her childhood friends. Which in itself was familiar, like an old, worn pair of shoes that pinched because they were too small.

Getting up to use the washroom, she felt all eyes on her backside, and then Patty smiled at the irony and how the tables had turned. She was judging her old classmates for seemingly having empty lives, as she had once been judged. As Patty applied fresh lipstick and more rouge on her cheeks, she paused, giving herself a once-over in the mirror, and made the realization that nobody was small and insignificant. She smiled with approval at herself and thought true success was liking yourself, liking what you do, and how you do it. Patty came to the conclusion that everyone was living their best life.

Patty thought of her mom and the young woman she used to be. She whispered, "What happened to you, Mom?" She wanted to leave, not say goodbye, and get on a bus. She could visualize herself taking a Greyhound to the Hillsprings airport, getting on a plane to L.A., and sliding contentedly into Albert's arms.

During the past week, immersed in her mother's tragic life, Nelson's meltdown, and new and old friends, Patty had failed to think about her boyfriend much. After only one week away, she suddenly missed everything about California, especially who she had become, the career woman Patricia Krakatoya. She smiled at the thought of Albert and how he always called her *Patricia.*

She concluded that the most significant part of the whole trip to MeadowBrook was not the high school reunion, but rather it was staying up all night talking to Nelson. It had not been her lifelong dream come true, but nevertheless had felt rather monumental, and it was actually a relief that he was not interested in her romantically.

Their late-night conversation had revealed so much to Patty. They talked about Nelson's grandmother and the backwards injustice of when she was institutionalized, over rumours that she was a murderer.

Patty shared her thoughts on the legal system, detectives, and working at a news station. She explained her transformation after leaving MeadowBrook ten years earlier, and told Nelson she had no regrets. Nelson agreed and said leaving was the best thing he had ever done.

They both surmised that the judgment, gossip, and narrow-minded thinking of growing up in a small town had given them a limited view of themselves and the world. Each had since developed a new perspective and realized they were not the stereotypes they had once bought into.

Nelson divulged that his obsession with Darcie Richmond had become a crutch and a narrative he could not shake. He linked his infatuation with his mental health and wondered if he had slipped off the deep end, as his grandmother had done. He explained to Patty that the telephone call he made to her at the jail was his attempt to get back on track.

Nelson wondered if he had ever been on track in the first place.

As morning broke, Nelson thanked Patty for listening and stated that he had never told anyone his true feelings. She shared how she had been obsessed with him for most of her life. The astonishment on Nelson's face was comparable to winning the lottery for Patty. Nelson then gave Patty a once-over, looking her up and down as if seeing her for the first time. Patty thought to herself that normally, a gaze like that would have felt obtrusive and inappropriate. Then smiling, she'd said, "It's about damn time you noticed me!"

He apologized by saying, "Well, I have wasted almost my whole life longing for impossible things, with so much anger and rage, worry and self-loathing. I hope I never think about someone else as much as I have thought about a girl who never even knew I existed." With an exasperated sigh, Nelson looked into Patty's caring brown eyes and continued, "For what it's worth, can you please forgive my ignorance, that I never noticed you?"

He hung his head. "Sometimes we search a lifetime for what can be right under our nose the whole time."

Patty only smiled and chose to say nothing.

And that was that. Without embracing or making any future plans, they said goodbye. Each left the bench and walked in different directions, going their separate ways.

After taking a few steps, Patty turned around and said, smiling, "Hey Nelson, you know the old saying, 'life's a journey'? Well, it just so happens in our case, nobody had the courtesy to tell us our paths would be a construction zone!"

Nelson nodded and smiled back, responding, "Yeah, you got that right, and hey, something tells me we are both going to be okay."

Leaving the small two-stalled bathroom with the cracked mirror and empty paper towel dispenser, Patty walked out into the restaurant and saw the empty table where her friends had sat. All that was left were leftover plates of cold hash browns and dried-up egg bits. She spotted her old friend Jan waiting for her. Looking up as Patty approached, she said, "Sorry, Patty, they all needed to leave, but I'm still here."

Patty sat down next to her friend and said, "That's okay. I'm happy for some time alone with you. We have so much to catch up on. How are your mom and dad? I have so much to tell you about mine."

***

After the late-night feast at Robinson's Diner, Dakota invited Darcie to sleep over, but she was reluctant to say yes, even though she could see herself spending an eternity at his beautiful eclectic home. Just thinking about his menagerie of pets brought a glow to her face that spread throughout her being. As her heart swelled, Darcie smiled and thought, *What's not to love about this man?*

Looking at Dakota admiringly, she reflected on how much they had in common, from playing the guitar under a star-studded night sky, to believing in the healing principles of meditation. They shared the philosophies that what goes around comes around, and that a greater existence beyond themselves was universal and ever-present. When she discovered he was a vegetarian, the deal was sealed for her.

However, Darcie's first priority was her mother and ensuring she got the care she needed.

In the morning, waking up in her old bedroom and hearing the sound of wind chimes outside her window instantly put a smile on Darcie's face. Her mother's mystical hippie ways had not changed.

Lingering on the futon sofa bed, she squirmed slightly and missed her old mattress on the floor. Then she noticed the warm morning sun outside the window and the tinkling of the bamboo pipes sounded to her like church bells on a Sunday morning. She remembered how her mother once said, "Wind chimes expel negative spirits and attract loving spirits to any space, and if you listen closely, their sound in a gentle breeze has a calming effect, bringing peace to the environment." Darcie soaked up the familiar harmonious jangle and felt immense gratitude for her mother.

Reveling in the peaceful morning, she reflected on the past week. Darcie was astounded at how quickly Dakota forgave her for running away on grad night. They picked up right where they'd left off, just like a made-for-TV movie, the sappy plot wrapped up in less than two hours even with commercials.

On the other side of the coin was her brother and the entire Fasp family. Darcie had no desire to get to know her biological father, even though the truth of the matter pained her heart. John Fasp seemed more like a grandfather figure to her—and a mean, disgruntled one at that. Yet, she made a point never to say never.

However, the question remained: What if her mom had given both her and Johnny to their father, together, like a package deal, two for the price of one? Brief thoughts of what it would have been like to grow up on the farm with a twin brother and six other siblings gave Darcie pause and stirred up fleeting regret and melancholy.

Shoving down thoughts that would not serve her well, Darcie was excited to get reacquainted with Johnny for the time being. All her mixed emotions toward him over the years made sense now. She understood why she never wanted to date him and how they could often finish each other's sentences.

Eventually, Darcie flung her legs off the side of the futon, stood up and stretched, and threw on some cutoffs and an old Led Zeppelin tee. She went into the bathroom, pulled her long mane of hair into a high ponytail, splashed cold tap water on her face and brushed her teeth. She had forgotten how much she loved her mom's cinnamon organic toothpaste and made a mental note to buy some.

As she made her way into the kitchen, Darcie hoped her mom still drank coffee.

Unfortunately, after scouring the cupboards, the closest she could get to the pick-me-up that only caffeine could give her was a cup of black, loose-leaf tea. Darcie made a cup for both of them with a large dollop of honey, and mugs in hand, she lightly tapped on her mom's bedroom door with her foot. Nancy immediately responded and said, "Come in, sweetheart." When Darcie entered, she paused. There, sitting crossed-legged on her bedroom floor was her mom, who still looked so young. Darcie's eyes filled with tears when she was reminded again that her mother had cancer.

After handing her mom the tea, she climbed under the still-warm blankets just like she had done as a little girl. Darcie patted the bed and said, "Get in, Mom." Nancy obliged. Snuggling into her daughter's body, she listened intently as Darcie went over the night's events like she was reading from a well-loved fairy tale. Darcie allowed her voice to escalate in the dramatic parts and soften with concern while describing the jail.

She then steered the conversation to Johnny and told her mom how happy she was about meeting up with him and Margarita. She went on to say how sweet it was that he tried to defend her from Nelson's advances. Even though it was a little over the top and unnecessary, Darcie said she understood that he meant well.

Darcie then exclaimed, "Mom, did you know they're leaving for Argentina tomorrow morning?" Before Nancy could respond, Darcie went on to say, "Mom, please come to the picnic at the pond today, because afterward, Dakota and I are cooking dinner for Johnny and Margarita at Dakota's place. Please say yes. We don't know when we'll see them again!"

Nancy responded tenderly, "Yes, of course I'll come, darling. I wouldn't miss dinner with my two kids and soon-to-be daughter-in-law for anything in the world. However, I would rather not go to the pond. The heat and sun don't agree with me right now. But yes, of course, to the dinner. Besides, if I'm going to be a grandma and make trips to Argentina, I better catch up on everything I have missed."

The room fell silent as both women knew Nancy's days could be numbered; therefore, future travel may not be an option.

Initially, Darcie had a hard time imagining her mother as sick, and then at some point, something in her shifted to having a hard time visualizing Nancy being well. She shook the negative thoughts from her brain and forced a vision that the same time next year, her mom's cancer would be long gone. Even though the prognosis was not good, Darcie intended to get more details and be her mom's advocate.

Curled up next to her mom, Darcie rested her head on her mom's head and felt a lump growing in her throat. She didn't know if it was sorrow or gratitude, but she said a silent prayer to the universe, *"Please do not take my mother yet. There is still so much she wants to do."* Then she corrected herself, *"There is still so much WE want to do."*

Before getting ready for the picnic, Darcie shuffled through her mother's record collection and found what she was looking for. She had absent-mindedly been humming the song since she listened to it on the airplane—"The Circle Game" by Joni Mitchell. The album cover was memorable. Darcie remembered many years ago studying the outline of a woman and a hodgepodge of a colourful life, but it was not until all the recent changes for Darcie and her mom that she came to understand the lyrics and the creative album art of *Ladies of the Canyon.*

Everything about the song was relatable. It gave her pause and a desire to take out her journal. Finding it at the bottom of her duffel bag, Darcie found a pen, and in point form, she wrote down the words, *seasons, captive, time, game,* and *Dakota.*

***

Tracy and Kent were making up for lost time. They shared their thoughts on politics, the economy, their religious beliefs, music, books they've read, and their favourite television shows. He liked *Johnny Carson* and the 6:00 news. She liked *The Golden Girls* and *Sixty Minutes.*

Tracy told Kent she always knew they would one day be a couple, and Kent said, "Ditto to that!"

She brought Kent to one of Susan's aerobic classes, and they laughed and laughed through grapevines, squats, lunges, and the V-step. Since Kent was the only man on the floor among twenty women, Susan made a big fuss over him from her teaching spot on the stage.

Into her microphone headset, she teased him about being the only guy and referred to him during squats and push-ups, stating, "C'mon, Kent show us what you got!" He rose to the occasion and showed off just enough to get a laugh, but not too much to embarrass Tracy.

Meanwhile, both women were pleasantly surprised and impressed with Kent's coordination, energy, and determination. At the end of the class, Kent thanked Susan and commented on how fit both women were. He said he would attend more classes provided he did not have to wear spandex tights and leg warmers.

After the reunion, Kent listened while Tracy tried to unravel the events of the night before. She eventually came to terms with the event being enjoyed by most and being a great bonding experience for the ten of them, disconcerting as it was. Kent apologized for being a part of the Nelson fiasco; Tracy relayed her appreciation that he was only trying to help.

***

Tim and Marnie stayed up most of the night talking in her apartment living room. Tim explained how they would have called it "pulling an all-nighter" in his day.

Tim knew he was safely relaying details from his childhood that were completely unknown to his little sister. He candy-coated certain parts and was brutally honest in other areas. He told Marnie how out of place he had always felt, like an intruder and never comfortable in his own skin. Consequently, he had no idea who he was supposed to be.

He explained how their father always expected perfection, yet Tim only delivered disappointment. Therefore, feelings of failure followed him from MeadowBrook to university and then on to California. Tim dug deep, went to places he had never gone, and shared with Marnie how low he had become.

When he became quiet, Marnie knew there was more. She braced herself, put her hand on Tim's arm and gently said, "It's okay. You need to talk about it. I'm here for you, and I always will be. I want to be your sister and friend, so please let me."

With trepidation, Tim told his much younger and seemingly innocent sister how he grappled with suicide. Without wanting to frighten her, he skirted the details and then described how he succumbed to living because he was even more afraid of death than staying alive.

Seeing the shock on her face, Tim quickly added that performing, singing, and dancing gave him an outlet and always brought him out of the difficult times and slumps.

Marnie cried right along with her big brother as they hugged.

They sat for a while, not speaking. Just being in each other's presence was comforting. The time was right to be tuned in to each other, and aware of their brother-sister bond.

Tim changed gears, turning the conversation around, and got Marnie laughing at some of his auditioning horror stories. He described the many times he was turned down because he was too good-looking and too good of an actor. She belly-laughed at his retelling of the time he dressed as a lollipop for a toothpaste commercial and a banana for a Fruit of the Loom underwear ad. He carried on with examples of fellow actors in the auditioning room, practicing lines, being either overly friendly, or rude and obnoxious.

Tim summed it up and said, "All in all, Marnie, I figured out that I confused my mistakes with my destiny rather than allowing them to empower me."

Both siblings felt immensely grateful they had found each other.

At 7:00 a.m. Tim made his sister a special breakfast of huevos rancheros and coffee with heavy cream.

Marnie planned to visit Tim in Florida and hoped he would come home more often. Tim was reluctant to commit to anything but said he would be ecstatic if Marnie visited him in Florida.

The picnic at the pond would be their last time together before Tim left, and even though Marnie was not a part of his graduating class, Tim insisted she attend. "You can be my significant other because you are the most significant person in my life!"

They decided to catch a ride with Susan, Dwayne and their four children in their Econoline van to the picnic at the pond.

***

Waking up together in Branda's hospital room, Amanda and Brad had spent the night not talking but felt closer because of it. Nevertheless, they were groggy and disheartened about their daughter's situation and knew their strained marriage needed a lot of work if it was going to survive.

Neither one wanted to attend the picnic, and with feelings of nostalgia, Brad said, "Hey, let's blow it off, go for a jog, make some popcorn and participate in a little afternoon delight like we used to do during our good old college days!"

Amanda sighed and smiled. Without responding, she knew what Brad suggested was the last thing she wanted to do. Even just thinking about it made her cringe. Regardless, she felt flattered that he was thinking about them as a couple.

They simultaneously commented on their need for a shower, yet only Amanda wondered how Bram had made out at her mother's house the night before. She started to think about the upcoming day's activities in addition to laundry, grocery shopping, and meal planning for the upcoming week. All of this, combined with squeezing in time spent at the hospital and worrying about Branda.

Eventually, they both decided the picnic would be fun for Bram and perhaps it would be good for them to spend time together as a family. Amanda suggested Brad go home and shower, and she would stop by the Frugal Grocer to pick up picnic supplies, and then stop by her mom's to pick up their son. They would take their own vehicles and meet up at the pond.

Once again, Amanda took care of organizing the family. However, for what seemed like the first time, Brad felt guilty. Clearing his throat just before leaving, he turned to Amanda and said, "Hey, I realize that you do way more for our family than I do, and I'm sorry I haven't been there for you and for the kids as much as I should." Pausing as if trying to find the right words, he told Amanda he would try and help out more around the house, and suggested that after the picnic, he go back to the hospital so she could go home and get a good night's sleep.

After Brad turned to leave, Amanda ran after him and said, "Wait!" Walking urgently toward him at the end of the pale green hallway, she embraced her husband, something she had not willingly done in months. Looking up into his face, she said, "I want to make our marriage work. I noticed a few other couples last night and thought of how we used to have what they have. I would like to get it back."

Brad did not agree or disagree but said in a kind, gentle voice, "Life could be so much simpler if we could live it backwards."

Brad turned his back to Amanda, and walked to the elevator, while she stood staring at the space between them, confused. She thought his comment made no sense and Amanda wondered if they were even on the same page.

All Brad could think about while getting into his brand-new sports car, was how Amanda always compared them to other couples. Putting the car in gear, he chose not to go home immediately and took a drive instead.

Pushing in the cassette tape, he turned the volume up and, with the top down, enjoyed the sun on his unshaven face and the breeze in his unkempt hair. Taking the back roads, he sang along with the band Kiss to "I Was Made for Loving You."

As he bellowed out the lyrics at the top of his lungs, he was not thinking about Amanda.

Taking a detour from his intended route, Brad decided to drive past Virginia's house like he had done many times before. Stopping out front, he turned the radio down with the tail end of the song asking a question. Changing the lyrics, Brad sang under his breath, *"I can't you get enough of you, Virginia."*

***

When Patty got to the pond, clad in her red bikini and matching red sarong, there was so much going on that she went unnoticed. Even her new friend Darcie was distracted with helping some kid blow up a monstrous dingy. There was a serious game of badminton underway, lawn chairs being set up, and food tables getting organized. Music was blaring and burgers were sizzling.

Patty stood for a moment in the shade of a low-hanging weeping willow tree and became annoyed with all the fussing about. She wished her boyfriend Albert was there and was pretty sure Nelson would not show up. "Why would he?" she said under her breath. Patty knew from their conversation the night before that Nelson had no desire to make amends with his cellmates or the woman he had disastrously proposed to. His whole idea to show the graduating class of 1978 his success story had become a sham. He was embarrassed and wanted to visit his grandmother, the notorious Gladys Farnsworth, instead.

Without giving anyone or anything another thought, Patty took off her wrap skirt to display her tanned, fit body and tiny red bathing suit. She then waded into the water and started swimming. She figured she could go across the pond to the other side and back again before being observed or recognized.

A summer breeze dipped into the MeadowBrook valley and glided across the water's surface. The pristine pond had a calming effect, and Patty was glad she took the plunge. As if the warm airflow curled into the secret corners of her mind and whispered, *"Swim Patty, swim, keep going, swim farther..."* she felt wooed and set free. She followed the promptings of the breeze, persistently kicking her legs and moving her arms in unison.

When she was halfway across the untouched water basin, she could hear voices from the shoreline yelling at her. She momentarily wondered if they were calling out for her to come back. Ignoring the soundscape as it grew fainter, Patty's long, lean arms pulled her forward, and her strong legs propelled her body like a fine-tuned machine. She felt powerful and buoyant. Invincible and courageous.

Coming into focus was the other side of the pond. The spring rain had deepened it and the passing of time had made it smaller than Patty remembered it to be. Seeing the highway, the off-ramp, and the giant welcome egg on one side and the farewell egg on the other side reminded Patty of the small town she would be saying goodbye to. She could hear the hum and roar of the motorists: semitrucks, campers and trailers, travellers and residents.

The voices from the beach had died down, and Patty was relieved, especially since everything about the day so far had reminded her how anxious and eager she was to return to L.A. She had started to think of it as her home, whereas only a few days earlier, she had still referred to California as her home away from home. The sun-drenched state of orange groves and sandy beaches was a refuge of anonymity and a place where people left her alone. She liked it that way.

As she got closer to her destination, Patty noticed there was no beach or bank to speak of, so she decided that treading water and intermittently floating on her back would allow her a moment to catch her breath. Then she would make an about-face and return to the picnickers and party people at the beach.

The underwater vegetation had suddenly grown thicker, and the water was not as sparkly as it was only a few strokes earlier. Patty stopped abruptly. She recalled how most people referred to the body of water in two parts: the *swimming side* and *the swampy side.* Never before had she heard of anyone swimming across, and she could understand why. She wondered if she had made a mistake.

The widespread, unruly weeds made Patty's imagination suspect there might be creatures lurking beneath the surface. She instantly became skittish as her thoughts took hold. Rather than be afraid, Patty decided to see for herself. Filling her lungs with a big gulp of air, she held her breath, stretched out face down, and opened her eyes in the water.

It was initially murky. However, when her eyes adjusted, everything became clearer but with a slight greenish hue. She remained as still as possible, and then, out of nowhere, she saw the most out-of-context sight. Its enormity startled her, so she screamed underwater, expelling bubbles and air until she had to come up and take a breath.

Treading water, her heart pumped into her water-logged limbs, and she knew she had to submerge her face again to take another look.

***

Shortly after 1:00 p.m., in the ever-present warmth of the early afternoon sun, Tracy gathered all the returning grads together to make a speech.

Over breakfast that morning while discussing the upcoming picnic, Kent suggested she not make a big deal about the interruption the night before—especially since her new boyfriend was front and centre of the police debacle. He winked at Tracy while taking a swig of coffee. Tracy smiled and said, "Yes, great idea." She asked his opinion as to whether she should make a little joke or just brush past it and move on to the task at hand.

Kent replied confidently, "I have one hundred per cent faith in you, however you want to word it. I will support whatever comes out of that gorgeous mouth of yours."

Tracy rolled her eyes and smiled lovingly.

So, at the pond, holding drinks, paper plates, and condiment-laden burgers, people stood, sat on blankets, or loitered around the food table while Tracy began to speak sincerely.

"Hey, MeadowBrook grads! Welcome to our farewell picnic! Thank you so much for being here and for contributing. It is wonderful to meet your families and taste all your delicious food!" She continued on in a light tone, "Well, we made it through the last ten years, and most of you made it past getting thrown in jail last night…"

Tracy paused to let the laughter settle, and before she could continue, she heard someone yelling incoherently. Bodies and faces turned toward the water and the splashes of the approaching swimmer. People started to move to the shoreline to offer assistance, and everyone was confused.

Tim was wading in when someone said, "It's Patty! Patty Krakatoya! What the hell is wrong with her?"

As Patty emerged from the tepid water, she could hardly breathe and was in obvious distress. Gasping for air while trying to speak, she placed her hands on her knees and bent forward with rounded shoulders. Patty exclaimed, "Somebody call the police..." Her normally suntanned body was pale, and water streamed from her expensive bikini and messy long blond hair. Her face was contorted in anguish as black mascara smeared down her cheeks from her false eyelashes.

As Patty's laboured breathing regulated, she was able to stand up and finish her sentence. "I found him...it's him, I know it is...over there on the other side of the pond near the highway in a submerged vehicle, an old car. I'm certain it's a Pontiac Parisienne!"

Silent bewilderment was followed by an outcry of chaos, overwhelming the crowd.

Everyone knew exactly what and who Patty was talking about. They had all grown up under the absent reign of William Farnsworth. Stories, folklore, and parental fear had, in one way or another, affected all the residents in MeadowBrook since 1953, and the graduating class of 1978 was no exception.

Tim tried to take charge and suggested someone run over to the Fasp farm, and use the telephone to call the police.

Still sitting on a blanket, Johnny looked at Darcie, Dakota, and Margarita, and said, "Holy shit!"

Dwayne looked at Susan. "I am not going to be the one to ask to use the phone. John Fasp nearly bit my head off for calling him last night about the fight. No, thanks. I do not want to rile up that grumpy Gus again!"

Someone suggested it might be faster to drive to the police station, while another person vocalized that Patty needed to stay there to give a statement. People spoke all at once, their voices amalgamated in the disorder of a worn-out story that had lost itself in many translations, only to be revived by this staggering new discovery.

It was Patty who immediately thought of Nelson, especially since she knew he would be visiting his grandmother, the woman who just happened to be the main suspect in the mystery.

Meanwhile, Tracy looked at Kent and said, "Are you kidding me? Not another interruption at one of MY events!"

Kent responded in his usual confident and sarcastic tone, "Well, baby, if anyone can handle it, you can. Why don't you stand on that old tree stump over there and start dishing out orders?"

Tracy took Kent's suggestion and hoisted herself up onto a fallen weeping willow tree. Placing two fingers in her mouth, she whistled loudly to get everyone's attention. Kent's heart swelled with adoration for Tracy, and he could only smile from ear to ear, despite the seriousness of the situation.

Once everyone had settled down, Tracy began, "Hey, it's me again!" The collective laugh that erupted from the crowd seemed to be the release that everyone needed. She continued, "Look, some of us just need to avoid getting involved. It has been my experience that too many cooks spoil the broth. So here's what we are going to do..."

After speaking to the group as a whole, Tracy spotted Johnny and spoke directly to him. As she signalled toward Fasp Farms, Tracy kindly said, "Hey Johnny, since your house is just over there, could you please be the one to call law enforcement?"

Glancing back at Patty, Tracy wondered why, in the heat of the afternoon, she was shivering, and then Tracy realized she might be in shock.

Pensively scanning the crowd, Tracy announced in an authoritative voice, "Can someone please get Patty something to wrap herself in? Patty, stay here. Dakota and Kent, please go find Nelson."

Patty blurted out that Nelson was probably at the hospital visiting his grandma. Everyone fell silent and then Kent looked at Dakota and said, "Okay, man, we better get going. Is it okay if we take your truck?

At the same time, Tracy said, "Okay, good. Since we know Nelson's at the hospital, you guys better go there first!"

Everyone busied themselves following Tracy's orders.

Johnny got up from the blanket he shared with Margarita and looked down at her sheepishly. He felt ridiculous leaving her again in a crisis, so he said apologetically, "Can you stay here, babe, and maybe hang out with Darcie? I won't be long." Reluctantly, he set out down the gravel roadway to his parent's farm. The familiar driveway was where he'd learned to ride a bike as a kid and his dad's truck as a teenager. It was also where he'd staggered home when he was too drunk to drive.

Even though he had always looked forward to going home in the past, an unveiled history of lies and deceit had replaced any desire of ever wanting to come home in the future.

Contemplating his youth, Johnny knew his dependence on alcohol and pot were a numbing antiseptic for his past hurts. He conjectured that leaving MeadowBrook for good would be the purifying solution. He thought of Margarita, the baby, and Argentina—three surefire reasons to abstain from drugs and alcohol.

As Johnny got closer to the property to make the phone call, he thought how the situation was paradoxical. He had always avoided the police at all costs. Therefore, he couldn't help but smile and shake his head at the irony of deliberately phoning them this time.

Meanwhile, the last thing he wanted to do was alert his family, so even though he walked briskly, he felt like a prowling cat as he skirted the parked vehicles and made his way around to the back door of his own home, the place he built with his dad and brothers. He would soon be leaving the quaint dwelling for good, even though it had always been expected that he would raise a family there.

Once in his kitchen, it already felt foreign to him.

Johnny called the police detachment and spoke in a monotone voice. "Hi. There's an issue at the pond, the big swimming hole by Fasp Farms, off the highway. You better get someone over there right away."

The dispatch operator sounded annoyed when she said, "So what's the problem?"

Johnny was no longer interested in being on the phone, so he raised his voice and said, "Somebody found a 1953 Pontiac submerged in the pond. They think it's

William fucking Farnsworth!" Without waiting for a response, he hung up.

After he put down the receiver, Johnny went upstairs to his bedroom and threw his duffel bag on the bed. He could feel trepidation creeping in, then his usual stirrings of anxiety. He thought of the weed already rolled into a joint waiting for a match.

Taking a few deep breaths to erase his thoughts of lighting up, Johnny surveyed the room and noticed Margarita's belongings on the floor in a messy open suitcase. Her well-travelled backpack sat next to it. Instead of packing up his few things, he first emptied Margarita's suitcase and neatly refolded each article of clothing, placing everything back inside. Even though she didn't wear perfume or fancy lotions, Johnny could smell her sweet essence on every lacy top, T-shirt, and embroidered skirt. He noticed her journal, a tattered notebook covered with pencil drawings of sunsets and a sketch of a man he thought looked like himself. Immediately, Johnny felt curious about the contents inside but deliberately chose not to open it. He gently placed the book in amongst Margarita's sandals and peasant blouses.

Johnny carelessly grabbed a few things of his own and took their bags downstairs, placing them on the front porch. Leaving them there, he went back inside and over to his stash. Speaking out loud as if it would be more convincing, he said, "Okay, this is one last joint, just to get me through, then I'm quitting."

Feeling the burn to his throat and the anxiety leaving his body, Johnny ascertained that making a smooth, non-confrontational departure would be best. He hoped he was doing the right thing leaving with Margarita, and he hoped he would not one day regret it.

Looking at the bags, he spoke to them. "Nope, no goodbyes." With that, he picked up their few belongings and walked briskly back to the pond and the woman he planned to spend the rest of his life with.

***

Tim got a blanket for Patty and brought her a cup of lemonade. Marnie leapt to his side and assisted Patty to a lawn chair. But she was too excited to sit down.

Dakota and Kent briefly hugged their significant others and strode to Dakota's truck with purpose. Kent commented on the vehicle and said, "Nice ride. How much did they ding you for the beast?" Dakota responded with a smile and a shrug.

On the silent drive over to the MeadowBrook hospital, both men separately went over in their minds how they were going to approach Nelson. Each had an entirely different plan. And neither had a very good track record.

Meanwhile, Amanda looked at her watch and wondered why Brad had not arrived at the picnic yet. With a furrowed brow, she sat listlessly, utterly uninterested in the goings-on around her. She spotted her freckled-faced, towheaded little boy playing at the water's edge with a small plastic shovel and red bucket. She thought about her storybook romance collapsing around her like a stomped-on sandcastle.

Susan took everything in and knew there was a news story in all of it. She wished she had something to write on. She spotted a group of children colouring. One of the kids was her own. She knelt down beside the busy little bees and asked if she could borrow a black crayon. In seconds, Susan was given a brown paper bag to write on, and she started jotting down notes.

She surmised that her article would make headlines if Patty's discovery and assumptions were correct. Susan visualized the front page and used her crayon to write: "Breaking News! Mystery Solved! William Farnsworth's Body Has Been Found. Case Closed."

Chapter Ten

Living in The Past

> *"Keep a record of the lessons learned, think about how you can avoid making the same mistakes twice, and tell the naysayers to go straight to hell."*
>
> *—Gladys Farnsworth*

The purpose of the earliest mental institutions was neither treating nor curing the ill. Based on fear and ignorance, the mentally ill were considered social deviants or moral misfits who required punishment for some inexcusable transgression.

In the early 1900s, the Hillsprings Asylum was built to house an eclectic group of individuals deemed criminally insane and unfit to walk the streets. Conditions such as being born with a deformity, having a mental disability or emotional imbalance, experiencing extreme poverty, or having a criminal past—these were all reasons to be committed.

William Farnsworth declared the conditions at the asylum to be harsh, cruel, and inhumane when he was taken on a tour shortly after he incorporated MeadowBrook in 1930. Especially since it was demonstrated to him how the Hillsprings Asylum relied heavily on mechanical restraints such as straitjackets, manacles, waistcoat, and leather wristlets. Doctors explained to William the restraints kept patients safe, and shock treatment restored them.

But William stated in his ten-page complaint to the chief administrator, *"The use of physical restraints is a means of controlling an overcrowded institution. They are unnecessary in most cases and ineffective in nearly all situations."* He later went on to admonish the theory of demon possession and brought up the argument that perhaps the so-called crazy people were simply out of balance. He asked the mental health team if there was a more humane and kinder way to treat individuals who suffered from extreme outbursts and madness.

By 1940, ten years after first visiting the Hillsprings Asylum and from doing his own personal research, William was able to participate in closing down the facility and relocating the patients. After many years of painstakingly writing letters and meeting with qualified medical authorities and healthcare professionals, he was proud to shut the door on that chapter of history.

However, the real work began when it came time to transfer all those who were housed there.

First, each patient was assessed by doctors whom William hired, and depending on severity and probability of rehabilitation, they were moved to various places that would suit them better. William believed that with proper nutrition, exercise, and a healthy environment, almost anyone could be restored and made well. As a result, he also hired dieticians, herbalists, and a Catholic priest.

It was a vast undertaking, but William was gifted in delegating and treated the whole operation like a business.

There were many local residents who offered to help. The Fasp family took in those who could work the land, which included room and board. Earl Fasp, John Fasp's father and Johnny's grandfather, offered a helping hand whenever possible. He was generous and kind but mostly had ulterior motives. He liked to refer to his charity as "coming in from the side door," which was a less conspicuous means of entry. His goal was for those down on their luck or struggling mentally and emotionally to contribute to society and his pocketbook through hard labour. It was never known if the vagrants and mentally unstable truly wanted to be working, but over time it became known that Earl Fasp would help just about anyone, provided it helped him.

Shortly after the mental institution in Hillsprings was deemed unfit, the MeadowBrook hospital started a day program for those in need. Individuals would receive three square meals daily, a hot bath, medical treatment, and a trained professional to assess and guide them on the correct path.

It was all about moving forward, not backward or staying the same in an often-unnecessary drug-induced state. William was pleased and proud of his rehabilitation program, which was titled "Going in the Right Direction." Later, through financing from William Farnsworth and collected donations, renovations to the hospital were implemented, with beds for a complete psychiatric ward steeped primarily in naturopathic medicine.

However, with as many supporters as William had, there were just as many nay-sayers, pessimists, and people who were against him. Many were outraged by his modern views and feared that the inclusion of the unwell would be the downfall of society altogether. Regardless, William had the power and clout, so he kept his unconventional program going.

Shortly after Marvin got married, the Bureau of Investigations deemed William's disappearance a cold case. Aside from a small allowance from the grocery store, Gladys was living with little to no means. The house was in ruins and an eyesore. So she went to live with her son and daughter-in-law, Marvin and Diane. Unfortunately, Gladys needed round-the-clock care, and she became too much for the couple.

Gladys had taken to sneaking out at night with a shovel; every morning, new holes were reported throughout town. Eventually, the newspaper started a column called "Last Night's Dig." It had turned into a joke and a mockery of the family name, not to mention a danger to the residents. Pedestrians and motorists were breaking ankles and axles from the unexpected craters and gaps in the sidewalks and roads. It was speculated that Gladys was either looking for her husband or still trying to bury him.

At the same time, she had become somewhat of a celebrity and a hazard all in one fell swoop. Business sales increased at the Frugal Grocer in hopes there would be a Gladys sighting, and the town's maintenance department had to hire more workers.

Unfortunately, due to her wandering and digging obsession, Marvin was advised by the authorities to have his mother committed.

Some thought it serendipitous, while others deemed it happenstance that William Farnsworth's wife would end up in the place he had created out of compassion and a belief that there was no such thing as crazy, a word William considered to be in the ranks of other four-letter words.

Therefore, many years after the infamous founder had disappeared, Nelson's grandmother was placed in the psychiatric ward of the MeadowBrook hospital. Half the town of MeadowBrook still believed Gladys was a killer, while the other half thought of her as a sweet, kooky old lady. The paradox made for yet another popular topic of conversation and debate, and the ongoing arguments and questions over the long-standing cold case of William Farnsworth continued. Admitting Gladys Farnsworth was seemingly the only solution.

In spite of the rumours and opinions of others, overall Gladys was a fun-loving and kind person. She was the most favourite resident in the healthcare facility and was known for organizing sing-alongs, knitting circles, and board games. She had an infinite number of visitors and somewhat of a cult following. The newspaper had stopped writing about her and the whole story devolved into folklore, scary campfire stories, and hearsay.

Throughout the 1960s, Nelson's father Marvin visited his grandmother every Sunday, and Diane brought Nelson in to see her every Saturday. They liked to call themselves "The Gladys Farnsworth Tag Team." Gladys adored her son, tolerated his wife, and thought her one and only grandson to be an oddball.

In 1988, the day after the high school reunion, Nelson, the only Farnsworth heir, decided to reach out to his grandmother. He had hoped that Gladys could offer some clues as to why he felt so imbalanced and kept having uncontrollable outbursts. Nelson had many questions that plagued him. Was he following in his grandmother's footsteps? Did insanity run in the family? Had he been handed down the ancestral gene of mental instability?

In addition to the inquiries about his brain, he wanted to secure a loan or a handout to get his product, Nelzema, off the ground. Nelson knew he had to play his cards right, especially since it had been years since he had visited his grandmother.

The morning after the reunion, Nelson lolled in bed, as he had no plans of going to the grad picnic. He was not in any rush to face the day. He looked around his bedroom and noticed his Marvel comic book collection, all neatly stacked on his desk and bedside table. He smiled at the images of Iron Man, Thor, Hulk, Spider-Man, and The X-Men.

As Nelson recalled his simple, uneventful life, he wondered at what point everything had taken the drastic turn to run amuck. When he thought back to the days, weeks, and months he had stayed enclosed in the darkened basement with his comic books and television, he came to the conclusion that his isolation transformed into loneliness, culminating in a staggering amount of wasted hours spent immersed in plotting a relationship with a girl he had never spoken to.

Conclusively in the last twelve hours, an epiphany of sorts had occurred, and Nelson had Patty to thank for his clearer thinking.

Nelson's reminiscing brought a sense of warm nostalgia. He missed the simplicity of being a hermit. However, he finally understood that his lifelong infatuation with Darcie Richmond had spurred his pursuit of education and his desire to be successful. Even if for the wrong reasons.

When he thought of Patty, Nelson made a mental note to find his old high school yearbooks and look her up, as he could not place the woman he immensely enjoyed speaking with the night before. Her peroxide-treated hair and the sinewy, tanned body were foreign to him. Nelson thought it odd that he had no recollection of Patty

Krakatoya in his memory bank. And yet, as she described it, they were cut from the same cloth and could have been friends long before their chance meeting at the bus stop the night after his proposal scheme went sideways.

Nelson marveled at the perfect timing of their deep meaningful conversation that had been remarkably life-changing for him.

Emerging from the basement, Nelson discovered his parents sitting quietly at the kitchen table, waiting. As Nelson got ready to leave for the hospital, an unexpected sense of well-being washed over him. He was pleased that his parents had forgiven him for what they referred to as his "instability and poor mental health phase." They had a blatant discussion in front of Nelson, as though he were not in the room. Marvin and Diane stated that craziness and poor choices must run in the Farnsworth family. They summed everything up by saying to Nelson, "Blood is thicker than water, and you are the apple of our eye, son. All you need is our support and a little redirection. You've always been a special boy, and highly intelligent. Just keep on marching to the beat of your own drum."

All Nelson said in response was, "Yeah, I guess I will."

Whether Nelson agreed or disagreed with his parent's assumptions about him, he felt good to be waking up in his old familiar bedroom, and his exchange with Patty the night before had been utterly freeing.

Completely changing the subject in a lighter, cheerful tone, Diane said, "Now tell us all about last night's event. We want to hear everything. Did you have a nice time?" Before Nelson could respond, his dad chimed in and said, "So, did you dance with any pretty ladies, wink-wink, nudge-nudge, if you know what I mean?"

Nelson realized his father must not have told his mother about his entanglement at the reunion and being carted off to jail. So, he chose to go along with his dad's charade of not telling Diane what really went on.

Both parents laughed and Diane said, "Oh Marvin, that's our son you're talking to! Don't be crude."

Nelson paused, stared blankly, shrugged his shoulders and gave both his parents a wry smile. He had no intention of telling them the full truth. He knew they would never understand his obsession with a girl from high school or his short temper when things didn't go as planned. Besides, he thought, his mother would surely disown him if she learned about the police locking him up. Again. Instead, taking the cue from his father, he decided to skirt around what really happened at the reunion, have a hearty breakfast, and then go to the hospital to see his grandmother.

Nelson's mother asked again, "So, please tell us, how was the reunion?"

In his usual no-nonsense way, he said, "It was fine, just a bunch of boring people bragging about themselves."

Still trying to make conversation, but sensing that Nelson was not interested, his dad asked, "Oh, I see. So what are your plans today, Nelson?"

Not only did Nelson not want to reveal anything about the night before, but he definitely did not want to share his true intentions for the upcoming afternoon, so he was as vague as possible when he said, "Well, after I eat, I want to go visit Granny and ask her a few questions, and after that, I have no idea."

Diane prepared waffles, sausages, and scrambled eggs for breakfast, and after showering, Nelson walked into town and made his way over to the hospital.

***

As a rule, most small-town gossip reveals personal or sensational facts about others. People are known to stretch the truth or spread rumours that are not always factual. But it did not occur to anyone that a certain employee at the police station might overhear the call from Johnny that the police were needed at the pond ASAP. Or that someone else may have eavesdropped on a conversation between Dakota and Kent as they walked from the truck to the hospital to inform Nelson of the

1953 Pontiac Parisienne that had been discovered only ten feet underwater on the outskirts of town.

So, it was alarming to Patty when cars started pulling up in droves at the pond. Unbeknownst to anyone there, they were also flooding the hospital just as the unlikely pair of Kent and Dakota arrived at the admitting desk. They both wondered if they were doing the right thing, but Kent trusted Tracy's common sense, and Dakota always wanted to help. So, they checked in at the front desk, took the elevator to Gladys's floor, and then reported to the nursing station.

Dakota thought it ironic that Branda was at one end of the hospital and Gladys at the other. He speculated that Nancy might end up there someday soon as well. And then he wondered why he kept being asked to go there.

Gladys greeted them both with open arms. Even though none of them had ever met before, Gladys knew everyone and everything. She was as sharp as a tack, even though her behaviour suggested otherwise.

"Why, hello boys! If it isn't Kent Gordon! Lordy, Lordy, are you ever the spitting image of your father! And dear, sweet Dakota! I was so sorry when I heard about your dad. It seems like yesterday that I lived in my beautiful home and had you kids over for swims and picnics."

Before either of them could get a word in edgewise, Gladys digressed even further to her love of entertaining guests and all the grandiose meals she used to serve. Thus began a rant about the price of Campbell's soup. She finished up with a monologue about how chicken noodle soup was her favourite. She wondered if they used authentic chicken pieces, as it sure seemed like it.

When she stopped to breathe, Kent blurted out, "They found Willy, ma'am!"

Dakota quickly added, "Hang on, Kent, you're being misleading." He clarified, "What happened is they think they found the car your late husband William was last spotted in."

Gladys was excited and only heard Kent's first pronouncement, so naturally, she thought they had found her husband alive. She responded, "Oh, for heaven's sake, I knowed it all along. Where has the little dickens been holed up all this time?"

Then Gladys asked where Officers Malone and Brown were. Unbeknownst to Gladys, both men had retired many years earlier. Officer Malone had moved to a Florida retirement complex called La Boca Vista, while Officer Brown still lived locally and cared for his three grandchildren daily. Their mother, his daughter, worked as a waitress at Robinsons' Diner.

Both police detectives stayed in contact with the MeadowBrook police chief as old buddies and workmates. So, as soon as Patty's discovery was accidentally made public, Malone and Brown were notified. Officer Malone booked a flight and was expected in at 7 a.m. the following day, and Officer Brown insisted his daughter take time off because he had important police business to take care of.

Malone and Brown were thrilled with the recent development, albeit a little disappointed that they were not the ones to discover the submerged vehicle from thirty-three years prior.

Dakota gently nudged Kent's elbow and said, "Actually, we don't want to alarm you, Mrs. Farnsworth, or get your hopes up. We were actually looking for Nelson."

Seconds later, Gladys fainted, and two nurses ran over to revive her. At that very moment, Nelson abruptly came into the room, and when seeing Kent and Dakota, his two arch enemies, he yelled, "Hey, what the hell is going on in here?"

Nelson automatically assumed that Kent was trying to get money out of his grandmother and Dakota was there to spread lies about last night's fiasco.

Once Gladys came to, one nurse helped her sip orange juice while another nurse ordered everyone to leave to leave the room.

***

Meanwhile, back at the pond, Patty shivered, children ran around chaotically, and the reunion picnic had taken on an air of complete and utter discord.

Margarita stood on the periphery, stroking her belly, lost in daydreams of a reunion of her own. It had been almost a year since she had seen her family, six months since she had met Johnny, almost three months since she had become pregnant, and a long week since she landed in the strangest of towns with the oddest of people. In less than a year, her world had drastically changed; if she could, she would leave unannounced and never return.

Darcie stayed close to Margarita, but neither woman spoke. Instead, they were each privately in their own head, and amongst the calamity, Darcie's mind wandered to her mom, new brother, and hallmark romance with Dakota. Aside from her mother's imminent demise, everything about her life seemed right and on course. Unless, of course, her story was to take on a twist where she, the heroine, would go on to do something remarkable during the grieving process of losing her mother. Perhaps she would start a support group and call it, "Listening to Joni Mitchell Helped Me Cope" or "When Bad Things Happen to Good People, and You Can't Cope at All."

Her spirits lifted when she saw Johnny return from the farm. Looking up from her seated position, Margarita smiled. Johnny, with a sappy grin, stood there with bags packed, looking ready to go. As he helped his expectant girlfriend to her feet, Darcie, completely confused, leapt up also.

Before he could say anything, Darcie said, "What's going on? Where are you going?"

Johnny quickly responded, "Hang on, sis, don't worry. We're still coming to Dakota's for dinner, and then we're leaving for Argentina first thing in the morning as planned. I was hoping we could stay at Nancy's or Dakota's place. I can't fathom spending another second at that godforsaken farm with any of my so-called family members!"

Darcie couldn't think of what to say, and all she managed was to just stand there with a worried look and respond, "Oh, okay."

***

While watching Bram play at the water's edge, Amanda felt a slow-brewing panic rising within her. She imagined the keystone cops from the old black-and-white movies showing up at any time. She envisioned her marriage collapsing like an old Bette Davis saga, and the small-town mystery to be solved by the television personality Perry Mason. She wondered where Doctor Kildare was to fix her daughter. At that precise moment, she despised every happily-ever-after that ever was.

Meanwhile, unbeknownst to everyone—particularly Amanda—Brad had just gotten into a tussle with Virginia's six-foot-four football linebacker boyfriend.

On his way home to shower before the picnic, Brad had taken a slight detour and parked outside Virginia's home in true stalker fashion, slinked down in the driver's seat and hoped for a sighting of the woman he lusted after. Eventually, he was caught, because Virginia just happened to be looking out the window and recognized Brad's car.

She had grown suspicious at how attentive he was at work. Even though she thought Brad was kind and helpful, there also seemed to be something creepy about the older man who always seemed to be around. Virginia had started recording all of Brad's niceties, so when she saw his sports car in front of her house, she decided to finally tell her boyfriend.

Brad was wholly embarrassed when confronted, but instead of apologizing for spying, making up a fib, or speeding off, he decided to fight back, despite the fact that he was no match for someone bigger, stronger, younger, and angrier.

In one breath, Virginia's fiancé Simon reached into Brad's snazzy automobile and pulled him out by his shirt collar. Not known for his way with words, Simon bellowed, "Hey buddy, what gives? Virginia says you're bugging her, so you better back off!"

Brad was speechless as his face turned the colour of death, and sweat appeared on his forehead, trickling down the side of his face.

Winding up his football-throwing arm, Simon punched Brad square in the middle of his nose.

Needless to say, Virginia screamed at her fiancé to stop hitting Brad, and a neighbour called the police. Brad, in turn, was sure his nose was broken as he was hauled off to the police station for causing a disturbance. As he sat handcuffed in the squad car's back seat, wondering how he would explain the debacle to Amanda, he heard the call come in: "All available units proceed to the Fasp swimming hole as soon as possible."

Brad was instantly alarmed and anxiously thought of his wife and son. He asked the officers upfront if he could go with them to the pond. Both policemen erupted into sarcastic laughter and said, "Buddy, the only place you're going is to the station where you'll be dropped off, booked and detained for however long they decide. So you better simmer down!"

***

When the police arrived at the swimming hole, the flurry of picnickers, partiers, and interfering townspeople only added to their job of getting to the bottom of what the problem was. The pond was well known for reports of teenage disturbances, tomfoolery, and an occasional false alarm, so the two on-call officers were skeptical, wondering if there was a genuine situation.

Once the uniformed officers were spotted on the scene, bystanders began clamouring to be heard and everyone pointed to Patty.

She was no longer quivering, and to be taken more seriously, Patty had thrown on her wrap-around skirt and T-shirt. Anticipating law enforcement, the minutes felt like hours, so she'd gone over everything in her head while she waited. Patty was determined to give an accurate statement, fully aware of the enormity of her findings. She told herself, *I will dive down again if they want me to!*

It was Tracy who took the lead policeman over to Patty, and as if on cue, she began relaying her discovery. She spoke calmly and enunciated every word as if she was a reporter from the 6:00 news.

"It was hot when I arrived, so I entered the water right away. I am a very strong swimmer, but halfway across, I almost changed my mind and turned back. When the water became murky close to the other side, I thought I'd made a mistake going as far as I did. However, it was not until, out of curiosity, I ducked my head under the water and opened my eyes that I saw it. I knew right away it was a car wreck and only because I've studied the Farnsworth case for years did I ascertain it was probably the car related to the William Farnsworth case. Under the circumstances, I was elated and then frightened, so I swam back as quickly as possible to get help."

It was immediately decided that a crime scene was located on the other side of the pond. With more than a few busybodies and looky-loos already trying to swim across, the police rapidly called for backup, and then started yelling in their authoritative deep voices at the people on air mattresses and rubber dinghies to get out of the water. It was pertinent that the physical evidence for the criminal investigation was not disturbed.

The police spoke into their loudspeaker, "Please return! I repeat, all swimmers must return and clear the water! It is crucially important that nothing be disrupted!"

It was determined the initial responder needed to take witness statements, and more police were called in to block off the highway adjacent to the scene.

The tension was high, as everyone, especially law enforcement, knew the first crime scene back in 1953 was botched and reported as a catastrophe. Some news outlets back then had even called the MeadowBrook Police Department "bumbling idiots."

***

After Kent returned to the pond, Tracy ran into his arms and buried her head in his chest. Only two weeks into their relationship, Kent had never seen her be any way other than stoic, strong, and in charge. He adored her confident and decisive nature, so Kent was taken aback at her display of vulnerability.

It only made him adore her more.

Taking her face in his hands, Kent gently said, "C'mon, let's get out of here."

Tracy thought it irresponsible of her to leave, but when she scanned the crowd, along with the flashing lights, yellow caution tape, and news cameras, she said, exhausted, "Yes, please, let's go!"

It was unlike Tracy to abandon an event, at least not without delegating first. But upon Kent's suggestion, she let him take her hand and felt good about throwing all caution to the wind. As they headed toward Tracy's pink catering vehicle, Kent said, "Hey, I bet you didn't know I make a mean pasta carbonara."

Tracy responded, "Good, I'm starving!" as she handed Kent the keys to her vehicle.

***

Amanda was worried about Brad and his absence from the picnic and remembered he had promised her that he would stay at the hospital that night so she could get a good night's rest in their own bed. So Amanda packed their belongings by herself and carried everything, including Bram, to the car.

Driving home, she looked forward to a cool shower, an easy dinner of soup and grilled cheese, and an early bedtime for Bram. When Amanda unloaded the car, she was unnerved and had begun to worry extensively in regard to Brad's whereabouts, so she thought of making a call to the hospital for fear he had been in a car accident. Once inside, Bram got his pyjamas on, and Amanda glanced at the telephone, willing it to ring. Instead, the flashing light on the answering machine indicated there was a message.

***

Susan chased after Tracy before she and Kent drove away. She wanted to reassure her best friend that she and Dwayne would take care of packing everything up. Besides, Susan wanted to stick around the flurry of detectives and forensics investigators because, as a journalist, she hoped to climb aboard one of the rowboats the police had brought in for the dive team.

Dwayne immediately started cleaning up the picnic site, and afterward, he told Susan he would take the kids home, feed them supper and put them to bed. She could not believe how fortunate she was. When they said goodbye, they kissed and lovingly embraced as if they were newlyweds.

***

Dakota, Darcie, Johnny, and Margarita had no desire to stick around and knew Nancy would be waiting for them. Dakota had prepared tofu burgers and marinated eggplant earlier that morning, and Nancy promised to bring a salad.

The happy, weary couples climbed into Dakota's pickup truck and made their way to Nancy's apartment. Johnny suggested they stop along the way to pick up some beer.

Darcie felt ripples of excitement mixed with dread at the prospect of telling her mother what happened at the pond. She knew her mother would be rattled, but hopefully relieved.

Dakota manoeuvred his truck around the police barricade, onto the highway, and through town to pick up Nancy. Darcie sat snuggled up against his side, hoping it would always be her place. She anticipated the evening ahead and could feel a desperation brewing to reacquaint with Johnny and learn more about his upcoming travel plans. Darcie went over a mental list of everything she wanted to talk about, past, present, and future. She worried they would not have enough time to cover everything.

***

Gladys pleaded with Nelson, "Please, you must get me out of here! I need to see William one last time. I need to tell him I forgive him for abandoning me. Please, I beg of you, Marvin!"

Nelson realized his grandmother had mistaken him for his father, her only son. He also knew he could not get her out of the hospital, nor did he want to.

Instead, he said, "Granny, it's me, remember? Nelson, your favourite grandson."

Gladys flew off the handle and went into a rant. "Why, you little deranged brat! I never liked you, and I told your father that mother of yours was ruining you!"

Nelson was completely and utterly taken aback. Mouth agape, he left without saying another word. He had no inclination to find out what was at the bottom of the pond, so instead, he walked over to Patty's street and sat at the bus stop where he had seen her the night before. Nelson set his sights on waiting for her. However, he had no idea that Patty was immersed in her own drama and would not be going back to her parent's home for quite some time.

***

Through all of it, Tim and his little sister Marnie ended up helping whoever needed a hand. Marnie offered lemonade and plates of food to the bystanders, and Tim assisted the police in carrying boats and underwater gear to the water's edge.

He was asked to accompany the officers in the boat, and when he looked to his sister for approval, she nodded and eagerly said, "Go for it!"

They both stayed until well past midnight, when they decided to go home, even though there would still be many days of the police investigation.

In a temperate climate, it usually takes anywhere from three weeks to several years for a body to decompose. The body breaks down more slowly if death occurs underwater. As a submerged corpse decays in water, bacteria in the gut produce methane, carbon dioxide, and hydrogen sulfide. This combination makes the body float up to the surface. However, it depends on the temperature of the water and how deep the bodies are submerged. Sometimes the weight of the water pins the bodies down for eternity. If the windows are closed and sealed tightly, less damage will occur to the contents.

Amongst the few remains found in the glove compartment and trunk were William's ID in a plastic wallet, the car registration, $20,000 in cash, and a photograph of Gladys as a pigtailed young girl. The paperwork and money were deemed useless from years of water damage.

The forensic team speculated that when their car hit the water, William Farnsworth and Jane Doe were both struck on the head from the impact, causing blunt force trauma. Conclusively, even though the evidence was scant and all that remained of the bodies were a few detached bones, it would take many more months for the autopsy results to be made official.

The newspaper later stated that, unfortunately, the woman and supposed driver of the vehicle could not be identified.

The disappearance of William Farnsworth was solved, and the case was officially closed, yet the mystery and speculations continued. Some still wondered if Gladys had something to do with his death, while others ruminated on who Jane Doe might have been and what her motives were. Many were relieved that a killer was no longer lurking, and local business owners cashed in on the publicity and attention generated from the small-town scandal making the national news. Upon the mayor's retirement, he commissioned June 14th to be William Farnsworth Day, and Patricia Krakatoya was awarded the key to the city.

***

The day after the picnic, on the drive to the Hillsprings airport, Tracy drove the speed limit and manoeuvred the hills, twists, and turns like a driving instructor. Her foot was steady on the gas pedal while both hands gripped the steering wheel in the 10-2 hand position. With a lump in her throat and a happy heart, Tracy dutifully drove her fiancé Kent Gordon to catch his plane.

Meanwhile, Kent shifted in the passenger seat and fiddled with the radio. He was pleased that Tracy was taking her time, as he was not in any rush to leave. Years earlier, her fastidious nature would have driven him stark raving mad, but since his transformation and new lease on life, Kent had difficulty finding any fault with the woman he was destined to spend the rest of his life with.

Neither spoke, but both felt a comfortable, compatible warmth with the other.

Suddenly, out of the silence, Kent blurted out, "Dammit!"

Tracy's concentration broke, and she quickly said, "Whoa, what's the matter?"

Before Kent responded, he found the radio station he was looking for, and with a sigh of relief, he said, "Okay! Got it! Sorry about that, sweetie! So, remember when I told you about my Kent Gordon Five-Step Program when I first arrived?"

Tracy smiled warmly and said, "Yes, I remember."

Kent continued, "Well, one of the guys I scammed in Grade 12 is the dude who started up the local radio station. I thought while we were driving it would be nice to support him, so I just found the station. Is that okay with you?"

Tracy could find very few things that bothered her about Kent. And since he wanted to support a local business, she was definitely on board. Tracy pondered the networking side of Kent and liked his ability to start a conversation with just about anyone. She pleasantly observed that neither of them was shy or meek, and they both enjoyed connecting, commanding the lead, and helping others.

As her vehicle clocked miles toward their eventual goodbye, Tracy felt a thought needling her, words she could easily go without saying. They had both avoided discussing what a long-distance relationship would look like and the fact that she hated to fly. But she was distracted from her worrying when Kent turned the radio up all of a sudden.

The D.J.'s commentary carried a wry, sardonic tone: "Good morning, all you farmers and ranch hands! How the heck are ya? DJ Chris is coming to you live at KTS9 radio in downtown MeadowBrook, home to Fasp Farms fresh eggs and never-ending brooks and streams. This morning we have a request going out to our very own

Tracy Hansworth, from the love of her life Kent Gordon, with the message, 'This one's for you, baby! Please don't forget about me.'"

DJ Chris added, "Well ain't that sweet, and here it is, from the hit movie *The Breakfast Club*, 'Don't You Forget About Me,' by Simple Minds."

Kent spoke above the music, "Please don't forget about me, Trace. We can make a great team. I want to know everything about you, inside and out. There are a lot of things out there that can pull us apart and a lot of people may say a lot of crap about me, so please remember the tender things we have shared…"

Tracy could not believe what was happening. Before Kent could finish and before Tracy could respond, she saw an exit and took it. Pulling over onto the shoulder of crunching gravel, the whirring in her brain and Simple Minds lead singer Jim Kerr worked hard to distract her. When she put the vehicle in park, the dust circled the van like a symbol of magic and mystique.

Tracy felt like climbing onto Kent's lap to profess her love and beg him to stay. Instead, she looked over at him in the passenger seat and allowed the song to finish. Even though she was flattered and slightly embarrassed, Tracy said, "I have been waiting for you, Kent Gordon, for what seems like a lifetime. So now it's my turn to ask a question. I quote, 'Won't you come see about me?'"

For the moment, she allowed her right hand to leave the steering wheel and reach for Kent's hand. She squeezed it and then placed the back of his hand on her cheek.

When the song ended, DJ Chris returned on the radio and said, "You know, I had the pleasure of going to school with Kent and Tracy, and I'll be honest, I did not care for either of them." His loud guffaw could be heard through the airway. And then his voice softened as he continued, "Napoleon once said, *'One must change one's tactics every ten years if one wishes to maintain one's superiority.'* So folks, take it from me, the world hates change, but people do it every day, and all it means is that if what was before wasn't perfect, change will make it better. Kent is living proof that a person can change by merely changing his attitude. I want to wish you both the very best."

Tracy was finally satisfied that she and Kent were a committed couple. Making a U-turn, she drove her vehicle back onto the road to the airport.

DJ Chris had another request, so he said, "The phone lines are buzzing today, folks! The next song is a request from Nelson Farnsworth, and we all know who he is! Okay, MeadowBrook, Nelson has requested this song as a tribute to our hometown. This one's for you, MeadowBrook, from the grandson of our founder, with the tagline, "Who's doing your wash?" 'Dirty Laundry' by Don Henley!"

Nelson had sat by the radio all morning in his parents' kitchen waiting to phone in his request. He was disheartened about everything.

His intentions were to give the town his grandfather founded a jab to the heart and a kick in the mouth. He hoped the song "Dirty Laundry" would be hurtful to those who spread unflattering facts, questionable secrets, and private matters.

With the message being that dirty laundry should be washed at home and not aired for all to see, Nelson surmised that he and Don Henley had both been kicked when they were up and even more so when they were down.

***

The ten-year reunion weekend had been a success for some, disappointing for others, and life-changing for many. Memories were stirred up, past hurts were addressed, and lovers were reunited. Enemies made friends and certain friendships ended. Some issues went unresolved, and some hearts were broken in the process. History became the present and latched onto the present time as it stood still, if only for forty-eight hours.

Some say a close-knit community is defined by the number of people in it who rely on one another day in and day out. Others profess it is the connections made and a shared history that bind citizens together. But most will agree there are always differences and similarities among the people who live in the same small town.

Unfortunately, throughout time, communities have found it much easier to label a person with a stereotype than make an effort to really see them.

There are always many unanswered questions. How important are first impressions? Does our first impression reflect how we view each other? Does the way we speak, think, or look even matter?

For now, we will ponder the many questions that plague us from our past, or maybe we will leave them alone in the dark corners of our minds until we reunite, perhaps in another decade or lifetime.

Every book seemingly has an ending…or perhaps the ending is just another way to say goodbye until we meet again.

Epilogue

Tim left MeadowBrook and never returned until his father's death and funeral, which went hand in hand with the twenty-year high-school reunion. Both events happened during the same week at the end of June 1998. In the interim, he travelled with his theatre company throughout the United States, Canada, and Europe. Over the years, Tim performed in *Fame*, *Jesus Christ Superstar*, *Hair*, *Godspell,* and *Hairspray.* He became close with the troupe, and his fellow actors became like family. They spent Christmases together and supported each other through grueling rehearsals, dodgy hotel rooms, good reviews and bad ones.

Everything about Tim's career felt serendipitous, and looking back, he decidedly would not change a thing. He was proud of his hard knocks and painful past, as they made him who he had become. He was elated with his career as an actor and dancer and grateful for each day.

Eventually, Tim purchased a bungalow on the boardwalk of Venice Beach, and always kept a spare bedroom available for his little sister.

Meanwhile, Marnie continued to work for Tracy at Events by Tracy, and spent a lot of time managing the business in Tracy's absence. Marnie used all her vacation days to visit Tim, wherever he was in the world at that time. They became closer and considered themselves "best friends," regardless of their rocky childhood and ten-year age difference. Marnie never married but had a few long-term boyfriends, some of whom met Tim's approval. Those who did not were quickly left by the wayside and never spoken of again.

Tim and Marnie's mother kept in touch with them and sometimes joined Marnie on her visits to see Tim. Their father never made amends with either of his children and died a lonely and miserable old man.

Tim kept his romantic life and relationships private but brought his partner Richard to the twenty-year high-school reunion.

***

Nelson struggled to get over Darcie and Patty, the only two women he had ever been interested in. Unfortunately, Nelson's mental health got worse before it got better. Directly following the reunion, he spent a few months in the MeadowBrook hospital psychiatric ward and became close with his grandma. He had a strong faith in the doctors and psychiatrists, whom he felt listened to him and helped him to heal.

Nelson's father, Marvin Farnsworth, built him a laneway house behind the family home in MeadowBrook and tried unsuccessfully to convince Nelson to take over the Frugal Grocer. Nelson perpetually refused. But he enjoyed living near his parents and rarely missed a Sunday dinner of chicken stew, biscuits, and gravy.

Gladys lived to be ninety-eight, and it was noted that she always had the most visitors of all the elderly residents. She had become somewhat of a celebrity and took on a Joan Crawford dramatic way of speaking. Gladys refused to see guests or callers if she did not have a full face of makeup on.

Eventually, Nelson's product, Nelzema acne medication, became a huge success. Teenagers worldwide were healed from acne and scars. Unfortunately, in the late 1990s, the stock market dropped, and so did Nelson's skincare line. He had already made a significant amount of money, so he didn't mind working trade shows with his claim-to-fame balms, salves, and ointments.

Nelson stayed in MeadowBrook even though his heart still broke every time he saw Darcie, and his anger flared at the thought of Dakota. Nevertheless, they were always kind and cordial to Nelson, even though he snubbed them on many occasions.

He never married, and it was speculated he never dated. The Farnsworth name went down in history just like the disappearance of the town's founder, the late great William Farnsworth.

The small-town gossip mill continued, but as MeadowBrook grew, the rumours and scuttlebutt lessened. Townspeople became more open-minded, especially when all the old fogeys began dying off.

***

Johnny kept his word, left MeadowBrook and never went back. He fled to Argentina with Margarita, and even though they loved and adored each other, Johnny's deep-rooted pain got in the way of maintaining a healthy relationship.

As she suspected, Margarita's family accepted Johnny, and he fit in well. Unfortunately, Johnny was arrested for drug possession in his newly adopted country. Due to his grandmother's influence, he did not consider marijuana an illegal drug and fought for legalization. However, law enforcement in Argentina did not share Johnny's views.

He was convicted, sentenced to two years in prison, and got out for good behaviour after eighteen months.

During this time, Margarita waited for him, and Johnny got clean while incarcerated. While in prison he read *I'm Dysfunctional, You're Dysfunctional* by Wendy Kaminer and *Stop the Insanity* by Susan Powter. Her famous quote, *"You can accomplish things you never thought possible,"* became his mantra and he believed in the power of change through hard work and self-control. As part of Johnny's release, he reported to the parole board weekly and was able to show proof that he was rehabilitated. Johnny started AA and NA meetings in the local church basement in Margarita's village. He became a fisherman alongside Margarita's father, and he continued to play his guitar. He practiced dancing the tango with Margarita regularly and learned how to make empanadas with her grandmother.

Everything Margarita described to Johnny about her home life before they met was accurate. The laughter, affection, food, and music of her culture was what ultimately redeemed Johnny.

Darcie and Dakota visited many times, and once, before Nancy was too sick to travel, they brought her along with them. She relished every moment.

Before he passed away, John Fasp Sr. ended up on Johnny and Margarita's doorstep. He came bearing remorse, apologies, and regret. Father and son shared one week of bonding, healing, and forgiveness. Johnny took him out fishing and Margarita made him help her in the kitchen. Before he left, he said in earnest, "I am truly proud of you, son. I only wish I could have been half the man you are."

Margarita and Johnny married before their first child was born, and after Johnny was released from prison, they had two more.

If asked, they would both say they lived happily ever after, with a few bumps along the way.

***

Kent's whirlwind romance with Tracy Hansworth consisted of a two-week courtship, marriage proposal, and long goodbye. However, they managed to keep it going and their relationship grew, regardless of the long distance between their homes and careers.

Kent got his pilot's licence, and Tracy took an "Overcoming your fear of flying" counselling course.

After one year of back-and-forth visits, they were married. It was Kent's idea for them to say their vows up above their birthplace in a hot air balloon. His grandiose romantic concept paid tribute to seeing Tracy on the cover of the *Women in Business* magazine back in the late '80s when he saw her hot air balloon layout and had the instant epiphany that Tracy was the one for him.

They built a house in MeadowBrook on the outskirts of town, which enabled them to add an airstrip. Kent could then travel back and forth to New York in his own twin-engine airplane.

However, after their first child arrived, a boy, Kent left New York for good and set up an investing business in MeadowBrook. Kent named his business Five Steps with Kent Gordon. The name of his company was a private joke between him and Tracy, but his agency with its five easy steps toward financial success took off, and Kent helped many people. His concept really worked. The first four steps consisted of executing a plan to tackle debt, saving for emergencies, facing your fears, and building an investment portfolio. The fifth step was a play on words called "Putting your money where your mouth is."

They went on to have another child, a girl. As soon as their children were of school age, Kent ran to be elected as a school board trustee, and Tracy became the head of the Parent-Teacher Advisory Council.

They enjoyed family dinners and holidays with Kent's parents. Tracy's father worked on their vehicles and anything that needed fixing around their house. Be that as it may, Tracy and Kent tolerated her mother and sister, but they were never as close as they had once been, even though the couple tried many times.

Kent and Tracy socialized with Susan and Dwayne, Darcie and Dakota, and once visited Johnny and Margarita in Argentina. While there, they chose to stay in a five-star hotel.

***

Dakota and Darcie never married, but they lived together as a married couple. They said that eventually they would do the paperwork and tie the knot, but felt there was no rush, as their love was a union between their hearts and souls, with respect and friendship at the forefront.

Dakota continued with his teaching, taking in misfit animals, and thanking the universe every day of his life for his many blessings.

He eventually got into politics and instigated many changes in the Indigenous community where he grew up. Street lamps were installed, clean drinking water became a right, and all train crossings were made safer. He also started a conservation program for wild horses.

Over the years, Dakota continued to be a friend to all but explored his comfort level in all situations by setting better boundaries. His propensity toward self-reflection, instilled by his father, had guided Dakota to create a framework of helping others, volunteering, implementing change, and still taking time for himself.

Shortly after Darcie moved in with Dakota, they invited her mother Nancy to live with them. She helped with the garden and planted healing herbs, seasonal vegetables and perennial flowers.

Dakota and Darcie never had children of their own, but they fostered many. His siblings, nieces and nephews, cousins, and all their friends were welcomed into their home with open arms. The many visitors and those who temporarily lived on the property nicknamed Dakota's home "D & D's Home of Peace, Love, and Tranquility." Less formally, everyone referred to the hobby farm as D & D's.

***

Immediately following the grad farewell picnic at the pond, Susan was assigned the story of the William Farnsworth case at the *MeadowBrook Gazette*. She collaborated with Patty, and the two women created a three-page storyline. Patty had saved all her homemade scrapbooks from her childhood, so she shared with Susan all the information she had gathered when she was obsessed with the town founder's disappearance. Patty found the old scrapbooks in her parents' attic, which turned out to be an ultimately cathartic experience. Susan's news story consisted of William's history before MeadowBrook, the town's founding, his marriage to Gladys, and his eventual disappearance, complete with the conclusion of being found at the bottom of the Fasp Farms pond. All of William Farnsworth's accomplishments and scandals were documented and communicated with accuracy and solid reporting, including photographs.

Even though Patty moved back to L.A., Susan kept up with her career. She visited Patty a few times as a professional journalist and friend.

Susan kept up with her fitness career and eventually became accredited to train and certify those interested in becoming fitness instructors. Susan went on to implement step classes, Jazzercise, and Zumba at the fitness studio where she taught. Eventually, she also became a personal trainer, all the while being a hands-on mother and weekly newspaper columnist, penning her well-loved articles for her column, still titled "Sarcastic Susan."

She tried on many occasions to make amends with her mother, and even though they became cordial, it was never the mother-daughter relationship she had with her own two daughters.

Susan's sisters and their children met for Sunday picnics at the pond in the summer and took turns hosting dinners at their homes in the winter.

The three sisters had twelve children between them and enjoyed their family get-togethers immensely.

Unfortunately, Dwayne was diagnosed with a heart condition and had to retire early with a disability pension. Susan cared for him until his death, and she refused to date or remarry after his passing.

As soon as their youngest graduated high school, Susan got the travel bug and travelled with Tracy to New York and various places in the world where her dear friend Tim was performing.

Susan and Tracy planned the twenty, thirty, and forty-year class reunions together. Each one was more elaborate than the last.

***

A lifetime of hard work and early-on celibacy proved to be the perfect combination for Tracy's career, personal life, and general well-being. Teenage insecurities and a nymphomaniac mother and sister were her guides for what **not** to do, and a roadmap to decipher where she was going.

Tracy effortlessly grew her event planning business. She learned how to delegate duties, and after meeting Kent, he taught her how to set up boundaries and take time off. She started a four-day workweek, and because most events were on the weekends, she promoted Marnie as her right-hand woman and primary assistant. She hired a fresh-out-of-high-school student to take care of all the franchises, driving from city to city to collect franchise fees and make notes on discrepancies if they were not adhering to the franchise agreement. Tracy revamped the franchise manual, upon Kent's savvy business advice.

Tracy continued to be best friends with Susan, but after her first romantic encounter with Kent, she refrained from sharing intimate details with her worldly, sexually experienced confidante. At the start of travelling back and forth to see Kent, Tracy found Susan's advice detrimental to her overall love-making experience. Tracy was showing up in New York in uncomfortable garter belts, fishnet stockings, thongs and bustiers. All because of Susan's advice, much to Kent's dismay and Tracy's discomfort. Eventually, she was able to find a balance between work, romance, and sharing details of both with her dear friend. Once her wedding date was set, Tracy and Susan agreed to disagree on how sex between two consenting adults should be performed and were able to laugh at their differences in opinion.

Tracy did not believe in happily ever after, but she put a huge value on unconditional love—with conditions. Respect, space, forgiveness, and always working through disagreements were values she stood by.

On every anniversary, she and Kent went up in a hot air balloon to commemorate Kent's realization that Tracy was the one for him. On their 25th wedding anniversary, Kent got permission from Brad, the head of the MeadowBrook High PE department, to take Tracy into the equipment room in the school gym to relive the night he proposed.

Tracy and Kent acquired financial success and tried to help others to the best of their ability. She always strove to be a good mother, devoted wife, and business owner.

Tracy and Kent's children remained in MeadowBrook and their son became a lawyer, their daughter, a nurse.

***

After Patty's significant William Farnsworth discovery, she stayed in MeadowBrook for an extra two weeks to work with Susan on the newspaper story. Consequently, she was fired from her L.A. newsroom job for not returning when expected. At the same time, Albert flew to MeadowBrook to share his undying love for the woman he knew as Patricia.

Subsequently, Albert met Patty's mother and father. To kill two birds with one stone, Albert asked her parents for Patty's hand in marriage. She thought it old-fashioned and archaic, but at the same time could hardly wait to show off her engagement ring to Pastor Herman. She had heard through the grapevine that his marriage was on the rocks, which made Patty feel bad, but she was able to look on the bright side by showing off that nerdy, foregone failure Patty Krakatoya had found love and success.

When Patty and Albert got back to L.A., he surprised her with a three-bedroom ranch-style house in Pasadena. Patty had no idea Albert had money. They tied the knot in Vegas, and when they returned, Patty got a job at a TV station as a commentator for a true crime investigative reporting show. She came up with the opening theme song for the program: "Running Down a Dream" by Tom Petty. Not only did it have a catchy chorus, but on a more personal level, Patty had been chasing her dreams and working on mysteries for most of her life.

Patty became highly respected as a television journalist and reporter.

Albert went on to continue his education and eventually became a sports broadcaster.

They had one child. Patty pleaded with Albert to call their son Noslen. He had no idea that his eight-pound baby boy was named after Patty's childhood crush Nelson, with some of the letters transposed. Unfortunately, what proceeded was years of bullying for her poor son, and Patty wondered if she had cursed her son with a name that could be made fun of, as if history had repeated itself.

Noslen eventually grew out of his awkward stage and went on to become an orthodontist.

Meanwhile, Patty's mother continued to be on and off the booze wagon, until she caught pneumonia after passing out in a farmer's field in the early winter of 1995. She died in the hospital with her husband at her side. Patty and her mom never did connect as a loving mother and daughter. Patty had given up on her shortly after the ten-year reunion.

The silver lining was that after Noslen was born and her mother passed away, Patty's father retired, sold their family home in MeadowBrook, and moved to be closer to Patty and her little family of three. He spent time combing the beaches with his metal detector and babysitting his grandson. Noslen referred to his grandpa as "Papapa Toya." He had become the boy's saving grace throughout his years of being bullied and taunted for his odd name.

Patty did not return for the twenty-year reunion but enjoyed keeping in touch with Susan. She still wondered about Nelson and what might have been.

***

Amanda and Brad separated for fifteen months directly following the ten-year reunion. During this time, Amanda went through a healing transformation with the help of a supportive network of family, friends, and co-workers. Having grown up in MeadowBrook and becoming a teacher there, Amanda was well-known and loved by many. Her family, especially her two sisters, stepped up to the plate with Bram and Branda, helping with hospital visits and school pickups. Her parents invited her and Bram over for barbecues and Friday night movie nights, and Amanda's co-workers at MeadowBrook High hired a cleaning service to come to Amanda's house weekly for one whole year, paid in advance. In retrospect, Amanda's time as a single mother was the best year of her life.

After she took Brad back, the couple still struggled with finding happiness. Eventually, they got separate bedrooms and developed their own interests and friends. They stayed together for the sake of their children. They didn't hate each other and called their marriage an "arrangement." Neither dated anyone else.

Branda eventually recovered and became cancer-free by the time she turned four years old. Amanda was so thankful that she turned to God and started to attend church and a weekly Bible study group.

By the time the twenty-year high school reunion rolled around, Brad asked to go to church with Amanda. By then the kids were teenagers and they both went to youth group. Bram went overseas with a group called

YWAM—Youth with a Mission—and Branda wanted to follow in her parents' footsteps and become a teacher. She was not an athletic jock like her mother but excelled in all other subjects. When Branda entered MeadowBrook High, she and Amanda waved at each other in the halls and would often sit in Amanda's car during lunch hour. They were very close.

After their kids graduated, Brad took a one-year sabbatical from teaching so he could travel. Amanda stayed behind and kept the home fires burning. Upon Brad's return, he asked if they could renew their vows. So, after twenty-five years of marriage, they went on a second honeymoon that was unequivocally better than the first. They kept separate bedrooms but joked with each other about making conjugal visits to each other's bedrooms.

***

Darcie settled into an amiable relationship with Dakota. Together they worked the farm and still hiked the foothills behind their house like they had done when they were teenagers.

She volunteered at the high school teaching dance, and picked up a few classes at the ballet studio in town, instructing interpretive movement. Darcie started a weekly poetry club, with their meetings taking place in the gazebo she and Dakota built on the property. In the spring of every year, she organized an Art Walk, where artists would come from neighbouring towns to set up a booth in the park at the centre of town.

Nancy spent her final years enjoying her time with Darcie and Dakota. She helped take care of the animals and garden when she could, and rested on the terrace overlooking the backyard and lush plants when she was not well.

At one point Darcie thought about having a baby, but it just didn't happen, and she was okay with it. The animals, kids at school, and children from the dance studio were her life, and some referred to her as a mum in her own right. She was Auntie Darcie to Johnny and Margarita's children and felt happy and content with her life.

Darcie eventually sold her Kitsilano, Vancouver, apartment, and with the money, she treated Dakota, Nancy, and herself to a month in Argentina to visit Johnny, Margarita and their children. Once there, Dakota helped Johnny renovate his moderate home by adding another bedroom. Darcie insisted on paying for all of the supplies. Nancy planted eucalyptus and a monkey puzzle tree to commemorate their visit.

The women and children spent mornings at the beach and they all gathered in the evening for long extended mealtimes together. After dinner, Johnny demonstrated his tango dancing, and they all played musical instruments. Darcie laughed until she cried.

They spent time memorializing the past and celebrating the present. Lots of sharing, healing, and grieving occurred. The trip was cathartic for all, and it was decided that Darcie and Dakota would repeat their visit at least once a year from then on.

Over the years, she would occasionally see her biological father John Fasp in town or at a community event, but she could never find the gumption to approach him. She regretted not having the providence to know he would not live forever. After John Fasp died, she embarrassed herself by weeping loudly at his funeral. She could barely walk and needed Dakota to steady her. By that time, Darcie was sure that everyone knew about her father's sordid past, and yet she felt no shame or malice toward the man who gave her and her brother life, if nothing else.

***

On behalf of the MeadowBrook Graduating Class of 1978, "Never feel sorry or unhappy about something you did or did not do. Life is far too short to regret what might have been!"

About the Author

After graduating high school in 1978, Karen Harmon went on to travel and attend college, and began a career as an aerobics instructor in the 1980s when curly perms and leg warmers were the going trends. She became involved in the disco scene and the many unsavoury characters that went with it. Karen became a single mother at the age of 32 and went back to college to obtain a degree as an Education Assistant.

Karen currently works in a high school and enjoys being in a fun, busy place of learning. She is reminded daily of her own high school experiences and revels in how many social aspects have not changed, and yet how young people have evolved and grown to make for a much healthier, inclusive environment.

Karen enjoys blogging about the past and has found writing to be a cathartic, life-changing and entertaining pastime. During the writing of Class of '78, all of Karen's fictitious characters developed into real people she looked forward to hanging out with every time she turned on her computer. Each personality was created from Karen's memory bank of people and experiences she encountered during the 1970s and '80s. She often stated, "Writing Class of '78 was like watching a well-loved movie or episodic series."

Karen currently lives and works in North Vancouver, British Columbia, and is writing the prequel to the Class of '78. She still teaches fitness and enjoys her husband and family of three adult children.